DIG OR DIE

A NOVEL OF AMERICANS IN FRANCE

IN WORLD WAR I

By
KENNETH REDLINE

DIG OR DIE

AUTHOR'S DECLARATION

Published by Fox Hollow Press

Interior design by OPA Author Services, Scottsdale, Arizona

Cover Design by John M. Coopey, Mesa, Arizona

Attention Corporations, Universities, Colleges and Professional Organizations: Quantity discounts are available on bulk purchases of this book for educational and gift purposes, or as premiums for increasing magazine subscriptions or renewals. Special books or book excerpts can also be created to fit specific needs. Contact Fox Hollow Press.

Printed in the United States of America

American Expeditionary Force in France, 1918

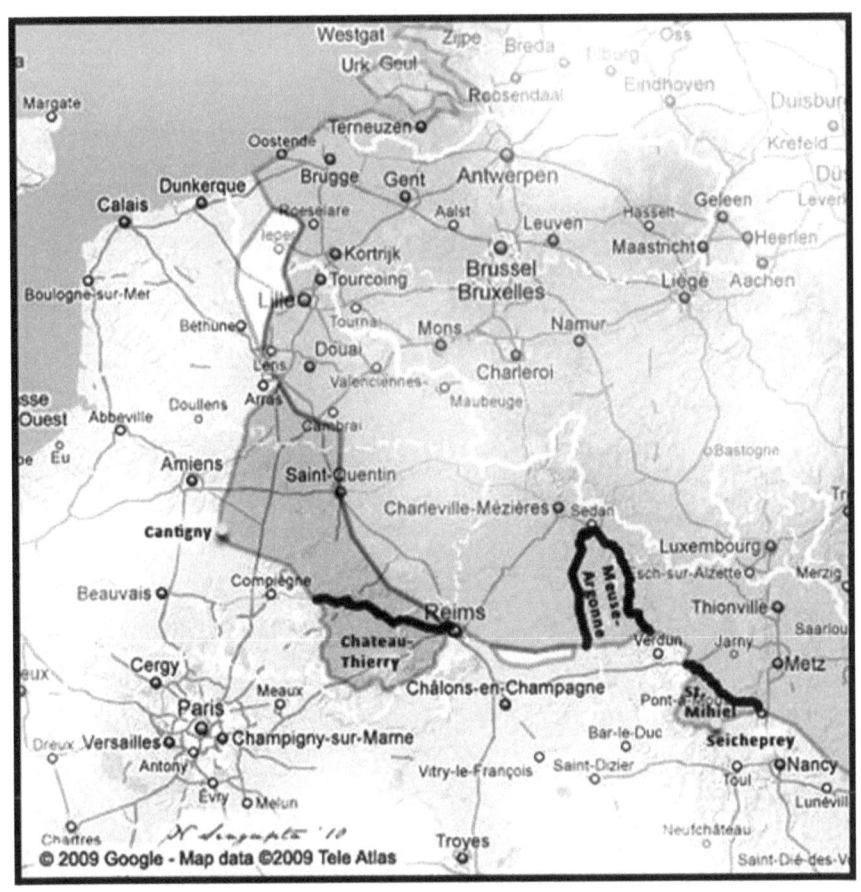

Map of France showing the main offensives
in which the Americans participated:
◆ Cantigny – May, 1918
◆ Chateau-Thierry – July and August, 1918
◆ St. Mihiel – September, 1918
◆ Meuse-Argonne -- October and November, 1918

DEDICATION

To the men of Company C, First Regiment,
U.S. Engineers, 1917-1918
May they rest in peace

ACKNOWLEDGEMENTS

The most important person to thank for this work is Kenneth Redline. A lifelong student of history, he was adamant about accuracy and authenticity. His clear memory for details, his adherence to the facts and his geographic clarity carry this work on its own. I checked the facts, the chronology and the geography and found that he knew what he was talking about – without exception. As his editor, I worked on syntax, word choice and rhetoric, but I left the facts to him – and the story. It's his story, beyond my ability to improve, real and true, not only for times, places and events, but for the gut-wrenching honesty it reveals.

In addition, as there are always people who make a book possible, I thank my book designer/proofreader, Paul McNeese of OPA Author Services, for his enthusiastic support of this project and my son, John Coopey, for his inspired cover design.

INTRODUCTION

My father, Kenneth Redline, was a man whose life took some unfortunate turns. Born in Altoona, Pennsylvania in 1896, his father died when he was not quite five years old, leaving his mother to raise him and his brother by running a boarding house. At fourteen, he was enrolled at Thaddeus Stevens Trade School in Lancaster, Pennsylvania where he spent the next four years learning the bricklaying trade. A gifted athlete, Ken played both football and baseball at Stevens, but baseball was the love of his life. After graduating from Trade School, he enlisted in the U.S. Army on November 5, 1915 at Fort Slocum, N.Y., to play baseball. The Army had teams that played in the north in the summer and in the south in the winter, and all Ken wanted to do was play baseball.

But the summer of 1916 found him attached to Black Jack Pershing's Mexican Expedition in pursuit of Pancho Villa. That operation ended just before the United States declared war on Germany, thus entering World War I. Since they were already trained, Ken's unit, Company C of the First Engineer Regiment, attached to the First Infantry Division, was one of the first AEF units to arrive in France in late August, 1917.

Dig or Die is more memoir than novel, and more a soldier's poignant account of his experiences as part of the First Division in the war. His discharge papers read like a chronology: Luneville Sector (defensive), Nov. 1-10, 1917; Luneville Sector (defensive), Dec. 13, 1917; Toul Sector (defensive), Jan. 15-Mar. 31, 1918; Montdidier Noyon (defensive), Apr. 21-Jul. 7, 1918; Aisne-Marne (offensive), Jul. 18-24, 1918; Saizerais Sector (defensive), Aug. 7-24, 1918; St Mihiel (offensive), Sep. 12-13, 1918; Meuse-Argonne (offensive), Oct. 1-11, 1918; Army of Occupation, Dec. 1, 1918-August 15, 1919.

He was there, through it all, and he survived. His proudest accomplishment was having served his country with steadfast loyalty and devotion to duty. . He only rose to the rank of corporal, but he was awarded the Purple Heart, the Bronze Star and the Silver Star for his conduct in the face of the enemy.

After the war, Ken returned to Altoona, married and fathered eight children. The Great Depression hit the family hard, for Ken had bought two lots in the Juniata section of Altoona and built two two-story brick houses in the late 1920s, one for his family and one to sell. He lost both properties in the early days of the Depression and was without regular employment for more than five years before being hired as a janitor at the Altoona Post Office in 1935. He gradually pulled his family out of poverty, first as a mailman and later as a railway mail clerk, but he never achieved the kind of economic status most people associate with success.

As far as I know, he wrote *Dig or Die* during the dark days of the Great Depression, when writing must have been a way to escape the economic realities of unemployment. I was born in 1941, and I don't know of any writing taking place in my lifetime. I knew he'd written a book, and that it was stored away in his closet, but I never saw it or read it. He may have sent it out for publication, but if he did, it was never returned because the only complete copy that I know to exist is written in longhand in pencil on newsprint. After his death in 1970 one of my sisters had acquired the manuscript and passed it on to me several years later. I decided to transcribe it to the computer so that I could make copies for my siblings and other family members. It took a long time, and when I finally finished the transcription, I realized that I had something more than just a family keepsake.

So I decided to honor my father by bringing his work into print in commemoration of the 100th anniversary of American involvement in World War I. I am privileged to be his editor and publisher, but you are privileged to be his readers.

Judith Redline Coopey
Mesa, Arizona
January, 2017

CHAPTER I

BAR-LE-DUC
AUGUST, 1917

Name: Emmet (Judy) Redding. Age: twenty-two. Status: Corporal, U.S. Army Corps of Engineers. I joined the Army in 1915 to play baseball, and I did—for a while. Big adventure, this being in the Army—playing ball and chasing Pancho Villa around Mexico with Black Jack Pershing. But then the war got in the way. This is the story of the war and me. The Great War. World War I. The war to end all wars. So they said.

"Come on, sister, fill 'er up. How's a soldier ever gonna get a drink out of a tiny little glass like that?" Sergeant Mac MacCarthy of the 1st Engineers, First Division, A.E.F., openly criticized French liquor glasses. To be disparaging was one of his outstanding qualities. To appear crabby and surly were others, all surface actions designed to hide a decent and generous nature.

The tavern was full that day—the general meeting place for the men—and we'd just returned from a practice march. The weather was warm for late August. Since I wasn't much of a drinker in those days, after a few sips of beer I put down my glass and turned to chew the fat with Tony, a reluctant transplant from South Carolina, and enjoy Mac's tirade—delivered in English so as to make little or no impression on the buxom French barmaid, one of three who assisted the elderly proprietress of the "estaminet".

"Hey, Judy. How's everything?"

Roddy Hite straddled the chair next to me.

"Not bad. Not bad at all. Sit down and rest your feet. Where's Red?"

"That's a hell of a question. Where would he be? You know Red and women. He'll be along shortly."

"That son of a gun," drawled Tony. "Gotta admire his charm. Put him down in the middle of the ocean and he'd come up with a woman on his arm."

"Each arm," corrected Roddy. "What're you guys drinkin'?"

I pushed back from the table. "Nothing for me. A little bit of this stuff goes a long way."

I used to like a drink with my buddies back home, but my experience with alcohol was pretty much limited to a beer now and then. I'd heard about how the army could change a man in that regard, but I thought I was pretty settled about the matter.

"Okay, suit yourself. How about you, Tony?"

"Make mine beer."

Roddy moved to the counter to put in the order.

"Hey! Hey, boy! Make room for a thirsty man." Red Conlon strode through the door, spied our table and seated himself with a swagger, his flaming hair slicked down under his overseas cap, blue eyes twinkling merrily. Roddy returned to the table, eyes on Red all the way.

"Old Rudolph Valentino himself." Roddy enjoyed a jab at Red now and then. "How're your love affairs, if I may be so bold as to ask?"

"Oh, you may be as bold as you wish," Red replied with calm assurance, "but I don't have to reply."

A good old farm boy from some little dink place in the Midwest, Red's prowess with women belied his humble roots. "How ya gonna keep 'em down on the farm?"

After the barmaid set two glasses of beer on the table and turned away, Red, looking neither to the right or left, lifted one and sucked it up.

Roddy confronted him with feigned indignation. "Why, you nervy devil! Who invited you?"

Turning to the girl, he held up one finger. "Encore un."

As I wandered over to Sergeant Mac's table, he looked up and smiled a greeting. "What's goin' on over there among you snot- nosed kids?"

"Watch."

Roddy Hite had moved away from Red's table. All unsuspecting, Red sat there sipping his purloined beer, exchanging a few words with Tony, who caught my eye and winked. As we watched the barmaid make her way among the tables with a sweating mug of beer, Tony rose as though to speak to me, barely hiding a grin.

The girl set the beer on the table, now empty except for Red, and stepped back expectantly. "Voilà, m'sieur. Deux francs, s'il vous plaît."

Red looked up in surprise. Bested. None of us would be back until the score was settled. As the room erupted in laughter, Red looked around, embarrassed. Then with great ceremony he reached into his pocket and brought out a fistful of banknotes, selected a two franc note and handed it to the girl with a flourish. Smiling broadly, she reached for the money and stuffed it into her bosom, giving Red a 'serves you right' look.

"Watch this, Roddy!" Red rose from his chair, threw both arms around the girl, pulled her close and kissed her heartily on the mouth. Struggling to free herself, she broke away and slapped him a resounding blow on the cheek.

Bellows of laughter filled the room. Roddy Hite bent over, hands on his knees and yelled, "I saw it, Red! I saw it all!"

Outside, a bugle sounded first call for retreat and the café emptied as if by magic. The troop drew themselves up in quick but grim military formation. It'd been all training so far, but beneath the fun and games lurked the knowledge that war awaited just over the hills, where the rumble of guns, muffled but constant, promised to introduce us.

After supper, as I sauntered aimlessly down the village street, Tony called to me.

"Hey, Judy! Wait a minute."

"What'd you want, Johnny Reb?"

"Oh, nothin'. Nothin' in particular. You're on guard tonight, aintcha?"

"Yeah. Why?"

"Well, I was just thinkin'. I'm on, too, you know. Third relief. If you stand my first trick, I'll stand your second."

I considered his offer. It would keep me on from eight 'til twelve, but after twelve I'd be through for the night. I eyed him with suspicion. "What's up your sleeve?"

"Come on, Damn Yank. Don't act so dumb. You know what's up my sleeve."

I laughed. Of course. His lady of the moment. But the idea of unbroken rest after I came off post was appealing. The rest of the company didn't know it yet, but I'd met a Parisienne damsel in the next village. I could slip over there after my tour.

"Okay. Bargain. But be sure you're on deck at 12 o'clock."

Pretty loosely organized, the guard tour went from 6 p.m. to 6 a.m. It wasn't really guard duty in the strict sense—more of a patrol. The thing was to watch for fire or whatever Heinie might dream up. The patrol leaders awakened their men and posted them, then were free until the next posting.

After I'd posted my relief at 8 o'clock, I wandered around the village, keeping within call. About a quarter of the men in our company were seasoned veterans. Regular Army—a lean, hard-bitten bunch for whom soldiering was a trade. Some could remember San Juan Hill, the defeat of Aguinaldo, the occupation of Vera Cruz, or the bitter fighting in the rice paddies and marshes of China and the Philippines. Tanned and weatherbeaten, lithe and agile, they moved with an air of confidence that promised a cool head in a crisis. Just being around them assured a recruit that the future would take care of itself.

The rest were duration-of-war men who'd enlisted at the first call. Neither blaring bands nor waving flags influenced their action. They joined because their country demanded it. "My country, right or wrong," — loyalty their highest value.

I stood with the regulars, even though my reason for joining was for sport. It was just bad luck that a war broke out right in the middle of my baseball career. After a few months of training in the States, we'd arrived in France, where we continued our training in the art of warfare under the tutelage of French veterans bearing scars from Loos, Lens, Verdun, the Somme. In fact, there was hardly a battle that hadn't left its mark on our instructors and, while we listened intently to the voice of experience, we were painfully aware that such experience was mostly of defeat. I wondered how men who'd been ground under the heel of the enemy could advise us on how to win. But they were to mold us—raw Americans that we were—into a cohesive machine destined to astound the military world with its efficiency and precision under fire.

At 10 o'clock I found Tony's men and relieved the posts of the guard, then strolled through the village to the bank of the Rhine-Marne canal, which crossed the valley from north to south. I was hardly settled in when I heard light, quick footsteps approaching along the hard tow-path. They stopped abruptly, but I made no move. A feminine voice called guardedly, "Judy? Judy? C'est toi, n'est-ce pas?" She put a heavy emphasis on the last syllable. Jud*ee*.

"Oui, ma petite. C'est moi."

She sat down beside me, talking in undertones. Her name was Antoinette de Gardelle, of Paris. Staying with an aunt in the village across the valley, she was a comely girl, anxious to please and willing to break with tradition…just a little. Her aunt kept a close eye on her comings and goings, but after auntie fell asleep, Toinette found her own way of passing the time. Sitting on the canal bank in the hot hazy night, we took off our shoes and dangled our feet in the cold water.

She was teaching me French, but there was no need for me to reciprocate, for she was fluent in English, having attended a finishing school in Switzerland, where English was the common language. My French lesson was accompanied by much quiet laughter. The evening passed, filled with flirtation and fun, but as twelve o'clock neared we put our shoes back on and I walked her along the canal bank toward her village. When we reached the point where the canal entered the town, I kissed her goodnight and she ran down the canal bank, pausing at the first building.

I called to her. "Demain soir?"

"Ah, oui. Demain soir." Amid a flutter of white, her skirt bouncing up to reveal her petticoat, she disappeared behind the buildings.

I trekked back to our village just in time to turn the guard over to Tony.

"Where've you been?" he asked.

"Down by the canal."

"Who with?"

"No one."

"I betcha," he snorted. "I betcha you were down by the canal. I just bet you had a swell time sittin' there countin' the stones on the bank, all by yourself. Now I'll tell one."

"Well, in any case, you're on guard and I'm goin' to bed."

CHAPTER II

BAR LE DUC
AUTUMN, 1917

The days passed quickly as, in our pursuit of the art of modern warfare, we practiced combat formations, offensive and defensive tactics, and patrolling. Our French allies let us know soon enough that what was all right in the Mexican Campaign was all wrong here. The importance of concealment, the use of hand grenades, and the handling of the automatic rifle were drilled into us so thoroughly we could load, unload and sight in our sleep. When our instructors staged a liquid fire demonstration, we witnessed a cone shaped column of flame near one hundred feet long, tapering from a few inches to eight or ten feet in diameter, hot as hell. Even from where we stood—a hundred feet away—we were duly impressed. Of all the terrifying weapons, this was the worst—truly no plaything.

We spent our days studying war and our nights relaxing any way we could. We visited the café, sipped beer, laughed, joked, and exchanged quips with the barmaids. The weather stayed warm and delightful all through September. After nightfall, men slipped quietly away to meet the local girls along the canal bank, a favorite haunt for seekers of romance.

The pine grove across the valley was another. Antoinette and I spent many a pleasant evening on top of the high hill overlooking the village. She usually brought some small sweet cakes while I would contrive to contribute a bottle of wine. I was acquiring a taste for French wine. Our 'language lessons' yielded reasonably understandable conversation as we enjoyed our wine and cakes and exchanged tales of Paris and America. Like most Parisians, Toinette loved her native city and never tired of describing its wonders.

But Toinette wasn't all fun and games. Sorrow often sneaked into her voice, revealing a weary indifference to daily affairs. Her whole family, except her mother, had been lost in the war. At times, she seemed happy enough, but it was short-lived, before the inevitable relapse into gloom. Though she seemed to enjoy being with me, she also seemed distant, her mind wandering as she listened to my talk. She accepted my caresses without protest, but didn't reciprocate. She seemed willing, even glad to be with me — swell company when she was happy. But her mood changed to indifference — if not outright anger — without warning. Tonight, disheartenment held sway. The early October chill reminded us that this would probably be our last trip up the hill. As it grew dark we sat silent, watching the lights of the village come to life, one by one. Finally, I turned to her.

"What's wrong, Toinette? Don't you like me?"

Her regretful smile chilled me even more than the night air. "Like you? Yes, I like you. Else why would I see you?"

"But you're so quiet and sad when we're together," I took her hand in mine. "Sometimes I think I'm poor company."

She replied after a long, thoughtful moment.

"Yes, I am sad. I'm sorry for our whole generation. Just a few years ago I had many friends my own age. Where are they now? Dead. Dead at the Marne, in Flanders, at Verdun, at the Somme. Their bodies rot on every battlefield in France. My father. My two brothers. My fiancé. Everything is gone, destroyed in the jaws of war. Now, in this valley, I see thousands of Americans. Every day I see them. Young, lighthearted, in the full strength of youth. Where will they be a year from now? Do you know?"

I shook my head, unwilling to give the expected response.

"Well, I do. Some will be lying in hospitals, their bodies broken and mutilated; others will return to their homeland insane, their minds shattered beyond repair. Others will add their numbers to the thousands already buried in shallow graves from Switzerland to the North Sea. Some few, and I hope that you will be among them, will still be fighting—but fighting for what? Why? Because some arrogant rulers cannot agree?"

She hesitated, while I sat quiet. Her words struck me with such force, there was nothing left to say. It was the reality we all knew but did our best to keep down, drowning it in laughter and beer.

She sighed, then spoke again. "You ask me if I don't like you. I'm afraid to like you. Liking might develop into love, and of what use is love? To see your love taken away to slaughter is too much to bear. Love should lead to marriage and happiness, but how can we look forward to such things when we can't be sure even of tomorrow?"

I reached over and placed my hand over hers in the dark. We sat thus for a long time, each lost in our own thoughts; hers of the past, mine of the future. No word passed between us.

Finally, she stirred. "Come, Judy," she whispered. "We must go."

We rose and made our way slowly down the hill. At the bottom, she stopped and turned to me. "Forgive me, Judy. Forgive me for making you sad. Come, we shall go to my aunt's house. Auntie is a sound sleeper. I'll make you coffee with rum. It will make you happy again." There was an endearing sweetness in her effort to cheer me.

I was soon seated in her aunt's kitchen, eating hot, buttered bread and drinking coffee liberally spiked with rum. A gradual warmth stole over my body, improving my mood. From Toinette I'd gained a better understanding of the French people and how they'd suffered over the past few years. Scarcely a home in the nation that couldn't tell a story like hers.

Near midnight, I kissed her good-bye and trudged along across the darkened valley to our village. No light showed at the café, but as I passed the rear door I heard the murmur of voices. These "estimets" were supposed to close at nine o'clock, but for the select few, they were open any time. I rapped on the door. Three distinctly separate knocks. Shortly, the door opened a crack and a cautious voice inquired, "Qui est là?"

"Le Corporal Judy."

I heard the chain unhook, and the door swung wide.

"Entrez, m'sieur." The proprietress herself smiled as she motioned me toward the main room. "Vous promenez ce soir," she said with a benevolent grin. "Avec Antoinette, eh? Antoinette est très jolie, n'est-ce pas?"

"Oui," I answered, taken by surprise. How did this old hen ever learn about Toinette and me? "Shh," I admonished her, my finger to my lips. "Sa tante ne sait pas."

She nodded and smiled her understanding as I entered the room where the 'select few' spoke in whispers and undertones. Tony and Red Conlon moved over to make room at their table.

"Where were you?" Red demanded.

"Over at Ligny. How's chances for a beer?"

"Ligny? What the hell were you doing over there?" Red's voice had only one range: loud.

I smiled. "None of your damn business."

"Hell, you were probably visiting the hospital over there or something."

"Or something."

"Okay, soldier. Sit down."

Tony eyed me with suspicion. "Ligny, huh? Listen, Damn Yank, you might kid these other guys, but you can't kid me. What the hell *were* you doin' over at Ligny?"

"Studyin' French."

"Yeah, I guess. Blonde or brunette? Five bucks says she don't live in Ligny, either."

"All right, smart guy. Find her, then."

"To hell with 'er. I've got one of my own."

"Yeah, with three sons in the army and two married daughters." That one always worked on Tony.

"Oh, you go to hell, you Damn Yank," he growled and returned to the business of getting drunk. My attitude toward alcohol was beginning to waver just a bit, so I joined him in another beer.

Later, we sneaked back to our billet by an alleyway, aware that everyone knew what was going on — but nothing would be done unless we became too brazen.

Falling temperatures, brisk winds and crisp, frosty mornings indicated that October was nearing its end. We rehearsed in earnest now, hiking with full pack, digging trenches on three- and four-day maneuvers. Not far from the village was a complete system of trenches we'd carved out of the stony soil by hand. In a four-day sham battle, the white army held this trench, with the blue army in assault. The affair ended in complete failure for both sides. The only branch to function efficiently was the culinary department. Not one hot meal, nor one served on time, gave the cooks a perfect record for consistency. A wandering cow that got tangled up with one of the outposts on the third night nearly demoralized both armies.

As we cleaned our equipment for the next mock war, we took turns poking fun at Red. Word was, he knew more about the cow episode than he was willing to admit.

"How'd that cow come to get up there, Red?" Jack Bartlett wanted to know.

"How would I know? Walked, I guess." Red evaded the question.

"Yeah, I guess she did, but who was on the other end of her tether?"

"I dunno."

"Well, then, answer me this." Jack moved in like a district attorney, fixing Red with a baleful eye. "Where'd you get that canteen full of milk, and how did you just happen to get to the outpost right before the cow did?"

Looking around with a grin, Red replied, "Manna from Heaven, Jack. Just Manna from Heaven."

The whole billet erupted in laughter. I was still grinning when the door opened and First Sergeant Stubblefield entered, glanced around, then raised his voice so all could hear. "None of you men leave this village until furthah ordahs," he announced in his clipped Texas accent. After a quiet conference with Mac, he left us.

"What is it, Mac? What's the dope?"

Mac, besieged with questions from every side, looked around, his face blank. "Why, it's what you heroes have been waitin' for. The company has orders for the front."

The room instantly hushed, each mind suddenly filled with its own thoughts. Here it was—the thing we'd been waiting and training for. What we'd been hoping for and fearing at the same time. That steady rumble and roll we'd heard for months now would cease to be a thing apart. We'd be right in the middle of it.

The letter writers got busy right away. I never was much of a letter writer. Told myself there'd be time for writing later. I'd intended to go over and see Toinette that night, but it wasn't going to happen now. The bugler's call to mess interrupted my thoughts, so I picked up my mess kit and wandered up for supper.

After we'd eaten, Tony, Mac and I stopped by the café. There really wasn't anything else to do.

"Here, young fellow. Give this a try."

Mac handed me a drink of brandy, fiery stuff that burned all the way down and made my eyes water.

He roared with laughter. "Boy, you'll see the time when you'll take three times that much at one swallow and never bat an eye."

"Maybe I will—when I have a little more hair on my chest."

"That's the stuff. Put it there." Mac grew up tough in South Boston. Rough, crude, always ready for a fight. All I knew was, I wanted him on my side when things got nasty.

The café was only about half filled, and the talk was quiet. Little or no laughter. Mostly speculation about what time we'd depart. Sitting near the edge of the group, I noticed one of the barmaids standing in the rear doorway, trying to attract my attention. She glanced about as if to make sure no one was looking, then made furtive beckoning motions to me. I got up and walked casually to the doorway, where she lifted a tray full of glasses from a table in a small back room. As she passed me, she murmured, barely audible, "Go down to the canal."

I went out the back way into the dark, misty alley. When I reached the canal, I found Toinette standing on the far bank, wrapped in a raincoat. She motioned for me, and I crossed the little bridge to her side. She grabbed my hand, saying nothing, just holding my hand, looking into my eyes.

"You are leaving."

"Yes. How did you know?"

"Oh, we know the signs. There were French staff officers here yesterday. Then, this morning, the mayor told us the billets would be vacated."

"Do you know when we leave?"

"Yes, early tomorrow morning, before light."

"Well, my sweet, you're better informed than we are." I raised her hand to my lips and kissed it. "How do we travel—on foot?"

She offered up a sad smile. "No. By camion—in trucks."

"I'm glad you came. I'd meant to come over tonight, but we have orders not to leave the village."

"I know. I can't stay long, but I wanted to see you once more. I'm sorry you have to leave."

"I'm sorry, too, Toinette, but it's war. That's what we're here for."

"Yes, that is so, but you've been a good friend to me."

"You've been swell to me, too." I reached up and removed one of the collar ornaments from my blouse. "Here, take this to remember me by. It's not worth anything, but when I'm rich and famous, you can show it to your grandchildren and say, 'I knew him when.'"

. She smiled and reached out her hand. "Au revoir, Judy. I must go now. My aunt is not well and she needs me."

I kissed her hand again. "Good-bye, Toinette, and good luck."

On impulse I drew her gently to me, clasped her in my arms and kissed her forehead. "Goodbye, Toinette. Goodbye."

Her eyes misty, she reached up and touched my cheek "Be careful, Judy. Goodbye."

She slipped from my arms and hurried along the canal bank, turning to wave before she disappeared. I returned the wave and made my way back to the café where Tony and Mac had saved my seat. Neither said anything. After a quiet hour or so, we settled our tab and moved up the street toward the billet, watching a string of trucks rumble into town. Mac eyed them for a second, then turned to Tony and me.

"There's our trucks." He nodded, his tone quiet. "Revielle at two, I guess."

After making sure everyone was present in the billet Mac repeated the announcement he'd made in the street. "Revielle at 2 a.m. Put everything in your packs. We're not coming back."

CHAPTER III

ARACOURT
NOVEMBER, 1917

Mid-November brought chilling and torrential rains. The sun that warmed us in the pleasant little valley where we spent the last few months deserted us now, taking with it the spirit of cheerfulness and gaiety that had prevailed since we got here. It rained for days, cold, chilling downpours that froze us to the bone, started our teeth to chattering and sent shivers chasing up and down our backs. We were altogether miserable.

Once the weather turned chill and wet, I found a drink of rum, gin or brandy brought a tingle of warmth. I guess that's how a guy learns to drink.

We rested in a little town just behind the lines. That rolling rumble that'd been part of the background since we left the coast changed to resounding crashes.

One day a few of us braved the elements to walk out and inspect the many shell holes around the village. One, about ten feet in diameter and approximately the same depth, looked fairly fresh, with black lumps of earth around its edge and the strong stench of high explosive lingering. We gazed into the chasm, mostly curious.

"Hell," Roddy Hite observed, "a hole like that saves a hell of a lot of digging."

"You're damn right. Digging is the curse of this war." That was Red Conlon adding his two cents.

Roddy nodded. "I'm inclined to agree, but I'll bet the shirt off my back that the time'll come when you'll dig and be damn sorry you can't handle a half a dozen picks and shovels at once."

Red grinned, producing a bottle of cognac from under his raincoat. "Maybe you're right. What say we dig into this now, though?" We sat on the edge of the shell hole, passing the bottle and musing on our fate.

When we returned to the billet, I made sure the men had their equipment made up and ready for departure. We were going into the line tonight, and it being our first outing of this kind, I was meticulous with the details. Then, too, I'd just been made a sergeant and my shoulders hadn't yet learned to bear up under the responsibility.

We were assigned to relieve the first battalion, who'd been holding the lines for a week. Gresham, Enright and Hay, the first Americans killed in action, were buried at a little town called Bathelemont, just across the hill.

We set out in a driving rain immediately after dark—raindrops, large as peas, driven by a venomous wind, stinging our faces and rattling on our helmets.

"Devil blow me blind if this ar'n't a nice mess. Not 'arf, it ain't."

This outburst came from the cockney, Bones, a veteran of the Turkish campaign with the British in the Dardanelles. He'd been discharged from the British army on disability, so on a visit to the United States, he'd enlisted in the American Army. How he ever passed the doctors was a mystery. Subject to balmy spells as a result of his head wounds, the boy was a tiger in a fight in spite of all that, which, after all, is the main requisite for a soldier.

Bones' outburst touched off a volley of growls and curses. I chuckled, hiking along in the file closers. A soldier swearing and complaining, no worries. He was just taking advantage of his natural prerogative. A man who wouldn't growl and bitch about a soldier's life probably wouldn't fight, either.

The column had slogged about a mile through the mud when Sergeant Mac dropped back to my side, wasting no time in preliminaries. "Where's Tony?"

"Up the column someplace."

"No, he ain't. He didn't answer the roll call and Dave Evans is trying to cover for him. Think you could find him?"

I was pretty sure I knew where the missing could be found because I'd spent most of the day with him. I knew the last place he intended to visit before we left, and there was an even chance he'd still be there. Well, there was only one thing to be done. Much as I hated it, I'd have to fall out and go back for him. The prospect was anything but pleasant. Two extra miles on a dark rainy night, with artillery supply wagons and ambulances splashing me in up one side and down the other. One thing sure, that damn South Carolina Reb would stand me to a drink or I'd break him in two. I turned to Mac.

"Keep covering for him. I'll have him back before morning."

"Okay, but be quick. You know how it is in a case like this. People that never wanted him before are sure to start asking for him now."

I slipped quietly out of the ranks and lay in a ditch at the side of the road until the company passed. When the road to the rear was clear, I made my way back toward the village as fast as I could slog.

When I arrived at the place we left from a good hour before, I approached a house a little past the center of town and rapped on the door.

"Entrez." A low, husky feminine voice.

I opened the door and found myself in a very tasteful — if simply furnished — room, the home of Yvette, a young woman of considerable physical charm and questionable moral standards. She stood at the table in the middle of the room, looking puzzled to see me. There was no sign of Tony. He was headed here when I left him this afternoon — said he'd stay until we assembled to move up. I questioned the girl in my halting French, suspicious as to what she might be covering up.

"Où est le corporal Tony?"

A look of alarm spread over her face. "Pas ici."

"I see he ain't here, but where the hell is he?" In my exasperation, I reverted to the language in which I was most comfortable.

"Il est parti." Aware I wasn't satisfied with her first statement, she elaborated. "He's go a neuf heures."

So, he left at about nine o'clock, did he? He certainly should have caught the company then, for that's when we pulled out. Outside was a chilling downpour and a dark muddy road at the end of which was war, and my dumb ass friend Tony was somewhere trying to get himself in a jam. Damn Reb.

I turned back to Yvette, who looked sincerely worried about Tony. I wondered if maybe they had something going, a wonder in this time and place. Getting serious with anyone in the middle of a war is dumb. Getting serious with a French lady of the evening in the middle of a war is even dumber. But I had to admit Yvette was a pretty girl, probably making a living any way she could. I wondered if Tony'd considered how she'd get along once we were gone.

"You take care of yourself, Yvette. Maybe someday I'll bring Tony back and you two can have a nice reunion."

Scouring my pockets for money I came up with a fifty franc note I'd been carrying around waiting for a reason to spend. I handed it to her. "Here. You'll need this more than I will."

Her face lit up. "Oh, merci. Merci, sarjong. My Tonee, he ees good man, sarjong. Don't be too mad at heem."

"I know he's a good man, but right now he's a pain in the ass. I gotta find him before he gets his sweet rebel ass in more trouble than he can handle. Bonsoir."

As I lifted the latch to leave, she followed me to the door. "Cherchez dans le café."

I slogged on over to the gin mill, where upon entering I spied my quarry in the far corner, a pair of high-priced boots under his arm. With his other arm he made threatening gestures toward a little wizened Frenchman.

"Hey! What in God's name goes on here?"

"Hello, there, Damn Yank. You're just the guy I want to see." Pretty well crocked, and in a convivial mood, Tony commenced an explanation. "I'm gonna kill this guy if he don't gimme these boots." The Frenchman could bank on the fact that Tony meant it.

Slowly, I unraveled the story. When Tony came in to get a drink before joining the company, he'd met this old Frenchman, the village cobbler, on his way to return a pair of boots he'd just repaired for one of the majors billeted in the village. Tony struck up a conversation with the old codger, became enamored of the boots in an alcoholic way and tried to buy them. Such an idea was preposterous to the little old man, one Jules Pierre St. Ettiene, a reputable businessman.

"Such a transaction would never do. It would be a direct violation of business ethics, not to be thought of. No! No! Never! Impossible. Absolutely no."

My private opinion was that fear of the major's ire was the only thing keeping the deal from going down. So Tony figured to get the little man drunk and steal the boots. Good luck, Tony. Jules Pierre St. Etienne was small, wizened and scrawny, but his drinking capacity would put even Mac to shame. By the time the company had formed and moved out, Tony was still committed to winning the game. He got a little anxious when the cobbler showed no signs of inebriation, but he wanted those boots, dammit! About the time I arrived, he'd decided his only alternative was to resort to force. The situation called for quick and decisive action, so I walked into the middle of things, picked up a square gin bottle, took a quick drink and grabbed Tony by the arm.

"Give him the boots. Get your pack and come on. There's a war waiting." I yelled like a drill sergeant.

"Hell, Judy. Give me five minutes and I'll have them damn boots."

"You don't have five minutes. Come on—now—or I'll bust your damn head with this bottle."

He knew me well enough not to mistake this for an idle threat, so he threw me a surly glance and then, as the humor of the situation dawned, grinned like the dumb yokel he was.

"Okay, Judy, okay. What the hell kinda war is this, anyhow? Won't wait for a guy to get a pair of boots."

"If you need boots, the U.S. Army will provide."

I made him pay for the bottle of gin, and we left the café amid continued grumbling and grousing. We splashed our way up the road amid a torrent of cuss words, some of which I'd never heard before. Must be southern. But I'd bet he was glad I didn't leave him there to face a squad of MPs.

We had practically no chance of overtaking the company. It was seven kilometers from the frontline to the village, and the average marching pace of a fully equipped company was four kilos per hour. It'd been a good two hours since I left the outfit, so they should easily have reached their destination by now. Tony and I sloshed along the road in the dark, giving way for transports going up or for ambulances coming back.

Night after night these roads were congested with endless traffic in both directions. Food, ammunition and other supplies going up—empty carts, caissons, ambulances and worn out equipment (including men) coming back. At midnight it seemed the roads would never be cleared and the enemy need only lay his guns and blast away to annihilate everything for miles in both directions. But somehow he seemed to miss the road more often than he hit it, and by daybreak the unutterable confusion of traffic had miraculously melted away.

As we plodded along in the dark for an interminable age, I pulled hard on my cigarette to see my watch in the glow. Two hours since we left the village; we should be nearly there. Tony stood quietly by, for the exertion had worked the liquor out of his brain and he was about as normal as Tony ever got.

A narrow side road meandered off to the left, and a solitary form, indistinguishable but for the glow of his cigarette, hailed us from the darkness.

"What's your outfit?" It sounded like Tommy Connors, a sergeant in the third platoon, but as one of the cardinal rules of soldiering was never to give out any information, no identity, numbers or disposition of troops, I wasn't about to be caught napping.

"Q troop of the mounted submarines," I replied.

I didn't have long to wait for a reply. "G'wan, Judy, you son-of-a-bitch. You're drunk. Did you find Johnny Reb?"

I handed him my square-faced bottle. "Yeah, I've got him. Where do we go from here?"

My only answer was a gurgle, followed by a gesture toward the side road.

"Up this godforsaken path somewhere. I don't know how far. Dave Evans asked me to wait here for you. He'll have someone on the lookout."

We mucked our way along the path in single file for half a mile before Morrie Muller, a Jewish kid from Hoboken, halted us and led us down into a communication trench, which we followed for another kilometer before we reached the front line. The trench was already organized, the men on post and guns in position.

At four I took the relief and filed down the trench. Each member of my relief stepped up to his place on the fire step as we reached his post. After he'd assumed his position, the man he was relieving stepped down.

The troops stood to at that mystical hour just before dawn, when the shadows merged with the faint light of coming day, the most advantageous hour for an attack, which is why every available man on both sides, from Switzerland to the North Sea, was at his position in his respective trench, fully armed and alert, ready for what the next hour might bring.

The day was wet and dismal, with intermittent showers driving furiously across the landscape, pursued by a wind that swept everything loose before it and plastered our slickers around our bodies like shrouds. We encountered the company commander, Lt. Smith, in the trench, accompanied by 1st Sgt. Stubblefield. Stubby was a recruit with me in Texas a couple of years before. The lieutenant gave me a nod. Saluting was generally dispensed with on the lines.

"Well, sergeant, how are things?" he asked. He was just as new to this as the men, but he was a good officer — concerned that his unit perform well but not yet confident in his own leadership.

"Everything's okay here, sir, but this weather does beat hell!"

"Yes," he agreed absently. "It is rather mean." He turned away, then stopped and came back. "By the way, sergeant, have you seen Corporal Lambert this morning?"

"Yes, sir, he was down in the dugout just now, sir. Shall I call him?"

"No, don't bother. I heard he'd missed the company when we left the village last night. I just wanted to be sure he's with us."

"Oh, he's here, all right. He hiked right beside me all the way up." At this statement Stubby Stubblefield shook his head in silent mirth, covered his face and turned away.

There was a twinkle in the lieutenant's eye, too. "I'm glad the rumor was unfounded, sergeant. I'd hate to have a man get in trouble at this stage of the game."

As he followed the lieutenant past me in the narrow ditch, Stubby paid me silent tribute with a wink. I moved on, inspecting my posts, satisfied with my handling of the truth.

Done with my inspections, I entered our dugout—about twenty feet down, snug and warm. At one end an air shaft leading up to the surface served as a flue, effectively carrying off the smoke from our fires. The place was uncommonly dry, an excellent feature. I descended the steps, followed by a sudden, whistling shriek as three shells buried themselves with a deafening blast just to the rear of our trench. I entered the dugout fully convinced that we were now sure enough soldiers.

CHAPTER IV

ARACOURT
NOVEMBER, 1917

Daybreak. The rains had finally stopped, leaving the world clean-washed and crisp. Heavy frost coated the parapet of the trench, biting our noses and making our eyes water. Men shivered and stamped their feet in stiff shoes in a futile attempt to warm numbed toes. We were formed in our trench: Two machine guns and two squads of riflemen. The entire party in command of Lt. Weyandt, a swell officer, was going up to man a strong point about three hundred yards in front of the line. We'd heard an enemy raid was in the works. If it happened, we'd be in position to deliver strong fire onto the flank and rear of the attackers.

Once assembled, we moved up the trench to a junction where a communication trench led to the strong point, Lt. Weyandt in the lead. I brought up the rear to make sure the party reached the post intact. As I waited for the section to file past, some of the men threw jabs my way.

"Hello, sarge. How'd you like to be back in Texas?"

"Got any gin left?"

"Where's your square-face bottle? I hear you're deadly with 'em."

I got a laugh out of it. "Go on. You guys been readin' my mail?" I fell in on the rear of the column. "Who has the guns?"

"Hite and Lambert."

Roddy and Tony. I was pleased. Up to then, I wasn't sure those two were with us. You never knew about them, especially Tony.

As we turned into the communication trench the rising sun, shining straight down the trench, caught the reflection of our bayonets, taking away any the element of surprise.

With the head of the column about two-thirds of the way up the trench, a shell came screaming from the right, burst a little ahead of the detachment, then another farther ahead. The column stopped, the rearmost men looking to me for instructions, but my ignorance of the situation was about the same as theirs. They'd been taught to look to their non-coms in times like this. Unfortunately there was no one for me to look to. Aware that indecision on my part would lead to confusion on theirs I assumed an attitude of confidence, told them to stand fast, then hurried up the trench to where I saw Roddy Hite standing at the head of the rearmost squad. "Take my place at the rear and bring the men on up the trench."

I stopped near the middle of the outfit. "Any damage here?"

"I don't think so," someone said, "but if them babies come any closer, someone is liable to get damaged quick and conclusive."

Even though shells continued to fall fairly close, the men remained calm. In front of me was a man named Kohl from Tony's squad. I wasn't sure whether to move up and report to Lt. Weyandt or return to the rear. The shells came closer together now. Up at the head of the detail a great mass of earth lifted high in the air, disintegrated, and settled back in dust. Another one hit ten yards to my left. Rounding a traverse, I heard one blow a little behind me.

Suddenly the world in front of me exploded with a gigantic roar and a loud clang, and I ended up on my knees in the trench facing the rear, drunk and disoriented. I couldn't get up. The world tilted this way, then that. In a dream-like state I regained my equilibrium and sense of direction. Out of the jumble of screeches and noises, one persisted – a human voice in mortal agony.

Behind me a man named Meadows hunkered down on the bottom of the trench, his face blanched, agonizing screams issuing from his throat. At each scream a gush of blood spurted out from beneath his overcoat in an ever growing pool at his feet. His face, a flaccid shade of white, seemed all eyes and mouth. God, so this was war. I moved to help him, shaking and cold. As I turned I heard a low moan from the other direction, where Whitey Kohl leaned on his arms, braced against the side of the trench. His shoulders shook as a low, moaning whimper reminiscent of a puppy's whine emanated from his throat.

"How's things back there?" It was Lt. Weyandt. God, I was glad to hear his voice.

"Bad! Two men hit. I don't know how bad."

"I'm comin' sergeant." God bless you, lieutenant.

In the meantime, Meadows' cries weakened. I turned to him just as he sagged into the mud of the trench mingled with his own blood. I stooped and took one arm over my shoulder, running my other arm through his crotch, and straightened up. As I rose and moved toward the rear, the lieutenant stepped around the ruined traverse, taking in the situation at a glance.

"Good boy, sergeant. Here, you two men take hold of Kohl. Vance is dead. Two men are bringing him back." The lieutenant's crisp voice and decisive manner did wonders for my confidence, and without quite knowing how, I retraced my steps along the way we'd passed so shortly before, surprised that shells were still falling, for I hadn't consciously heard one since the 'big one'.

As we turned into the front line with our burdens, creating a sensation, soldiers shouted questions, but we didn't respond, knocked dumb by what we'd just seen. We shook our heads and plodded on our way.

"Who is it?"

"Are they hit bad?"

"Which shell was it?"

"Boy, they sure were hittin' that trench with 'em."

"Damn shame."

Questions and comments filled the air—offers of help that we refused, for to shift our burdens would cause more pain. The distance, actually not more than a kilometer, seemed endless. Our burdens grew heavier, and when I deposited mine on a stretcher in the first-aid dugout, I was wet with sweat.

A French doctor, a captain, bent over Meadows and, after a brief inspection, straightened up and spread his hands. "Kaput. Il est morte. C'est fini."

"He's dead. It's over."

I couldn't believe it. The examination so quick and perfunctory. I thought he must be mistaken. "C'est certainment?" My pigeon-French got my question across.

The doctor glanced sharply and nodded. He leaned toward the wounded man and gently removed a blanket spread over him. One quick glance assured me that there was no mistake. Where there should have been an abdomen, there was just a bloody pulp. The piece of shell, after hitting him below the pelvis, took an upward course, spinning its way through his intestines until it reached the breastbone where it broke through. The sight rendered me helpless, cold, clammy, as though I were falling into a black pit.

The French Captain took my arm. "Voulez-vous boire?" he asked.

Not waiting for a reply, he poured a slug of brandy into a tin cup and handed it to me. I drank, grateful for the warm glow that surged through me. Small comfort, but comfort, nonetheless.

"L'autre est mort." He motioned to the body of Vance.

I nodded. The other doctor who'd been working on Kohl looked around and smiled.

"Your friend is not keel. Hee is moch hurt, the sit down, 'e will be no posseeb for a long time." He was trying to explain that the shell removed Kohl's buttocks as neatly as he, a surgeon, could have done the job himself. Long association with such scenes made these men unbelievably calloused to the terrible sights they saw. It was a wonder they could produce the marvels of surgery that they did.

As we left the aid station, I was surprised to see the sun still low on the horizon. I looked at my watch. It'd been exactly thirty-one minutes since we formed to move up to the strong point. I wondered how so much had happened in so short a time. Less than an hour ago strong and healthy, now two dead and one crippled for life. All this in the space of a breath. I tried to sort out my feelings and realize that all this had really happened. Welcome to the war.

"Boy, they sure play for keeps up here, don't they?" A voice at my elbow disturbed my thoughts.

"Yes, and warnings are short." I looked at my companion, Jones, an infantryman of the old school. Tough and hard, with enough military knowledge to command a battalion, but still a private. Liquor had kept him down. I knew the type.

He took hold of my arm and spoke earnestly into my eyes. "Listen, soldier, you're young and hold a rank. Maybe I shouldn't try to give you advice, but let me tell you something. You mentioned a warning a minute ago. I knew we were going to be shelled way before it hit."

"How?"

"Never move into the sun with a bayonet exposed to the light. We had sixteen men with their rifles hung over their shoulders, bayonets fixed, facing the sun. It flashed off of those bayonets like a heliograph machine. The enemy was sure to see, and that's why we got shelled. I knew it would happen as soon as I saw the sun shining from behind the enemy lines straight into our faces."

"Thanks. I'll remember that." A lesson driven home with such force would never be forgotten.

"Another thing. Never be afraid to take cover. It's not cowardly; it's just good sense. A live soldier is a menace to the enemy; a dead one is no good to anybody."

As I thought this over, he continued, "Did you hear the shell that did the damage this morning?"

"Yeah, I heard it."

"Did it sound different than the ones that landed farther away?"

"Yes. Louder and more piercing, sort of a shriek after it reached a certain point."

"Exactly. When it reaches the top of its trajectory and starts down, it shrieks. On the way up, the sound diminishes. When it gets over the hump and starts down, the nearer it gets to the ground, the louder it gets. When you hear a shell coming and its whistle gets louder and shriller, flop down as flat as you can and try to bite yourself in deeper. See this?" He reached into his pocket and produced a piece of shell about four inches long, jagged and sharp.

"Where'd you get that?"

"Dug it out of the trench wall a while ago at just about where my belly would have been if I hadn't flopped down when I heard her put on the brakes. It was smoking and steaming there in the trench wall, and I dug it out to remind me that the length of my life will pretty much be up to me."

Impressed, I asked. "Where'd you learn all this stuff?"

"In church," the laconic reply.

I questioned him no further, figuring him for one of those venturesome souls who used to slip across the Mexican border where a good shot could command twenty dollars a day in gold for his services. I'd heard rumors while stationed on the border—had even been approached in a half-hearted way, but that kind of life can get you killed.

Absorbed in our conversation, I wasn't paying attention to what was going on up ahead. The wham, bang and crunch of exploding shells re-awakened me to the war. The rumored raid was on. We found the front line fully manned. Riflemen sat on the ledge, some standing in the walkway, stamping their feet, while men on post stood on the fire step, erect and alert, grim determination on their faces. The shelling—fairly heavy—lacked this morning's accuracy.

Next I heard Stubby drawl at me in his Texas accent. "I heah y'all's been havin' doin's up theah this mawnin,' sawgint."

"Too much doin's for me."

"Yeah. Too bad abote them fellas, but thet's wah, I guess. You fellas're to go on up to the strong point. Rest of the detail got up all right."

We moved along the trench and into the sap that took us to join our outfit. As we passed the scene of our recent misfortune, I noted four places where direct hits had damaged the trench, the smell of high explosive still strong in the air. When we passed where they were shelling now, a twitchy feeling ran up and down my spine, my limbs trembled and my ears tuned to catch the first faint whisper of an approaching shell. At the strong point the men greeted us with nods and quiet words. The recent experience had subdued them into thinking harder than most had ever thought before.

We were positioned in a large circular hole, over six feet deep and about thirty feet across. Mounted guns, on all sides of it and in every direction, commanded an excellent field of fire. The side of the hole facing the enemy had been undercut to about six feet, forming a roof or overhead cover about four feet thick. This section was maybe sixteen feet long, and men off duty could snatch a brief rest in its shelter. Camouflage hid the hole from the enemy, providing a shallow sense of security.

When I rejoined the company, Lt. Weyandt called me into the shelter to go over the plans for defense. During a lull, he straightened up and asked quietly, "What about Meadows?"

"Dead."

He nodded. "And Kohl? Will he live?"

"Yes sir. Crippled, but he'll live."

"And you, sergeant?"

Surprised, I asked, "What do you mean, sir?"

"Well, that shell hit closer to you than anyone else." Handing me his trench mirror, he turned away. I frowned and looked at my reflection.

My face black, my eyebrows vanished, a streak of blood ran down from under my helmet across my left temple. My face was splattered with dirt and mud. I looked half dead. When that shell burst, the heat of the explosion burned my eyebrows and eyelashes away and the smoke blackened my face, but where was the blood coming from? I look up, puzzled, as I handed the mirror back.

"You can wash in there, sergeant." He motioned toward the overhang under which sat several basins and buckets of water.

As I moved toward the bench and unbuttoned my blouse, the lieutenant followed me, standing nearby. Tony lounged on a dirt shelf, hands behind his head, watching. I reached up to take off my helmet. What? My hand ran over something cold and rough. I snatched the helmet off and stared at a three cornered piece of shell sticking in the tough steel just above my left temple. It had penetrated just far enough to cut my scalp.

The morning's episode flashed vividly back. Meadows lying saturated in his own blood, his piteous screams ringing again in my ears. My stomach twitched and retched so I couldn't control it; I groped my way out of the shelter fighting for control. Lt.

Weyandt stood by, a hand on my shoulder, for which, even in this embarrassing state, I was grateful. Tony followed me out, caught my eye and motioned to his canteen. The lieutenant noted the gesture and stepped back into the shelter, while Tony gave me a big drink. Slowly my stomach stopped its infernal jerking and twitching. I sat on a stump, head down, spent and exhausted. After Tony gave me another drink, I started to feel better.

"What the hell's wrong with me?" I asked, embarrassed by my apparent weakness.

"Little case of shell shock, my boy. The Frog doctor noticed the symptoms and called up the company. He also told us about the piece of shell in your tin hat. You'll be all right now, once that takes hold." Solicitousness was very unlike Tony.

"Yeah, I think I will. But ain't I a helluva soldier?"

"Well, you're a little high strung, but you'll get over it. You're all right as long as there's something to do. The feelings erupt when there's a lull. Just nervous reaction. Anyone would feel the same. No reflection on you." Somewhere in the dark reaches of my brain I marveled at Tony Lambert waxing philosophical.

His words comforted me, such serious talk from a clown like Tony. Lt. Weyandt returned, telling me to take things easy for a while. We manned that strong point for three days, and when the company was relieved we returned to our village for a few days of polishing and drilling.

As day followed day, the future became the present and the present became the past. We'd now occupied the sector for six weeks, alternating between our little village, the support positions, and the front line.

We felt ourselves change in subtle ways. A hard, ruthless and unmistakable quality began to take shape. We knew how it felt to pour bullets from smoking hot gun barrels as the enemy advanced. We knew how it felt to prowl that silent strip of misery between the trenches known as "No Man's Land," where a careless move or an ill-timed word could spell death. We knew how it felt to follow a thundering, crashing barrage over to the enemy's position and engage him in hand-to-hand combat. No doubt about it, we were becoming soldiers.

CHAPTER V

ARACOURT
DECEMBER, 1917

We learned the simple joy of returning to our village, where we could buy omelets, pommes de terre, a chicken, or a rabbit stuffed with chestnuts. Just to be warm, dry and fully fed after what we'd been through were blessings, joys no civilian could know.

One such evening we were grouped around a large table in the cafe. The madame of the establishment had outdone herself in her efforts to show us her appreciation for our fighting alongside her countrymen. Roast rabbit, chicken, potatoes fried as no one but the French can fry them. Crab salad produced from heaven only knows where, and, wonder of wonders, a French woman's conception of an American pie. Of course, there was liquid refreshment in abundance. My self-imposed teetotaling had all but eroded away.

The occasion was a farewell party for Roddy Hite, who would leave us the next day for a job at division headquarters as an artillery observer. Tony, Mac, Red Conlon, Roddy, Morrie Muller, Tommy Connors, Stubby and I gathered to send him off, as the company waxed sentimental.

Mac rose to propose a toast but stopped in mid-sentence, hesitated, staring at the door. There on the threshold stood Yvette, the young lady of the evening whose house I'd tried to rescue Tony from. Dressed in some sort of white filmy thing, she was transformed into everything desirable in a woman. Her lips slightly parted, her eyes shining with eagerness, she looked like a little girl playing grown up. She advanced into the room a half smile playing at her lips. Up until then we'd had the place to ourselves, but, after all, it was a public place, so this couldn't be called an intrusion. Still, it felt a little uncomfortable. Moving to the head of our table by Stubby, Yvette picked up his glass almost apologetically, looked toward Mac and smiled.

"Ah, sarjong, you make thee bonne chance, how you call heem? Thee gud luck, no? Permittez-moi s'il vous plaît."

"Ha, she wants to make a toast. Let 'er go. Good girl, Yvette. Let 'er rip!" Encouragement from every side.

She stood for a second, as though lost in thought, started to speak, then hesitated. "Mon pappa ees die from thee Somme et ma mama ees feel ver bad from heem die. She die aussi. But me, Yvette, she's no die. She's leeve. Peut etre eet ees more better she's die."

"No, no. You're all right, Yvette. Go on. Give us the toast. Let's have it." Again encouragement from the men.

Smiling around the table, she raised her glass in one hand and recited, without a trace of accent: "Hokay, like you say eet, very gude. Thees thing is no moch, but I like heem. I hear heem one tam from les Anglais."

"Here's to the sands in the hour glass,

That measure swift time as it flies,

Here's to the men gone west today,

And here's to the next man that dies."

All the frivolity left the celebration, and a stunned silence settled on the room.

"Now why the hell did she have to do that?" Red Conlon asked. Every man at the table was thinking about the sad events of the past few weeks, and I was furious that she would cast such a pall over a party. I called her over, ready to bawl her out proper and send her home. She came and stood by my chair, looking down at me with the poignant sadness in her eyes that was so common to the women of France. As my anger abated, all desire to deal harshly fled. I wanted to put my head down and cry. Instead, I patted her on the shoulder.

"That was swell, Yvette. That was a damn nice toast."

Brightening visibly under praise, she regained her sprightly air. "You teenk so. Sarjong? I like heem, too."

"You're all right, sister. Sit down and get your belly full of chow."

No one objected. She ate daintily, but from the amount of rations she stored away, it was doubtful she'd eaten all day.

By midnight gaiety returned, and we all escorted Yvette back home, a noisy, irreverent gang of American boys. After she went in, someone suggested chipping in for a Christmas present, and Mac passed the hat, collecting more than three hundred francs. He rolled it up, weighted it down with a stone and dropped it through her transom. We heard a gasp as it hit the floor. As we scattered to our billets, Mac put our thoughts into words. "Maybe the poor kid can sleep alone while that lasts."

The next night we moved up again. It was New Years Eve, and we'd been relieved in this sector. That day Yvette told me she'd use our Christmas gift to move to a cousin's in Vitry La Francois. Said she'd have left long ago but for lack of money, but stayed these last few days to thank us when we came out of the lines.

The next day we moved again, destination unknown. We'd been told it would be a more active front. This sector was known as a quiet front. Yes, even on a quiet front, a man can die.

CHAPTER VI

GONDRECOURT
JANUARY-MARCH, 1918

Resting in the rear sounded good, provided we could actually rest. No such luck. In this new sector, we were subjected to a never-ending round of drills and 'training'. It galled us to have to listen to instructors who'd never even been at the front. All of the petty abuses of authority, forgotten at the front, came back to life here in the rear. Rank reclaimed its privileges. Everything irksome to the soldier's mind was trotted out and enforced. Almost made us homesick for the front.

There were some compensations, though. We spent the nights in the cafes, relaxing with our buddies. One night in Gondrecourt, Tommy Connors regaled us with the story of Jock Flock, a Scotsman who'd joined the company a few days ago and, like all recruits, had a lot to learn. A notice had been posted on the company bulletin board stating that new men had been saluting cavalrymen, probably because cavalrymen wore leggings and orange hat cords, hard to distinguish from the gold hat cord of a general. Having read the notice, Jock Flock determined to be alert against saluting a cavalry soldier.

That evening, young Mr. Flock was on his way from the mess hall to his billet, full fed and comfortable. Since the weather'd been damp and cold, most personnel wore overcoats and slickers. Jock was swinging along, happy and carefree, hardly noticing the portly figure approaching, swathed in a long slicker. Past middle age, the man wore an iron gray mustache, not a presence any old soldier could mistake for a cavalryman. As they met, the older gentleman looked closely at Jock, strutting briskly along, without a glance in his direction. Suddenly the stately gentleman wheeled around and bore down on Jock with a voice like thunder. "Don't you salute officers?"

Jock looked him up and down, still seeing nothing to denote officer status, and immediately retorted, "T'hell with you, buddy. You goddamn cavalrymen can't fool me!"

The general, near to apoplexy, raised his arms to heaven, struck dumb by this monumental insult. Then he spied Tommy standing by, hugely enjoying the scenario, and beckoned him over. Tommy approached with a snappy salute.

"D-d-do you know this man?" Still beside himself, the general could barely speak.

Tommy, hoping to keep Jock out of trouble after he'd provided such a swell show, evaded the question, doing his best to duck a direct order for punishment. "Not for certain, sir. Probably one of the recruits from one of the companies hereabouts, sir."

The general chewed his mustache, wanting satisfaction for this gross offense to his rank. "Ascertain that man's company, sergeant, and report him to his company commander for punishment by my order. Then see that the distinguishing insignia of rank are explained to him."

"Yes, sir!" Tommy saluted again and marched Jock away before the irate general could add any afterthoughts. Once they were out of sight, Tommy turned Jock loose with a shove and a dope slap to the back of the head, then, leaning against the wall of a nearby building, laughed himself silly.

We turned to Jock, present and still slightly uncertain. "'Ow the 'ell are you gonna tell 'e's an orfficer when 'e's all wrapped up in a raincoat, sergeant? 'Ow you gonna do it?"

"By his belly, me lad, by his belly," Mac informed him, to the sound of more laughter. "A fighting soldier never carries a front like that, and particularly not a horse soldier."

I was only vaguely interested in the conversation as I had a mission in mind. As soon as the opportunity presented itself, I slipped out of the café, bound for a little shop around the corner where a sign in the door glass declared, "English Spoken." I entered to the tinkle of a little bell and seated myself at a small round marble-topped table.

The establishment was run by Madame Cecille Maureauge and her daughter, Georgette. The madam was a well preserved woman somewhere in her middle forties, while Georgette was a gorgeous twenty-two. I heard footsteps coming from the rear and as I'd hoped, it was Georgette who came to serve me.

"Ah, sergeant, it is you. What can we do for you?"

"You can get me a cup of coffee and rum, mostly rum, if you please. Then you can sit and talk with me, if you will."

"Ah, you soldiers. Are you sure you want any coffee at all? I've heard it spoils the rum."

"Well, I can do very well without it, but I'd like some Benedictine and the pleasure of your company. It's soon time for you to close, isn't it?"

"Oh, it's long past closing time," she replied, setting my Benedictine on the table and closing the shutters. I just kept open, hoping that—" she hesitated, a shy smile playing at the corners of her mouth.

"Hoping what?"

"That someone—"

"Who?" I took her hands as she stood beside me. "Who, Georgette? Me, perhaps?"

She nodded, turning her face away. I gently pulled her down to my knee, caressing her hair. Slowly she began to relax until, as I sipped my drink, she nestled comfortably in my arms. A short kiss—she was hungry for affection—and more. These French girls had lost so much—with each caress she became more responsive. I asked her for another drink. She kissed me and disappeared, returning with my Benedictine and a glass of cherry brandy for herself.

We moved to a sofa along the wall, wrapped in an embrace. Abruptly she looked up at me and whispered, "Sgt. Judy."

I didn't expect her to know my name.

"Yes?"

"You will never leave me?"

The same old question, but wasn't this a little soon? "But, my sweet, I am a soldier. I must go with my company."

"Yes, yes. But that is not what I mean. You will always come back to me?"

"As long as the enemy lets me, I'll come back."

"Yes, for as long as you live you must come back, for I love you. All the time I see you on the street, I love you. The first time you come in the shop, my heart almost stop. If you do not care for me, I would die." She wrapped me in a generous hug which I returned with fervor.

I was thinking I just might be able to love her—very comfortably love her. Or would this be just the same old story? Well, time alone would tell. For now, there was love to make.

Resisting my rising passion, she demurred. "Not here. Not here. Come, we shall retire."

"But, your mother."

"Ah, she is visit my Aunt Margot at Abainville."

Abainville was the next town down the road, so we were secure for this night at least. I wrapped her in my arms—and so to bed.

We were awakened in the morning by the bugles in the street blowing first call for reveille. I dressed hurriedly, kissed my newfound love, and hastened up the street to stand the call with my company. My absence from the billet overnight having been noted, I was the target of hoots, laughter and a couple jabs in the ribs.

That evening I returned to the little shop where I was smothered with attention. Madame Cecille, returned from Abainville, witnessed the attachment with nods and smiles. I'd been duly accepted as a member of the ménage, and when I gave Georgette a handful of money, my position was doubly assured.

After a very tasty supper, madam engaged me in English, not so fluent as her daughter's but very understandable. After we'd talked aimlessly for a while, she leaned forward, smiling roguishly and said, "Sarjong, you are acquaint with the sarjong that is—how you say—like this?" She made a figure in the air with her hands which I took to signify rotundity.

"Yes," I said with a smile. "I think I know who you mean."

Mac was not what could be called fat by any means, be he did incline to roundness. I dug out a snapshot of him, taken just before we left the States.

"That is heem! That is heem! I—what you say, I like heem—is it not?"

"D'you want me to get 'im?"

"If you would?" Her coy expression, assured a roguishness hidden away somewhere behind that smile.

"I'll be right back." Think of that, I chuckled. She liked old Mac, the toughest bruiser to ever come out of South Boston. I found him in the cafe, sitting apart, relaxed, smoking. When the gang spied me, I got the ribbing from every side.

"Judy, the family man!"

"Did she run you out already?"

"Who untied the apron strings?"

"Take me over and let her meet a real man!" It was half fun and half envy.

"I've got a nice warm bed, and the cooking's swell," I retorted as I sat down beside Mac.

"Well, old heart breaker, what's on your mind?"

"Nothing much. I just came over to deliver a message."

"A message? What the hell kind of message?" He was immediately alarmed for the word message spelled front to him.

"Oh, just a friendly message from a lady."

"Who for?"

"Well, Mac, after me, who's the best looking guy in the outfit?"

"After you? Why, you homely bastard, if I had a dog with a face like yours, I'd feed him strychnine."

"Oh, so you think you're better looking than I am, do you? Well, then the message must be for you. Come on."

"Wait! Not so damn fast! Where're we goin'?"

"Here's how it is, Mac. Madame Cecille, who runs that little coffee shop is lonesome and she asked me to bring you over."

"The hell she did." His round face lit up. "Say, she's pretty nice, ain't she? Well, what're we waitin' for? Let's go!"

We slogged across the muddy village to the Maureauge household where Madame Cecille went to great lengths to welcome Mac and make him feel at home. We spent the evening around a table in the shop, enjoying the company and the refreshments. In the morning the madam fixed coffee for us before we went out. It looked as though a happy sojourn in Gondrecourt was assured.

We stayed in the village for nine tedious days, putting up with the Army's ideas of what we needed, but at least spending our evenings in ease and contentment. We had four new officers assigned to the company, but Lt. Weyandt had been appointed battalion adjutant, a great loss to us. Our new officers were all fresh from training camp, bringing with them a training camp's concept of war. We tried to teach them what they needed to know, an impossible task, for what they needed to know could hardly be expressed in words. It came through experience, and then more as instinct than conscious knowledge. These officers were there to see that we had food, clothing and an abundance of ammunition. Theirs were the thousand and one details of modern warfare, so in the last analysis, our lives were in their keeping.

My new platoon commander marched up the street, resplendent in a tailor made uniform, brand new boots and Sam Browne belt. I saluted him without ceremony, and he returned in kind. "Sgt. Redding, I believe?"

I seldom heard my surname anymore. Redding sounded strange.

"Yes, sir."

"I've heard of you."

He was a decent looking lad, fresh faced and blue eyed, but weak with self-importance.

"Lt. Smith says I should rely on you sergeants." His tone, like a teacher talking to a pupil, grated on me.

"Well, we're all in the learning game, sir," I answered, thinking that the price we would pay for lessons from this guy would be way too high.

"I am glad of that." He drew himself up. "I expect full cooperation from all ranks, and I assure you that I will not be patient with those who make mistakes."

"That's fine, Lieutenant but you'll find that the enemy usually takes care of mistakes much quicker than you can."

He gave me a sharp glance. "I'm glad to have met you, sergeant. I'm sure we will work together very well."

"I'm sure we will, sir."

"Just one other thing, sergeant." He held up a finger to detain me. "I've heard some of you men take a drink now and then. Unfortunate. I don't approve and will not be lax in any case of intoxication."

"I have never been intoxicated in my life, sir, and in my experience it isn't customary in the regular army for an officer to pry into the personal habits of enlisted men until such habits show signs of conflicting with duties. Sir."

Dumb arrogant bastard. I'd already forgotten more than he'd ever know about war. He glowered and, controlling himself with a visible effort, turned sharply on his heel and stalked away, missing my parting salute which I executed in a most military and deferential manner. Apparently my early disposition to avoid hard drinking lay in the muck somewhere, but I resented being considered a problem, especially by one who barely knew me or my performance.

On my way to the parade ground, I ran into Kaynes and Morrie Muller. "Who's the new shavetail?"

"My son, you have just had the honor and privilege of conversing with his excellency, the Lieutenant Melvin, sent over here by the war department expressly to win this war."

"The hell he was. Who taught him the business, his mama? He tells me he's down on liquor."

"Yeah. He is," laughed Morrie. "So am I. Let's go down a little." We repaired to the cafe to discuss and cuss new officers in general and Lt. Melvin in particular.

CHAPTER VII

MONTSEC
JANUARY-MARCH, 1918

We were back on the lines again, in a sector west of our former position. Georgette and I had bidden a fond and tearful farewell, pledging our undying loyalty. She knew that as soon as I came out of the lines again I'd try to win myself another home, and I knew that my place in her heart would be filled before the week was out. In spite of this, we staged a touching scene in the back room of the café. Her mother gave me a bottle of cognac wrapped in brown paper, which I placed carefully in my pack, thanking her profusely.

"Bonne chance, sarjong." she said in a quiet murmur.

"Bonne chance a vous, ma mère," I told her and was on my way.

Digging, wiring, wiring, digging. The war consisted of nothing but dig, fix wire, stand to and stand down. The trenches here were in a swampy section and constantly needed repair. Winter being the season of continual rain, in some spots the bottom of the trench was waist deep in cold, thin mud or thick water. If a man was unlucky enough to slip off the duck board, he was in for a cold, dirty bath and no mistake. Trenches were continually caving in, and we eyed the high hills of Montsec above us, occupied by the enemy, with envy.

Mac, wearing a sheepskin coat and a pair of hip boots, came sloshing up the trench one morning with a squad of six men.

"Well, kid, how you doin'?"

"Who the hell cares? Anyhow, what could you do about it if you did care?"

"Try this." He offered his canteen.

"Oho! Good cherry brandy." I shut my eyes and let it run. "What's goin' on around here? Who are *these* guys?"

"I'm takin' a little patrol job tonight. We're on our way back to battalion to get the dope."

"Leave the canteen here. I'll catch you on the way back."

"You go to hell," he grinned, sloshing up the trench, the muck flirting with his boot tops.

Because an observant enemy was quick to notice movement, and just as quick to discourage it with a few shells, no unnecessary activity went on in the trenches during the day. The less shelling, the less digging we had to do to repair the damage, so we were more than content to spend the daylight hours in our dugouts, leaving only the men on post in the trench.

So far I'd escaped trench lice, but one look at our new dugout told me my time had come. Even though there'd been some heavy fighting here in the past, this sector had been stationary for some years, during which this hole in the ground had been occupied by dozens of outfits. Each had added a little something to the infestation of vermin. Lice were thick on the bunks and among the blankets. I didn't know how I'd escaped so far, but I knew my days of comparative comfort are over.

I joined a blackjack game centered around a candle stuck on a helmet.

"Hot dog! He's broke himself." Scotty Baugh chuckled as the dealer dealt himself a card.

"Pay everybody."

The dealer paid all around, and the game went on.

"What do you play?" the dealer asked.

"Ten francs."

"And you?"

"Fifteen."

"How much to you?"

"Five."

So it went until each man had made his bet before he got any cards. We played with intensity, each man eyeing the dealer's exposed card and weighing his chances carefully before asking for a 'hit' which could improve his hand or ruin it altogether.

Jack Hardy looked at me with a grin. "Nice mam'selle you had in Gondrecourt, eh, Judy?"

"Nice room, too."

"Oh, I'll betcha," he mused. "Plenty vin rouge, too, huh?"

"You know me. I'm a liquor drinker myself. I leave the watery drinks to you smooth faced kids."

"Tough old Judy Redding, the guy with hair on his ears." Hardy's manner leaned toward the provocative.

"Wait'll Lt. Melvin catches up to you. You'll be a water drinker!"

"You're darn right." Mart Keough added. "He's a regular grape juicer. Caught Dave Evans sucking on his canteen this morning and asked him what was in it. Dave says, 'good ole rum,' so he told him to empty it."

"What did Dave do?" I held my cards awaiting the answer, which came from a dozen sources: "Told him to go to hell!"

"Then," Jack went on, "the lieutenant told Dave he was under arrest and would be tried when we moved to the rear. Dave kind of laughed and told him he should say 'if' we move to the rear."

"That bastard ain't gonna live long if he don't change his bloody ways." The comment came out of a corner of the dugout. Bones, sitting up on his bunk looking down at us recalled, "I remember a bloomin' aws like him was wif us in the mucking Dardanelles. One morning they found 'im. Not 'arf shot up 'e warn't, and go blimey, they were all infield bullet 'oles." He laughed a softly gruesome sound. "The bloody bastard, 'e never bothered nobody else."

I knew what Bones was talking about, but that kind of thing can lead to something no one wants to remember.

"Can that crap. Any more talk of shooting people and I'll find a nice little wiring job for you. Remember, we're all in this war for the same thing: to survive. Maybe he doesn't like us a damn bit better than we like him."

"Sure. Sure, Sarge, we know all about that, but I still bet you a hundred francs he changes his ideas or dies damn sudden."

"Well, be damn sure you butchers give him time to change his ideas before you do any shooting."

I rolled up in a blanket in my bunk, ready to give myself over to fatigue. Before dropping off to sleep, my mind wandered back to more pleasant times, my home town—a gritty Pennsylvania Railroad town at the foot of the Alleghenies, my old girlfriend, Claire. Her old man wanted to marry her off to a prosperous butcher and every time I turned up on the scene, I raised hell with his plan. Her letters were filled with the day-to-day—nothing of consequence. She lived in a world so far from mine I could hardly remember it. Under family pressure she'd probably marry her peddler of puddings and grow fat.

"Oh, well, there are plenty other women." I rolled over to get some sleep.

That night I did my tour in the trenches. We didn't have any working parties out because of Mac's patrol. It didn't do to have the area in front of the trenches too thickly populated. Parties were hard to identify and two parties from the same outfit could get confused and shoot each other up. Mac's patrol had been out about two hours since midnight so we expected them in soon. They came and went by a drainage ditch running out under the barbed wire directly in front of my section of trench. It was so miserably cold the dampness was creeping into my bones. I heard someone sloshing along the trench so I lowered myself from the fire step. The new comer moved around the traverse into our bay of trench and almost bumped into me. I recognized Lt. Melvin's voice: "Who's that?"

"Sgt. Redding."

"Oh, I was looking for you, sergeant. How is everything?"

"All's well, sir. Mac's not back with his patrol yet."

"Well, they should be in soon. Two hours is the rule." He seemed anxious.

"When you're out there, lieutenant, you can't just regulate your schedule by the clock. Lots of things can slow you up."

"Yes. Yes, I know. Beastly cold, isn't it, sergeant?"

"It's always cold up here, lieutenant."

"How do you men keep warm, anyhow?" He sounded wistful as if the most important thing in the world was to get his feet warm. I knew the feeling.

"Well, mostly, lieutenant," I said, taking a chance, and handing him my canteen, "we use this."

"What is it?" He drew back, fear of temptation written all over his face.

"Brandy."

"Oh, I never touch that stuff. It's poison." Like a Sunday School boy, he was determined to stay true to his childhood convictions.

"Lieutenant, there's nothing in the world that doesn't have its uses. This, I think, was expressly made for men shivering in trenches, numb with cold. General Grant used it. Why not us?"

He hesitated, then slowly extended his hand for the canteen. I unscrewed the top and passed it to him. He raised it to his lips and took an experimental sip.

"Why it's not bad," he said, licking his lips. "Burns a little, but it's not as strong as I expected."

"I wouldn't drink it if it tasted that bad." I took a good big slug, proud of my skill in dealing with this Boy Scout. I handed him back the canteen; he took another sip and returned it.

Up the trench a few yards, at the end of the drainage ditch, I heard the man on port challenge in a whisper. "Halt! Who's there?"

"Shut up, you slack brained son of a bitch! Any more noise from you and I'll kick your damn fool head off." No mistake. Mac had returned from his patrol. I was relieved of my worries for this crusty purveyor of tough talk, upon whom I found myself relying more and more every day. Good old Mac.

The party filed past in the narrow ditch, one man bleeding profusely at the neck and another holding his arm in his hand. Mac hurried by with a grim nod to make his report.

I stepped up on the fire step beside Tony, the gunner on post. "See anything?"

"Not a thing." Tony peered deep into the darkness. "How long've we got yet?"

"Fifty-five minutes." I checked my watch to make sure. We did four hours on and eight off. This gave the men a good rest between shifts, more important than the layman might think.

Mac must have had trouble. He was due in at two, and didn't get in till after three. Crawling around in the mud between the trenches clear over to the enemy barbed wire to find out what he was up to was asking for trouble, discomfort and often death. I must have been a morbid sap, else why did my thoughts always end up dwelling on death?

Probably because deep down we knew death was the ultimate end for all of us. We'd escape for a while, tasting of the joys between the terrors, but in the end—Poof!—someone else would take your place, not only with the outfit, but in feasting on the delights we thought were ours alone.

"Hey, Judy. You asleep?" Tony spoke softly from his place on the fire step.

"No, just thinking."

"Well, while you're thinking, just think it's darn soon time for the relief."

"Gripe and bitch. Gripe and bitch. Gritch, gritch, gritch! Listen, guess what I did a while ago."

"What?"

"I gave Lt. Melvin a drink."

"The hell you did!"

"I sure did, boy, and he took it like a man. There's hope for the lad, Tony. There's hope."

"Well, what the hell do you know about that?" Wonder and admiration in his voice. "How'd you do it, anyhow?"

"I just let him get damn good and cold and then made the suggestion." I groped in my pack. "Pull in your ears, Tony. I'm gonna kick off a flare."

I loaded my flare pistol and moved down the trench a few yards. Pointing the pistol upward in the direction of the enemy lines, I pulled the trigger. After I shot, I trotted back up the trench to Tony's post. The flare reached the zenith of its arc in a shower of sparks. The enemy was likely to shoot at the base of this display of fireworks. As usual, he didn't disappoint, but his efforts were wasted. Maybe he'd be luckier next time. Tony and I watched as the flare opened high in the heavens and floated gently earthward. Nothing could be seen in the bright, eerie light except the gaunt branches of a dead tree here and there and our own barbed wire, stark and stiff in the cold, white light. Far off was a dim blur, the enemy's wire. In between nothing moved. Tony fired off a burst to keep the gun warm. We pulled our feet out of the muck repeatedly, trying to stir up a little circulation.

Far to the rear a throbbing hum, faint at first, gradually increased in volume until a squadron of planes passed overhead—large planes, probably bombers with fighters above.

Our own planes. We tried to pick out their shapes as they passed in front of light spots in the sky.

"There's a soft job," Tony sighed as the throbbing beat faded into the distance.

"Best job in the war," I agreed. An aviator would probably never know what a good job he had. They only had to fly a few hours each day, their only menace the other airplane. Three hots and a cot. The war's aristocrats.

Tony and I stood looking into the darkness in silence. Tony was quite the good looking southern boy, blue eyed, black haired and roguishly handsome. He'd broken a heart or two in his time, but he was always a gentleman, full of consideration and respect for women. It was bred into those southern boys like corn pone and fatback. He wasn't a Southern Gentlemen in the economic sense, but he did them proud in decorum.

Scattered shellfire chattered a little way to the east. Flares went up here and there. It was almost peaceful, and we were lost in our own thoughts, enveloped in a strange contentment. The bond between us allowed communication without words. My best friend, Tony understood me as no one else did. There was a difference between his friendship and Mac's. Mac mothered me and braced me up, but Tony understood without words and made me feel okay about my shortcomings. I don't think I could have made it without him. He knew my fears—the extent and depth of them, and I knew his. He knew I had to stay half drunk for a month after that shellfire up near Aracourt or I'd never have dared stick my nose out of the dugout. His manner didn't give me away. We trusted each other with our lives. No words. No public demonstrations. Just good, solid understanding and unwavering friendship.

He stirred and fired a burst, stamped his feet and cursed. "Christ Almighty, how long are we on this stretch for, life?"

"They're coming now," I heard the clank of equipment from up the trench.

After we were relieved we clumped down into the dugout, where Mac was drinking coffee and rum and regaling the troops with a tale of the night's patrol.

"What happened? I saw you had a couple of casualties."

"We mixed it with a Heinie patrol over near their wire."

"How many hurt?"

"Two. Schorach got a bayonet in the neck and Carlin got a broken arm from a rifle butt. We had a prisoner, but he kicked off before we could get him back."

"Tough."

"Yeah. I'll say. They caught us over there in that little swale. They must have heard us and sent out two patrols to get us between them. Well, O'Malley caught sight of the one coming through the wire, and we started to draw away from them and damned near bumped right in to the other bunch. We had to fight like hell for a while to get away."

The warm dugout candlelight threw faces into bold relief — faces that had developed a lean and hawk-like quality, a ruthlessness in their bearing. Here they sat, not an hour back from an expedition of death, but strangely enough the conversation turned not to death, but to life and love. Oh, woman. The sphere of your influence reaches beyond your wildest dreams.

Bruce spoke, as usual, of his girl back home in Alabama. In fact, he'd scarcely stopped speaking of her once since I'd known him.

"And, boy! You ought to see those big blue eyes of hers. Gee, if I could just see her for a minute."

"Aw, you take your women too serious," Mac told him. "You gotta learn to love 'em and leave 'em in this game. You ask anyone."

Bruce was not convinced. "No, sir, boy. Not me. I couldn't leave her. Why, buddy, if she was to quit me now, I'd go nuts!"

"Well, you better be nuts, then. She's probably sleeping with a shipyard worker right now."

"Like hell! Not my girl!" Bruce shouted. The dugout burst into a roar of laughter.

"Ask Judy," someone said. "He knows all about love."

I looked around. It was Tony, sitting on a bunk, his feet dangling over the edge and an impish grin on his face.

"Me? I don't know anything about love."

"Hell, no. You don't know anything about love. But every place we stop long enough to sleep, you don't end up sleeping alone." Tony was just getting wound up.

"That's not love."

"No? Well, what the hell is it?"

"I'm just learning the language."

"Oh, so you don't believe in love? Well, Bruce does."

"Yeah, I guess he does," I agreed. "And I'll bet before he's through with this war he'll be damn sorry he ever heard the word. Love. Humph."

"Tony's still thinking about Yvette." Morrie Muller climbed up to a top bunk. "Don't worry, Tony. She's sleeping warm."

Tony threw him an angry look, jumped down from the bunk and stomped up the dugout steps. Somewhere out there someone started to sing. What gets into these guys? Singing!

"Well, for Christ's sake! Who put the nickel in the hurdy-gurdy?" Red Conlon didn't appreciate singing.

CHAPTER VIII

MONTSEC
JANUARY-MARCH, 1918

March came along, bringing with it the promise of spring. Shells popped over intermittently and now and then we heard the twitter of a bird. Oh, it was good to be alive these days, even if we did lead a miserable life.

My earlier aversion to alcohol had given over to a constant buzz which got me through the long days and longer nights, so when Mac and Tony called me to a sunny angle of the trench to offer me a big drink of fresh rum just brought up from the rear, I took advantage.

In the eight weeks since we took over this sector, we'd gone far on the path to wisdom. With about four months of trench warfare behind us, we felt invincible, ready for anything. We'd made raids, been raided and repulsed one fair sized attack. Because of quite a few casualties, particularly when a 210 dropped in our bay of trench one night and killed eight men and wounded four, our section had been brought up to strength with men from other sections.

That's how I happened to be bunking with John Gallagher from Tyrone, a town not far from my hometown of Altoona, Pennsylvania. A replacement for one of the corporals, he seemed a little homesick, so I told him to throw his blankets in my bunk, and it seemed to help him adjust. His youth and innocence made me want to watch out for him. He didn't smoke, drink, chew, swear or try to dodge duty, all very unusual in this man's army.

After leaving Tony and Mac, I passed down the trench to arrange for a covering party for that night's working party when Lt. Melvin appeared around the traverse.

"Good morning, lieutenant." We'd become good buddies since I showed him how to keep his feet warm.

"Good morning, sergeant. How are you this fine morning?"

"In the pink, Lieutenant. Absolutely in the blooming old pink."

"I'm glad to hear it. You know you're down for a covering party tonight?"

"Yes, sir. So I've heard."

"Have you picked your men?"

"Yes, sir. I've got four guns and twenty-four riflemen. Each man has two hundred rounds and two grenades, and two men will carry a bag of grenades each."

"Right. Now at four-thirty this afternoon I'll meet you in the trench and point out the area, and you can plan the disposition of your men."

"Yes, sir. I'll be here."

I slipped down to eat a bite of corn bill at the dugout fire.

"Boy, we sure made a human out of Lieutenant Melvin."

I said that to John, who sat on the bunk cleaning his rifle. He was going to shoot somebody with that thing yet.

John gave me a smile and went on with his cleaning, stopping to offer me some candy from one of his innumerable boxes from home. His mother, sister and girlfriends kept him well supplied with cookies, candy and wool socks. After sitting around for a while I crawled into the bunk to sleep before the long night ahead. My God, how I did itch, but then better than two months without a bath *should* make a guy itch. Suddenly I tore open my shirt for a closer look. A bath would do me no good. I was lousy.

Evening. The sun low on the horizon behind us. I met Lt. Melvin and we laid out the positions. We left the trench at ten o'clock crawling on our bellies under cover of darkness. At ten-thirty the working party would come out and work till two in the morning. We'd follow them back at two-thirty. Movable panels were placed over the barbed wire to ease our exit and return. Everything was ready. Lt. Melvin had charge of our covering party and Lt. Crockett the working party. I smelled bacon frying back in the dugout—reminded me of my mother bustling around in her kitchen back home. I wished I could go down to enjoy a bite before we set out on the night's business. No such luck.

Black night. Silence in the bay of trench where half a hundred men stood waiting, prepared to file out into the darkness. It was no less dark here in the trench but contact with each other and the protecting walls created an illusion of security, a haven that'd be left behind once we filed through those gaps in the wire. I'd had the feeling before. Once beyond the sheltering maze of wire, I'd be seized by helplessness—loneliness—like there was no one to lean on. If we were caught out there and attacked by the enemy, it meant annihilation. I felt infinitesimally small, a helpless creature toyed with at the mercy and whim of our adversary. Once our position was established, the feeling would pass and we'd gain strength from each other, once more a formidable fighting machine.

A star shell slowly curved up from the enemy lines to burst and flood the ground with radiant light. Its illumination didn't reach our wire, but made the men cautious—the best possible thing for them.

Lt. Melvin filed past the men to my side. "All ready, sergeant?" This was no longer new to him, and he wasted no time in preliminaries.

"Yes, sir. All ready."

"How are the men?"

"Good shape, I think, sir. Some may be a bit jumpy, but that'll wear off."

"Yes, it generally does. A few nights ago we had trouble keeping them awake after the first two hours. All right, sergeant. Move them out."

I motioned to the men nearest me and we silently slipped over the parapet and out through the lane in the barbed wire in single file. Once in position, we deployed on a predetermined line with two machine guns on each flank. Two of the guns were placed to command the center and two protected our flanks with the riflemen stretched out between them. The lieutenant asked for the patrol and I called for John Gallagher. He and four men moved out ahead about a hundred yards to patrol back and forth parallel to our line. Their job was to see that no prowling patrol or enemy attacking party would get within striking distance.

The spring air was soft and balmy and after looking over our dispositions, I lay down beside Tony at his gun.

"Nice night."

"Swell."

"Not much doing in the line of dirt, either," he continued. "I hope the job is like this all night."

"I hope so, too, but you can't tell. Some are and some aren't."

Soon muffled tappings and scrapings told us the working party was out doing a job on the wire.

An enemy machine gun started to hammer, muffled at first, then louder, then suddenly sharp, loud and insistent, then quiet and muffled again. I dug my toes in and felt Tony wiggle himself flat to the ground to let the burst pass over us.

"Some guy warming his gun, I guess."

"Humph, took a damn long burst to do it with."

"Wonder if he hit the working party." We listened as the quiet sounds of industry still came faintly from the rear. No harm in that quarter.

Silence once more, so I decided to look over our party again. As I belly crawled to the center of the line, word passed that the lieutenant wanted me. I hurried to the other end where he waited.

"I think the patrol's in trouble, sergeant. I heard something that didn't sound right."

I listened for a time but didn't hear anything. I looked at the lieutenant.

"We'll have to send another patrol to see what happened. Send two good men, sergeant."

"Yes, sir." I passed the word along the line for Mitchell and Bones, the best hand-to-hand fighters in the outfit. This assignment called for quick, decisive action and above all, silence. They'd try to establish communication with the patrol we thought was in trouble. If they ran into the enemy, there'd be only one course of action: kill or be killed. No prisoners taken. The action was swift and deadly—silence paramount, for the sound of a shot would bring the artillery of both sides into play and then nobody would have a chance.

Bones and Mitchell stripped themselves of everything—rifles, bayonets, helmets, ammunition—anything that might encumber or make noise. They carried only entrenching pick handles with spikes driven through the thick end, the heads filed off, the ends sharpened like something out of the Middle Ages—a 'knob duster'—quick, silent and deadly efficient.

When they were ready, I gave them last instructions, useless, as all concerned were aware. They knew as much about what they were going to do as I did, and were far more capable of doing it. No need to tell a man to be careful of his own life. No matter how many other lives were in his care, he'd guard them no better than his own.

Bones grinned as I slapped his back. They crawled slowly out in front and melted into the darkness. I heard a sigh beside me. Lt. Melvin. Only a few months away from a sheltered home life, he'd just ordered two men to possible death. Their quiet obedience and matter of fact acceptance of what the next hour held in store brought the lieutenant to grave respect.

'What do you see, sergeant? Anything?"

"Nothing, sir."

I peered into the darkness as though what was happening out there should be visible. There was no sound, but my senses told me things unseen and unheard were going on out there in the darkness. Restless, I fidgeted, constantly shifting my gaze. I couldn't be still, so I moved to see to things along the line, crawling slowly toward Tony's gun.

The men were all lying stretched out with their rifles in front of them, surprisingly well hidden. I felt better. As long as I kept moving, my mind occupied, there was nothing to indicate any further mishaps out front.

Suddenly a scream — long, drawn out and shrill — pierced the night, then a dull coughing grunt, and silence. The hair rose on the back of my neck as electric chills ran through me.

"Christ, that did it. We'll get artillery now." I cowered down expecting to hear the approaching whine of shells, but nothing happened. I waited. Then I figured it out. There was an enemy party on patrol. Our own artillery knew we were out and wouldn't fire without a signal. The enemy must have been in the same fix. I dug in my elbows and pulled myself along toward Tony.

"What's the dope?"

I told him what I knew.

"Well, someone just got his out there, and we'll have news damn quick."

"That's right. Take care of yourself. I've got to get back to the lieutenant. If anyone comes in on this end, shove them along the line as quick as you can."

"Okay. Be careful."

I moved back up the line. Here came a man crawling as fast as he could to meet me. Anderson. "Hurry up, Judy, the lieutenant wants you," he panted. "Bones and part of the patrol are back."

"Where's Mitchell?" I asked, hurrying along behind him.

"Dead. Stabbed, I think."

When I reached the lieutenant, he was all action.

"Alert the men, sergeant. There's a large enemy combat patrol out. Gallagher reports about three hundred men."

So Johnny was back safe. So much for worrying about him.

The lieutenant continued, "I sent word to the working party to retire. We'll follow as soon as they're safely in."

I hurried along the line making sure everyone was awake. Here and there I had to shake a man out of reverie. A few offered quiet comment.

"What's the dope, sarge?"

"Whites of their eyes, eh, what?"

"Yeah, but don't shoot 'til you get orders or until the machine guns go into action."

We weren't here to start a fight, just to cover the working party as it filed back into the trench.

Suddenly and without warning, pandemonium broke loose. One moment the dark silent mystery of night; the next, hell let loose its fury, the shriek, roar and crash of exploding shells, whining pieces of red hot metal. Not a series of noises, this. Just one long detonating crash. I saw a body lift from the ground and slam back down again. The light from the shell bursts provided a continuous red glare. This was no bombardment. This was a barrage, and we were right under it, and this was no patrol; it was a raiding party. This was their barrage and they'd follow behind it loaded for bear. Here we were, caught out in front. What a hell of a jam.

I lay against the earth, engulfed in fear, surrounded by friends but unable to communicate in this fury of shells. We might as well be separated by a thousand miles. I was tempted to signal for a counter barrage from our own artillery, but we were so far in front of our own lines, it would either fall behind us or right on top of us. I knew this enemy barrage would move on past us onto our front line, but when it did, we'd have the enemy raiding party to contend with. We were outnumbered by better than ten to one before this artillery fire hit us. God only knew how we'd compare when it was over.

I was surprised that my mind even worked in this fury of high explosives. The strong smell of chiddite stung my nostrils, my eyes burned, and I couldn't seem to orient myself. I tried to make my way to Tony because when this let up, machine guns would be our only salvation. I crawled and gasped and fought my way along, trying to melt into the ground, like being tossed and buffeted about in a stormy sea. I lost my sense of direction, turned about by the gigantic concussions all around me. Christ, couldn't I move any faster? Suddenly I saw Tony's gun position and struggled with my last ounce of energy to reach it. I didn't think I was making progress, but the mound which was Tony's gun seemed to slide steadily toward me. It was right in front of me. I saw a dim figure tugging and hauling among some bodies, piling the bodies of freshly killed men about the gun to protect it from anything except a direct hit.

I crawled right up and put my mouth close to his ear and yelled, "Give 'em hell!"

He shrugged and shouted something I couldn't hear. The din was too great. I turned and crawled back the way I'd come. Tony lay down behind his gun. The explosions didn't shake me so much now. Sure enough, the barrage was lifting and falling to our rear. Well, now for it.

The world in front was suddenly flooded with a brilliant white light. Both guns on the left hammered out their chorus of warfare and sudden death. I watched the enemy advance. He didn't know we were there yet. Rifle fire cracked up and down the line. Tony's gun came into action in a long burst. Where was that fourth gun? When it suddenly it came to life, relief flooded over me. All four guns in working order. Good! Those Heinies would sure as hell know we were here.

Our crossfire caught them bunched in a compact group, and they seemed to melt away. I heard their cries, elated. Yell, you Bastards! We had to take it a minute ago. Now, God damn you, you take it! I ran along the line toward Tony's gun, unable to keep still. I fired my pistol, reloaded and ran on. Ah, there he was, hunched over his jumping, bucking gun. It shook and danced like something alive. In the light of the flares, I could see his lips move, but I heard no sound.

The enemy spread out, intending to make a fight of it. Harder to hit now. I ran along the line urging the men to pick their targets, surprised we hadn't lost more. The lieutenant moved toward me with a flare pistol in his hand and placed his mouth against my ear.

"A barrage is our only hope, right, sergeant?"

"Yes, sir, if we can get it in the right place."

"I think we can. I sent a runner back to phone in our position to the artillery."

"Well, let 'er go, lieutenant."

I was still exhilarated, in the midst of an adrenalin rush, unable to keep still. The lieutenant pointed his flare pistol in the air and a stream of sparks streaked upward, burst into five stars and slowly descended. The stars hadn't touched the ground when the whine and roar of approaching shells, this time from our side, filled the sky. We dropped down, not sure where they'd land. They passed over us with a rush and suck of air that almost took our breath, to crash right on the enemy positions.

"There, you bastards! See how you like it." I shouted in relief.

Lt. Melvin looked at me, frowning.

"Have you no pity, sergeant?" he asked quietly. With that, the rush subsided and I suddenly felt small and humble.

Under cover of our counter barrage, we assembled our party and slipped back into the trench. Their barrage now fell to the rear of our front line—regular raid procedure, designed to isolate the section to be raided. Of course, their artillery, not knowing the outcome of the raid, went right through with their operation on schedule.

Tired, weak and nauseated—the feeling of exhilaration gone—normal reaction set in. My stomach started to twitch and jerk—not as bad as the first time. I sat down on the fire step. Shells banged and crashed overhead. This wasn't a good place to be, but dejected and dispirited, I took a big drink from my canteen and covered my face with my hands. What the hell was the use, anyhow?

What was this? My face wet and smeary, I ran down the dugout steps to find a mirror, searched my face, one side of which was smeared with bits of hair and flesh and blood. I never felt it hit me. Horrified, I ran back up the steps to the trench. Mac stood on post, his eyes scanning the darkness.

"Well, for Christ's sake," he growled, "you coming unraveled again?"

"Look at my face."

"Well. There's water in the dugout."

His refusal to see anything unusual served to calm me, and I went down the dugout steps to clean my self up. Tony was there, his face streaked with sweat and powder smoke. He greeted me quietly. The men lay around, quiet and subdued, utterly exhausted.

"How many got back?."

"Twenty-six." Tony said it flat, without emotion.

"Who all got it?"

"Kyle, Jamison, Mitchell, Edwards and Mart Keough from our section. I don't know who from the other sections."

"Tough."

"Yeah. Damn tough. And what's it all for, anyway? We do this so some white-livered son of a bitch back home can lie in bed in safety." I understood his bitterness. I felt the same way.

CHAPTER IX

MONTSEC
APRIL, 1918

News, rumors and counter rumors. The enemy attacked from Arras to St. Quentin. Shells have fallen on Paris. We would have to move. The air, now definitely spring-like was filled with stories that sprung from nowhere.

I met Red Conlon 'reading his shirt' in the warm sunlight.

"What's the latest?"

"I dunno," Red replied. "They tell me there's still a war on." As he spoke, two shells buried themselves in our barbed wire, not a hundred feet away. "Say, Judy, did you hear how far the Heinies have advanced up north?"

"I heard about twelve kilometers up to yesterday. The British and French are slowing them up and making them fight for all they get."

"Well, we ain't gonna be here long."

Morrie Muller came down the trench to join us. We all had our shirts off now and were reaping a harvest of lice. Some we cracked between our finger nails and some we burned on a cigarette.

"I saw some strange officers back in the second line this morning. Americans, too. I think they were liaison officers from a division coming up behind to relieve us." Morrie always was a fountain of information—something about his boyish face made him trustworthy—a keeper of secrets.

"Might be, but if we're relieved here, where'll we go?" I wondered.

This division was in great shape right now, and ready for anything. The men had all been under fire; all had seen men die. We were fully hardened to modern warfare.

"Hey! Did you guys hear the news?" Scotty Baugh ran up the trench as fast as he could tear. "There's gonna be an armistice."

This was the most common of all rumors. It popped up about once a month, but that didn't deter Scotty from repeating it with enthusiasm.

"Where'd you get that? Out of the latrine?" Red could be disparaging when he wanted to be.

"No. An ambulance driver told Anderson that he heard two Frenchmen celebrating."

"Probably celebrating payday," said Muller. "But anyway, the way the Heinies are gaining in their drive, the war might be over damn sudden."

"Yeah, that's right." Red pulled his shirt over his head, his voice issuing forth in muffled tones. "And we'll all be prisoners of war."

"How are they goin' so damn fast?" Lafferty wondered, a replacement who still thought the enemy would scare if you yelled boo at him. "The French and British should have stopped them in their tracks."

"Well, when Russia collapsed, that freed up about seventy-five enemy divisions for this front. They kept those divisions out all winter, fed and rested them all that time. When they started their drive the other day, they had the better part of a million men—fresh, strong, full of ginger. There's no reason why they shouldn't move right along. The Allies have no reserves and can't relieve tired outfits with fresh ones. So if you're in front of their push now, you just have to stay there and take it."

Lafferty looked thoughtful, then brightened. "There's lots of Americans coming over. It won't be long before we have plenty of reserves."

"All I gotta say is, they better hurry up." said Muller. "I don't want to wind up in any German prison camp."

"Oh, I don't know. I've heard that frauliens don't make bad bedfellows." That was Red, always thinking of the ladies.

"Hell of a chance *you'd* get to find out," Muller chided.

Red grinned and moved off. I followed him down the dugout steps, but our conversation came to an abrupt end when I heard my name called at the top. I climbed up to see what Lt. Melvin wanted.

"Have the men assemble their equipment, sergeant. We leave here tonight."

"Yes, sir."

He hesitated, then went on. "I'm leaving, too, sergeant."

"I'm sorry to hear that, sir." I meant it, for he'd turned out to be a fine, humane officer, one in whose hands I was now willing to place my life.

"I just wanted to tell you goodbye," he continued, "and to tell you that my service with you men has done more for me as an officer than all the training schools in the world. I was pretty bad at first, wasn't I?"

"Well, there *has* been improvement, sir. But you weren't *so* bad, and I am glad to have served under you, sir."

He laughed. "Well, sergeant, before this turns into a mutual admiration society, I'll be going. Tell the rest of the men goodbye for me."

I went down the dugout steps. "You guys get your junk where you can find it. We're getting relieved tonight."

Joy greeted my announcement. No one knew where we were going and no one cared. The only direction we could go was back. That meant a few days out of the mud away from the constant threat of death or torn, bruised, bleeding bodies. Already the men started to enumerate the delights of the rear areas.

"Oh, boy. Wait till I get my feet under a table," cried one.

"You said it. And a bath. I'll soak for a week."

Tony came down the steps. "I hear we're pullin' out, Judy."

"That's right."

"When?"

"Tonight."

"Where to?"

"I dunno, but I wouldn't count on too much. You know we still got a war on."

"Yeah, I know. I just wondered if we might get back far enough for a trip to Vitry le Francois."

"That might be arranged." If we got within a few miles of the place I figured I'd tell him to take a day off. "Do you ever hear from her, Tony?"

"Yeah. Regular." A quiet response.

"What's she have to say?"

"Oh, nothing much."

"Well that's the way with a girl. They get a guy going and then just string him along."

"Oh no, Judy. You're dead wrong. She's not stringing me a damn bit."

His voice was low and earnest. It was clear he'd fallen. I just hoped he could tell a good woman when he saw one. Hell, Yvette could be a French spy for all he knew. But, what the hell? I wouldn't try to talk him out of it if I could.

That night we were relieved by the 26th American Division which had moved down from the Chemin de Dames area. As we marched out of the rear area, someone, I didn't know who, turned and shook his fist toward Montsec. "So long, old boy," he cried, "we'll be back and get you."

The gift of prophecy might well have been his.

CHAPTER X

CANTIGNY
MAY, 1918

Hay foot, straw foot, belly full of beans, hike, hike, hike. Dusty roads, muddy roads, unending roads, stretching forever in front of us like ribbons to eternity. For seventeen days we marched, resting here for a day, there for a day. Now airplanes buzzed above us in greater numbers, the dull rumble of the guns a constant crash and bang. All signs indicated we were close to the front.

This time back of the lines was a total washout. We hadn't stopped anywhere long enough to do anything except get cleaned up. Gripe all you want, soldier, it can't be helped. Yesterday we sighted a squadron of British fighting planes returning from the front, doing rolls, loops, dead leaf falls — cutting all the capers known to aerial combat as if they were celebrating something. Today we got news that Baron Von Richthofen was shot down yesterday. The legendary Red Baron. We figured the squadron we saw must have done it.

April 25th at midnight or later, we moved into our positions in support, shells whining and banging incessantly. Quartered in the ruins of a little town called Broyes, we settled ourselves in a large, L-shaped dugout under a house. It was dry, thank God, so we counted ourselves lucky, lit some candles and stowed our equipment around on the bunks.

In the interim between getting settled and what was to come, Red Conlon and Tony opened a major discussion on the merits of rum versus cognac. Red was for rum. When they asked my opinion, I pleaded that it would be impossible to render a just decision without having a sample of each. This brought shouts of derision.

Bones sat on his bunk, humming softly to himself while Brice and Harris made coffee. Brice looked at me. "Shot of coffee, Judy?"

"Sure. You got anything to go with it?"

"You'd be surprised." A sly look. "Ta daa!" He lifted a package wrapped in brown paper.

"What the hell is it?"

"Chicken, boy. Chicken!"

"Where'd you get that?"

Harris chimed in. "Never mind now, *sergeant!* What you don't know won't hurt us."

"G'wan. Tell 'im, Harris."

"He doesn't need to know." Harris, the mystery man—distinguished looking, fine modulated voice and quiet manner—well educated if I was any judge. What he was doing as a private, I'd never know.

So Brice took up the story. "Harris told an old lady back in the last town the story of his life," he chuckled. "And she cooked up this chicken for him."

Harris sat quiet, eyes downcast, almost as though he were embarrassed.

"What the hell kind of story was it?" asked Tony, curious as I was about Harris. "Nothing to interest you."

Harris went on slicing the chicken. There wasn't much for so many, but we made it go as far as we could. In the meantime, my curiosity aroused, I figured I'll try to get Harris's story out of Brice. I moved over and sat down beside him, my steaming cup of coffee in hand.

"What's with Harris, anyway?" I asked in low tones. "Is the law after him?"

Brice leaned back with a laugh. "Anything but, fellow. Anything but."

"Well, then why the mystery?"

"Well, it's like this. Our friend Mr. Private Second Class Harris is a mislaid preacher."

"The hell he is!" I'd expected almost anything but this.

"Damn right. And what's more, he could make some of these narrow-backed chaplains eat their Bibles, too." Brice was full of admiration for his bunkie.

Highly intrigued, I figured to learn what was behind this 'mislaid preacher' sooner or later. Should be interesting.

Bones stretched, let himself down from his bunk and began a retelling of the story of the Angel of Mons, which immediately stoked a discussion of the supernatural. Red Conlon joined in, going on about how he came to fire on a raiding party some time back while I was on duty and Red was one of the gunners in the trench. "Remember that night, Judy?"

"Sure do."

"Well, there I was standing in the trench, dark night, not many flares on account of a patrol that was out. I couldn't see a thing and the harder I looked, the less I saw. After a while I thought I saw something white moving over toward the enemy lines. I would watch it awhile and then lose sight of it. Then I'd see it again. I couldn't make out what it was—just looked like a formless white cloud. Then it moved steadily in our direction, and as it came closer it took on the shape of three white horses. Well, I wondered what in hell three horses would be doing running around between the trenches."

While Red related his tale I wondered if there was anything to these visions—if they really did mean anything. Was it his imagination, or did some occult influence really go to work in times of great mental stress to warn us of impending danger?

Meanwhile, Red continued. "Then these damn horses came right up to our barbed wire and seemed to disappear. They appeared again farther out and came up to the barbed wire again, but instead of disappearing as before, they hesitated. They walked right through the barbed wire. Right through it, mind you, without making a sound. Well, that's where I figured they were trying to warn us or something. When three horses can walk right straight through the wire, it's time to shoot, and I did. I never had the least idea there was a 'Jerry' raiding party out, but there was. I caught them fair and square just as they were strung out in a lane they'd cut in our wire. And let me tell you, that raiding party sure got ruined sudden and complete." Finished, Red looked around for approval.

Heads nodded and others contributed similar experiences. It all seemed rather creepy to me. But then what wasn't creepy here in this region of death and destruction? The nights always felt clammy, like anything could be hidden in the mist. Sometimes when we were on patrol or some risky night job, it seemed as though the fingers of death rested lightly on our necks, ready to close at the whim of the grim reaper. When the job was done, and we reached the haven of our trenches, the deadly caress seemed to relax, with a grisly promise, "Next time."

Before daylight came we had surveyed our new surroundings between shell bursts that had been coming all night long. Tony and Mac arrived from across the street with news.

"They knocked off fifty-one of company A with one shell this morning. Thirty-three dead and eighteen wounded."

"Anyone we know?" I asked.

"Sure," Tony replied. "Hobart, Davison, Rogers and Sgt. Buss, that I know of." All friends of mine. Slowly but surely the old blood was being whittled down. Soon I'd be a stranger in my own outfit.

Late in the morning we were called to company headquarters to meet the new officers and learn of our whereabouts. Our post was in front of the deepest advance made by the enemy in his big attack of March 21st. The city of Montdidier was just a few kilometers behind his lines and directly in front of us. The village of Cantigny was practically in the enemy's front line, a very active front—constant artillery fire and minor movement all along the line.

Our new officers would be permanent. In the past, we'd been acting as a sort of training outfit for officers. They'd come and stay with us for a few months, get some experience, and then go take over outfits of their own. This was all over now; these officers would stay with us until removed by one cause or another related to the hazards of war.

Capt. Dunkel, company commander, ran the show with our platoon leader, a freckle-faced little Texan named Courland. I liked his looks. He shook hands with me and Mac when we met and I noticed his uniform was the same material as ours and sort of a sloppy fit. No elitist, he. Eyeing us up and down, he drawled, "Ah've heard of you gen'lemen, and ah b'lieve we'll get along."

"We always have," Mac grinned at a twinkle in the lieutenant's eye.

Shells burst continually in the village. A white dust arose from the incessant vibrations, covering everything with a fine coat of chalk dust like the erasers back in school. Walking back to the dugout Mac commented. "Well, soldier, it looks like we've really got some war on our hands here."

"Yes. I guess we have."

"What do you think of the new platoon commander?"

"Looks all right to me." The beautiful spring morning set my mind to wandering back to trout fishing in a crystal clear

Pennsylvania creek, reveling in the soft spring sunshine. The fresh green of the landscape and the clean, sweet smell in the air took me away for a while. Lieutenants and the trappings of war and bloodshed faded onto the distance for a few short moments. Then a screaming shell crashing into the apple orchard behind us rocked me back to the present.

"Dreamin' again," Mac derided. "Some day you're gonna start dreamin' and wake up with a harp."

"Doesn't make much difference, does it? Just make room for some other poor sucker to take my place."

"Yeah. That's right. Someone will take all of our places sooner or later."

I was surprised to hear Mac give voice to such thoughts. He wasn't much of a thinker—always seemed too tough to waste a moment brooding over his own demise, but if it was action you wanted, he was your man

John Gallagher yelled from the dugout doorway. "Hey, sergeant. You're wanted at company headquarters."

What? I was just getting back from there. I retraced my steps, leaving Mac to go on alone. Capt. Dunkel greeted me when I arrived.

"Sergeant, take your section and report to Lt. Davies at the crossroads outside of town. He'll give you further instructions."

"Yes, sir," I hurried back to the dugout, formed the section, and moved them to the crossroads, where I found Lt. Davies and a section from the fourth platoon.

"Move 'em up, Sergeant. Establish a line along the crest of that low rise just in front of the town."

I look where he pointed. On top of the rise stood an old chateau, its grounds right in our line of digging.

As we moved up through the lawns and driveways, shells fell around us—big ones, throwing up great blobs of earth and shaking the ground. They weren't thick enough to be called a barrage, just a good, heavy, harassing fire. As soon we reached our position, we laid out a line and started to dig, the shells providing a great incentive. Everyone dug. I had a hole deep enough to cover me in a crouch in no time. Two men teamed up to dig each hole, then we connected them to form a trench, widening and deepening as we went. For now, our main objective was to gain some protection from the murderous shell fire.

I'd have liked nothing better than to hunker down in the shelter of my hole, but as the senior non-com with the party, I had no choice but to go up and down the line, assisting the lieutenant and watching over things in general. Laying aside my shovel, I crawled out of my burrow, then slid back in, unscrewed my canteen, and swallowed a sizable slug of brandy. No longer a novice drinker, now it took much more to do me any good. I waited a few minutes for the drink to take hold, scrambled out, and walked down the line of holes. Three men had been hit, one badly. I told the two with cursory wounds to carry the serious one to the aid station. Farther on I encountered Lt. Davies, standing around looking helpless. This was his first taste of heavy shell fire, and the expression on his face made me glad for the drink that warmed my guts and stiffened my backbone.

As I approached, Sgt. Jim Tracy and Cpl. Hanks were digging a hole beside where the lieutenant was standing, their faces grimed with sweat and dirt, working like sand hogs or sewer muckers.

Lt. Davies bent over and shouted, "Start another hole now, sergeant. That one's big enough."

What did he mean, start another hole? A look of surprise came over Jim's face. "What, Lieutenant?" he yelled.

"I need a hole," cried the lieutenant. "I can't stay here, can I?"

So a man was supposed to risk his life to dig a hole for some shave-tail lieutenant? I tapped him on the shoulder.

"Every man digs his own hole, sir," I shouted. Jim gave me a grateful look.

The lieutenant looked bewildered. "But, sergeant, I'm an officer. I can't dig a hole."

"Well, that's just too damn bad, lieutenant," Jim yelled from the shelter of his hole. "You'll dig now. You'll dig or you'll die."

The lieutenant grabbed a pick and started digging with an effort more frenzied than effective. Satisfied that the lesson had been learned, I moved on down the line. The work progressed well under the spur of the bombardment. Another man was hit—Hague. One look told me he was done for. Still, I called Bones and Anderson to carry him down and ask for a couple of first aid men to come up here.

This shell fire was too well directed to be accidental. We were under observation from someplace. I moved back along the line to where the lieutenant was still digging his hole. The exertion had taken his mind off the danger. He looked up at my approach. "You'd better get under cover, sergeant."

"Thanks, sir, I will," I said, dropping into his hole, which was practically no cover at all.

"This is pretty bad, sergeant. What do you think we should do?"

"Do ya think we could get a little counter artillery fire?"

"We might if the artillery could get a fix on the batteries firing at us."

"They probably can, sir. The artillery has the enemy's active batteries pretty well taped."

"Call a good man to act as runner, then, sergeant. We'll try it."

I called Hunter and sent him on his way to a telephone to call artillery brigade headquarters and explain our predicament. Shortly, the shelling slowed down, but it didn't stop completely until after we'd finished our job and filed back down into the town.

On the way down the slope I heard some man repeat to his buddy, "You'll dig now, lieutenant. You'll dig or you'll die," as quiet laughter broke out.

CHAPTER XI

CANTIGNY
MAY, 1918

Hell's Half Acre, the Devil's Elbow, Shrapnel Hollow, Dead Man's Curve, Death Valley—names on maps with a potent meaning to us, christened by events we were glad we hadn't witnessed. With the roads under constant bombardment, our food was conspicuous by its absence. Chow details were continually being shot up, so instead of one hot meal every twenty-four hours we were lucky to average one in seventy-two hours. We'd taken on a permanent coating of white dust. Men, hollow-eyed and hollow-cheeked, thought only of food. We'd been issued a big two-litre French canteen, an extra one that I kept filled with liquor and the other filled with water. I'd come to the conclusion that I'd rather be disgraced as a rum sot than a coward.

One early morning, John Gallagher and I walked along the Serviller-Villers Tournelle road on the way back from a wiring job. With the breaking day the irresistible dewy freshness of early summer issued forth. I stopped to take a drink from my large canteen while John watched—a funny kid with a shy way about him, fresh faced and innocent. He still called me sergeant.

"So, John, what made you join the army?" I was always curious about how each man got here. Great stories.

"You know why anyone joins the army in time of war."

"No, I don't. I've read a lot of reasons from people who never saw the army except in pictures, heard a lot of reasons from men who would never give their real reasons. Now, tell me your real reason. Did the flags and the music stir you up?"

"No." The word was terse and final. "There were no flags flying or bands playing where I enlisted. I joined the army because it's a man's patriotic duty to help his country in time of need."

"Well and good, but you were too young for the draft. Why not wait?"

"What if everyone waited? You say yourself that every man must do what he can to end it — quick and decisive, regardless of the cause. Besides, when people try to force their will on the world, it's a man's duty to meet force with force. Gotta stand for the idea that the world belongs to everyone, not a chosen few."

"So, how do you feel about conscientious objectors, then?"

"I think about ninety-five per cent of them are only conscientious of their own skin."

I smiled as we walked on amid increasing shell fire from both sides, now a steady roar. None fell that close, but the shells passing overhead created a steady swishing howl, the sky a vaulted dome where the wind shrieked and wailed continuously. John moved over to a clump of bushes to relieve himself. While I waited, a low, sibilant whistle, disconnected and oft repeated, akin to the twitter of birds, mingled with the roar.

John heard it too, and called, "Gee, it's funny how the birds stay around in all this noise."

The noise came again, and this time I caught an ominous rat-tat-tat, sharp and menacing. The Germans were sweeping the road with indirect machine gun fire. The birds we heard were bullets, the whistling, their song of mutilation and death.

"Come on, John, unless you want to stay here forever."

He tore out of the bushes, fastening his breeches on the run. We did a quarter mile in nothing flat. Once out of machine gun range, we slowed to a walk.

He turned to me with that shy grin. "Close, eh, sergeant?"

"Yeah. Too damn close. But you know how it is. Close don't count."

We reached the dugout and found, wonder of wonders, chow got up during the night. 'Pittles' Hanks was keeping it warm over a fire in the dugout and dished it out as each group arrived from their missions.

I passed my mess kit and settled myself comfortably on the dugout floor. This was the life: warm, dry and comparatively safe. A mess kit full of slum in front of me and every prospect of a good sleep during the day. I ate slowly, gloating over every bite and savoring every morsel. This was my first hot meal in forty-eight hours, and God only knew when the next would be. Napoleon was right. An Army moves on its stomach. A man can endure unbelievable discomfort as long as he's well fed.

Coming down the steps with his party, Mac cried. "I smell slum! Lead me to it!"

Pretty soon Tony wandered in and sat down beside me with a full mess kit. "How's it goin,' Judy? Nice war we got here. Lost nine men up the valley last night."

"What? Shellfire?"

"Nope. Machine guns. Indirect fire. Two dead. Seven wounded."

"Who's dead?"

"Anderson and Carlson. Anderson was perforated across the chest like two sheets of toilet paper. Fell in two when we picked him up." Tony said it matter-of-factly, talking with his mouth full.

Hanks straightened up and glared at him. "Shut up, you damn undertaker. I'm eating. Damn it, I don't like guys breaking in two with my meals."

Tony jerked a thumb in his direction. "What the hell's the matter with him? Goin' dainty on us, hey?"

Red Conlon mopped up his mess kit with a piece of bread and stuffed it into his mouth. "Come on, Judy, open up that canteen. I gotta have something to top off a meal like that."

I uncorked the big French canteen and passed it around.

Mac stretched out luxuriously on his back and sighed. "I'm sure gonna enjoy a little rest."

"Not right now, sawgint." Damn Stubby had sauntered into the bunker unnoticed. "All you sawgints be ovah at company headquartehs in half an houah. Y'all got some bidness to talk ovah."

We turned to each other, generally annoyed at having our rest snatched away at the last minute. These conferences were not social occasions. Something was up, that's what.

"I'm going to get some sleep, seeing as how I'm no sergeant." John Gallagher pushed me aside and climbed into the bunk.

Then Tony chimed in. "Yeah, me, too. You damn sergeants run us corporals ragged, but even at that you're just a gang of Cascarets."

"What the hell do you mean, Cascarets?" Mac asked. "I thought Cascarets was a laxative."

"Right." Tony grinned "You work while we sleep."

Everyone laughed. The dugout had filled up since dinner. All who would return from the night's work were back—well fed—and the food spread contentment in tired bodies.

"Hey, Judy, who'd you sleep with the last time out of the lines?" Red Conlon, eyes twinkling, brought up a topic sure to create interest.

"John," I replied.

"What? No 'demoselles? You're slipping."

"You go to hell." I remembered those days of endless hiking and no relief all too well.

As we sergeants gathered our gear for the meeting, every-thing got quiet.

Then Skinny Ketner started telling Bones about an amorous adventure, forgetting the entire dugout was listening. "When I got in bed and put my arms around her and started to kiss her,—boy, it was just like losing yourself in—well, I don't . . ." He noticed the silence and looked around, red faced, at a loss for words.

"Go ahead, Skinny, you're doin' great," I told him. "Quite poetical, you are. Let's have the details. What did you tell her?"

"To hell with you guys." He turned over on his bunk, facing the wall.

Tony was up on his elbows, his face one big grin. "Ask Mac his technique. He's the guy can get 'em. Remember that Mama he had in Gondrecourt?"

"You shut up, fella, if you know what's good for you," Mac growled. He was better known for his fighting ability than for his amorous successes.

"Come on, Mac. Give us the dope. How do you do it?" Tony always got a kick out of riding Mac.

"Yeah, help us out. We like the ladies, too." Insistent clamor aimed at Mac.

"Well, I'll tell you guys." Mac mused, stretching his thick arms. "I just walk up to 'em and say, 'Listen, sister, I'm a man of few words. Let's go to bed."

"How simple. What if they say no?" Tony didn't let up easy.

"Well, then, they just say no. Too bad for them." Mac looked at his watch. "Come on, Judy, it's time for us to go and tell 'em how to run this war."

We moved out into the debris of the street, stopping to pick up Dave Evans on the way. When we reached the headquarters dugout, most of the other sergeants were already there.

The company commander addressed us. "Gentlemen, it has been decided by the powers that be that it would be to our advantage to take the village of Cantigny, just to the rear of the enemy's front line. We've been picked as one of the units to make the assault in a few days. I've called you here this morning to impress upon you that this is the first independent offensive undertaken by the AEF. The eyes of the world will be upon you. The prestige of the entire army rests on your shoulders. No man in this command will, by any personal action, place the reputation of the United States Army in jeopardy. This is our trial by fire. We'll rise to the challenge and emerge with our heads held high. No further night duties until after the operation is completed. Knowing that I can count on you for your full cooperation and support, I thank you. Dismissed."

The skipper turned on his heel and disappeared behind a blanket partition into the rear dugout. We looked around at each other and filed up the stairs.

"Well, I can get me some shuteye now." Mac broke the silence.

That's right, I thought. We'd rest today. Nothing to do now but rest and wait. But could I rest, or would I just lie and roll and toss? I wished I didn't think so much—or that I was like Mac, who never worried, never thought one moment beyond the present. Well, I was at least going to try to sleep. God knew I was tired enough.

Descending into the dugout, we were greeted with a clamor of requests for information.

"What's the dope, sarge?"

"What's comin' off?"

"Come on, come on, tell us."

"There is no dope." My tone was flat, unemotional, unlike the turmoil that roiled inside. "We're goin' over the top in a few days, that's all." The men fell silent at the news.

"That's right," Mac told them. "Heinie's been lookin' down our throats for a long time. Now we're goin' where we can look down his."

I took advantage of the silence to roll into my bunk, but it was no use. I couldn't sleep. The longer I lay, the more I was beset by fear. I didn't get it. I didn't particularly dread any one thing, but I lived with a nervous terror of putting myself out there where the enemy could wreak its vengeance. Fear of the unknown, more than anything, I guessed. Fear of how I'd perform.

I gave up trying to sleep and went out to wander around the deserted town. This did no good either, so I returned to the dugout where I spied my canteen. Oh, that was what I needed. I let the fiery stuff run down my throat until it choked me. I sat on the bunk, my legs dangling over the edge and drank myself into a stupor.

"What price a croix de guerre, Judy?" Morrie Muller grinned up at me.

It'd never do to let anyone see how I felt, so as usual I replied with a bravado I didn't feel.

"Croix de guerres ain't my meat," I told him. "I'll take the diamond rings and watches. You can have the medals."

"Well, while you're hunting around for profit, don't overlook Joe Dalbert. He cleaned up a crap game for about six hundred francs."

"You don't say. I'll remember that. It'd be a damn shame to bury all that money in case he cops one."

"Yeah, or let the chaplain get it."

By then the rum had taken a good grip and I felt better. I lay back on the bunk and in no time passed into blessed, restful oblivion.

CHAPTER XII

CANTIGNY
MAY 1918

On a beautiful, soft, early summer night, with just a hint of a moon hanging low and the sky plentifully sprinkled with stars, we waited in a large quarry for the signal to move to our jump-off positions. Artillery fire was light for now. The men were quiet—self-contained—here and there the sound of a low voice or a suppressed laugh. Just another night at the front. The stars paled and twinkled as they faded out of view, and the sun rose slowly above the horizon. Movement down the company. Capt. Dunkel crooked his elbow to look at his watch, then motioned with his arm, swung his cane and strode off. The column followed, single file on our way to the jump-off.

Suddenly, with no warning, the world was engulfed in a gigantic cataclysm of sound. Like walking in our sleep, we saw other men moving, their equipment swaying, saw them gesture to each other, but no sound could be heard above the deluge of noise flooding over us. I looked at my watch: 5:45. We'd have an hour's preparatory bombardment before we went over. It'd just started, so we had an hour to reach the jump-off and get set.

Here and there we caught a glimpse of batteries of 75s as they hurled steel toward the enemy, their positions precariously close to the front lines. The gunners sacrificed everything to the God of Speed. Some in their undershirts, some stripped to the waist, dripping sweat and smeared with black powder stains, they tore open the breech block, slammed a shell home and

WHAM! The gun hurtled back in its recoil and waited for the repeat operation. Like the ticking of a clock in its regularity and like the promise of doom in its thunder, a battery in action was fascinating to watch.

Stumbling along like sleepwalkers, we entered a shallow trench on the edge of the wood, followed along it, and shortly arrived in our jump-off position. I sat down on the bottom of the trench and took a last tug at my canteen. The feeling in my gut reminded me of the way I used to feel before a football game at school. I'd stand back near the goal posts and look around at the other backs to see if their knees were shaking, too. I hoped this feeling would wear off as quickly as that one did. My spine tingled, my knees felt tense, and my teeth would have chattered if I hadn't kept them clenched.

The men looked calm, self-possessed. No sign of weakness in my section. Feeling so all gone myself made me look closely for signs of it in others. I met Tony's eye and he gave me a wink. The damn Johnny Reb wasn't even scared. Neither was Red. Chewing tobacco with deliberation, he munched and spit, munched and spit, as if the most important thing in the world was to get in a certain number of chews before we left the trench.

The bombardment was terrific. I stole a glance over the parapet at a plain, sloping toward the village of Cantigny, a gently swelling stretch of land that seemed to bubble and boil like a witch's caldron. Shell bursts, smoke and dust hung over the plain like something transplanted from hell.

The captain came along the trench. "How's your watch, sergeant?"

I compared mine with his. He went on past, then swung around and came back. "You know your job, sergeant?"

"Yes, sir."

"Fine. How's your section?"

"They look all right to me, sir. To tell the truth, sir, I think I'm worse off than any of them."

He looked at me sharply, then smiled. "Don't be so quick to confession, sergeant. If I felt like you look, I'd think I was all right."

I grinned. The captain still lingered near.

"How's Mac, sir?"

He gave a little laugh. "No fear about your tough friend, sergeant. He's an efficient fighting machine. Not a nerve in his body."

As he moved on I noticed a change in the sound of the artillery. It swelled in density and rapidity until it obliterated everything else in the world. I took another peek out front where the shells were bursting in line about seventy-five yards out. Our barrage was started. We'd go soon. I looked for the captain and motioned to my watch. He held up two fingers. I started to move the men, met Lt. Courland doing the same thing. He shouted something, but I didn't hear. Then, above all the bedlam of noise, came the shrill blast of a whistle. The men crawled stolidly out of the trench. We were off.

The barrage moved steadily forward, and we timed our pace to its advance. I counted twelve tanks stretching out on both flanks, clanking along like prehistoric monsters, nosing almost vertically down into holes and out again, then rearing up and over obstacles that should have turned them over on their backs. Strange, mechanical freaks, they offered us formidable protection, and as long as they kept moving they injected fear into the enemy.

My section was divided into three combat groups. I herded them along and kept them spread out—not too fast, or we'd get hit from our own barrage, and not too slow or we'd be too far behind and lose its valuable protection. Rat-tat-tat-tat. A thin whine of bullets. The enemy sprayed our barrage, conscious of what was behind it. The fire was too thin to be effectual, but nevertheless, a man fell here and there. Not many, just here and there. We were lucky, for from the time we left the quarry not one enemy shell came near us. Our guns kept them down in their holes. They told us we had the support of four hundred guns — about four thousand shells per minute.

Our advance was slow and a little monotonous. I saw Hanks take a shot at something with his rifle. Off to the right, a figure in grey popped up from the ground, spun and fell. Elated, Hanks gestured to me; I nodded and grinned. The tank ahead of us shot off toward the left, its one-pounder belching. One group moved off to the right, where a hand-to-hand fight took place in a shell hole. No organized system of trenches here. The front line was just a series of connected shell holes and strong points, and we moved from one to another, grabbing shelter where we could until we were almost to the ruins of the town.

Again I heard the whine of machine gun bullets, but something wasn't right. Those bullets weren't coming from the enemy lines, but from our rear. There they were again. We threw ourselves flat and looked around. I didn't see any gun, but one group broke off to our left and another directly to the rear. Someone threw a grenade, then another. Now the German machine guns appeared, cleverly concealed in two shell holes about a hundred yards apart.

Our guys on the left made a rush under the protection of a shower of grenades. Bayonets lifted and fell, a rifle butt flashed in an arc. The gang to the rear lay down, throwing grenades. Suddenly they made a rush. Bayonets and gun butts again — then both parties returned to our position. There was nothing left but what looked like some piles of old grey rags where the guns had been.

The line moved steadily on. Three or four riflemen took on a stuttering machine gun until suddenly the gun lay silent, its nose swung up in the air, the gunner collapsed over the breech, blood gushing out of his mouth. Another one leaned stiffly forward on a bayonet sticking out the back of his neck. An American crawled aimlessly on his hands and knees, his face a bloody mask. We moved steadily forward, watching a series of vulgar, hair-raising vignettes.

Crash! A grenade exploded close on my left. We were already at the edge of the ruined town. My section's assignment was to clean out the cellars on one side of the street. The first cellar had two entrances, so I left one group at the first and moved on to the next, where I left the second group. The last group took station at one entrance of the next cellar, while John Gallagher and I moved to the other. I shouted down the stairs. No answer. I shouted again.

"Let me go down after them, sergeant."

"What the hell's the matter with you? Are you nuts?" I shouted. "They'd kill you the blink of a gnat's eye."

"Well, I don't like to see them bombed like rats down there." Always decent, even in the face of death, that was John Gallagher.

"All right! Don't watch," I yelled, pulling the pin on a grenade and tossing it down the stairs, followed quickly by another. Commotion below as the grenades blew, and I shouted to the other group to watch their entrance.

"They're coming!" cried Brice, and I moved over to their position. Seven dirty faced, ragged-looking German soldiers rose out of the rubble, hands in the air.

"Any more?" I asked.

One of them must have understood me, for he shook his head. "Nein. Alles tot."

"Chase them toward the rear." Taking out my pistol, I descended the cellar steps. My two grenades must have lit right among them, for there were five unquestionably dead men strewn about the cellar. I went through their pockets, taking watches, pocketbooks, two good rings—stuffing whatever I found into my blouse.

The three groups had already moved on to the next cellars, so I hurried up to the street. In the middle of the road an American and a German ran full speed at each other, collided head on, knocked each other down, got up and ran on. It was a world gone mad, hand-to-hand fighting everywhere. Germans caught in their dugouts emerged into the street to fight it out in the open rather than be bombed in their holes. A huge man, his sleeve gone to the shoulder, a bloody trench knife in his hand and his arm covered with blood to the elbow, tore madly down the street, tripped, fell, sat up — and started to sing. He sat there singing madly as the war made its way around him.

A tank came crashing through a wall, sidled up to the ruins of a house, and stopped. Machine gun bullets rattled off its sides like hail on a tin roof. I saw the snout of a machine gun under a pile of rubble on the other side of the wall. Slowly, inexorably, the muzzle of the tank's 75 depressed, swung into line. The machine gunners started to file out, hands in the air, but it was too late. The 75 belched once again. All that was left was a horrible shambles of arms, legs and bloody torsos to mark a circle about the spot.

Distracted by the horror, I turned suddenly to find a man bearing down on me, bayonet leveled. With no conscious effort I raised my automatic and shot. Dust flew from his tunic but he came on. I shot again. He jerked with the second impact, but kept coming. I shot a third time and jumped aside barely in time as his bayonet just grazed my breeches. He lunged past me to crash into the side of the tank, where he fell, twitched once or twice and lay still.

Trembling like an Aspen leaf, I looked around, but the fighting had died down. Troops were busy here or there consolidating and organizing the position. They threw together a couple of strong points out at the edge of town. Two planes flew low over the village, the first I saw, but the men said they'd been with us all morning.

I returned to the man I'd shot, turned him over, and took off his helmet. No older than me, he had crisp, curly black hair and nice features. I took his watch and pocketbook, and then noticed the ribbon of the iron cross on his coat. It was the work of but a moment to fish under at the end of the ribbon and pull the medal out. As I straightened up, the door of the tank slid open and two Frenchmen stepped out, gave a bored look around, then stepped over to me.

"Cigarette, m'sieur?" One of them begged a smoke.

"Oui," I handed him a pack.

"Un bon combat ici aujourd'hui, non? Tout va bien." he went on.

"Oui,. Tout va bien," I echoed. "Avez-vous des vins?"

He looked at me curiously. "Oui," he smiled. "Venez ici" He let himself back into the tank, and I followed. Courteous and deeply grateful for our help, the French knew they were on the verge of losing the war, so they didn't try to hide their appreciation for the American presence.

The tank officer handed me a canteen of good brandy. I took a drink and offered him two more packs of cigarettes for enough brandy to fill my canteen, which was about two-thirds full of rum. He agreed and the exchange was made. I had no idea what kind of drink I'd get by mixing the brandy and rum, but I wasn't much concerned about the quality of the drink as long as I could replenish my supply with authority.

As I stepped down from the tank, the Frenchmen leaned out and shook hands. "Au revoir, m'sieur. Bonne chance!"

"Au revoir." They clanked away toward the rear amid clouds of dust.

There was a typical Frenchman, I thought. Just as unconcerned as if he were in a Paris café instead of in the middle of a fine, first-class slaughterhouse.

I found the section and we dug in just in front of the village burying ground. Red Conlon asked me for a couple of men to go for water. I sent Harris and Brice, thinking he'd found a pump in working order. In a short time they returned with a barrel of beer they'd found in one of the dugouts. I shouldn't have let them keep it, but what the hell? In this sun it wouldn't be fit to drink before the day was out.

Our guns still pounded the enemy rear, but they'd stop soon to cool and be cleaned. That's when we'd get it. We dug and sweated under a hot sun. I looked at my watch, shook it, couldn't believe my eyes. 8:25, one hour and forty minutes since we'd gone over the top. In that hundred minutes more than a thousand men had gone to their deaths with many more mutilated beyond belief, and, if I was any judge, the worst was yet to come.

Lt. Courland came along, jubilant. "Sawgint, y'all know ouh platoon has not lost a man."

"Well, that's great, sir."

"That's what ah thinks, too," he smiled. "You know this is my first battle, sawgint."

"Mine, too, lieutenant."

After he left I urged the men along with their digging. Our fire had slackened by about half, and that meant trouble. Tony set up a gun, wiped his lips, and threw me a wink and a nod. I suddenly remembered the beer and decided to have a mug before it got too warm. I slipped down to where the men hid it in a corner of the cemetery wall, filled my canteen cup and drank. It was still cool and refreshing. Then, as I turned to go, three shells landed in the town. I hadn't traveled fifty feet before more arrived. By the time I got back to the section, they were dropping all up and down the line. They didn't have our range too well yet, but we were in for it, nonetheless. Suddenly they started coming in numbers, big and small, hitting right on target.

CHAPTER XIII

CANTIGNY
MAY, 1918

We lay down in the bottom of our holes and took it. One crash after another, not as thick as barrage fire, but good heavy-duty drum fire. Now came a cry for stretcher bearers. I got up to see who was hit, but I couldn't do it. The old fear was back. It was more than flesh and blood could bear—to force myself out into the open of a hell-roaring inferno. Now I knew how those poor bastards on the other side felt this morning. Somehow I found my feet and ran, stumbling toward the cry for help. I heard a shell coming—close. I flattened myself on the ground just as the earth rose in front of me, sifting down a fine mist that obscured everything from sight. The world spun round and round as I lay there trying to hold on to the ground to steady myself. I crawled to my feet and, staggering like a drunk, I fell and tried to rise again. It was too much. I gave up until my equilibrium slowly returned, the spinning sensation slowed down, and I could crawl along the line of holes looking for shelter.

"Here, sergeant. In here."

I dimly made out John Gallagher crouched in a hole. Once I was in, he took a handkerchief and wiped at my eyes until I could almost see. My ears rang so bad I couldn't hear the explosions that rocked and shook the earth.

John spoke and I could hear his words plainer than the bursting shells. "I thought you were done for, sergeant."

"Where'd it hit?" I asked. "I heard it coming, then—Wham!"

"It hit right in the next hole."

"Who was in there?"

"Mason, George and Lenhart."

"They're all gone, then. I saw bodies in the air."

"Yes. They're gone."

No need to comment. A chill ran down my spine. I took a good stiff drink from my canteen and crawled out of the hole to move along the line. Hines was bleeding at the nose and both ears from shell concussions. I told him to go to the rear if he thought it was worth the risk in this shell fire.

He shook his head. "I joined this army to fight, and when I go to the rear, I'll be carried." Plenty of guts, that boy!

The faint odor of mustard gas tickled my nostrils. If they gassed us, they wouldn't counter attack right away—foolish to run their own troops into the gas. They'd have to fight in their gas masks, the same as we. Where was the lieutenant? I wanted to ask him about the gas.

My brain whirled from the continual concussions. Oh, Christ, won't they ever let up? I couldn't stand it. I thought I'd go crazy! My hands shook. I had to force my legs to move as I emerged from the hole and lurched toward the town in search of Lt. Courland. Two close ones came over together. I ducked flat and lay there, watching my hand shake on the ground. I tried to stop it, but I'd lost control—like it wasn't my hand at all. I thought maybe I was crazy now. Even so, I'd have to be on my way. Oh, Yeah. I was going to tell the gas about Lt. Courland. No. Tell Lt. Courland to get some gas—that must be it. But where was—?

"Judeee!" A shout pierced the din to bring me back to myself. I rolled over and looked up. There was Red, between two stretcher bearers, blood streaming down his face, and the shoulder of his coat a dark red blotch.

"Oh, Christ, kid. I thought you were dead, lying there so still," he moaned.

"No, not yet, I guess." My brain slowly began to function again. "How bad are you hit?"

"Not bad, Judy, not bad. Just enough for a nice trip to the hospital."

I looked to the stretcher bearers for confirmation. "He'll lose a few teeth, but his tongue still works. The other one broke his collarbone."

"Can he take a drink?" I wanted to do something for my buddy before he left for who knew where.

"Sure. So can we," said one of the stretcher men.

Hell, I let myself in for it that time. "Well, here you go."

They all took a pull at my canteen. Part of Red's leaked out of his cheek. Maybe it'd help sterilize the gash. He made a wry face at the sting of it, and they moved off.

"So long, Red. Take care of yourself."

He turned. "Never mind about me. You take care of yourself. I'll be in a safe place."

I watched them struggle up the slope, expecting every minute to see a shell get them, but they made it to the woods safe, and I was relieved — no, thankful.

I finally found Lt. Courland, dust covered and grimy.

"Mawnin, sawgint."

"Hell's fire, lieutenant. Its past mawnin' now, ain't it?"

He looked at his watch. "Yes, it is. It's 1:15."

I told him about the gas.

"Yes, I noticed a faint smell myself. No heavy concentration, though."

"What do you think they'll do, lieutenant? Try to gas us or counter attack?"

"Counter attack, in my opinion. When you get a chance, inspect your section and see that the men are well placed. Count them and report back, will you, sergeant?"

"Yes, sir. Right away."

"Well, don't take any chances with this shell fire."

That tickled me. Telling me, the most frightened man in this outfit not to take chances! By the time I got back and started counting the men, the shelling had died down. I looked toward the enemy lines. Sure enough, our artillery was laying down a line of shells in front of the German positions and he was on his way with his counter attack. I blew my whistle and yelled with all my might. Heads popped out of fox holes, rifles laid on the edge in readiness. An air of grim determination took hold.

"Hold your fire, men. Wait till they get closer, then make every shot count." It was the captain, strutting up and down behind us as if on parade.

Their barrage came closer but not so thick. Then I heard our own shells passing overhead, concentrating on the enemy artillery, making it hard for him to fire his barrage. Good, we were not alone in this. A feeling of confidence settled over me. I moved down to Tony's gun.

"Hello, Damn Yank. What are you gonna do?"

"I'm gonna shoot that damn gun." A sudden impulse had taken hold of me. "You keep me in barrels and we'll give 'em hell!"

"Hurry up, then."

A crackle of fire broke out. I glanced around in time to see the captain wave his cane. Pulling back the catch, I pressed the trigger and the gun began to jump and buck. The enemy advanced in waves through a thin barrage. I depressed the muzzle till I saw dirt fly up at the feet of the advancing men, then I raised it a trifle and let her go in a long burst. Another burst and another. Men fell kicking as the first wave melted under the withering fire. Rifle fire swept over us and the enemy barrage dropped down right on top of us. I saw Brice knocked clear out of his hole by a rifle bullet. The gun bucked and jumped in my hands. Boles kept feeding the gun, even though his ears were bleeding. Christ, we were getting hell, and no mistake. Tony changed barrels in an instant and we were off again. The enemy waves broke up into little groups. Another wave advanced to the aid of the first. We'd never hold them off.

"Steady, men. Hang on." It was the captain, still strolling up and down, calm and collected.

My gun hammered out short bursts now, shooting at what was left of the first wave. Then a long burst into the new wave, now short ones into the isolated groups lying on the ground.

I heard the captain's voice again, a note of triumph in it. Hell, he must be able to see something we couldn't.

"Now, men," he shouted. "Give it to them. Give it to them, men. Pour it to them, sergeant. Pour it in there."

I couldn't see what he was so excited about. The enemy seemed as thick as ever to me. Suddenly he jumped across a hole and moved out in front of the company.

"At 'em, men! Up and at 'em!" The whole line of defenders seemed to catch his enthusiasm, for as far as the eye could see, men surged out in front to meet the enemy in hand-to-hand combat. Bayonets, rifle butts, knives, pistols, bare hands and even teeth came into play. There was nothing for us at the gun to do but hold our position and watch. The artillery fire had moved to our rear, so we had an unobstructed view. I yelled to Tony to watch the gun as I moved out front with the section.

Two men lay on the ground locked in mortal combat. The American had the enemy's throat in his teeth, worrying it like a dog trying to tear a chunk out. An enemy soldier hit one of our men on the chin with his rifle butt so hard his throat broke open and his head lay down his back between his shoulders. Three Germans had a man cornered in a shell hole. My first shot caught one of them; my second missed. The American was Mac.

I lay down, steadied my automatic on my other hand and fired. My target spun around and went down as if he'd been hit with a sledge hammer. Just ahead, a man walked along holding his groin. As he came closer he took his hands away, revealing genitals shot away. Then small groups of enemy soldiers started to run back toward their positions. The fight seemed to be slowing down. I turned back to the gun as a hand dropped on my shoulder. Startled, I spun around, my gun raised.

"Easy, Judy. It's only me."

I looked half dazed at Mac, then at the other men. All wore the same expression—eyes narrow, lips slightly parted, saliva drooling from their mouths. Harsh guttural sounds issued from their throats, the hair risen on the back of their necks.

Mac was coming out of this stage, his voice still thick. He swayed as he walked, like a drunk. We moved back to our holes in silence. As I dropped down by the gun, he put his hand on my shoulder again.

"Thanks, kid. I couldn't handle them all."

For four days we held our positions under shell fire and counter attacks with only two day's reserve rations, about enough for two meals. Their artillery kept up such a barrage on our rear it was impossible to supply us with food or ammunition. Thick tongues and cracked lips told of lack of water. None of us had had two hours of unbroken sleep since we made the attack. Exhausted, dejected and miserable, we knew if Heinie put over one more counter attack, he could have this damn town without any more argument. After four days without water or food, our ammunition practically exhausted, word came that we were to be relieved.

We moved back, forty-seven strong out of two hundred who went over.

Tired—impossibly, incredibly tired. Black lines of dirt and sweat cut deep into our faces. We were thin, emaciated, tattered and torn. If addressed, we didn't respond, for the effort was too great. We had only curses for those who might fawn upon us and glorify our achievement, but we took and held the town.

CHAPTER XIV

PARIS
JUNE, 1918

Tartigny Wood, reserve positions in the rear, luxurious to stretch out in the sun and rest, relax and feel the strength flow back into our limbs. I lay on the grass, reflecting on our status. Our company of two hundred and fifty men and seven officers had been reduced to a company of ninety-seven men, fifty of whom hadn't taken part in the attack. Three officers survived. The captain, a gallant soul, had been killed just after he leaped across our holes to engage the enemy hand to hand. Lt. Stark was hamstrung by a bullet and I didn't know what happened to the others. Red? Gone — to a hospital. Morrie Muller gone with a piece of shell in his side. I guessed I was lucky, or was I? Maybe the lucky ones got it early. We, the forsaken, went on, only to meet the same fate after months of physical and mental torture. Mac, Tony and John were left, thank God. Harris was still in the section, but I didn't know him very well. These friendships came and went at the whim of fate.

I drowsed, for after all, it was still good to be alive.

Funny creature, man. Endowed with superior intelligence, he'd struggle to survive against any odds, even though he knew the end was inevitable. I wondered over this. Poverty-stricken slum dwellers struggled to prolong a life with no tangible compensation. Why? I guessed man did what he had to from day to day and, in doing his best for as long as he could, justified his existence.

"Hey, Judy." Someone called me.

"Over here." I rolled over and got up. John Gallagher stood in the path looking older than the fresh-faced boy I'd met a few months before. War ages you.

"The new captain wants you."

"We got a new captain?"

"Yep. And I think you'll like him." His still youthful face lit up in a smile. "Hurry up. He wants you right away."

I buttoned my blouse and trekked up the path to the company headquarters, which was housed in a large iron shelter. I entered and, lo and behold, there was Lt. Weyandt, who'd been with us on our first front. A lieutenant no longer, he wore captain's bars. He rose to meet me, his hand outstretched, smiling. I could have jumped for joy. My first impulse was to throw my arms around him, but I restrained the urge.

As we shook hands, he slapped me on the back. Such familiarity from an officer to an enlisted man said much about how war bonded men. I was overjoyed to see him, like a long lost brother.

He grinned—his eyes suspiciously bright. "I'm proud of you. I heard grand accounts of your conduct in the advance."

Overwhelmed and uncomfortable with praise, I deflected it with a wave of my hand. "You can be proud of Mac and Red and Tony, too, sir. And John Gallagher."

"Yes. Yes, I'm proud of all of you. My first company, and now I get to command it. I'd hoped for it when I heard of Capt. Dunkel's death. Poor fellow. He was a good man."

"More ways than one," I agreed. "Christ, captain, I'm tickled to death you're back with the company. I don't know what to say. Oh, hell. I'm gonna take a drink."

He laughed. "Well, sergeant, considering the occasion, we might have one together. I gotta talk to you anyway because I have a job for you."

"Fine." I accepted his invitation. We both knew it wasn't considered good discipline for an officer to drink with an enlisted man, but there were exceptions to all rules. I followed him into his quarters in the rear of the shelter where he burrowed deep into his bedroll and came up with a bottle. Aha, Benedictine. My favorite tipple.

He filled two small aluminum cups, extended one to me and held the other high.

"Here's to the sands in the hourglass, that measure . . ."

I stopped him. "Not that one, captain, please. Reminds me of too many old friends."

He sobered instantly, the smile fading. "Pardon me, sergeant. That was thoughtless. I didn't realize."

"It's okay, sir." I was ashamed of how sorrow could get hold of me when I let myself think of those bloody, misshapen heaps of rags I used to call friends.

We sat quietly. I downed my drink and refilled my cup. The captain drank his and set it down. We each attended to our own thoughts in silence. Finally I spoke.

"The captain mentioned a job."

"That's right, sergeant. Take two men and go to Saint-Nazaire after two Ford ambulances. You can drive, if I remember correctly."

"Yes, sir. I can drive." I could scarcely believe my ears. This job would take a week at least. Saint-Nazaire was the port where we landed. I began to figure—one day from here to Paris, one day from Paris to Saint-Nazaire, four days for the return trip. Even if we left Saint-Nazaire the day we arrived, the trip would take at least a week. A full week of regular meals, beds at night, baths, lights, everything that made for comfortable living. Too good to be true. The captain smiled at what he knew was passing through my mind.

"Who are the men, sir?"

"Take your pick, sergeant. The only requirement is that one be able to drive. The other will act as a general helper."

Suddenly I had the germ of a brilliant idea. Tony! Tony — sick for a sight of his girlfriend Yvette, and I could make it happen.

When I mentioned Tony, the captain nodded assent. "And who else?"

"I don't know yet, sir. Maybe I better go out and look around."

"All right, sergeant. Let me know who you want and have them here tonight at ten o'clock. You'll go from here to Breteuil by truck and from there by train. Your travel orders will be ready."

I went out into the sunlight, my heart pounding. I looked around, trying to decide on the third man. Ah, there was Harris — as good as anybody. I called him over.

Cleaned up and shaven, having somehow got hold of a clean uniform, he came up smiling. "What is it, sergeant?"

"I have a job for you." Usually such a statement meant bad news. Harris showed no emotion as he awaited the outcome. Any order I might have to give him would be received with stoic calm.

"Can you drive a Ford?" The question jolted him. He looked at me in surprise.

"Yeah, I can drive a Ford."

"Then you, Tony and I are going on a trip to Saint-Nazaire." Together we marched on down to Tony's billet where I gave them the plan.

Tony was pleased beyond words. "Why you old Bastard. How'd this happen?"

"Wait until we get under way before you get so happy. I've got a plan for you." We trailed off to our billets to get ready. Later, I went to the company office to hand in the names of my travel mates.

Long before the appointed time we assembled at the company headquarters awaiting transportation. An ammunition truck rolled up and, while it was unloading, the captain came out and shook hands all around.

"Well, good-bye, sergeant. Have a good time while you're gone, but keep out of trouble."

We climbed aboard the truck and were on our way to the town of Breteuil, the railhead for the division, only a short ride away. We spent the evening in a café sitting around a table, congratulating each other on our good fortune.

I leaned toward Tony. "Listen, Johnny Reb, I've got a plan."

"Yeah? What is it?"

"Well, how would you like to see Yvette?"

His face lit up. "I'd give anything in the world just to see her for an hour."

"It's like this. There are only two ambulances. Harris and I can drive them back. What's to stop you from grabbing a train in Paris tomorrow and going to Vitry La Francois to see her? Harris and I can return that way and pick you up on our way back."

He looked like he could kiss me. "Would you do that, Judy? Gee, you sure are a friend."

Having agreed on the plan, we settled ourselves for the night. In the morning we caught a local train to Beauvais where we boarded the Paris express. Every turn of the iron wheels moved us farther away from the reality we'd come to know so well. The incessant booming of the guns, physical discomfort bordering on the unbearable, and the constant fear of death.

This was my first visit to Paris, and after seeing Tony aboard the train for Vitry La Francois, Harris and I moved about the city taking it all in. It was full of Americans who'd have been worth more at the front than here and a throng of YMCA people who seemed like tourists wanting to visit the war as long as they didn't have to experience the hardships or discomforts—a soldier's everyday lot. On hand more out of curiosity than charity, as soon as things got ugly, they'd scurry for the comfort of three squares and a bunk. Somehow that irritated me. I'd seen too much horror not to be offended by those who thought they were experiencing the real thing.

Harris and I dropped into the Café Brisbon on the Rue des Italiens. It was comfortably full of men in all uniforms and—for me—fascinating Parisian women. As soon as we were seated I scanned the room for feminine companionship. No likely prospects. Prostitutes there were in plenty, but commercial wenches had to be a last resort.

I noticed Harris's eye roving over the women as steadily as my own. "Looking for a girlfriend?"

"Why not?" he answered with a nod.

"I thought you were an ex-preacher." His ready interest caught me by surprise.

"I am," he laughed. "Don't assume members of the clergy have no interest in romance. Some preachers get around."

I raised my eyes.

"Yeah. Like that," he nodded.

I was looking at a roguish eye and bewitching curve of a cheek from behind the shoulder of a French Captain. I shifted my chair to get a better view of the party of three, the French officer and two delightful-looking girls. From my new vantage point I had an unobstructed view of the girl who may have appeared ordinary to some, but to me, five months removed from female association, she looked like an angel. She looked up. Was I mistaken, or did a faint smile play around her mouth as her eyes met mine?

Music started and couples got up to dance. How was this done in France? Did I just go and ask her to dance or must we be introduced? Well, I'd always had plenty of crust. She couldn't do any worse than say no. I rose. Damn, too late. She was dancing with the French captain again. The captain didn't appear that interested, even though she danced with verve and a captivating grace. As they moved past our table, I caught an elusive fragrance—infinitely dainty and altogether charming. Again they danced by, this time on my side. I saw a glint of light, and something dropped to the floor. I retrieved it at a bound—an earring. My elation knew no limits. Harris watched, laughing.

"Right on the job, Judy, eh what?"

"I'll tell a man. Ain't she sumpin' to look at?"

"Yes, not hard to take. So you think you're the fellow to take her?"

"Well, boy, I'm sure gonna give it a try."

Would that damn music never stop? Didn't these French musicians ever get tired? I sat and fumed while the dancing continued forever. Ah, at last the music stopped, and they moved toward their table.

She sat down and the officer moved round to his chair and took up conversation with the other girl, plainly where his interest lay. I gave them a decent interval to get settled and moved over to their table, noting that my lady's eyes twinkled with amusement as I approached.

"Pardonne, mam'selle."

"Yes?"

"Your earring, I believe." I held it out to her.

"Oh, thank you. I didn't know I'd lost it. Where did you find it?"

"You're more than welcome. It was on the floor near our table."

"That was very careless of me." Suddenly I realized that we were speaking English, and hers was impeccable.

The captain checked me out, taking in my uniform, insignia, general appearance. Evidently he wasn't displeased with what he saw for he motioned to the waiter.

"Would you care for a drink by way of thanks, sergeant?" he asked with a friendly smile. He spoke English, too.

"Just a small one." I glanced over toward Harris, who motioned for me to push my campaign.

"What is your organization, sergeant?" asked the captain.

There it was again. To answer would be to give military information. These people appeared to be nice, cultured French people, but so would enemy agents. I was wary at once.

The captain noticed my hesitation and laughed. "Very good, sergeant. Let's just say the American of Cantigny."

"Why say that, sir?" I asked, wondering if this was a ploy to get me to relax, or if there was something about my uniform that gave that away.

"Because I was there last week myself—with my group of tanks. If I'm not mistaken, I recall seeing the same insignia you wear among, shall we say, the frolicking throng."

CHAPTER XV

PARIS
JUNE, 1918

Boy, I really was among friends, so when the music started I turned to the captain for permission to ask the lady to dance.

"To be sure. To be sure." He rose with a sweep of his arm. "It will entertain her and relieve me. There is little joy in squiring one's sister."

Needing no more encouragement, I turned to her and held out my hand. We whirled away, lost in the lilt and rhythm of the music. I was too delighted to speak, even though—with my hike-worn legs and hobnailed shoes—I was no Fred Astaire. She didn't seem to mind as she looked up at me, laughing.

"Are all Americans what you call—uh, opportunists, sergeant?"

"They would be in a case like this, I think."

"Oh, and they have smooth tongues as well." She was enjoying this.

"Just to smooth people," I answered, at which she smiled again.

We danced in silence for a while, her faint perfume, the joy of her nearness intoxicating me.

"Good talkers and nice company. What else can they do?"

"Who?"

"Americans."

"With time and practice we might learn to dance."

The music ended too soon and I led her back to her table.

She smiled as I turned to go. "Oh, I enjoyed that very much. We must have the next one."

We had the next one and a dozen more after that. I looked around for Harris, but he had disappeared. Well, he knew where to meet me in the morning.

As soon as the music started, we moved out for each dance. In a good two hours since the first dance we hadn't missed one yet, good friends by then. She hummed the music for a few seconds, then looked up at me.

"You Americans are very entertaining. You can talk, you can fight, you seem to drink very well, you dance nicely . . ."

"And we're great lovers."

She straightened and looked askance at me. "You wouldn't push a poor girl into anything, would you, sergeant?"

"No. Just gently lead her," I laughed.

We moved into a secluded little alcove where there were no tables or chairs, dancing slowly in one spot, her soft, smooth cheek against mine. I raised my head and when she looked up I lowered my head and our lips met gently, brushing across each other and then clinging in a long, warm kiss. Smothered with emotion we embraced, still holding each other when the music stopped. We moved back to the table, our heads spinning.

At the table, the captain and his lady were ready to leave. My young friend gave me a reassuring glance as they engaged in a volley of French too rapid for me to follow. Then my sweet lady suddenly broke into English.

"But I am not going home to dinner. Sergeant Redding and I are going to have dinner and dance afterward. He will see me home." She smiled in my direction.

The captain looked compliant. "I do not wish to impose on you, sergeant, but you see how it is. My little sister has a mind of her own."

"It's no imposition at all, captain," I assured him. "I'll be only too glad to spend the evening with your little sister."

We bid our adieus and they wandered out the café door, obviously lost in each other and probably relieved to be rid of us. We sat down, lingering over one more drink as I squeezed her hand under the table. She suggested a small restaurant nearby for dinner, and we stepped out onto the boulevard into a sublimely sunny afternoon. This much I knew—her name was Jeanne Trevost and she lived on the Boulevard du Clichy.

We strolled down the wide avenue basking in contentment. If this were the reward for every battle, bring on your battles. We walked slowly, taking in the scenes. The Seine sparkled in the sunshine. The Cathedral of Notre Dame rose in Gothic splendor on the Ille de la Cite. Everything about this city spoke of culture, class. I felt completely at ease there, even though my knowledge of French language and culture was almost nil. There was something mystical about Paris on a sunny afternoon. Jeanne delighted in showing me the sights, famous and infamous. I pressed gently on her arm, and she responded with pressure on my hand. I saw so much in her eyes, big and brown. Curiosity, intelligence, mirth, sadness.

"Sergeant, what is your age?"

"Twenty-two."

She looked pensive. "You have lost many friends these last few weeks."

"Yes, we have."

"Oh, it is sad. My brother, Rene, told me of your battle last week. So many killed and all so young. Oh, it is too, too bad."

"Let's forget about that," I told her. "I'll be back there soon enough. Right now, let's just enjoy this time together."

"Oh, I'm sorry," she cried and gave my arm a squeeze. "We will put the war aside. We will be very happy, like children at play."

In the midst of our conversation, I felt a gentle tap on my shoulder and looked around to see a YMCA girl at my side. Plain and a little on the hefty side, she matched my stride and took her place on my left with Jeanne on my right.

"Where are you going, soldier?" she asked, obviously bent on missionary work.

Right away I was irritated at her breach of courtesy and made no effort to conceal it.

"What business is it of yours?" I asked sharply. "If you must know, we are going to dine."

"Do you know that girl?" She wagged her head toward Jeanne as though indicating some low form of humanity. What made these people think they had a right to judge? Or to interfere in the lives of others?

It was plain she was set on saving me from a fate worse than death. I decided to humor her a bit to see how far her impertinence would take her. I glanced at Jeanne, observing in bewildered silence.

"Fairly well," I replied. "Do you?"

"No, I do not. But wouldn't you far rather be with a nice American girl than with a French tart?"

"Tart?" I studied her. She wasn't ugly, but everything about her spoke of church. War did one of two things. It either sent you scurrying back to church or it put the whole question of religion to rest.

"Where would a nice American girl want to go?"

"Why, we could go to the Louvre and see all the wonderful paintings, and then we could see the Pantheon de Guerre."

Jeanne stood by taking this in like a little thoroughbred. Sensing that I could take care of myself, she gave me space to pursue my little game.

"The Louvre, the Pantheon de Guerre," I murmured as though intrigued. Then I turned on this female meddler with venom.

"Listen, sister, it's been five months since I have had any friendly contact with a woman. In the last few weeks I've seen hundreds of men die bloody, horrible deaths. I want to forget that. I want love, laughter, beauty and gaiety. I want to be loved and kissed and fussed over. And what do you want me to do? Look at pictures and marble statues! You should remember this. I'll probably be dead in a few weeks — violently and painfully. Who the hell wants to die with memories of pictures and cold stone statues? As for this girl with me, I've no reason to assume that you come of any better upbringing than she. She at least has the decency to mind her own business."

I took Jeanne's hand and we walked away some distance before stopping to browse in the book stalls and look at the water color renditions offered for sale. She glanced at me several times but didn't speak. Angered at these meddling, self-righteous fools, I wondered what business they had over here, anyhow. Finally Jeanne broke her silence.

"I wouldn't want you angry with me, sergeant," she murmured, laughing gently.

Her laughter improved my mood and by the time we'd walked a few blocks I was happy again, just to be with her. We stopped in a restaurant where the ground floor was crowded, but a balcony surrounding the room on three sides offered a place for comfortable privacy.

"Let's go up there." Jeanne pointed to an empty table.

After ordering we sat and talked while my eyes roved casually over the crowd below. This seemed to be quite a stylish place. A few civilians, but no enlisted men, nothing but officers, which didn't bother me, but I did find myself searching for just one common soldier. Ah, there was one, way over there in the corner with a party of French people.

As I gazed, he turned to look directly at me. By all the Gods, it was Harris. Now how'd he get there? And with a great looking party like that, too? I promised myself to give that backslid son-of-a-bitch a word or two about this. He saw me, smiled and waved. I waved in return and motioned for him to keep looking as I brought Jeanne over to the balcony rail to point him out to her. He clasped his hands over his head in a gesture of congratulations. His party noticed and they gazed up at us with smiles.

"Is that your traveling companion?" Jeanne asked.

"Yeah, that's him."

"Very distinguished looking."

"Here, here."

"But I don't think he would be as much fun as you."

"That's better. You sounded treasonable at first."

"Do you know the people he's with?"

"No. I've never seen them before."

"No?" she smiled. "Well, I'll tell you. That very beautiful lady in blue is the niece of the minister to the Argentine. The other is the daughter of General Duval, who is retired from the Army."

So, I thought to myself, nice people we common soldiers travel with. Our meal arrived and we returned to our seats. Jeanne ate with the dainty poise typical of French women—part of their charm for me.

"Your friend has been to Paris before," Jeanne commented.

"I really don't know," I answered. "Why?"

"Oh, he must have been. Otherwise he would not be acquainted with those people."

"Old Harris gets around, but I don't think Paris is one of his stomping grounds."

"Impossible. One does not just scrape up an acquaintance with such people. He must have been at least introduced before."

I pondered this as we ate. Harris, man of mystery, must have been about thirty-eight or forty, so he'd had time to get around. I hadn't had a chance to get to know him very well, but his story got more intriguing all the time. I'd probably learn more about him later, but right now I had a pleasant evening to put in.

We moved to the lounge for coffee and liquor—the waiter brought a pot of coffee, a bottle of Benedictine and two glasses. Since leaving Breteuil I'd had a little beer and some weak wine. I hadn't even thought of liquor. This was proof in itself that my need for spirits was the result of the tensions of war. When I was away from the sights and sounds of conflict, I could do without the stuff.

Jeanne poured the coffee and we spent a cozy hour learning about each other. She told me about her brother, Rene, and that two other brothers had died in the war, but she didn't have much to say about her life beyond that.

I painted a picture of my home town, my mother and brother, and my favorite pastime, baseball. She listened attentively, smiling and nodding as though she'd never met anybody as fascinating as me. It went right to my head.

"What shall we do with the evening?" I asked.

"Dance," she replied immediately.

"What, no Follies Bergère? No Moulin Rouge? No trip up Montmartre Hill?"

"Would you like that, Judee?" She put a delightful French accent on my nickname.

"Not in particular, but I thought those were the customary places for people on their night out."

"They get a big tourist trade, but we are not tourists, are we?"

"I hope not. Shall we go back to where we were?"

"No, I have a better place. One where we can dance and have a booth to ourselves."

"Booths are my weakness. Just lead me."

She smiled a bright, happy smile. Laughing and talking, we moved out onto the boulevard, where the Eiffel Tower stood lit up in splendor against the darkening sky. Jeanne hailed a taxi and we were off to our evening destination.

We arrived at the entrance to a large café, the center room of which was a black marble dance floor. Booths lined the side walls, each set off by a six foot partition with a door in the end, which could be closed or left open. Inside hung a velvet curtain to ensure privacy, regardless of whether the door was open or closed. A tiny bell summoned the garçon when one wished to be served, and at each summons the waiter left a small saucer on the table. When the score was settled, these plates were counted, and the amount stamped on each plate summed up.

As we entered a booth, I kissed the back of Jeanne's neck as I removed her light coat. She reached back and touched my face with a gentle hand. How lucky could I get? I rang the bell and a waiter appeared. I glanced at Jeanne. "What do we want to drink, champagne?"

"Do you like it?"

"Not particularly, but it seems the thing when one is going to be merry."

"Well, what do you like, sergeant?"

"You."

Her smile sparkled. "But, I'm afraid you would find me a little too solid to drink."

"Possibly. Possibly."

The waiter stood by, patient, though we knew we couldn't keep him waiting forever.

"How about some malaga?" I suggested this heavy sweet wine from the south I'd tried when we were fresh off the ship.

"Fine," she nodded.

"Un flacon du Malaga, et des petits biscuits," I told the garcon. He nodded and departed.

"Did you hear the man? You sounded like a Parisian born."

"Listen, sweet woman, speaking of speaking, how about your English? You know all the words, where to put them and how to say them. What's the answer?"

"The answer is seven years study of English, plus three summers in the United States. My father has spent much time in your country."

"Oh, so that's it. What is your father?"

"A Frenchman," she answered evasively and gave me a smile that told me gently but plainly where the boundary lay.

I didn't mind. If she wanted to keep her father a secret, that was okay. I didn't plan on dancing with her father anyway.

"When were you last in the States?"

"Last summer. Papa had business there, and he took me with him. We returned in September."

"What did you like best over there?"

"Coney Island!" The answer was quick and decisive. "I spend days there every time we go."

I mulled this over. She was in the States until last September. The French mission, headed by Marshal Joffre, was in the states last summer. Part of the group stayed through September. By putting two and two together I thought I could figure out pretty close who Jeanne Trevost's father was.

"Judy, don't think so deeply. No matter who I am it need not make any difference tonight." Enthralled by her sweet smile, I took her in my arms and kissed her.

The music started and we got up to dance. I felt conspicuous—the only American in the place. "Feels like everyone is looking at me."

She smiled. "Don't let it worry you. Those are looks of admiration."

"Who, me? I'm just another soldier off on a spree."

"Yes, but they know you were at Cantigny, and Cantigny is still fresh in their minds."

"How do they know I was there? I haven't talked to anyone but you."

"Well, my brother Rene recognized you. Your friend has friends here. When you two walked into the café this afternoon, it was whispered among the tables that here were a pair of Americans from Cantigny. I bet you anything you want that before the evening is over, you'll see that I'm right."

"What if I was? Cantigny was a small operation. It was only a front of about a kilometer and the advance wasn't very deep. If we'd liberated miles of territory, I could understand the importance. As it was, though, the operation was a mere flea bite on the enemy's butt."

She shook her head. "No, darling, you underrate yourself. To us, the battle of Cantigny was a promise of victory. To the enemy, it was the forecast of defeat. Why, do you think, did the enemy make such desperate attempts to retake the town and nullify your gains? Why do you think he bombarded you so heavily? Rene doubts that you will ever be subject to such merciless artillery fire again. He watched from a hill back of your lines after his tanks were withdrawn, and at times everything was obscured by smoke and flame, nothing could be seen but a rolling cloud of smoke and red flashes of shell explosions. He told us that more than six hundred guns were concentrated on your positions. Why do you think this was?"

"To tell the truth, I was so busy trying to keep my skin in one piece, I gave practically no thought to the whys and wherefores."

"Well, I'll tell you why. It was the American Army on trial. We'd been promised great things from the Americans. The enemy people had been told you were no good, that you would collapse under pressure. To prove it, the Germans couldn't afford to let your offensive succeed. In spite of all he could throw at you, you held; your offensive was a success. It promises France more and greater help and spells failure for the enemy. The newspapers here in Paris printed the news of the battle all over the front pages. Each day's progress was reported, and there was great joy when, on the fourth day, news came that the battle was over and that the Americans had held their positions."

"And so now we're heroes, eh what?"

"Exactly. We French appreciate what you've done, coming here to our rescue. When Rene described that awful bombardment, I thought you must be a race of supermen. I pictured you as great, deep-chested, hairy giants. Instead, I find you're just sweet, fun-loving boys."

"And here I was, thinking myself a tough, hard-shelled old soldier. Sweet, fun-loving boys, huh?"

"And," she looked down at her lap. "I decided then that if ever I met one of the men from that battle, I would do all I could to give him a few hours of joy and happiness in return for the days of misery and horror he endured for me and my country."

She looked up with a shy little smile. "So you see, Sgt. Judy of Cantigny, I do not make a habit of going around scraping up acquaintance with strangers."

"Yes, I see. Then I hope I haven't been too forward, a little too bold."

"No, no. I think I'm very fortunate in the man which destiny chose to send me from Cantigny. Your attentions have been anything but objectionable. You have been very sweet."

As I sipped my wine she nibbled a cake watching me.

"Have I spoiled our evening with my seriousness?" she whispered.

"No, not at all," I shook off my sobriety and sprang to my feet. "The night's young. Let's dance."

She slipped into my arms and we glided out onto the floor passing the night as dance followed dance. Jeanne was tireless and I, after days with a pack on my back on hard roads, could have done this forever.

I lost track of time as we ate, drank, danced and talked the night away. By eleven o'clock we were still in our booth, enthralled with each other, but this couldn't last the night. Each time I looked at Jeanne, I felt a joy that would stir the soul of a statue. This was the life.

"Would you care for something else to eat?" I asked. "If the answer is yes, name it."

"We might have a crab-meat salad."

While we waited for the garçon, I reached over and took her hand. We sat in quiet contentment as the music stopped and the master of ceremonies made an announcement. Jeanne straightened up suddenly and looked at me, smiling proudly.

"There. What did I tell you?" she exclaimed.

"Why? What did he say?"

"He just announced that the Royal Garden Cafè had the honor and privilege of numbering among its patrons this evening a member of one of the American battalions which recently captured and held the village of Cantigny against powerful opposition. He said that, with a lady friend, this gentleman occupies the fourth booth from the front on the right side, facing the stage. Now we must draw the curtain and let them have a look at you."

"Don't. Don't," I pleaded, embarrassed. "This is more attention than I deserve."

"Never fear. They are anxious to show their gratitude. Let them thank you."

She slid the velvet curtain back, throwing the booth open to public view. There was applause and craning of necks and as we stepped out for the next dance a polite patter of more applause, accompanied by a chorus of 'Vive!' and 'Bon!' There was nothing I could do. A friendly demonstration with no polite way of escaping it, so I took it in the best possible way. When we finished the dance and returned to our booth I sat down beside Jeanne instead of across from her. Public acclaim forced us to leave the curtain open wide, so I slipped my arm around her and she sidled close to me.

"Damn that curtain," I muttered. "I wish it were drawn."

She looked up at me, her eyes shining. "French people are very tolerant, sergeant."

I kissed her gently, and then again. She responded with another gentle caress of my cheek.

CHAPTER XVI

PARIS
JUNE, 1918

"Well, Jeanne, it's time to be thinking of unpleasant things. This has been the swellest day of my life and I'm sorry it must end."

"Yes, it must end," she echoed quietly.

"So now, darling, if it pleases you, I'll call a cab."

"What for, sergeant?"

"To take you home as I promised your brother I would."

"But it's only midnight."

"I know, ma cherie, but I promised your brother I'd see you safely home. If we wait longer, he'll think I'm not a man of my word."

"What will you do after you've left me at home, then, Judy?" Her question unnerved me.

"I'll probably have a drink or so and go to bed."

"With whom?"

Ahhh, the discerning little beauty. She read me like a book. Should I lie to her or tell her the truth? I decided on the truth.

"Well, my dear, it's this way. You've given me an unforgettable day's pleasure. I enjoy your company and cherish your friendship. I think I come nearer to loving you at this moment, than any woman I've ever known—as near to loving you as possible on such short acquaintance. So I am going to take you home."

"A very pretty speech, sergeant. A nice sentiment, very prettily phrased." She was serious now. "But, listen. I know what you want and I know what you will do as soon as you leave me. I like you very much and I'm not going to let you leave me to pick up some woman of the streets. When you retire for the night, if you are accompanied by anyone, it is going to be me."

She took a deep breath. That speech cost her some effort.

"But, Jeanne, think of your reputation—your family. Think of your brother, of your mother and father. Remember, I promised Rene to see you safely home."

"Yes. My family. My mother is dead. My father is away for weeks. I live alone in a big house. René comes home on leave and spends the night with his mistress. I have stayed out all night many times before. Rene doesn't know when I come home or if I never come home."

I kissed her. "You're too sweet a girl for such things."

She clung to my neck and whispered, "Judy, tell me the truth. Don't you want me?"

"Want you? Sure, I want you. I want you so much I ache, but my brain tells me I shouldn't take you."

"Well, it is settled, then. Come, we will dance a while yet."

We danced one or two dances, but our rhythm was gone, our minds somewhere else, far afield from dancing. I held her in a fervent embrace and buried my face in her hair.

When the waiter arrived to settle my bill, he spoke rapidly to Jeanne for a moment and she turned to me, smiling. "He says the management is happy to have served one of the men of Cantigny and that there is no charge."

In gratitude for the kindness, I requested that all the help in the establishment be given a drink at my expense. I gave the waiter a hundred franc note and told him to keep the change. He was very pleased.

The waiter called a cab, and I directed the driver to take us to the Hotel du Grand Concourse on the Sebastopol by way of Jeanne's house, an imposing edifice set back from the street amidst a grove of Linden trees. She stopped in for a few minutes and returned with a small bag. We drove on to the hotel, where we engaged a small, two-room suite. After settling in we relaxed and talked for a while before Jeanne went into the bedroom and emerged a few minutes later, clad in a soft, filmy pink negligee. She handed me a small package and smiled as I opened it. A suit of silk pajamas and a robe. They must have been her brother's, for when I took them into the adjoining room to change, they fit me like a tent, but any sleeping garment beat army underwear.

When I returned to the sitting room, Jeanne was curled up in a large chair, sipping coffee. I slipped into the chair beside her and took her in my arms, intoxicated by her delicate fragrance. I pressed her to me, delighted and excited by the feeling of her firm breasts against my chest. I kissed her face, her neck, her shoulders, stroking her tenderly. She returned my caresses as I lifted her from the chair and carried her into the bedroom.

Morning dawned as only morning in Paris can, sun streaming in at the windows amidst the clangor of char people and delivery wagons. No shells, no rattle of machine guns. No listing of the night's dead or wounded. Ah, this was swell.

I turned my head to look at Jeanne, sleeping like an innocent babe, her breast gently rising and falling, her eyelashes resting on her cheeks. A shame to waken her. I tiptoed to the outer room and pushed the buzzer for the waiter, who appeared within a moment. I didn't know what to order, but I decided on coffee and hot hard rolls with butter, hoping Jeanne would like them.

I went into the bathroom and indulged in a hot, fifteen-minute bath before I awakened her. When I returned to the bedroom she was sitting up in bed, stretching her arms out to me, and I crawled in beside her. The waiter arrived with our rolls and a bed table, and we ate and chatted in comfort, far removed from the muck and misery of the trenches.

Jeanne looked at me over her coffee cup. "Have a good night, darling?" she asked.

"Swell, sweetheart. All too short, but swell."

"Too short," she echoed pensively. "I'm afraid all of our time will be too short."

"Listen, darling, you wouldn't by any chance be in the market for an elegant husband, a little war torn and frayed around the edges, but still serviceable, would you?"

"You don't mean that, Judy, dear."

"Well, it was said in fun, but if you'd like to consider it seriously, you may."

"You don't know what you're saying." She was serious now. "Remember the French women of my generation have little hope of marriage. All their prospective husbands have been sacrificed to the war. Too many would snap up such an offer in a hurry."

"Well, darling, since that's the way it is, you need look no farther. You're a sweet gal. You're good company. You're pretty as hell, so you can lead me down the aisle any time you want."

"Judy, darling, do you mean that?"

"Sure, I mean it. It's only fair to warn you, though, that you'll probably be a widow within a year."

She put her finger to my lips. "Shhh. Don't think about such things. Let's think that you'll be one of the lucky ones and won't even get a scar."

"Okay. And you'll be Madame Sergeant Emmet Redding, U.S.A.?"

She snuggled into my arms and shivered with delight. "I'll be glad to. When shall it be?"

"Well, there is a little matter of catching a train to Saint-Nazaire scheduled in a couple of hours so it can't be today. But you write to me and I'll let you know when I can come to Paris. When I can make the trip, you have a preacher and we'll march up the aisle."

"Judy, you're a darling, but there are obstacles. I have my work, and it might be a long time before we could both be in Paris at the same time. I will write to you, and you must write to me. If you are still of the same mind a year from now, I'm sure I shall be. It would be unfair to take advantage of your offer now."

"Hell, I'll be rotting in some shell hole a year from now ."

"Let's hope not, Judy. René has been in the war for over three years, and he can still relish his women. Just take a little extra care."

As we embraced and lay down again, I kept a wary eye on the clock. My train would leave at eleven; it was now eight-fifteen. I took Jeanne in my arms and for a sweet interval we basked in oblivion to the world about us. All too soon the hands of the clock pointed to nine-forty-five.

"Are you going to the station with me?" I asked as we rose to face the world.

"All the Gendarmes in Paris couldn't stop me," she smiled.

A short time later we settled ourselves in a cab for the journey to the Gare du Austerlitz. Riding along the broad avenues of Paris on a beautiful summer morning could only be compared to a trip through fairyland. Trees lined the boulevards, their lovely shades of green a never-ending delight. Jeanne was radiant. I stole glances at her, enjoying the sparkle in her eyes and the flash of her teeth as she smiled. Before long we arrived at the rail terminus, where I told the cabby to wait, that Jeanne would return with him.

We entered the waiting room and a sudden thought struck me. "Jeanne, can I give you something?"

"What do you mean, Judy?"

"Well, money or anything."

"Judy." She threw me a reproachful look. "I thought you knew better than that."

"I do. I'm sorry, but I want to do the right thing, in any case. Now look here."

I took half a dozen diamond rings wrapped in an Army handkerchief out of my pocket. I chose one, white gold with a large solitaire setting, and held it up for her to see. "Suppose I just slip this on your finger? That would make us really engaged, wouldn't it?"

"You darling, Judy. What a beautiful ring! Where did you get it? You're too sweet for words."

"Shhhh. Never mind."

I wished I had something not purloined from a dead man — something mine and hers alone — but I pushed the thought out of my mind. I needed to tie her to me, to keep a hold on this sublime interlude. Someday, I promised myself, someday I'd put a ring on her finger to obliterate all this might remind us of.

Harris walked down the platform with two young women and a French major. We greeted each other, and, no surprise to me, the others of his party already know Jeanne. We laughed and chatted for an enjoyable ten minutes before it was time to board our train. One of Harris's lady friends stole a quick glance at the ring on Jeanne's finger. Jeanne didn't seem inclined to hide the token of our betrothal.

Finally the train arrived and, unable to delay any longer, we moved toward the Paris-Orleans Express, waiting by the platform. Hands were shaken all around, goodbyes were said. We collected our equipment and Harris climbed into the coach. I started to follow, but on the lower step I stopped and looked around. Jeanne stood watching me with shining eyes. Disregarding Harris's friends and all the other onlookers, I reached down and folded her in my arms. One long lingering kiss. She sobbed quietly, "Oh, Judy, darling, you must come back."

"I'll come back, sweetheart, never fear about that." I kissed her again.

We parted and I boarded the coach and followed the corridor until I came to the compartment Harris had preempted for us. He had the window open and was talking in rapid French with his friends. I looked about for Jeanne, still standing where I left her. She came by the open window and as we talked in low tones, I caressed her with my eyes. She was interested in Harris's conversation with his friends and gave them an imperceptible nod.

"They are talking about us, darling," she said in English.

"Good or bad?"

"Neither. Just asking about you. Your friend is not doing our cause any harm." The train started to move. She walked slowly beside it and then, as it gathered speed, she stopped, waved and was lost to view.

I closed the window and sat back in my seat, feeling unspeakable loss. I knew how these things worked. She'd forget me with time, and I wouldn't be able to forget what a glorious girl she was. Living could be swell, I reflected as the wheels clicked over the rail joints, if it weren't for the damn rotten war.

CHAPTER XVII

PARIS TO SAINT-NAZAIRE
JUNE, 1918

To hell with it. I needed a drink. I rummaged in my rucksack for my canteen, unopened since we left Breteuil.

Harris gave me a look. "What's up, sergeant? Didn't you have a good time?"

I took a good stiff drink. The stuff tasted odd after two dry days. "I guess I had too damn good a time. Too good to give up."

"From that ring on her finger I'm guessing there's already a commitment there."

"Sort of, yes. But it'll probably never amount to anything. You know how it is. She lives in Paris and I go to war."

"Yes. Yes, I know."

After a short pause, Harris asked, "Are you aware of who she is?"

"Jeanne Trevost. Lives on the Boulevard du Clichy."

"No, I mean who she really is. My friends know her well."

That brought me around. I was curious about those friends of his. "Yeah, that's right." I pressed him. "How'd you meet those 'friends'? You did pretty well for a stranger in Paris."

"So did you. But I'm not exactly a stranger in Paris. I studied there for three years. Made a lot of friends. There are still a few left in spite of the war."

"That's right. I forgot you were an ex-preacher." A hint of derision in my tone.

"What do you have against preachers, Judy?"

"Nothing against an ex. Just against the still active."

"What's wrong with them?"

"Hypocracy, I guess. And undeserved respect. They preach a lot of things they don't believe themselves, set themselves up as authorities. I figure if you're going to be an example, you should live up to your principles."

"Practice what you preach, eh?" Harris didn't seem to take offense.

"Right. Don't act all pious and sit in judgment unless you've kept your own slate clean. And even if you have, leave the judging to God."

"My gosh, Judy. You certainly go to the crux of the matter."

"Don't get me wrong. I'm not knocking Christianity. If the preachers taught the religion Christ taught, everything would be swell, but they don't. Christ was a purveyor of love and peace. Is it love and peace to vilify others, call them wanton and sinful and preach our Christian duty to punish them? Maybe we're the ones who are wanton and sinful. Maybe everyone is. The enemy chaplains probably preach the same message to the Bosch. Who knows who's right? In the meantime, men go on killing each other with the blessing of their religion, and preachers sanctimoniously fan the flames."

I warmed to my subject. "Remember that Chaplain Bannon that came up to Broyes to bury that gang that got killed by a shell, right after we got here? Remember how scared he was? As soon as we came under artillery fire, he hurried up and skipped everything he could to get away quick. Started to back up as soon as he began the service, and by the time he was finished, he was damn near back to Serviller. Now, if he believed so strongly in his creed and was so sure of going to heaven, why didn't he have the courage to read a funeral service? God knows, my belief in religion is damn small, but even without it I can face death a lot longer than it takes to read a funeral service."

Harris looked out the window for a while before he responded. "Don't you ever get scared, Judy?"

"Don't I ever get scared? Hell's fire, man! I'm scared all the time. Why do you think I keep sucking on a canteen full of liquor? Without it, I'd bawl with fright every time I heard a noise. As long as the liquor holds out, I'll get through."

Harris continued to gaze pensively out the window, then he turned, facing me. "Sergeant, I appreciate your candor, both about yourself and the clergy. Some of the things you're talking about were the same things that made me leave the ministry. Insincerity. Sanctimoniousness. Sitting in judgment. Unearned respect. Seems if you just turn your collar around, people think you know all the answers. But when you come right down to it, preachers are the same as the rest of us—ignorant, scared and uncertain. It's about character, Judy. Some have it and some don't. In every walk of life."

I uncorked my canteen, took another drink. I was in good shape now. I could go on with the discourse, but Harris gave me a solemn look. "I wouldn't take any more now, Judy."

"I won't," I replied, but we both knew I would. Sooner or later, I would.

CHAPTER XVIII

SAINT-NAZAIRE TO
VITRY LE FRANCOIS
JUNE, 1918

We arrived at Orleans a few hours out of Paris where we changed trains, taking the Angers-Saint-Nazaire Express and in less than an hour arriving in Saint-Nazaire.

The change in the port since we'd landed there last August was unbelievable. This was just another French port of no importance except for ship building which was practically at a standstill. Now all was changed; the port looked like a piece of the United States, with American uniforms everywhere. Great docks and miles of warehouses lined the wharves filling spaces recently transformed from open fields. Stevedores worked three shifts—around the clock—unloading an unending stream of supply ships. Cognac, which used to sell for from six to ten francs a bottle, was now twenty-five to thirty.

I presented our orders at the RTO office and they sent a man to guide us to the Motor Transport Officer to have our papers examined and stamped. Another guide took us out into a great park of vehicles—trucks, touring cars, limousines, ambulances, motor cars of all descriptions. Finally, our guide stopped in front of a brand new, shiny Ford ambulance, checked a number on his list, and moved on to the next. "Here they are, sergeant. Shall I wrap 'em up?"

"No, never mind. Heine will wrap them up when we get 'em there."

He laughed, made some entries on our papers, and handed them back.

"Will you leave now or in the morning?" All the formalities having been taken care of, we were anxious to be on our way.

"I think we better leave now."

It was about six pm, but I was concerned about taking a roundabout route to pick up Tony. The ambulances were equipped with lights, so we could drive at night until we got closer to the front.

The MTC sergeant handed me a bundle of printed slips. "These are requisitions. When you stop for gas or oil, fill one out and leave it at the station. Here's a list of supply stations."

"Well, I guess we're all set, eh, what?"

"Yep. Just crawl aboard. We'll gas you up at the gate."

I started my motor, pushed in the clutch and we were off, stopping at the gate to fill up on gas before moving out of town. As soon as we reached the outskirts of the city, I stopped. Harris pulled up behind me and climbed out.

"Say, sergeant. You did that in a holy hurry."

"Well, if we're gonna pick up Tony in Vitry Le Francois, we'll have to make time from here on. Can you drive till midnight?"

"Sure, but what about gas?"

I scanned the sheet. Sure enough, both Vitry Le Francois, and Angers were on the list.

"We can stop at Angers for gas. We should make it by about ten o'clock. By midnight we should be nearly to Tours."

"Okay, sergeant. You say it, I'll play it."

I took a little drink from my canteen and reflected, "No use going without food. What do you say to stopping in the next village to eat?"

"Okay by me," he answered. "Although after what I had to eat last night and today, I don't think I'll ever be hungry again."

After a short drive we stopped in a small village, where we enjoyed a dinner of omelets, fried potatoes, bread, butter and coffee. We got right back on the road and arrived at Angers at ten after ten where we found the supply station and had our gas and oil replenished.

"Where you gonna sleep?" the soldier-attendant asked.

"Red Cross hut," I told him.

"None of your damn business," I breathed to no one in particular. What he didn't know wouldn't hurt us. We spun along toward Tours, but weren't there by midnight, so I stopped and went back to Harris.

"Are you sleepy?"

"No. Not yet."

"Neither am I. Let's keep going, and when you get sleepy, blow your horn. I'll stop and we'll put up for the night."

He agreed and we kept driving. Some time near one o'clock we passed through the darkened city of Tours and kept right on toward Orleans. It must have been about two-thirty when I heard the horn honking behind me. I stopped and got out.

"What'd you say?" I shouted, walking back to his car.

"How about you?"

"Yeah, I'm sleepy."

"So am I."

Pulling to the side of the road, we dragged out our blankets, rolled up in them, and stretched out on the grass. We could have slept on the litters in back, but the thought of that gave me the shivers. I'd take the grass and the starry sky. One moment I was awake. The next I was sound asleep.

Two days of driving late into the night brought us to Vitry Le Francois. Tony'd left word at the supply station telling us where to find him. We were soon thumping the knocker on the door of Yvette's house.

Tony opened the door, his face radiant. "Hello, you Damn Yank," he cried. "Hello, Harris. Come on in."

When we entered, Yvette stood shyly on the far side of the room. I went over and shook hands with her. "How are you, Yvette?"

"I am well, sarjong, and you?" She was very quiet, even subdued.

"Oh, I'm swell. How's Tony been treating you?"

"Ah, Tony, he is verr nice to me. All the Americans are verr nice to me."

Her English had improved since our last meeting. "You speak swell English, Yvette."

She was pleased. "Yes, you think so? I have work in a little store here. The proprietor speaks English and we talk with each other."

I turned to my old buddy. "Come on, Tony, let's go catch a drink before we clean up."

He looked to Yvette for approval, but she shook her head. "We have brandy in the house, sergeant."

"Yes, I know. But our friend Harris doesn't drink, and we wouldn't want to offend him."

"Doesn't drink? How is this thing, Judee?"

"I guess he's just never found any use for good liquor," Tony said.

"Oh, not like you," she exclaimed, her eyes widening.

"No, not at all like Tony." I laughed at the remote possibility of a teetotaling Tony.

A man who had no use for alcohol, not even light wines or beer was strange to Yvette. She looked at Harris with curiosity.

"But what does he drink?"

"He drinks water, tea, coffee, or maybe chocolate. He doesn't eat little babies, and young girls are safe with him."

"But not with you." She got a kick out of putting me in my place.

Tony's laugh was hearty, but a little too loud. I sensed something not quite right, so I wandered over to stand by him. Harris moved over to wash in a large basin, setting on the broad windowsill.

"Listen, Johnny Reb, what's up? Something doesn't smell right around here. I sent you down here to fix things up with Yvette. Is there a hitch I should know about?"

He was reluctant to talk .

"Come on, Tony, you can trust me."

"Yes, damn it, I can. You know what the trouble's about. I asked Yvette to marry me and at first I thought she wanted to, but then she seemed to back off."

"Back off? Why?"

"She's afraid her past will interfere. Scared she's not good enough for me."

I winced. "Oh, hell. Tell her there's nothing to worry about."

"I did, but she's still all wrought up about it.

This was what I was afraid of. She'd had a hard life with this war. People survived any way they could. I wasn't such an old guy myself, but I'd been around a bit, which made me feel older, and I knew how it was.

I sat down at the table and called her over. "Where's that brandy you were talking about? Me here for an hour with an inch of dust in my throat and not a drink yet. What the hell kind of a joint is this?"

She looked puzzled, but brought me a bottle of cognac.

"Sit down here, Yvette. I want you to meet my friend Harris."

Harris looked at me with a raised eyebrow.

"Yeah, you, Harris. This young lady needs a talking to—from a real, honest-to-goodness American preacher."

Harris still looked lost.

"You know. About how war changes people. Makes them do things they wouldn't normally do. Makes them regret things. Makes them feel low and unworthy."

Harris seemed to get it now. "Yes, that's right. We don't know what life's got in store for us, so we can't say never. Things happen. We do what we have to—to survive. It doesn't mean we're not good people. Hell, ask Judy. Every soldier alive has done things he never would have done in civilian life.

Yvette stood close to Tony, listening. She was a gentle soul and the thought of violence, even to a fly bothered her. She turned to me.

"Sarjong, you try to make me feel better, I know. But I break the commandments. How can Tony want a wife like me?"

I took her hand. "That's Tony's business. That's all past, anyway, Yvette."

Harris rose and led her to the next room. Tony and I stood quiet, waiting. After about five minutes, they emerged from the room hand in hand, Yvette smiling shyly.

"The preacher say I am forgeeve. Say God know I'm good person. Say I can marry Tonee."

Tony let out a yell. "Whoooee! Thanks, Harris. Come here, Yvette." He took her in his arms and planted a resounding kiss. "Now that that nonsense is over, let's have a drink!"

We spent the rest of the afternoon in the village, giving Tony and Yvette time to themselves. Harris and I found a room in a little inn and got a good night's sleep to prepare for another long day's drive.

When I returned to Yvette's in the morning, she greeted me with a gentle smile. Tony was full of himself, so I gathered they'd reached an understanding. As we were getting ready to leave, Tony took Yvette in his arms and kissed her. He turned to me. "We're gonna get married, Judy."

"Okay, but not today. We're takin'off."

"Oh, no. Not today. The banns have to be published first," Yvette said.

"I'm gonna try to get leave for a few days next month. We'll have the ceremony then." Tony was full of plans.

We shook hands and went to our ambulances, Tony riding with me. He waved to Yvette as we drove away.

At about three p.m. we arrived at Regimental Headquarters, where we were told to take one ambulance to the company and the other to battalion headquarters. At dusk we finally arrived at the company, now in reserve positions in and about the village of Coullemelle.

The captain seemed glad, and maybe a little relieved, to see us. "Well, sergeant how was the trip?"

"Fine, captain, fine."

"How long were you in Paris?"

"About twenty-four hours, sir."

He grinned. "Did you see my girl?"

"I don't know, sir. We saw a million or so. Maybe one was yours."

"No doubt. No doubt." He laughed, then turned solemn. "Say, sergeant, this man Harris, what about him? What sort of man is he? Would he make a good non-com?"

"You bet he would, sir, no doubt about it. He's all wool and a yard wide. Under a bombardment he sticks right there, and he's not half full of liquor when he does."

The next morning Harris's name was posted on the bulletin board to be made corporal.

We soon fell into the same old round of duties: front line, reserve, support, five to seven days of each. In June, the enemy made a determined thrust on our left, but the French fought him off with a little assistance from us.

This was one hell of a sector. They shelled right on the roads now, and they'd snipe at one man with their 155s. We ate when we could, and I drank all the time.

Word came down that we were to be relieved, but I didn't believe it. We'd been here seventy-six days and moving us to the rear would cause a mountain of confusion and consternation. We were more like apparitions than men. Chalk dust had seeped into the fabric of our clothes until they weren't olive drab, but gray. It seemed also to have worked into our skins for faces were gray, cheeks sunken, eyes hollow. Continual shellfire had wreaked havoc with our nerves. If we weren't relieved soon, we might as well be left there forever.

CHAPTER XIX

COULLEMELLE
JUNE, 1918

After seventy-seven days of hunger, nervous tension, broken rest, unrelenting toil and mental torture—with death for a bedfellow—two divisions of Alpin Chaussers took over our sector and we marched back of the lines for a week of reveling in luxury. Three meals a day, plenty of rest and, above all, bathing facilities.

To top it off, we got replacements. On a warm June day I leaned against an old stone building that served as company headquarters watching the new men fuss with their equipment under the watchful eye of Sgt. Stubblefield. Stubby worried first one, then another, keeping up a running fire of talk.

"Heah, you, that ain't the way we roll ouah blankets in this outfit."

"It's the way they showed us at Camp Upton."

"Well, ya'll ain't at Camp Upton now. What'd ya'll do befo' yuh got in de ahmy?"

"I was a barber."

"Ah thought so. Well, y'all ain't no babbah now. You ah gonna *git* close shaves, not give 'em." He turned to me. "What y'all laughin' at you Damn Yank?"

"I'm laughing at General Stubblefield whipping the Army into shape."

"Well, nemmind. Y'all can laugh now, but when y'all got 'em up at the front and I'm down in headquarters dugout, then I'm gonna laugh."

Tommy Connors wandered up beside me. "How do they look, Judy?"

"Pretty young, but potentially full of the old pepper."

"Yeah, I guess so. I used to be full of the old pepper myself. What are they, draftees?"

"How should I know? Ask Stubby. He's got their pedigree."

"Hey, you," Tommy shouted to one of the nearest recruits. "Were you drafted or did you enlist?"

The recruit looked up. "I enlisted."

"By God, I don't see how you did it at your age," marveled Tommy. "I guess you want to be a hero, huh? Well, we could use a few heroes around here. The ones we've been usin' are gettin' kinda thin."

Some of the smiling kids gathered round, all ears.

"Look at 'em" Tommy remarked. "Look at 'em laugh. By God, I'll bet they won't be able to laugh like that two months from now."

"Why not?" I asked. "You still laugh. I still laugh. This war is just a damn fake anyhow."

"Yeah, thass right. Thass right. You sound mighty damn big back here, but when we're up at the front you don't act like it's any damn fake."

"That's because I want to last." I changed the subject. "Hey, Tommy. Watch me pick up this 'demoiselle." I nodded to a comely peasant girl approaching carrying a bucket of water.

"Yeah? Says who?"

"Says me, punk. Watch."

She approached, smiling, and I fell into step beside her, smiling, too. "Bon matin, mam'selle. Permittez-moi porter de l'éau." I aired some of my choicest pigeon French.

"Never mind. Never mind that guy and his bedroom French. Gimme that bucket." Tommy brushed past me, took the bucket in one hand and the girl's hand in the other and, with a triumphant grin over his shoulder, walked her up the street.

Stubby loved a joke on me. "Aha," he grinned. "Kinda slow on the triggah then, wahn't y'all, sawgint?"

I laughed too, feeling a rare sense of well-being. My gaze wandered down the street, where all phases of life in a French village carried on as though the world was not coming to an end a few miles away. Toward the lower end of town, women washed clothes and gossiped around the community laundry pool. A sedate flock of ducks waddled across the road, no temptation to me now, but a week ago such an event would have resulted in at least one casualty to their number. A clanking noise came from the village smithy, where a one-legged ex-soldier held forth, boasting of his military prowess before the loss of his leg. Even the manure piles in front of each house, prize possession of the French peasant and bane of the American Army, seemed to evoke an aura of peace and good feeling. I stretched, enjoying the serenity. It was marvelous just to be alive. Hell, this wasn't such a damn bad war after all.

Stubby brought me out of my reverie. "Sawgint, deah," he said in a most dulcet tone, "Would it be askin' too much to request that y'all come down to earth long enough to show these seventeen men for your platoon wheah to go?"

"Yeah, it would," I told him. "Why d'you want me to take them down, anyway? They can't get lost. All they gotta do is walk down the street till they come to the 2nd platoon sign."

"Okay, okay. Save youah breath. I'll take them myself."

"Like hell you will. I'll take 'em."

"Thass what I thought all the time."

I turned to the group. "Come on, you guys." Surprised, they expected me to line them up in drill ground formation and move them away by command. We didn't do much of that up here.

When we reached the platoon billet, Mac was sitting on a bench in the sun, playing with two children of about four and six. They climbed over him and searched his pockets for candy and gum.

My mind wandered back to a hairy savage in a shell hole, a primeval brute swinging his clubbed rifle in deadly combat, his one object to rend and tear and kill as long as he had strength to move. What an incredible difference. How could this gentle, good-natured creature, bent on amusing two children, be that same terror-inspiring fighting machine?

He rose as we approached, having been made platoon leader since Dave Evans was wounded. "What have we got here, Judy?" he asked.

"Seventeen of the best," I replied. "Guaranteed not to shrink, rip, tear or cave in under shell fire. Eh, what, boys?" My remarks were greeted with smiles and laughter.

"Well, how many do you want for your section?" Mac asked

"Six."

"Any particular ones?"

"Just give me six good American names I can spell and pronounce.

"Why, sergeant? They all fight just as well as any of us."

"Not saying they don't. I just want to know how to say their names."

I left the new men to Mac's tender mercies and crossed the street to my billet where Marguerite, my young landlady, busied herself in her spotless kitchen. Due to my abhorrence of sleeping in haymows, I'd rented a bedroom for a few extra francs per week. Marguerite agreed to cook for me, but she seemed to think cooking covered a multitude of duties, including washing my clothes, shining my shoes, and making my bed. I spent a lot of time in her kitchen, watching her go about her household tasks. She brought memories of Jeanne and the inevitable comparison—unfair to Marguerite, for there was little in common there. Jeanne's delicacy and grace were beyond the ken of an uncultured Picardy peasant girl.

I sat on the broad windowsill and poured a glass of brandy. Marguerite asked me about the new men she'd seen me herding down the street.

"New replacements," I told her.

"Tres naïf," was her comment. "Tres jeune."

"Oui," I agreed. "But time will take care of that. Soon they'll be as old as the rest of us."

"Yes," she sighed. "War ages us all, especially you soldiers. My brother Jacques was called at nineteen. When he returned for his first leave eighteen months later, he looked like a man of forty."

I was in too good a mood for talk of war, so I rose and looked out the window until Marguerite put my lunch on the table. After I ate I headed out to give the new men a little schooling in the practical art of warfare.

We took them out of town to a large meadow, where we explained the Hotchkiss gun, showed them how to change barrels, and then let them shoot a few rounds. After they'd thrown some grenades we opened up a question and answer session. They asked. We did our best to answer without scaring them out of their shorts.

Capt. Weyandt watched for a while, then beckoned to me. "Have the new men fall in, sergeant, and I'll give them their commandments."

When the group had fallen into a semi-circle in front of the skipper, he looked at them earnestly before he spoke.

"Men, I have no long speech. I simply want to tell you that you've been assigned to the pioneer division of the American Army in France. This division has a record of achievement second to none, accomplished not by newspaper publicity, nor fond boasting by the folks at home. We hail from every state and territory in the union, so no one state or community backs us. Our record is a result of success in battle, courage, fortitude and self-sacrifice. We've demonstrated our ability to hang on and endure for hours, yes, for days on end, and then to strike swiftly and effectively."

He paused for a moment as the new men hung on his words. A faint smile hovered around his mouth as he continued. "Up 'til now, this division has borne the brunt of American participation in the war. We don't go in for the spectacular. Don't take unnecessary chances. Remember this: a man observed is generally a man lost, and a man lost is a wasted life. Penalties in this war are quick and final. Chances to rectify our mistakes are rare. We're fighting an alert and courageous enemy, quick to take advantage of our blunders, so letting down your guard for even a second can result in death for you and your comrades. Listen to and watch your non-commissioned officers and the older men. They are, any of them, as competent to command this company as I am, and I'm proud to commend you to their guidance and care. That's all."

He looked around the circle of faces and turned to me. "Take the company back to town and dismiss them, sergeant." Then in a louder tone, "All non-commissioned officers report to company headquarters immediately."

As soon as the men were dismissed a chorus of talk broke out, sizing up the captain. This was the first time some of the new men had met him, and they wanted to chew on their impressions of him.

"Seems like a fine guy. Straight shooter."

"Yeah. More like one of us than an officer."

Another chimed in. "Did you notice anything about his talk?"

"What do you mean?"

"Well, he didn't say 'I' once after he started. Everything was 'we' or 'us.'"

"Listen, you guys," Mac told them. "Everything you've said is true, and I'll tell you why. The skipper is one of God's corps. He knows who does the work, and he gives us credit. He knows damn well that without us behind him, he'd be a complete washout." He paused to let his statement sink in. Then with an abruptness that gave weight to his words, he went on. "But don't ever forget that without him behind us, we'd be just as complete a washout."

We left the recruits to digest the talk and made our way to company headquarters where the captain waited. "Men, there's a big allied offensive scheduled soon. We're to take part in the initial assault. We leave here in trucks tomorrow around sundown. Have the men get ready immediately after the noon meal tomorrow, all duties until then will be suspended. Let the men rest and relax. Just keep an eye on them in case they happen to get too enthusiastic in their recreation."

He looked around at us, smiled and continued. "I am not given to sentiment, men, but I'll take this chance to tell you that for what you've endured and for what you've faced without complaint, I honor you all. I probably won't have a chance to talk to you again until after the drive, so good luck and good-bye."

As we left I noticed orders on the bulletin board transferring Tommy Connors from the 4th to the 2nd platoon. This was good news as Tommy was an old timer and a natural born clown, so as long as he was with us we'd be assured of plenty of laughter.

The cooks announced supper and the company streamed up the street, mess kits clanking. I went over to Marguerite's and prepared for a comfortable night. Mac, Tommy and the gang would be in for a session of stud poker.

CHAPTER XX

SOISSONS
JUNE-JULY, 1918

The sun setting in the west threw a beautiful glow over the world. The road, lined with trees, was also lined with trucks for as far as the eye could see. As our group had already been counted and assigned to a truck, we awaited the word to start loading. I lolled on the grass by the side of the road and engaged the French truck driver in brief conversation. Riding in boxcars and in the rear of trucks was another of my pet aversions, so I casually reached in my pocket and drew out a full pack of cigarettes. I stole a quick glance at our chauffeur as I opened the pack, took out a cigarette, lit it, and returned the package to my pocket. Then, as though an afterthought, I looked up at the driver who eyed my smoke with interest.

I offered the pack. "Cigarette, m'sieu."

"Oui, et merci," he accepted.

After a few minutes, I casually asked who rode in the seat with him.

"No one. It is prohibited."

"Je comprends, tout droit," I returned. Forbidden or not, I was willing to bet that when those trucks rolled, I'd be on the seat.

After several minutes of aimless conversation, I asked if he liked his cigarette.

"Oh, yes, very much. American tobacco is very good. Much better than ours."

"How'd you like a whole pack?"

"Fine, but where would I get it?"

"Well, if I were to ride in that seat, a pack might fall out of my pocket."

He gave this lengthy consideration, Frenchmen not being given to snap decisions. I clipped another pack from my pocket, to show him I was well supplied. At last he gave in.

"Oui. Tres bien. You know how to get aboard?"

"Certainement. This isn't my first walk in the woods."

The trucks were loading now, and as soon as my men got aboard, I moved around to the blind side and sat down in the grass. As the truck jerked into gear I rose and stepped up on the running board. By the time we'd cleared the camp I was comfortably settled back against the cushions. The convoy was en route.

Riding through the night I tried to determine our direction by watching the stars, but due to a profound ignorance of astronomy, I couldn't tell the North Star from any one of a dozen, so I gave up. When we de-trucked in the morning in the midst of a great forest, I hadn't the slightest idea where we were. The driver enlightened me.

"Forêt de Compeigne."

Right on the front lines, somewhere between Soissons and Villers-Cotterets, a sector known for heavy fighting.

We slept all day, and at sundown the captain called us to his quarters and told us the offensive had been postponed until the day after tomorrow.

"I want all of you sergeants to take special pains with the new men—those we got after Cantigny—and especially those who arrived a few days ago. Do all you can to get them mentally prepared."

We returned to the company to find that we'd received a load of ammunition. The boxes were piled everywhere, so we had a time getting them sorted out and placed. As we worked, I debated with myself about what I'd say to these recruits. It was so easy to say too much and, after all, what was to be said? Noble speeches wouldn't take any ground, and noble speechmakers seldom got anything done except making noble speeches.

I decided not to say anything at all, just to let the question of what to say take care of itself. After the ammunition was distributed, someone built a small fire, since we were far enough to the rear that it was safe. I sat next to John Gallagher, with all of the new men grouped around, when one of them posed a question.

"Well, we'll soon know what a battle is like, won't we, sergeant?"

"Yes, you'll soon know," I answered slowly, wondering how many of them would survive to profit by their newfound knowledge.

"Day after tomorrow we go over." I was thinking out loud rather than trying to make an impression. "Don't anyone try to be a hero. All these so-called heroes do is draw fire, get themselves killed, and get their names in the hometown papers. We're not heroes. We're just a gang of soldiers working at our trade, but we work together. Don't try to rush any machine guns from in front. That's suicide. When you get so scared that your guts come up in your throat and choke you, just look at me and remember I feel that way, too. And above all, don't try to make a break for the rear. That's also suicide."

I stopped to dead silence. I'd said too much. I thought about the old outfit and wished they were here now. Anderson, Brice, Carlson, Morrie Muller, Red Conlon, Mart Keogh and the rest, a reliable crew. I was afraid these recruits weren't far enough removed from civilian life to be worth much as fighting men. As

Mac moved into the firelight and sat down, one of the recruits stood up.

"What's that light over there?" He pointed toward the front where a faint glimmer appeared and disappeared like a firefly — miles away.

"It looks like a lightning bug." Someone guessed.

Mac squinted toward the light for a few seconds. "That's exactly what it is," he said. "I can see his wings."

A shout of laughter went up and broke the tension, talk started up again and fear of the future was relegated to the future.

Slosh, slither, click, clack and click of equipment, noises peculiar to thousands upon thousands of men marching to battle fully equipped. Bayonets slapping legs, the squeak of pack straps, a sigh as a pack is shifted to a more comfortable position. There was only one road leading into our sector. One road to accommodate twenty-five thousand men, thousands of horses, and hundreds of guns. The only thunderstorm I'd seen in France burst upon us with the force of a deluge. In the lightening flashes, as far as the eye could see, the road was a confusion of artillery, machine guns, glistening helmets, shining slickers. Oh, for the brush of an artist.

We moved single-file along the west side of the road until, suddenly, the column of artillery to our right stopped. Someone broke through between the caisson in front and the gun team to the rear. The file of men followed. The caisson moved ahead, but the gun was held back by a human river flowing steadily before it. An artillery officer rode up, grasped the situation at a glance and tried to get his gun moving.

"Stop those men! Hold those men back," he shouted.

"Go to hell!" came a voice from the darkness.

"Who said that? Who said that? What outfit's that?" His outraged dignity immediately made him a target.

"Q troop of the mounted balloon corps," someone yelled.

"Who is that? Who are those men?" he called out, beside himself with rage.

"Christ and the 12 disciples. Who are you?" The reply emanated from the darkness.

"I'll have you tried. I'll have every man of you tried!"

Ridiculous.

"Go chew on a rope, you old bastard. The Boche is gonna try us in the morning." The voice faded into the darkness. Once again nothing could be heard but the snick, snack, click, clack of equipment. Here and there a chuckle broke into open laughter as we plodded onward.

Sweat ran into our eyes and down our backs and our breath came in shallow spurts. The rain stopped and stars peaked through the clouds to twinkle faintly in the sky. I was always amazed to observe night sky and think how steady were the stars in spite of the mayhem here on earth. Gun crews placed their guns here and there in the fields and the congestion on the road gradually diminished as outfit after outfit broke off to find their jump-off positions. Up until now, our movements had been perfectly cloaked by the thunderstorm, so no shelling yet.

We descended a slope into a deep valley. The sky began to pale as we turned and marched along the valley floor and through the ruins of a small town. Coeuvres et Valsery. I could barely make out the sign hanging askew on one of the houses. We turned a sharp right and started to climb the precipitous side of a ridge on one side of the valley — or perhaps ravine would be a better word. Part way up this steep slope we came upon dozens of large French tanks, well camouflaged but prepared to move. Here and there a motor drummed quietly. I watched the gunners straighten their ammunition belts and wondered if Rene Trevost was among them.

"Here I am," I thought, "climbing this damn hill while Jeanne is sleeping peacefully in Paris." Then another thought came to me. If it weren't for me and others like me climbing hills and preparing to fight, she and millions like her wouldn't be able to sleep peacefully in their homes. That thought lifted me out of my sullen mood. For once there was no place else in the world I'd rather be.

We climbed, grunting and struggling with the effort. Christ, this must be a misplaced Alp. How much farther to the top? Word came down to rest for five minutes. We sank down in our tracks, utterly exhausted. I lay on my back, gasping as though I'd never be able to fill my lungs with air again. Slowly, the gasping subsided into deep, panting breaths, which finally give way to almost normal breathing. I heard crackling in the brush, so I sat up and looked around as a group of French officers stepped out on the path. There was Capt. Rene Trevost, looking every bit as immaculate and debonair as when I'd last seen him in a Paris café.

"Captain! Captain! Captain Trevost!" I shouted.

He turned. "Why, sergeant, where did you come from? I was hoping to see you when I heard your division was in this campaign. How are you?"

"I'm fine." I wasn't sure whether to salute him or shake his hand. "How's Jeanne? Have you seen her lately? Is she still in Paris? Did she ask about me?"

He threw back his head and laughed. "Easy, my boy! Take it easy. Yes, I saw her last week, and she was in the best of health. She has left Paris. When I saw her, she talked continually of you. Does that satisfy you?"

"Yeah, but I'd sure like to see her," I replied, embarrassed by my impetuous behavior.

"She expresses the same thought regarding you." He smiled and offered me a cigarette. "You think a great deal of my little sister, is it not so, sergeant?"

"I'll say I do."

"Yes. Yes." His manner was pensive. "These things do happen, in war and in peace. A man and woman meet, fall in love and make plans for the future." He straightened up and looked at me, his manner changed. He smiled a half smile tempered by sadness. "Our future, if we could just see a little way into it—it is a precarious future, ours, is it not, sergeant?"

I was about to answer when a whistle blew and the men of the company struggled to their feet.

Captain Trevost thrust out his hand. "Well, gook luck, sergeant." His manner was brisk again. "I shall tell Jeanne of this meeting when I see her."

"Good luck to you, sir." I turned to go.

"And, sergeant . . ."

I paused, looking back.

"When you get to Paris again, be sure to look us up."

"I will, sir. I'll be glad to."

"Au revoir, sergeant. Bonne chance." He waved as I raced after the company, a new buoyancy in my spirit. This hill didn't mean a thing to me now. I could go over it in one jump. I caught the company as they filed into a shallow trench at the top.

The crest of the hill stretched in a wide plateau as far as the eye could see. To our left front were the ruined buildings of a small town, whose name I didn't know. I couldn't tell where the enemy lines were, either, for the entire hilltop was covered with waist-high wheat. As I made my way along the trench to my platoon, a strange silence enveloped everything. I looked to the east, where a great, blood-red ball, the sun, hung in the sky like a gigantic disk of burnished metal. The uncanny stillness gave me the creeps as I rejoined the platoon and ran into Capt. Weyandt.

"Ah, there you are, sergeant. How's your watch?"

"Mine says 4:28, sir."

"Check."

"What time do we go over?"

"4:35," he said quietly. "And sergeant . . ."

"Yes, sir."

"Watch for flanking fire from the village of Cutry."

"Is that it, there on our left?"

"Yeah, that's it. So long now, and good luck.

"Good luck to you, sir."

He moved away and I checked my watch again. 4:30. I turned my head to the rear just in time to see a rocket shot from a plane speeding toward us from the rear. Its lights were still visible when the gigantic noise of our barrage burst upon us. No preparatory bombardment here. Our barrage would play on the hostile trench for seven minutes and then move to the rear. We left our position at 4:35 and in two minutes were ready to rush the enemy trench as the barrage lifted.

I climbed out of the trench, watching for my men, and we moved forward through the wheat with practically no resistance. We advanced at a steady pace through a thin enemy barrage and no machine gun fire. The new men kept bunching up, presenting a good target, so I spread them out as we moved along. Suddenly the rattle of machine guns broke the air as bullets flicked through the wheat, but at that point the fire was weak and ineffective.

Something was missing, but I couldn't think what it was. Then I remembered. For the first time in my soldiering career I'd gone over the top without a good stiff drink. I raised my canteen and immediately remedied the situation. We lay down in the wheat, waiting for the barrage to lift from the enemy position about sixty yards ahead. We were too close—should have stopped a little sooner. Oh, well, we wouldn't be here long. I crawled around among the men, some of the new ones looking at me with wide, scared eyes. Abruptly, a whistle blew and we jumped to our feet and rushed the hostile trench. Heinie got one or two machine guns in action, but they didn't cause much noticeable damage.

"Keep them going, sergeant. Keep them going. Don't let them stop." The captain exhorted me to prod my squad into action. As we reached the trench, I ran along the ditch, herding the men past some already gruesome sights. We had to keep on the move. The groups behind us could deal with the men in the trench. As we advanced past the first position we met scattered artillery fire. Keep spread out. Tat-tat-tat-tat.

"Down, everyone! Automatic riflemen! Come on! Come on, automatic rifles! Hurry up!"

De Muth crawled up beside me, slamming his automatic rifle into position.

"Machine guns ahead somewhere. See them?" We peered through the wheat, bullets clicking past a few inches above our heads.

"There! See that? See that column of dust rising just to the left of that bush? See it?"

"Yeah, I see it."

"Well, sock it in there, boy. Their gun is raising that dust."

The automatic rifle began to stutter and hammer. Little spurts of dirt rose just in front of the telltale wisp. The machine gun fire slowed down, but didn't stop completely. I waited a minute, but there was no change in the rate of fire. I called for John Gallagher, Tony and Harris.

"Harris, turn your gun on the target De Muth is on. Tony, you and John take your squads and advance by alternate rushes. I'll go with John's squad."

Harris's gun was already in action, and the hostile fire slowed down still more. John Gallagher crawled through the wheat, his squad at his heels. He looked at me questioningly.

"Ready, sergeant?"

I took a deep breath—like diving into cold water, only much worse. God, I hated to get up and race toward that spitting, stuttering instrument of death. The urge to let them go alone passed over me. Even as the thought lingered, I answered, "All set, Johnny."

We rose and started to run at top speed, followed by the entire squad. Suddenly the wheat heads started to crackle and snick off around us. "Down!" I yelled.

As the gun continued to smash away at us I peered through the wheat to see what was going on. Here came Tony's squad, tearing past like the wind. Down they went. Now it was our turn again. Up we sprang. This time we got over a good stretch before we were forced to the ground again by that deadly whisper. Tony's squad passed us again on the dead run. I heard a grenade. Another. Then several in a bunch. I raised my head and looked to the left front, where the muzzle of a gun pointed up in the air.

"Come on!" I shouted, and we rushed the position. Tony's bombs had done all that was needed. Three guns and a dozen men lay in queer, twisted shapes, several only slightly wounded. I motioned to these to see to the seriously wounded and get them to the rear. The dead bodies yielded a diamond ring and a wallet that I slipped into my pocket.

The advance hadn't been bad so far. We counted noses and I found my section still in tact. Light artillery fire and scattered machine gun resistance from the enemy harassed us, but nothing serious yet. We must have taken them completely by surprise.

We continued to advance past a bunch of prisoners in underwear — artillerymen, caught in their dugouts. We halted at a position about in line with the enemy artillery. We'd moved three kilometers without serious trouble. A little fight here and there, but nothing to amount to anything. This couldn't last.

CHAPTER XXI

SOISSONS
JUNE, 1918

As we started to advance again, we came to a steep, narrow valley we had to pass through lengthwise. Withering fire met us as soon as we entered the mouth of the gully. A man near me coughed and fell. We were into it now—what I'd been expecting all day. Prickles ran up and down my spine; my mouth was dry. Their guns commanded our left flank with murderous fire. We lay down and pulled out our entrenching tools, each man trying to dig some protection from the annihilating fire. There wasn't much we could do but dig or lie there and take it.

Mac crawled over, protected by a fold in the ground. "What the hell are we gonna do, Judy? We'll be killed like rats if we stay here."

"Don't ask me. I know we'll be damn well killed like rats if we *don't* stay here. If we try to move now, we'll lose every damn man we have!"

"Hell's fire, man, we're losin' them right now! Listen to that!" A man screamed in pain.

"Just tell 'em to dig, that's all." I got to my feet in a daze, expecting to get hit every second as I wiggled my way along the section. "Dig, you guys," I yelled. "If you don't want to die, dig like hell!"

They dug, lying on their sides. Terrified as I was, I got a chuckle out of the memory of Jim Tracey's drawling voice. "You'll dig now. You'll dig or you'll die." I lay down in a depression and dug. As I raised my shovel a burst of fire scattered the mound of dirt I was piling up. Scared, I rolled over, my arm flopping up in the air as I rolled. The firing ceased. God, that was close! I wondered why they quit firing. Oh, yeah. My flopping arm looked like a limp body rolling. They thought I was done for.

Shouts and explosions indicated a fight on the side of the ravine over to our left. The intense fire slowed down, then ceased, and we moved forward. Directly ahead we saw the enemy haul their gun to bear on the group on the hillside. We rushed their position and McCoy, one of the new men, upset the gun. A German gunner put a pistol to the back of his head and pulled the trigger. Brains and hair flew like rain. Mac sunk his trench knife into the German's back and couldn't pull it out. Bewildered, I tried to watch every direction at once. When I saw an enemy rifleman crawling toward a tree, I grabbed their gun and heaved it upright. Another heave turned it around. I trained the gun on the crawling figure and pressed the thumb pieces. It didn't buck like ours. The man collapsed like a rag.

We kept moving up the ravine. A 77, firing down the valley, took its toll. Lt. Courland came across from the section on our right and told Mac to move ahead until we came to some shelter and stop there. Mac relayed the order to me, and I sent a runner to tell the first platoon moving on our left what to do. This ravine was rough country, making close contact impossible. Each section was more or less on its own, making slow and steady forward progress.

"Hey, sergeant! What's up?"

I looked around. Capt. Weyandt approached from the right, looking a lot more confident than I felt.

"I wouldn't be knowin' just what the general situation is, sir, but we just had a hell of a hot spell here."

"So I've heard. You in touch with the other platoons?"

"Yes, sir." My voice expressed more confidence than I felt. "By runner with the third and fourth platoon, and visual contact with the first platoon ever since we got in this damn gully."

"That's all right, then. How are your casualties?"

I looked around. "Damned if I know, sir. We've been so busy since we got in this Godforsaken valley, I haven't had a chance to check up on the men. We've had some hit, though."

"Yes, no doubt."

We moved along until, without warning, we got a burst from the left front and several men fell. Some just sagged to the ground, others spun and fell. Still others were knocked three or four feet by the impact.

Down we went, the captain still with me, using a stump for cover. I couldn't locate the bastard behind that gun, frying and crackling away at our section. Then a chau-chau burst into action. Our first platoon. The firing slowed while the automatic rifle hammered away. Then I heard grenades exploding and ventured a look.

"That's got 'im, sergeant. Let's go!" The captain was already on his feet. As we rose and advanced, the skipper moved over toward the first platoon. We came on to what looked like an old trench. Per our orders, we dropped into it and waited. We could see what was left of a village up ahead. A few minutes later, Lt. Courland dropped into our hole to tell us that village was the day's objective. We were to move within striking distance and stop. Then, when enough outfits moved up, we'd organize and make an all-out attack on the place.

I took advantage of the pause to count noses. We'd lost seven men, but I wasn't sure who. I did make sure that Tony and John were still with us before we started forward again. I noted that the shells from the 77 were no longer thundering down the ravine. Here lay a dead enemy with a good pair of field glasses around his neck. Must be a major or better, by his uniform. I slipped the strap over his head and hung the glasses around my neck. We continued our vicious fight up the gully against good troops, many of whom seemed to prefer death to giving up, even though their case was hopeless.

At last the order came to halt and dig in—not far from the town—a welcome respite. Tired to the point of exhaustion, where the strength would come from to make an assault on this town was beyond me. We lay in our holes, talking and munching hardtack. We hadn't eaten since last evening, and hunger was beginning to put a strain on us.

Shells fell in and around the town as our artillery pounded it with ever-increasing intensity. For an hour or more, a devastating bombardment fell on the village. We weren't bothered much by enemy fire, since we'd captured most of his guns in the day's fighting. Those he'd managed to save hadn't been placed yet, and replacement guns couldn't be brought from the rear during daylight hours.

Movement on the right. It was the captain standing up, looking at his watch. I told the men to get ready. The whistle blasted and men surged forward from everywhere. There must have been several thousand. Machine guns crackled and venomously intense rifle fire broke out. We'd lost plenty of men now, and no mistake. The dull p-lup of bullets hitting flesh kept reminding me that men were falling all around. I felt alone and helpless—men on all sides, but I still felt alone in a vast, empty waste. I saw a man pop from hole to hole and then disappear into the town. Crawling over piles of rubble on the edge of the ruins, we were checked by a withering blast of machine gun fire. Men fell and kicked, some screaming, some biting the earth in their agony, besieged by a storm of death and destruction beyond imagination.

I was terrified, appalled at the terrible anguish around me. I wanted to hide—jump in the first hole I saw. But on my right and left the line of attackers moved steadily on, heedless of the storm of bullets that threatened to overwhelm them. I rose and joined the advance. Great gaps appeared in the ranks, gaps that increased with each moment, but still the line moved, steadily, deliberately, and irresistibly forward. We reached the buildings and broke up into groups to rush into the houses, down into the cellars.

Our company was assigned to clean out a small area to the left of the square. Now the fighting was hand-to-hand. I carried a pistol in one hand and a grenade ready to toss in the other. Here came one of those French tanks, rattling and banging into the square. He nosed up to the side of a house, backed off, started again and moved right through the wall, whirled around and came out again.

An enemy soldier fixed the muzzle of a machine gun into position in the window of a house. I released the lever of my grenade, counted to four and tossed it in the window. The instantaneous explosion blew one man halfway out the window where he hung, limp and horrible.

Just when it looked like the fighting was dying down, it broke out anew. Why didn't we just give up the town and shell it some more? Then I thought of that magnificent, steady advance of men against that murderous fire. Should such a glorious action go for naught? No. We'd hold on.

My section shot, stabbed and bombed their way from house to house. Then we came to a house that offered no resistance, occupied by Americans. Everything had been cleaned out to this point, and from here on was someone else's territory. We sank down and rested, while sporadic fighting continued outside.

I looked over at Tony, his face black and powder-pitted. He rolled over on his back, his shirt bloodstained and torn, his hands bloody. "What the hell's the name of this town, d'you know, Judy?"

John Gallagher, having found water somewhere, was already busy removing the stains of battle. He looked up. "The name of this town is Missy Aux-, Missy . . . well, it's Missy something or other."

No one was interested enough to try to find out. We lay limp like spent balloons until Lt. Courland showed up to give us instructions for the night and early morning.

Then came a sudden commotion outside. "Everybody out! They're counter attacking!"

"God Almighty! More of it."

Since eleven o'clock the night before we'd marched ten miles to the front, fought our way forward for another five kilometers without food or water. A burning sun blackened and swelled the day's dead, and now we had to forego our well-earned rest to fight off a counter attack.

"S'Christ," I thought, "if we had all the damn curbstone patriots from back in the states over here now, they could prove their patriotism and we could take a much needed rest."

Keeping my thoughts to myself, I jumped to my feet. "Come on, men, if these babies want some more, we'll give it to 'em."

As we filed back up the cellar stairs into the street, Capt. Weyandt hailed us and gave Courland instructions. "Take your section back of the buildings. Deploy with your right resting on the ruins. Move forward as long as you can maintain contact."

We advanced accordingly and moved out past the edge of town. More hand to hand fighting. The enemy had brought up fresh troops for this special purpose. In clean uniforms, they grunted and cursed us. I distinguished the word schweinhund amid curses, grunts and yells. A big, blond man rushed toward me—then seemed to shrink as a bullet caught him fair in the face. Another guy used an entrenching tool to behead two men as quickly as could the guillotine. Men wrestled and struggled on the ground, but they were too many for us, forcing us back to the ruins of the town.

Now our machine guns opened fire from the windows and from the tops of the ruined walls. Two tanks waddled up through the debris littering the street, moving relentlessly forward, their treads crushing and spewing out the wrecked bodies of friend and foe alike. We moved forward behind them, joined by two more from the left, and finally drove the enemy beyond the village. We dug in quick in anticipation of another counter attack. The tanks moved back to the shelter of the ruined walls, where they took up a position in support of our flimsy line. I checked on the men, surprised to find that the section now numbered fourteen. We'd lost eleven. Christ, but I was tired.

CHAPTER XXII

SOISSONS
JUNE, 1918

All night long, patrols were out in constant contact with the enemy. Though we'd had command of the air all day, not so now. Through the night great large bombers, Gothas probably, soared over us dropping loads of death and destruction. They came in relays: first a small pursuit plane roared over and dropped a flare to light the ground below like midday and burn for three or four minutes. The bombers followed right after. No small bombs, these were gigantic ones that shook the earth, one after another, all night long. Rest was impossible. Anyone lucky enough not to be on patrol could only hug the bottom of his hole and hope. I heard one man praying, another crying like a baby. I felt like screaming. Would those awful concussions never cease? I uncorked my canteen and drank, again and again. This would be a fine outfit in the morning. No food, no rest, nerves shot and Hell awaiting us at dawn.

Day broke to the thunder of even more gigantic concussions. The enemy brought up fresh artillery during the night. These weren't 77s or 105s. Enormous shells rocked the earth and threw up great clouds of smoke and dirt as they exploded. Our only hope lay in the fact that they couldn't be handled as rapidly as smaller ordinance.

The company commander moved among our holes where we crouched munching on hardtack and raw bacon.

"Go easy on that food," he warned us. "We don't know how long it will have to last."

He beckoned and I crawled over to him. "Have the men stand fast when the advance starts, sergeant. We're letting yesterday's second and third waves pass through us. We assume reserve position today. Zero is 4:40."

"Yes, sir." A relief.

We lay side by side studying each other in silence. What do you say in such circumstances? All the trappings of rank dissolved. We were just two men, hoping against hope to make it home some day.

"How are you doing, Judy?" he asked.

"Well, I'm damn near starved, sir, and weak as a cat, but I guess I'll manage."

"Good boy," he jabbed me with his elbow and crawled away. I moved about spreading the welcome news among the section. As reserve troops we'd have things easier than yesterday. I looked at my watch: 4:25. Our artillery hammered the enemy positions incessantly. Their guns did the same to us, but fortunately they were over shooting our positions. As I crawled along, a shell landed behind me. I could have sworn the concussion lifted me two inches off the ground. I lay half stunned for a moment and then crawled into Mac's hole. A frightening figure with his sweat and powder-stained face and the stubble of a black beard beginning to show, to me he looked like an angel.

"How y'doin, Judy, old kid?"

"Pretty fair, I guess, Mac. How is it with you?"

"Not bad. Not bad. We've still got thirty-one men in the platoon. How about a drink?"

"Okay." I handed him my canteen. He drank and returned it. I took a small dose. I'd discovered that with my stomach so empty it took very little to have the desired effect. A little more would have made me woozy, which would have been worse than none at all. I walked a tightrope between sobriety and drunkenness, but I never let myself fall on the wrong side. Shells landed close. We scrooched down in our hole listening.

Mac cursed them. "God damn bastards." Then to me: "How's your section holdin'up, Jude? Them new men doin'all right?"

"Well, they seem to be doing all right for recruits, but they have to be watched close as hell, or they'll bunch up."

"I noticed, but they're pretty fair for new men."

"Yeah. They'll do."

The sound of our artillery changed to a steady, drumming crash. I peered over the edge of the hole to where the barrage was falling ahead. The advance was already under way. I marveled at how the gunners could drop their shells to form that curtain of fire. They'd moved the guns forward during the night, so close that the report could be heard distinctly. The sound of the guns so close behind us inspired a sense of security and confidence. Surely, we'd be all right with artillery that placed itself practically in the front line to render fire more effective. As I scuttled back to my hole, I thought "Boy, we got the best artillery in the world in this division."

I looked to the rear as the assault began. A sight for an artist again. Spread out, well aligned, they advanced steadily, unhurriedly. Some walked with a swagger, rifles at high point, sunbeams flashing on their bayonets. Here and there a helmet was tilted at a rakish angle, the early morning light reflecting from their worn tops. Shells burst among them, gaps appeared in their ranks, but still they moved steadily ahead, nervy and confident, walking to possible death or mutilation, but they neither faltered nor hesitated. Relentlessly, they moved forward, their progress as inevitable as the approach of doom. It was the first time I'd ever viewed one of our advances from the front.

They approached our holes and leaped over them, throwing comments at us as they passed.

"Good guys, you First Battalion."

"Swell job yesterday."

"We'll give 'em some more today."

Then I heard a shout that sounded like a battle cry, a sort of rhythm, like a chant. As I tried to distinguish it, an advancing man reached down and shook my hand.

"Well done, you men." An officer, he moved on before I could reply. Again I heard that cry, this time plainer, coming from the assaulting waves.

"Hell, Heaven or Hoboken by Christmas."

They shouted it again and again. The assault passed us, rolling inexorably on. As we waited for the supporting groups, I wondered if we'd looked like that yesterday. The awesome spectacle filled me with pride, for I'd witnessed the stark, raw, dauntless courage of men moving forward to battle, into the face of mutilation or death, the real test of courage.

Once the assault waves reached the enemy, the fighting was furious. The advance moved ahead, slow but relentless. As the support approached and passed by, we prepared to move. The way back was more or less uneventful. We moved along in the wake of the attack, at times subject to shellfire that caused some casualties, not very severe. Jerry was too much occupied with the attacking waves to spare much attention to us in reserve. We crossed the Paris-Soissons road. Fighting there had been terrific; the road and surrounding territory was littered with dead. Men, horses, guns, wagons, ammunition carts and several ambulances lay about in indescribable confusion. This was the enemy's main highway route, over which supplies were transported deeper into the salient. His troops fought desperately to defend it, the evidence of their gallant stand left as a testament for all who passed.

Tony stood beside me on the edge of the road, surveying the depressing scene.

"They sure put up a fight here," he ruminated, half to himself.

"I'll tell a man. Hey, look at John. What's he up to?"

Tony looked away to where John Gallagher tended an enemy soldier, painfully wounded about the face and neck. He'd bandaged the wounds and was trying to light a cigarette for the wounded man. Not a smoker, John had to make several attempts before he could light and place the cigarette between the lips of his erstwhile enemy. Tony and I laughed at the spectacle, not at the sight of one of our men caring for a wounded enemy, but at John's very evident distaste for tobacco.

"There's something you won't see six months from now," said Tony.

"What?"

"One of our men fixing up one of the enemy."

"Why not? We all do it, don't we?"

"Yeah, but six months from now the men we have will look at these things differently. We see the enemy as one soldier to another. We know he's put up with the same hardships we have. We admire his skill and courage—respect his loyalty to his fatherland."

He paused and I looked at him with curiosity. Tony didn't often open up and express deep thoughts. "You know," he continued, "they're teaching these new draftees to hate the enemy. To hate him as an individual and to deny any good in his makeup."

"What would you have them teach?" I asked. "To run over and kiss him when they meet, or invite him over for afternoon tea? I think he comes over too damn often without my invitation."

"Yeah, I know. I also know that we got a war on and . . ."

"Hey! You guys wanna get bumped off?" Mac's discordant voice, harsh with anger, interrupted our discourse. "Get the hell outta that. Don't you see that plane up there?"

We looked up, and sure enough, a Rumpler, by his large tail assembly, flew serenely around in a circle.

"Don't ya know what he's doin'?" Mac questioned belligerently.

"No, what?"

"Takin' pictures."

"Good," laughed Tony. "I hope he sends us one."

"By God, I'll make a picture of you with a punched in nose if you don't get under cover!"

We heeded his warning and went back to the section. The outfit moved along as the advance progressed but the resistance had stiffened considerably, and night fell amid a display of fireworks, magnificent in its unearthly beauty.

The third day, we moved up into the support position. Yesterday's support was today's assault wave. Advancing slowly, we took prisoners, bombed dugouts and strong points, mopping up after the front wave had passed on. Several times that day we were subject to heavy bombardments and machine gun fire.

John Gallagher and Tommy Connors approached me at the bottom of a sunken road. "Hear the news?" John looked like a dirty, wind blown scarecrow.

"What news?" I asked, too tired and hungry to be interested.

"The skipper's hit."

"The hell he is! How bad?"

"Well, he refused to be carried back, so it can't be very bad. I heard it was a machine gun bullet somewhere in the leg."

I was relieved the captain's wound was minor, probably enough to keep him out of danger for the rest of the drive.

I turned to John, struck by a sudden realization. "Who's company commander?" "Lt. Davies," he replied absently. "Gee, I'm hungry."

Christ! Lt. Davies. I'd rather it was Barney Google.

We moved along in the wake of the attack until mid afternoon, when we halted in the angle of a crossroad. I didn't like the look of the place. The artillery always had crossroads taped to a hair. With all those enemy balloons up, I felt trouble coming.

Sure enough, within a minute two shells arrived, then two more, then they were countless. Small ones, big ones, they shrieked and swooped down on us. Men were blown high in the air amid deafening noise. Great chunks of steel three and four feet long, sharp and jagged, flew through space. I saw Bill Whaley rise from the ground and fall back an inert mass. A man started to walk toward a shallow ravine two hundred yards to the rear and without warning his torso jumped in the air and fell, rolling to the ground, his legs and part of his body walking on for a dozen steps before they sagged to earth, where they lay jerking and kicking spasmodically.

I was cursing the lieutenant for stopping the company here when I saw him engaged in a fierce altercation with Stubby. Stubby turned away, blowing a shrill blast on his whistle, and pointed toward the ravine behind us, his meaning clear. The men moved back to take advantage of its protection. I hurried my section back and we were soon comparatively safe. Stubby called to me.

"Sawgint, go back to that crossroad and wait foah a runnah, will you? We'ah supposed to remain in the vicinity foah oadahs."

I returned to the crossroad and concealed myself in the ditch alongside the highway. The shelling had ceased, but not the cries of the wounded. I couldn't stand it. The first aid men were yet to arrive, so I crawled out of my ditch and moved among the casualties, doing what I could. I bandaged one here and another there, most of them so badly mutilated they were beyond help. I'd seen Bill Whaley get hit, no doubt that he was dead; both legs gone, one arm lying crooked under his body; the other hand gone at the wrist. The skin and flesh were stripped so that his ribs showed through, his neck peppered with fine holes. I was about to pass him by, when, unbelievably, he opened his eyes and recognized me. I crawled forward and knelt beside him.

"Hold everything, Bill. I'm going to bandage you." I bit my lip in an effort to appear calm.

He smiled weakly, and I swallowed the urge to sob.

"It's no use," he whispered, his voice faint and throaty. "Could you light me a cigarette?"

"Sure. Sure." I placed a lit cigarette between his lips.

As he inhaled, the smoke seeped out of the holes in his throat. I turned away to shut out the sight, but my gaze rested on the red head of young Reed, not more than seventeen years old, lying in a pool of blood. I walked over, but he was dead, his eyes staring, mouth open, lips drawn back. I returned to Bill. His head had dropped; the cigarette fallen to his chest where it lay, smoking, a brown spot where it'd burned his flesh. Dead. Sixty men rubbed out in twice as many seconds. Too many men to pay for one man's mistake.

A squad of first aid men came up the road on the run, Stubby and Tommy Connors with them.

"My God, Stub. What happened?" I asked.

Stubby looked like a mad dog. "Ah, that dumb son of a bitch. We had oadahs to remain in the vicinity of this crossroad and wait foah futhah oadahs. Ah tole 'im not to stop in the angle. Ah tole 'im we could move back to that gully and leave a man heah to wait foah the runnah. He got uppity and tole me that he was company commandah and that when he wanted advice he'd ask foah it. God damn his duhty haht, Ah'd like to make him count the men that's dead just because he's company commander.

"The lousy bastard. Well, he won't live forever. One more trick like that one, and I'm damn sure he won't."

The awaited runner approached along the main road, inquired for the company commander and the lieutenant appeared. He didn't yet seem to realize that the recent catastrophe was a direct result of his ignorance and high-handedness. He took his orders from the runner and, after signing for them, looked them over hurriedly. Beckoning us to follow, he double timed it down the road to the company.

When we arrived at the gully the lieutenant called for a squad from the fourth platoon to reconnoiter a section he pointed out on the map. The squad moved off to the left, and we sank down along the sides of the ravine. I took a pull at my canteen. It was getting low. It held two liters, but this was the third day without replenishment. I looked up Tony and John. Thank God they'd escaped that holocaust. We sat on the slope facing the rear.

"How many men've we got left?" Tony asked.

"Damned if I know. I haven't counted them lately."

"I'll count them now if you want me to, sergeant," John offered.

"Go ahead, if you want to, but for Christ sake, quit calling me sergeant."

He looked back, a hurt expression on his young face, putting me to shame for my irritation. He returned shortly with the count. "I make it eleven."

Eleven out of twenty-five and still we three hung on. It couldn't last. One of us would stop one before long.

CHAPTER XXIII

SOISSONS
JUNE, 1918

A sudden burst of shellfire on the far side of the gully, where a sunken road passed diagonally up a slope, caught our attention. We looked up to see a rolling kitchen drawn by four mules at the center of a mass of shell bursts. A cloud of smoke hid it from sight, so we waited for the smoke to clear. The vehicle lay on its side at the edge of the road, the animals down. Several small figures lay in the roadway as stretcher bearers moved to the scene. We watched in silence as the stretcher-bearers departed with their burdens. Tony looked at me. John was watching us both.

"Come on," I whispered.

We slipped quietly down the slope and crossed the ravine up to the road. A little distance down the highway the rolling kitchen still tilted against the bank. A shell whistled over and burst in the field beyond. We hurried up to the kitchen and removed the lids from the Dixies. What a sight for starving men! Steak, mashed potatoes, gravy, canned peas, bread, butter and coffee. We picked up a couple of discarded helmets, ripped out the lining, and filled them with food. What a repast! Intermittent shelling couldn't drive us away, and not until we noticed movement across the ravine did we return to the company, having eaten ourselves senseless.

Our reconnaissance party had returned and, when we re-crossed the gully, the outfit was getting ready to move out.

"Jesus Christ, Judy, where the Hell have you been?" Mac growled. "I've been looking all over for you."

"Never mind where I've been. D'you want to eat?"

He looked at me like the war had finally driven me nuts. "Do I wanta eat? Hell's fire, man, don't torture me!"

"Well, shut up and listen, then." I told him about the kitchen and showed him where it was. "You beat it over there and get a feed. I'll take charge of the platoon. You can catch the company later."

He needed no more urging. He and Tommy slipped silently down the slope.

We moved out promptly and, as luck would have it, before long the word was passed back for Mac. I answered the call by moving up to the head of the column. Lt. Davies' recent fiasco didn't seem to have had any appreciable effect on his judgment.

"Where is Sgt. Mac?" he asked.

"He fell out just a moment ago."

"Well, you'll have to do then. When he returns tell him we're moving to a position that was reconnoitered this afternoon. In the morning we join the assault."

"Yes, sir."

In half an hour Mac and Tommy overtook us, grinning from ear to ear. It was a shame we couldn't take the whole platoon over and feed them, but it would have gotten somebody killed for sure. Three days without a cooked meal and the men showed it—staring eyes, hollow cheeks, the personification of weakness and fatigue. They'd given beyond their strength, and now there was nothing left but nerve. Weak and tired as they were, when called on for further effort they drew on some hidden reserve, some undiscovered source that let them drive their worn out bodies to even further effort.

After another half hour we stopped in the shelter of the Paris-Soissons road, banked up higher than the surrounding country at that point, where we waited for darkness before moving into our position. It was fully ten o'clock when we resumed our march, the members of the afternoon's scouting party acting as guides. We crossed the road and made our way through fields, knee deep in grass. We halted often until we came to a line of fox holes occupied by the men of the 28th infantry. Here a hurried conference took place at the head of the column. I took advantage of the pause to gather information for my own purposes.

"Hey, buddy," I addressed a shadowy figure partly hidden in one of the holes.

"What d'you want?"

"Where are we?"

"Well, this is our main line, but we've got outposts out. Where you guys goin'?"

"Damifino, you'll have to ask his nibs, up front."

"Well, by God, you ain't goin'very far that way because Jerry's right on the other side of this field, and I think he's got outposts out, too."

We started to move again, but before we'd covered two hundred yards a guttural voice emanated from the night.

"Alte! Vos is?" The column stopped. I looked for the Germans to open fire immediately. I recognized the language and there was no reason why anyone else wouldn't, but the lieutenant seemed undecided—seemed to think this was a French outpost. What the hell? A Frenchman would have cried, "Halte! Qui vive?" Not "Vos is?" Ready to dive for the ground, I passed instructions back along the section to drop and roll at the first sign of trouble.

The lieutenant called for Coates from the first platoon to act as interpreter. He refused, saying, "I can't talk their language, lieutenant. I speak French."

"They're French." replied the lieutenant testily. "I'll call Munson if you're afraid."

"Okay, lieutenant."

Munson, a yes man and a suck, hurried to the head of the column in response to the summons.

The group that halted us remained silent. Old soldiers, too well versed in warfare to betray their own identity by firing prematurely, they stood by while this farce played out.

Munson's voice sounded clear on the night air. "Qui la? Les Francaise?"

The answer, immediate and unmistakable, was a blast of machine gun fire. I heard bullets strike living flesh with a dull p-lup. Men screamed as the hot missiles ripped through their bodies. Somewhere close by a man kicked the earth in his death agony. I dropped to the ground and rolled to my right. A storm of bullets whistled over my head. One clicked on the edge of my helmet, glanced off and buried itself in the ground under my right shoulder. The shock felt like a blow from a sledgehammer.

Flares went up on both sides, shedding a brilliant light on the scene. I saw the muzzle of a gun, steam rising from its water jacket, and then two more on its flank. I raised my head for a better look. Zing! Zing! Two bullets skipped off the top of my helmet and buzzed away like bees. I rolled farther to the right hoping I was out of the zone of fire and fairly well concealed by the tall grass. I ventured another look. Men lay all around, some wounded, some dead, some, like myself, unharmed but unable to move without drawing fire.

Flares still rose up from the front lines, illuminating the field like midday. A man, crazed with pain, leaped to his feet and rushed directly at the guns. A short burst and he collapsed like a rag. Two men crouched directly under the muzzle of the left gun, one so close the gun muzzle couldn't be depressed far enough to hit him. Partially concealed by the parapet, I doubted they saw him, split from his head to his crotch by hundreds of bullets. It took only an instant to grasp these scenes. As the flares continued to ascend, I reached down for one of my two grenades. Now, if those damn fools would just quit shooting flares for a minute, maybe I could manage this. In the darkness, my movements unnoticed, I waited for what seemed like forever.

The flares didn't show any signs of diminishing, so I'd have to take a chance. Slowly and with infinite caution I rolled over on my side. I pulled the pin from the bomb, held it for a second and then very carefully lobbed it toward the hole that sheltered the guns just like I'd lobbed the ball back to the pitcher in a game. Without waiting for the explosion I repeated the action with the second grenade. Rolling back to my stomach I raised my head in time to see the flash of my second bomb as it exploded right in the emplacement. Others had seen the explosions and now a perfect storm of explosions marked the site of the strong point.

I heard Stubby shouting to rush the position. I sprang up and rushed across the intervening hundred feet with all the energy at my command. We'd encountered and wiped out a strong point. Seven guns, eleven prisoners, and eight enemy dead were the result. Stubby ordered us back to the front line. I noticed that the company had dwindled perceptibly. When we arrived it seemed we'd played our skit to a very appreciative audience.

"Got you with your pants down out there, didn't he?" came a whisper from a foxhole.

"Yeah, that damn dumb Lt. Davies did it" The statement was made on no uncertain terms.

"How many did we lose?" I ask Stubby, who was busily trying to reorganize the company.

"Ah dunno, sawgint. The best count Ah kin get is sixty-one men.

I looked for Mac, Tony and John. Mac showed up immediately but Tony was nowhere around.

"I saw Cpl. Gallagher sittin' in a hole just a minute ago," someone close by told me.

We lay on the ground in the rear of the front line. Stubby was out with a patrol, trying to find our designated position for the morning's advance. I talked with the doughboy in the hole in front of me.

"How was it today?"

"It was just proper hell, buddy. Just proper hell."

"How deep was the advance?"

"Not very deep. Heine's fightin' like all hell, tryin' to keep us from cuttin' his railroad."

"Where's that?"

"Just ahead a little ways. We tried to cross it near sundown this evening, but he was too much for us."

"Get youah men togethuh, sawgint, weah movin'" Stubby's low voice ordered.

I moved in and, in low tones, called for the men of the second section, second platoon. Only eight responded, John Gallagher among them with a bandage on his wrist, hit by flying rock from a ricocheting bullet. His white face showed plainly in the starlight.

"Beat it to an aid station," I urged.

He looked at me reproachfully. "You know what we say about scratches and gas cases, don't you?"

"Yeah, I know, but you're liable to get gangrene. G'wan. Beat it the hell out of here."

"I'll go when I'm carried." His laconic reply and the finality of his glance ended that argument.

The word came to move, and we made our way to the left in single file. Our position was only a short way off, and in a half hour or less we were in place and organized for the morning's advance.

We had no officers left. Lt. Davies having committed his last blunder, lay at the scene, along with the bodies of the innocent victims of his stupidity and stubbornness. Stubby was now company commander; Mac and I were the only sergeants, and we had a grand total of three corporals. We divided our sixty men into two platoons. Mac took command of one and I the other. We made the corporals section leaders and the first class privates would act as corporals.

A pleasant respite followed, and we lay on the ground and in shallow holes, talking quietly. No one seemed sleepy. I couldn't understand it, for we'd had no rest for more than seventy-two hours. I was still worried about Tony and asked all around about him. Bones, the only old man in my section, filled me in.

"Go Blimey! Tony's done in 'e is. Got 'im fair, they did. Fair in the fyce. I seen 'im git it."

So, I thought to myself. 'Johnny Reb.' Now there was no one but John, Mac and me. They were whittling us down. I sat staring into the darkness, thinking about Tony with his grin and his wisecracks, lying out there in the dewy grass—just another bundle of old clothes.

"No! It can't be. It can't be," I told myself. But it was so. I uncorked my canteen. "Well, Tony, here's to you, wherever you are." I drank deeply, rising to my feet as I did. Returning to my seat on the grass, I reclined on my elbow. I didn't feel the least bit sleepy, but nevertheless I dropped off into a deep slumber from which I didn't awaken until morning.

My first realization was that I was in a fight. Someone pounded my face and I woke up slowly, rising from a deep abyss. Holding my hair with one hand, he struck my face with the other. I couldn't seem to get awake. My face stung and throbbed from the slapping, but my eyes were heavy, my vision blurred.

"Come out of it!" cried Mac. "You're the sleepingest damn Dutchman I ever saw. Wake up! We got a war on!"

I shook my head, numb with fatigue, not quite ready to adjust to my surroundings. Mac handed me a small bottle-shaped German canteen from which a strange smell emanated when I pulled the stopper. I tilted it to my lips for a good stiff drink. Wow, it choked me and brought tears to my eyes.

"Christ almighty! Liquid Fire! What the hell is that?"

Mac grinned. "I thought it'd wake you up. That's the good old original schnapps, my boy! Guaranteed to warm your feet, stiffen your backbone, cure gout, housemaid's knee, or fallen arches. You're awake now, ain'cha?"

"Yeah, I'm either wide awake or clear dead, and I'm not sure which."

"Well, we got some plans to go over for this here war before we take off."

"How soon do we go?"

"Four-Fifty." He looked at his watch. It was 4:38.

"Now look here, Judy. We got no officers left. Stubby is company commander; I'm first sergeant, and you're the whole damn gang of duty sergeants. Now, we want to show these apes that we're just as good without any sixty-day wonders as we are with 'em. When we start forward, you get your gang to the other side of that railroad over there and hang on. Once you get over there, by God, don't fall back for hell or high water. Even if we don't move another damn foot, hang on. On the other side of the track."

"Okay, Mac, but tell me one thing."

"What is it?"

"What are you gonna be doin' while we're hangin' on?"

"Oh, I'll be sashayin' around, takin' my morning constitutional."

"And we're to cut that railroad and keep it cut?"

"That's right. Say, did you hear about Tony?"

My head dropped. I'd forgotten. "Yeah, I heard about 'im. Damn shame."

"Hell, what d'you mean a shame? He's damn lucky!"

"Why? He's dead ain't he?"

"Well, if a dead man can walk to the aid station, maybe he is. I sure as Hell saw him doing that very thing last night."

"Did you, Mac? Did you see him yourself?"

"Yeah. Me. I, with my own eyes, saw him myself. I even helped wipe the blood off his face. He ain't hit bad. A bullet just sideswiped his cheekbone. He'll be back in a week."

"Yes! Tony alive!" Nothing could be wrong now. My mind filled with whole-hearted joy as I moved from hole to hole checking up on the occupants.

A whistle blew on the left, and a line of men rose from their holes and moved forward. A storm of rifle and machine gun fire broke out from the enemy positions. The advancing wave was swept away like dust before a windstorm, annihilated in an instant. Witnessing this catastrophe dulled my fervor for the fight. I looked around, hoping to spare the men the sight of the slaughter, but it was too late. In the midst of battle, if it registered at all, it was fleeting. We watched and waited for our whistle blast. A minute — two minutes — eternity. What was the holdup? A head popped up here and there. Someone had passed an order down the line. We were waiting for a machine gun barrage. I was glad to pass it along.

We didn't have long to wait. In no time we heard the sharp whistle peculiar to machine gun bullets fired at a high angle. We didn't know the barrage schedule, no details. Just go forward at the signal. When it finally came, we crawled out of our holes and advanced with an amazing spring of energy. These men, after four days of constant combat, hand to hand fighting, nerve strain, without food or rest, found some untapped reserve and moved forward, joking and cracking wise.

"Here's where I get me a Proosian," cried one.

"Yeah? Or a Proosian gets you!"

I glanced to the left. There was Mac, taking his morning constitutional, all right. Out in front, helmet tilted, shoulders swaying, he actually swaggered through the knee-high grass. He looked in my direction, caught my eye, waved and shouted, but I couldn't make out what he was saying.

Even with the protection of our machine gun barrage we were still getting popped aplenty. I felt a tug at my breeches and cursed the short bushes interspersed among the trees that caught and pulled at our clothes. We were so close now, we could see the Germans plainly. Suddenly, another whistle blew. We rushed forward. Men who were yards apart an instant ago were now locked in a deadly embrace. I carried a grenade in my hand with the pin pulled. An enemy figure jabbed at me with his bayonet. I released the lever and jumped to the side. He made another lunge and I threw the bomb. It hit him fair in the stomach and dropped at his feet. I fell on the ground and rolled to the right as a terrific explosion roared over me. My adversary had disappeared. We fought and gouged our way forward, stabbing, shooting, bombing like mad men. The enemy refused to give way, giving as good as he got. It was still two hundred yards to the railroad.

CHAPTER XXIV

SOISSONS
JUNE, 1918

The fight went on interminably. We lost all sense of time in the intensity of battle. Incredible that there were any of us left at all. I took aim at two men firing a light machine gun, hit one. The other raised his hands watching me with fear in his eyes. I moved over and took out my trench knife. He was thinking this was it for him. I sliced the suspender buttons off his trousers, pointed him to the rear and started him on his way with a well-aimed kick in the pants. His hands'd be too busy with his trousers to get into any trouble on the way back. I glanced up, surprised to see the railroad embankment looming over me. To the left the tracks curved toward our lines and some of our outfits were already across.

We threw ourselves down on the side of the roadbed and took advantage of it as a breastwork. Heavy fire came from the other side of the track. We tried to mount machine guns on the top of the hill, against withering enemy fire. We did what we could with our chau-chaus, but our ammunition was running low. I looked at my watch: 11:30. Six hours and forty minutes to advance three hundred yards, and we weren't even across the railroad tracks yet.

I slid down to the bottom of the embankment and sat cross-legged in the cinders. Mac crawled up beside me from the left. He pointed to a small hole in the crotch of my breeches, round and scorched around the edges. I turned the cloth between my fingers. Sure enough, a duplicate hole graced the rear. Hell, that damn bush that jerked my breeches this morning never grew out of the ground. It was shot from a gun barrel. I gave Mac a look of disbelief.

"Hell. Close don't count, Judy!"

"Yeah. But close can turn your hair gray."

We crawled to the top of the roadbed and lay there looking over the situation. Mac said we'd wait for orders—a good plan as I saw it, since further effort looked impossible.

I curled up with my rifle and dozed off, only to be awakened by a peculiar sounding shell burst on the far side of the tracks. No warning whistle. I looked around. Mac had disappeared. The men held a discussion about what kind of shell this was until Bones cleared it up.

"Go Blimey. They're Austrian 88s. We seen 'em on the Somme in 1916."

We peered over the top of the embankment as intermittent flashes lit the near horizon, each accompanied by a bursting shell. The guns fired point blank at us, but we were so tired and weak we could only hug the protective side of the roadbed and endure it. For hours we lay in the blazing sun, the top of our refuge swept by machine gun fire. We lay there, our faces gaunt and hollow-eyed. Dirt, mud and powder stains intermingled with bloody sweat. Now and then a man's limbs would twitch, then start to tremble with nervous exhaustion. Looked like we'd reached bottom.

I crawled to the top of the railroad to get a better view of our position. I hadn't seen Mac for a while, so I searched the meager remnant of our outfit for his familiar form. I heard a commotion at the other end of the company. One of the new men was fighting off two men holding him, his limbs jerking and trembling. He broke loose and tore to the top of the roadbed and into a storm of machine gun fire. He screamed once, spun around and fell face down on our side of the bank where his body slid down the cindery slope.

"Shit. When we have good protection they go nuts. If we don't lose 'em one way, we lose 'em another."

I turned to face Mac, who had shown up at my shoulder.

"Well, what do you expect, Mac? Here we are. It's a wonder we're *all* not crazy."

"I guess maybe we are. How's the canteen?"

I shook it. "There's still a drop for a soldier." I pulled the cork. We each took a drink and sat listening to the shell bursts, lost in thought. Finally, Mac stirred, heaved a long sigh, and looked sideways at me.

"Well, kid, hitch up your belt," he growled. "We're gonna take another crack at 'em."

"Who's gonna take a crack at who?"

He grinned the old Mac grin. "Yes sir, buddy. At 5:10 you and me and this here bone heap that was our outfit are gonna walk across this damn railroad and make it safe for democracy."

"Whose idea is that? Look at these guys! There's no fear, courage or strength left in any of them."

"I know," Mac said. "I know all about it, Judy, but I got orders by runner to advance our position to conform to a line on the other side of the railroad. I sent word back that the men weren't up to it. About a half hour ago another runner brought orders that we would advance as previously ordered at 5:10. So there you are."

"Well, I hope the bastard that ordered this rots in hell for forty thousand years."

"Oh, goodness! Not really!" Mac's sarcasm fits the moment. "Well, anyway, it's only 3:30 now, so we have time to make a few plans. You look the men over and have them get a little rest if they can."

I moved along the line of holes, counted the men and advised them to rest as much as possible.

"Are we gonna move again?" asked one.

"Yeah, we are. We're gonna take this damn railroad this evening."

"Damn little help I'll be. My reserve rations were gone two days ago. Look at that."

He held his hand out and watched it shake and quiver like a flag in the wind.

"Well, we gotta do it somehow." It was all the encouragement I could offer as I moved on.

Down at the far end of the company I met John Gallagher talking earnestly with two of the new men, all in the same hole. Just seeing him cheered me up. Knowing he was still with us made it better. I wasn't sure why I liked this fresh-faced innocent. Maybe deep down I wanted to be like him — honest and decent, incorruptible — but it was too late.

"What's the good word, sergeant?" He greeted me with his usual cheerful grin.

"The good word, Johnny boy, is — hold onto your hat and be ready to move forward at 5:10."

He looked at me aghast — his eyes wide in amazement. He swallowed hard. "That's good," he said. "This'll be our last assault. We'll be relieved as soon as we take that railroad."

"Maybe you're right. I hope so, anyhow." I didn't bother to point out that the railroad was already cut in at least half a dozen places and that this advance was but a line straightening maneuver and of no great importance to anyone except those who would lose their lives in its execution. I made my way back to Mac to report that we had thirty-nine men who, in their present condition, would equal about ten good men.

Mac grinned. "Ten's plenty."

As we lay in the grass listening to the shells, I silently gauged our chances. Mac seemed to have no fears about our forthcoming venture. After a long interval he rolled over and said quietly, "Five o'clock, Judy. Get'em up."

"Okay. Do we get a barrage?"

"I don't know. All I know is we advance at 5:10."

I got the men out of their holes and lined up at the top of the embankment. On both sides we noted similar activity among other outfits, leading me to conclude that this was a general line straightening action and wouldn't take long.

I glanced at my watch. 5:09. I watched the second hand make a complete circle. Promptly on the dot at 5:10 there came a rush of shells overhead and we crawled forward slow and steady, accompanied by as fine a barrage as we could wish for.

We took the Bosch completely by surprise, and sent them scurrying to get out from under our shellfire. We rushed them in groups of six or eight, took a lot of prisoners with very little hand-to-hand fighting. Three Germans in a shell-hole tried to right an overturned machine gun, but the rush of half a dozen men brought about an immediate change of mind. We moved forward an eighth to a quarter of a mile, crossed a shallow gully and came to a halt on the opposite side.

Mac yelled an order. "Have the men dig in and consolidate. This is our objective."

There it was again. Dig. We no sooner had one position dug and well organized than we move forward and had to dig again. Famished and exhausted, we still dug. I heard hostile artillery fire landing on the opposite side of the gully. I guessed we'd better dig.

After nightfall, our posts manned, I listened in vain for the sound of an approaching ration party. Disappointed, I drifted off into a deep and dreamless sleep, awakening at dawn with Mac shaking my shoulder.

"Come on, kid. Have'em stand to." Dirty, sweaty, with a long stubble of a beard, but still the same grinning, swaggering, unbeatable Mac. Inspiring.

I rubbed my eyes, greatly refreshed. He handed me his canteen and I took a good big drink and moved down the line, rousing the rest of the men. We were on alert till about 7:00, when we stood down and crawled back into our holes to await . . . what? The day passed quietly—we only had to fight off one half-hearted counter-attack. The rest of the time we spent hunkered down to avoid sporadic shellfire, speculating on whether or not chow would be up tonight.

Mac crawled over to my hole at about four in the afternoon. "How you makin' out, Judy?"

"Okay, I guess. What's the news?"

His grin was hiding something, and it must be good news to make him grin like that.

"You can shave and doll up, get ready to give the demoselles a treat. We get relieved tonight."

"The hell we do! Who's takin' over?"

"Scotch outfit, some division that has the Black Watch and the Cameron and Seaforth Highlanders in it. Hell, Jude, you'll die in bed yet!" Then, looking around at the poor remnants of our company, he added, "Tell the men to be ready to move at dark. Tell 'em to keep their heads down, too. We don't want to lose any more at this stage."

"Don't worry, Mac. I'll take care of that," I assured him.

As I moved along the line spreading the good news, hunger and weakness disappeared. A few minutes ago I was weak, sick and dejected, looking at a future that held another assault, and if I survived that, yet another and another until at last I'd succumb to the inevitable and end up one of the innumerable misshapen heaps that dotted the landscape.

Mac's news changed all that, for already the handful of survivors were busy visualizing the delights of the rear areas. Good food, baths, comfortable beds, luxurious living, and feminine companionship.

I dropped into a foxhole and gave the four occupants the news, then watched their instant reaction. "Hot Dog!" yelled Kline, a handsome lad from Cincinnati. "The minute I get away from this hole I'm goin' absent for a week!"

"Tut, tut, my lad. Such threats, and in front of a non-com, too."

"What can you do about it?" he asked, chin jutted out.

"I might report you."

"And what could they do to me if you did?"

"Try you by general court. You know, cowardice, desertion in the face of the enemy, mopery with intent to gawk, or what have you."

"Yes, yes, sergeant, go on. And the punishment?"

"Death, or such other punishment as the court martial shall decide," I solemnly recited the last sentence of each of the Articles of War.

He laughed grimly. "And what the hell have the Krauts been tryin' to do to me for the last five days?"

"Trying to kill you, of course."

"Well, then, what the hell is the difference whether I'm shot by a firing squad for having a good time or whether I'm shot by the enemy?"

"It's taken a damn long time for you to figure that out," I retorted.

"But it's not the same thing, is it sergeant?" When you're killed in battle that's an honorable death, but to die by a firing squad is a disgrace, right?"

I laughed a little too loud. It'd been a long time since I'd made any distinction between the honorable and the dishonorable dead.

"Well, either way, you're disgustingly dead." I crawled on to the next hole before I could be called on to explain.

At about midnight we were relieved by that famous Scotch division, marching right up to our holes, bagpipes in full blast. We lost no time in moving out, for those pipes were going to draw fire in a hurry.

We hiked back along a dirt road—twenty-three men out of two hundred who went over the top five days ago—gaunt, haggard, and weak. They staggered like drunks—some dozed off on their feet and when the column stopped, bumped into the man in front and fell down. When this happened we stopped, pulled them to their feet and slapped them awake. Even Mac couldn't awaken one sad trooper. He slapped and pummeled to no avail until I touched the lit end of a cigarette to the back of the man's neck, and he came around with a start.

We staggered on into the darkness, lurching and falling, rising, only to stumble and fall again. The man in front of John Gallagher fell and John tried to pull him to his feet but was so weak he fell on top of him. The column halted until we got them untangled and started again. Reaction was setting in.

The superhuman effort of the last five days took its toll. There was almost no conversation; men spoke in monosyllables, if at all. The road seemed endless as we staggered and stumbled along our way. An occasional shell came over to remind us that we were still in danger of death and destruction. These singles elicited no more attention than a cap pistol. I doubt if half of the men heard them.

As day broke we entered a large forest, far to the rear. I paused and turned to gaze back over those fields of waving wheat, scene of so much suffering a short time ago. In those miles of grain an epic had been written in the last five days.

CHAPTER XXV

PARIS
JULY, 1918

Sleeping men everywhere. They lay under the trees, along the edge of the roads, some even in the road, forcing wheeled vehicles to detour. They stretched out in a variety of positions, some on their sides, others curled into a ball, still others flat on their backs, limbs out flung, faces turned to the sky. I slept myself out, and to my surprise it didn't take long. When we arrived that morning I thought I'd sleep for a week, but I awakened early in the afternoon. My first priority was to clean up and repair the ravages of battle. A shave and a bath in a shallow creek improved my physical comfort, and for a moment, at least, I forgot the ordeal of the past few days.

The men still slept, so after I'd finished my bath I looked up the kitchen, running into Harris and Dave Evans at the cook fly. Tony and Harris had returned to company headquarters after having their wounds dressed, and Dave had just arrived with a group back from the hospital after Cantigny. We ate fried steaks between loaves of bread cut in half—a gigantic sandwich, two of which I cleaned up before the pangs of hunger were satisfied.

I moved to the company office where Captain Weyandt sat with his bandaged leg stretched out. He smiled as I saluted. "How are you, sergeant? Glad to see you back."

"I'm glad to see myself back, sir. At times it seemed sort of doubtful."

"Doubtful is hardly the word."

"How's your leg, sir? Much pain?"

"Well, I know it's there because it shows every sign of becoming a perfectly good leg again. For all practical purposes, that is. Of course, it'll never be much good for getting a job in the Follies, but I'll be walking as good as ever within a week."

"I'm glad it's no worse, sir." I turned to leave.

"Just a minute, sergeant. There's something else." His grave tone made me curious.

He eyed me steadily for a second, then asked, "Have you given any thought to how much you're drinking lately?"

"No, sir," I replied, somewhat taken aback. "Is the captain of the opinion that it's affected my work?"

"Nooo," the word was drawn out and thoughtful. "I can't say it has, but you're taking in more than good sense allows. In the last week you put away enough to float a battleship."

I didn't know how to respond. The captain meant well, but I felt he was off base, sticking his nose into my business. I nodded politely and took my leave to wander among the different outfits, startled and a little embarrassed at the episode. I wondered if I'd become a common rummy in the eyes of the men.

"It can't be," I thought. "I'm still too alert and active to be an alcoholic." My thoughts turned to Jeanne, wondering where she was—what she was doing. If I could just see her for a few minutes I could straighten this thing out. Reassure the captain. Get myself under control. Anyway, it was no use worrying. In a few months I'd be just another disintegrating heap of bones and no one would give a damn whether that particular pile of bones was an alcoholic or a saint.

My thoughts were disturbed by voices over near the kitchen—another group freshly arrived from the hospital: Bruce, Atkinson and Red Conlon.

Red's greeting was characteristic. "Christ almighty, Judy. Ain't you dead yet?" he cried. "Hell's fire, I thought you'd be pushin' up daisies long ago." Still rough around the edges, Red. You could dress him up, but . . .

"Not yet, Red. Not yet. How's Paris?"

"Oh, boy, you should know," he grinned. "How about a drink?" He produced a bottle. "A little of the product that made the Brothers Haig famous?"

Ah, good old genuine Scotch whiskey. Rummy or no rummy, I wouldn't refuse that.

After we drank all around I offered my hand to Ted Atkinson. "How ya feelin,' Ted? Okay?" He was only a boy, and I always did feel sort of fatherly toward him even though the difference in our ages couldn't have been more than three years.

"Yeah, boy, I'm in great shape," he smiled. "They tell me we been havin' quite a war up here the last few days."

"Just a bit. Like three or four Cantignys rolled into one. No food, no water, and hot as hell."

"Well, I'm glad you're okay. Where's Mac?"

"Sleeping someplace around here. Just go around kickin' butts until one comes up fightin.' That'll be Mac."

As we lolled in the shade, passing the bottle of Haig & Haig around, the steady bang of artillery made us wonder how that Scotch division was doing. According to all reports, they weren't having an easy time of it.

Stubby came down the path and stopped. "Git'em woke up and on theah feet, sawgint, weah movin' outa heah in trucks tonight."

"Okay, Stub. Where we goin'?"

"God knows. I don't. Back to the reah somewheah for replacements and new equipment."

I rousted the men out amid a chorus of curses, in spite of the fact that they were all glad to hear we were leaving.

Next morning, the sunrise illuminated rolling clouds of dust as we rumbled into a small village miles behind the lines. As usual, I was seated high and serene on the driver's seat. We de-trucked and make ourselves comfortable in an apple orchard on the outskirts of town, rolled into our blankets and slept until the cooks called mess.

After breakfast the company clerk put out the word that the captain wanted to see all the old men of the company. Wandering into the company offices I found Mac, Tony, John Gallagher, Harris and Red Conlon, all guests at the skipper's billet.

"Any of you men care for a drink?" he offered. He cast a glance in my direction, which, however, did not deter me from accepting the offer. The captain proposed a toast to old friends and we drank in silence; then he spoke.

"Men, you've all been with the company since we left the States. Leaves have been woefully few and far between. You've worked hard and fought hard, so it's only fitting that you should get a chance to play hard. I have no authority to grant leaves or passes, but I'm told we'll be here until we get replacements and new equipment—at least a week. Now, should you men disappear for five days and return not later than the end of the fifth day, I won't ask where you've been. But should any of you stay longer than five days and miss the company when we move, or be picked up by the military police, I won't be able to help you. If you want to take a little vacation under those conditions, I'll turn my back."

We stared in slack-mouthed disbelief.

"That goes as it lays, men, if you want to take advantage of it." Then, as an afterthought, he added, "Any of you need any money?"

As I ambled down the street toward our apple orchard, I stopped and turned about. Captain Weyandt still stood in front of his quarters. "Whatta ya want from Paris, Captain?" I shouted through cupped hands.

He smiled. "Just bring yourself back in good shape."

Mac, Tony, and Harris joined me and we walked down the street, pummeling each other in celebration of our unbelievable good luck.

"Forget that Paris stuff, Judy," Mac growled. "We got a job to do."

"Whattaya mean, a job to do?" I asked, afraid he meant a trip back to the front or some such nonsense.

"Why at Vitry Le Francois. Tony's gettin' married, and we gotta be pallbearers."

"Pallbearers? Don't you mean best men?"

"Hell, no. I mean pallbearers. Gettin' married and gettin' shot are just two different ways of doin' the same thing, ain't they?"

I nodded. "Maybe you're right. I've never been married yet."

"You haven't been shot yet, either, have you, sergeant?" Harris joined in.

"Well, partly . . ."

"Yeah, half shot all the time," growled Mac. "Come on, let's get this wedding party under way." We moved down the road, still reveling in our tremendous good luck.

Tony's getting married had completely slipped my mind. Here I was dreaming of a day or two in Paris with Jeanne and now I was supposed to give up that idea? Hell, no!

As we packed up for the trip to Vitry Le Francois, the company clerk brought our mail. I had a letter or so from home and two from Jeanne — one mailed in Paris only five days ago. The other came from Dunkirk, three weeks old. The later one said she'd be in Paris for four weeks and hoped I could visit her there. Wedding be damned. I was for Paris.

I found Tony getting ready, shining and cleaning his boots and uniform, joy radiating from his face.

"Hey, what about this wedding of yours?" I asked. "Is it on the up and up?"

"You bet your ass, Damn Yank. You should know. You helped arrange it."

"Okay. I just wanted to be sure. I don't want you city slickers playing horse with any wedding I help arrange. You're really gonna marry the gal, eh?"

"Sure am! And the sooner the better."

"Okay, then I won't need my shotgun. So when do ya think it'll be?"

"Well," he counted on his fingers. "This is Wednesday. We get there tomorrow. Give her a day to get ready. The wedding should be on Saturday. Why?"

I hemmed and hawed for a minute, then blurted out my story. "To tell you the truth, Tony, Jeanne's going to be in Paris this week, and much as I hate to miss your wedding I can't be in both places at once."

Tony gave me the eye for a second. "Sure, Judy. Go see her, just get your ass back for the wedding."

Torn between what might be the love of my life and loyalty to my best friend, I packed in a hurry and by eleven o'clock was on the road to Dammartin, where I could get the Paris Express. Luck was riding my shoulder for I hadn't been on the road more than ten minutes when an empty Cadillac pulled up beside me and stopped. It was Harris, shined up and looking spiffy in the driver's seat.

"Where the hell did you get this, Preacher man?" I asked, mystified.

He grinned. "I know people."

"People? What people?"

"Motor pool people, among others."

I hopped into the front seat beside him. "Man this preaching must be good business."

"It helps," he returned, still grinning. "Where we going?"

"I'm Paris bound, boy."

"Me, too! Nice of the captain to arrange leave for us."

"Who said anything about leave? We're on the loose, man. Just you and me against all the MPs in the world."

"We're probably laying up trouble for ourselves. Paris is lousy with MPs and the APM is clamping down on Americans tighter than a drum." He kept his eyes on the road as he spoke.

"Yeah, so I've heard, but I'll take a chance. You and I've been around a little. Here and there."

'Oh yeah, I know all about it, but I hear they're tougher in Paris now than in the old days. Red said there was a company of Marines, the Thirtieth, I think, doin' MP duty and acting like they're God Almighty himself." The preacher yawned and stretched his arm out the window.

"They always did think that. With all the newspaper publicity they get every time one of them skins a shin, they really believe they're fighters."

"They are," he grinned. "When three or four of them have a soldier down, they're great fighters."

We rode along in quiet, watching the tree-lined roads melt away. It amazed me, the serene beauty of this place while only a few miles away, hell was holding court. I leaned back in the seat and closed my eyes, trying to dispel the images that insisted on haunting me.

"You still believe in God, Preach?" I asked.

"Can't say I do anymore," he replied. "That's how I came to this state of affairs. Lost my faith and set out to find it in the real world."

"This enough real world for you?"

"Yeah. Plenty. How about you? You still a believer?"

"Naw. I never really was. My mother made me go to church and Sunday School when all a man ever really needed to replenish him spiritually was a fishing rod and a nice shady riverbank. Once I got out on my own, I made my own choices. If I ever were a believer, this war has wrung it out of me."

Harris drove along in silence, his hands casually holding the wheel. The road was straight, narrow and bumpy, but who were we to complain? Every once in a while we passed a French farm wagon pulled by a horse or an ox and driven by an old man in a loose smock and sabots. We waved a greeting—"Vive la France!" and continued on our way.

Harris had his own plans for Paris. One of the young ladies he was with the last time had a chateau outside Orleans, and the plan was to spend a few days there. He'd go on to Vitry with me, but the first couple of days were hers.

"Where does Jeanne live?" he asked as we approached the outskirts of the city.

I fished in my pocket and produced her address, carefully written on a slip of paper. Harris scanned it for an instant. "Fine, I'll drop you off at her front door around two."

"Boy," I mused, "is this luck or what?"

This morning I awakened without an idea in my head, and here I was at one p.m., practically deposited on Jeanne's front doorstep. This called for a drink. I opened my canteen, took a slug and offered it to him.

"Same old Judy," he grinned, waving the canteen away.

"Same old world," I returned. "Gotta grab your fun where you find it."

"That's right, and you'll get your share."

I nodded. "There wasn't much to laugh at in the past five days, so we have to cram five days' extra laughing into the next few days."

I lay back against the upholstery and relaxed — just closed my eyes and forgot everything as we sped along through the flat French the countryside in a half doze, letting my mind wander. I saw the river where I fished when I was a kid, the mountain we used to climb looking for teaberries, Tony, hunched over his gun in the bright light of flares, John Gallagher carrying the limp form of Morrie Muller on his shoulder, Yvette telling me Tony wasn't at her place, the gas attack at Vellers Tournelle, and I was dancing again with Jeanne. My life passed before me, a series of jumbled, disconnected events. A rough section of road jarred me awake and I reached again for my canteen.

"Think you'll smell fit to meet a lady if you keep on drinking?" Harris kept his eyes on the road. Why was everyone so concerned about my drinking? I was still competent, wasn't I?

"Oh, she doesn't mind. She says the smell is part of me, therefore acceptable."

"Amazing! She must be a pretty swell guy at that."

"Best in the world," I assured him.

"So I've heard. If I didn't know how easily you fall in and out of love, I'd think it was real this time."

"That's what I've been trying to tell you! I'm in love with the girl, and I don't care who knows it."

"That's great," he laughed. "Judy Redding, in love from the Rio Grande to the Rhine. Hey, what a title for a book." He rolled the words over on his tongue. "In love from the Rio Grande to the Rhine."

His teasing, along with the fact that I couldn't seem to convince him that this time it was real, got under my skin.

"Okay, friend, laugh if you want."

He laughed even harder, and I turned away to try to get more sleep as the road unfolded under the wheels. We passed through the scattered outskirts of Paris and rolled through the streets of the beautiful city itself. Harris made a left turn. "It won't be long now."

CHAPTER XXVI

PARIS
JULY, 1918

Preacher Harris drove through the city like he'd lived there all his life. Strange, how comfortable he seemed with the country and its people. I watched for street signs, and at the next corner there it was: Boulevard du Clichy. In less than ten minutes, we stopped in front of the large, stone house I recognized from my last visit. I told Harris to wait a minute as I jumped out and rushed up the walk to pound on an iron knocker, old enough to have witnessed the revolution. I heard footsteps, and Jeanne opened the door.

Ah, she was just as I remembered her. Too sweet to describe and radiant in the joy of seeing me again.

"Judy!" she cried, throwing her arms around my neck. "I am just this minute writing to you!"

"Don't bother writing," I whispered between kisses. "Tell it to me."

"Oh, I am so glad to see you." She snuggled close. "It has been so long and so ugly. That battle near Soissons, you were in there, were you not? Oh, I am so glad you are safe!"

I buried my face in her hair and breathed deeply, intoxicated by the nearness of her. I was suddenly and unpleasantly brought to earth by the blast of an automobile horn.

"Oh, that's Harris, the guy you met at the railroad station last time. You know, the one with all the friends. He drove."

"By all means, bring him in. Perhaps he would care for a drink," she said, instantly the perfect hostess.

I motioned to Harris, who came up the walk with a wide grin and a hug for my girl. "This dumb lug has done nothing but talk about you all the way here. I'll be glad to get rid of him and savor the silence."

Jeanne laughed, the joy of reunion evident in her eyes.

Harris turned to me. "Forget it. Forget everything I said this afternoon. I won't kid you anymore. I believe everything you told me."

"And you don't blame me, eh?"

"No. I don't see how you could help it. If I don't get out of here quick, I'll fall for her myself."

"Oh, sergeant, those smooth American tongues. I must become accustomed to them." Then remembering her role as hostess, she added, "Would you care for a drink, corporal?"

"Well, I guess—," Harris hesitated, glancing toward the car standing at the curb.

Jeanne was quick to perceive his hesitation. "You have plans of your own, no? Please don't let us keep you—and say hello to mam'selle Arlene for me." Her eyes twinkled at her friend's name.

Harris discreetly took his leave, and Jeanne and I were finally alone, holding each other with no intention of ever letting go.

"Oh, darling, isn't this swell?" I breathed.

"It is paradise, my love, but how long can you stay?"

"Well, I have five days, but there's one complication. Tony is bent on marrying his Yvette, so everyone is meeting in Vitry for the wedding on Saturday."

Her face clouded as she led me into the sitting room.

"These last six weeks have been terrible. All I've done is worry about you and René. Have you anything new of him?'

"No, nothing that could be called news. I saw him the morning we went over the top, but that's the last I know." Her brother René's tank outfit went in with our division, but by the end of the third day, there were practically no tanks left in action. I didn't tell her that.

I kissed her hair and stroked her shoulder, sorry I didn't have more comforting news.

"Well," she looked at me, her eyes misty. "One must be thankful for what one has. We cannot expect all of our men to be spared, and I am truly grateful that you have survived the last few weeks. At times the gunfire from up there rattled the windows here in Paris."

We sat in the firelight, not talking, blissfully content. Being with Jeanne brought peace and happiness I'd never known before. Too good to be true, yes, but I didn't care. My precarious existence had taught me not to think about the future. Now was enough. I stretched luxuriously and moved to pour a glass of brandy.

"Wait, Judy, wait." She stayed my hand. "If I remember correctly, you are partial to Benedictine, isn't that right?"

"That's right," I laughed, "but in the absence of Benedictine I find I can get along on brandy, rum, whiskey, cognac or what have you."

"Yes, but there is Benedictine," she smiled with sparkling eyes as she opened a wall cabinet, revealing a stock of wines and liquors that would have been a credit to a Fifth Avenue bar. She brought me a bottle of Benedictine. How good could it get?

"Tell me about those complications you mentioned a while ago," she said quietly.

True enough, I'd forgotten. I gave her a brief synopsis of Yvette's hard life, including her former means of earning a living. When I finished, Jeanne gazed thoughtfully into the fire.

"Isn't that grand," she smiled. "Her story is not uncommon. The war has devastated so many families and left the survivors to get on any way they can."

"Tony's so smitten he can't see straight. But I hate to lose even a minute with you. I wouldn't hurt him for the world—her either—but . . ."

"Oh, why, Judy, it is a simple matter. We will both go. We can leave here tomorrow evening by the Paris-Nancy Express and be in Vitry Le Francois early Friday morning."

"Sure! I never thought of that! There is one hitch, though. Remember, dear, I'm AWOL, and it's rather a ticklish proposition to ride on a train without leave orders."

Her almost merry laugh eased my concern. "Do not worry about that, my dearest. I can arrange things."

I looked at my watch. It was getting late, which brought up another matter.

"I guess I'd better go and arrange for a place to spend the night."

She gave me a reproachful look.

"But, you know you're going to spend the night here. We may never be together again and, as you say, there is no point in wasting a minute of it."

"I know, and that would suit me fine, but you know I'm a soldier."

"Soldier? Why, of course you are a soldier." She looked puzzled. "What is the man getting at?"

"Just this, sweetheart. Soldiers have been known to get lousy."

Jeanne smiled. "So, that is what bothers the man. We can remedy that. René, my brother, you know? The gentleman of the tank corps? He gets terribly infested with the things, so he fixed a room to change in when he comes home. Come. I will show you."

I followed her to the second floor, where she took me to a bathroom fitted up with steel lockers. She told me to hang my clothes in one. A steam line had been connected to the locker and when I got in the tub, all I had to do was turn the steam on and theoretically all the lice in my clothes would be killed. But, being soldier lice, they were tough and died hard.

Jeanne showed me clothes in the other lockers, so after finishing my bath I selected a flashy suit of red and black pajamas and a robe to match, a gaudy ensemble that made me feel like a brigadier general — at least.

I returned to the deserted sitting room, poured myself a drink and relaxed in sublime comfort. When Jeanne returned, bathed and clothed in a beautiful, filmy negligee that I wouldn't even try to describe, we reclined in each others' arms, blissfully content. Jeanne yawned delicately, and I found myself nodding off, so to bed. After the ecstasy and delight of making love, we lay in each others' arms and talked until the pauses in our conversation became longer and longer and we dropped off to sleep.

I awakened suddenly and sat up, startled. A crashing noise took me back to the front. I reached for my rifle. I couldn't find it! The enemy was attacking and I had no rifle. Slowly Jeanne's insistent voice penetrated my consciousness.

"Judy, it is all right. You are not at the front. You are here in Paris, safe with me. Wake up, Judy." As she tried to shake me awake, I still groped for my missing rifle. Sleep fell away, and I slowly recognized my surroundings. I grinned, embarrassed, and lay back down. It was after eight. I heard another crash, and this time I recognized the sound of a garbage collector dropping a can on the sidewalk. At the front, such a sound would have gone unnoticed, but here in a strange setting it had startled and unnerved me. I held out my hand, watching it shake, and wondered how long it would take to get back to normal — if ever.

Jeanne was very quiet. I thought she'd gone back to sleep, but no. She stirred and spoke quietly.

"War makes men terrible, n'est ce pas, Judy?"

"Oh, I don't know. What makes you think?"

"You should have seen yourself a moment ago. Your expression was horrible. Cold, hard brutality. It's hard to believe that you are the same person. Oh, why must men fight?"

"I don't know, my dear. It's one of the strongest human traits, settling disputes by combat. But then I have no dispute with the enemy. Our tobacco chewing politicians got us into this, and now it's up to fellows like René and me to get us out."

"You don't care much for politicians, then?"

I laughed. "No. Useless—nothing but word mongers, full of treachery and deceit. A common man has to show his fitness to hold a small government job—clerk, postman, even a janitor. But being a candidate for the most important offices in the land calls for no qualifications whatever. Any halfwit can run for any office, and if his mouth is big enough, he stands an excellent chance of being elected. So how can you expect anyone with a grain of intelligence to respect politicians?"

She gave me a quizzical smile. "So, my sergeant is something of a thinker, is he?"

"Just now and then, but when I think of what a soldier has to endure to rectify the mistakes of the politicians, my fury knows no bounds."

"You like war, though, don't you, Judy?"

Her question took me aback. I'd always thought I hated it.

"No." I spoke slowly, analyzing my real feelings. "There's a fascination I can't explain, but I don't think I *like* it."

"Yes, but look. You do revel in doing something that just everyone can't do, that some people are not strong enough for. You are proud of achieving an objective against impossible odds."

She continued, giving me pause. "When you have outwitted an enemy patrol or silenced one of his guns, that gives you great satisfaction, does it not?" She was certainly more perceptive than I gave her credit for.

"Yes, but the butchery and mutilation wipes all that out, and the inescapable fact that we can't last long has a bearing on the matter."

She considered my reply, then answered. "Yes, I suppose that is true. Still the excitement and challenge breeds affection for it. I see this in my brother. He comes home and is happy and content, just as you are now. Then after a few days he changes—becomes restless, fidgety, wearisome. Nothing occupies him for any time. He gets moody and irritable. And finally, when the time comes for him to leave again, he is actually happy to go. You and he are much alike. I believe you have some strange liking for war."

I was surprised at such talk from such a winsome, beautiful woman, for true to my upbringing, I hadn't expected intelligent conversation from that quarter. Beauty *and* brains. How lucky could I get? I stretched luxuriously. She smiled, and I drew her head down on my chest.

"Are you hungry, darling?" she asked.

"Well, I could eat."

"I'll beat you to breakfast," she cried, jumping from the bed and dashing down the hall toward the bath.

I followed at a more leisurely pace and we met again at the table. A breakfast of poached eggs, hard rolls and coffee satisfied my hunger for food. Just being with her went far to satisfy the other hunger.

"What would you care to do?" Jeanne asked as we sat looking out the side window at the street scene, just waking up. People on their way to work, rushing for the trolley. School children wandering by, their leather back packs fairly weighing them down, shouting greetings to their friends. It was hard to believe normal life went on with the war in such close proximity.

"We might dance awhile, just in case you're getting bored." I rose and took her hand. "Not that I need to do anything other than be with you."

"Well, we might go dancing later. At present I am well content."

The morning passed as mornings do. After lunch we went to the Gare de L'óuest to arrange for our trip to Vitry Le Francois, then looked in at half a dozen cafés, browsed the book stalls, wandered the streets, lost in each other. The June day was warm and a little breezy, perfect for walking and talking, and Paris was the perfect place for both. We revisited the place where I received such a pleasant reception on our first night together. Jeanne had fitted me out with one of her brother's uniforms to avoid trouble with the MPs, but the uniform was such a bad fit that if my fractured French didn't give me away, it surely did. The patrons of the café seemed amused at the spectacle.

We returned to Jeanne's house for dinner and spent the early evening talking in the sitting room. There was so much I wanted to know about this goddess who'd appeared out of the mists of war. At about nine-thirty we called a cab to take us to our train. It wouldn't leave until near midnight, but we were privileged to board after nine. When we arrived at the station a group of American MPs crowded around a turnstile, examining the papers of all Americans trying to board the cars. They had very little to do at present because the average soldier didn't ride the sleepers, but still it would be impossible to slip past them unnoticed. I mentioned this to Jeanne, and she just smiled and shook her head.

"Come," she replied. "There will be no trouble at all."

We retraced our steps to a small box office in the main station building where Jeanne talked with the officer in attendance. She then drew what looked like an identification card from her bag and presented it. He nodded, then pushed a button and a French soldier appeared and beckoned us with a smile. He led the way to a narrow gate to the train shed, unlocked it and stood aside for us. He escorted us across the tracks to where the sleeping cars awaited their passengers. With many bows and smiles he took his leave and we boarded the cars to find our compartment.

CHAPTER XXVII

THE WEDDING
JULY, 1918

As soon as we were safely in our sleeping compartment I took off my uniform and donned pajamas and a robe so that to any passing eye I was just a traveling Frenchman. As Jeanne busied herself with her bags I pondered the questions racing around in my brain. Who was this lovely lady? What was she? Where did she get the power to unlock gates? How could she travel freely when travel was so closely monitored by the authorities? During the day, all the places we visited were patronized almost exclusively by upper class French people—people of intelligence and refinement. Americans were conspicuous by their absence. Everywhere we went there was subdued elegance, and in every instance she was welcomed and well known. Waiters and managers addressed her with respect and deference. In one or two places, I, too, was addressed by name. I was mystified, to say the least.

Jeanne sat beside me where I sprawled on the berth. "What troubles my soldier?" she asked.

"Oh, nothing. I was just thinking."

"I could see that. And such deep thoughts, too, to judge by the frown. What were they?"

"Well, to be truthful, I was thinking about you."

"About me? The man is really complimentary. Who am I to inspire such deep thoughts to the exclusion of all else?"

"That's it exactly," I spoke honestly. "Just who are you? That's what I was thinking about. You live in a fine house in an expensive neighborhood. You move among refined, intelligent people. You have influence far beyond the ordinary, especially for a woman. You travel here and there with ease, even though travel is strictly controlled. Your word can open gates locked to ordinary people. How can you do these things? In short, just as you said, who are you?"

She leaned over and took my face in her hands. "Darling, I knew this moment would come. I never expected these things would pass unnoticed, and I have anticipated and dreaded it. For the present your questions will have to remain unanswered. I will tell you this much, I am involved in a patriotic duty but that is no cause for anxiety on your part. As to who I am, at present I am a woman in love. Because of that, I do things that would have been impossible even six months ago."

She kissed me with love in her eyes, then continued. "That is all I can tell you at present. You must trust me. If you really love me, you will trust and have faith in me. Later you shall learn everything you wish to know. Now I can tell you nothing more."

Moved by her sincerity, I pulled her to me and stroked her hair.

"It's enough, darling. I'll wait."

We lay in each other's arms and talked, listening to the clink and clank of the cars linked to the train as it moved out of the station into the darkness. Jeanne mixed me a drink, and we ate a light lunch before bed.

We were awakened by the porter announcing our arrival at Vitry in half an hour. Out the car windows, the sun barely peeped above the horizon. Jeanne was altogether captivating as she awakened with a drowsy smile. We made a hurried toilet and were ready to alight when the train stopped.

As Vitry hadn't been overrun with Americans yet, there were no MPs to contend with at the station, so we made our way to the street and on to the Hotel Continental. Once we were established in a comfortable room, I ordered coffee and rolls, after which I decided in favor of more sleep and Jeanne chose to take an early morning stroll.

"You are lazy, my darling," she chided me gently, "the morning air will be glorious."

"Maybe you're right," I smiled, "but sunrise strolls have been no novelty in my life lately. In fact they've been more or less the order of things, and the early morning air has proven decidedly unhealthy. Sleeping in a bed, now, that's a thought to tempt a soldier."

Jeanne smiled tenderly. "I know, dearest, I know. You would not mind if I walk while you sleep, would you?"

"No, indeed. Not a bit. Wake me when you return."

I slept for a couple of hours and was up and bathed, shaved and dressed before Jeanne returned, glowing with health and vitality from her walk along country roads. I waited while she freshened up before we set out to find our friends.

We were sighted before we even reached the house, and the entire crowd except Yvette welcomed us from the doorstep. She ran down the sidewalk to meet us, excited as a little child.

She caught me by the arm. "Sergeant Judy," she cried. "I am so happee. Oh, so verree happee."

"I'm glad you're happy, Yvette," I told her with a quick hug. "Here is a very dear lady I want you to meet."

Jeanne smiled beautifully and took Yvette in her arms and kissed her, saying, "Dear girl, I have heard much of you, and, believe me, I am glad for your happiness."

They led the way to the door, arms around each other, even though it was clear Yvette was more than a little shy in the presence of such a lady.

Inside, Yvette introduced Jeanne to Mac, John, Tony and Red, all of whom embraced her, talking and laughing at once. Overwhelmed with compliments, Jeanne retired to my side, shaking with laughter.

"Oh, Judy," she cried, "save me from these countrymen of yours. Such flatterers. They turn a girl's head."

"She speaks English, too," yelled Mac. "Of all the lucky devils I ever saw, that Judy wins the mothballs."

"She learned her English at Coney Island," I added.

"And the flattery from Judy." Jeanne clearly enjoyed the accompanying laughter.

Yvette came to my side, whispering, "Judee, I'm so glad you come. Corporal Harris, he comes, too?"

"Yeah. He'll be along. He has a little farther to come. How are things with you and Tony?"

"Oh, Tony, he is — what is it you say —, sergeant?"

I thought a minute, trying to find the word.

"You mean nice?"

"No, that ees not it."

"You mean good?"

"No, no. What do you say when you like something verree much?"

"Oh, you mean swell."

"Yes, yes!" she smiled. "That ees it. Tonee, he ees veree swell."

"That's fine! Glad to hear it. And how do you like my lady?"

"Ahh, she is wonderful."

Jeanne and Yvette were soon engaged in a torrent of French which drove us Americans to cover. We reformed on the doorstep.

"Judy, you bastard, where'd you ever find that girl?" Tony was full of joy for both of us.

"Ain't she swell, buddy?" I was as full of pride and pleasure as he was.

"I hope she's swell," Mac agreed. "And it's not just her looks, either. That gal's got something. What the hell she sees in a bum like you, I'll never know. She could do a lot better."

"Yeah, pick up with you, I guess."

"That's right," agreed Mac, and the laughter broke out anew.

I turned my head at the sound of a motor vehicle and saw Harris drive up in the Cadillac.

"Glad you could make it," called Tony, offering him a beer. Harris waved it away but grinned all around before reaching into the car and bringing out a stack of presents, wrapped in elegance for the wedding.

Yvette saw him and squealed with pleasure. "Harris. The Preacher man! You bring us joy!"

Harris gave an embarrassed grin and passed the packages to Tony, who passed them on to Mac, who looked around with a 'what am I supposed to do with these?' expression.

Red Conlon took up the conversation. "How long've we been over here, Judy?"

"Almost a year, why?"

"You've been on all the fronts, haven't you?"

"Yeah, that's right."

"You haven't been wounded yet either, have you?"

"Say, what the hell is this about? No, I haven't been wounded yet. What about it?"

"Well, you're soon due," Mac grinned. "I think I'll get me a new tailor made uniform and step right into your shoes after this next push."

"Why, you damn grave robber!" I got up and whacked him on the shoulder.

He dodged around the corner of the house and, as I followed, he produced a bottle of cherry brandy and we all shared a drink.

The women were in deep discussion over clothes and plans for the next day's event when we returned to the house. We draped ourselves over the furniture in comfort and engaged in rambling talk.

"Have any MP trouble in Paris?" Red asked.

"Nope. You?"

"Not to speak of," laughed Mac. "Red and I had to tame one down a little in Dammartin. Nothing worth mentioning."

"Mention it."

"Well, turns out we were accosted by an MP who insisted on seeing our papers. Seeing as we didn't have any, Red set upon him, took his gun, club and arm band and locked him in a wine cellar. Should have broken his head. A wine cellar is too good for an MP." A roar of approval rose, sure to make the neighbors wonder what sort of party this was.

The day passed with the women immersed in plans, while we Americans wandered off in search of amusement. We scandalized the natives and gained a reputation for being slightly crazy, but we managed to stay pretty much out of trouble, to Tony's relief.

Saturday dawned with a hustle and bustle as Yvette's relatives arrived for the wedding. Uncles, aunts, cousins, grandparents and whatnot, all gathered for a rare opportunity for celebration. One old gent, a veteran of the Franco-Prussian War, insisted on a personal recital of our war deeds from each of us. If we ran out, we invented some more, for he seemed to like his stories with trimmings. In return, he fought that war of 1870 over again for us, with gestures. We finally got him mildly drunk and deposited him on a bench in front of the house, where he sat stroking his beard, regarding all passers-by with a benevolent eye.

At three o'clock we gathered in the church for the impressive ceremony. Words rolled sonorously from the lips of the officiating priest, and while we didn't understand all of it, Tony made the proper responses at the proper time. Jeanne, moved by the ceremony, and, true to her gentle nature, turned to me with tears on her cheeks. I'd never understand women. They wept when they were happy, and they wept when they were sad.

After the wedding, we returned to Yvette's house, where the feast awaited. The old gent tucked his beard under his neckerchief and did serious homage to the meal. Where he put it, I couldn't tell. Mac and Red sat on either side, so I could see the old codger was in for a large time. Tony and Yvette came in for a good share of teasing, most of it in rapid fire French and some quite to the point, if Yvette's blushes were any evidence.

While the festivities were in full sway, John Gallagher and Harris left the room. I wasn't surprised, as neither drank. Mac stood up on a chair, trying to make a speech in French. What he lacked in vocabulary he made up in volume, and the effort was well received by the guests. Red Conlon proposed a toast to the bride and groom which had to be translated by Jeanne and Yvette and, as usual, the point was lost in translation.

There was a sudden commotion outside, and the rumble of a worn-out motor and the squeak of brakes announced the arrival of who knew what. The company rushed to the door and window where they saw John and Harris standing proud with an ancient Ford ambulance, procured from some unknown source. They'd draped the body with crêpe paper and hung evergreen branches all over it. A large sign informed the world that this was the wedding coach. John and Harris stood at attention, like two coachmen awaiting their Lord and Lady. After much urging and laughter, Yvette and Tony settled into the places reserved for them, and the rest perched wherever they could find room, and they drove off on a tour of the town. Jeanne and I stayed back with Red and Mac, who begged off with the excuse that riding an automobile upset their stomachs.

"Having a good time, dear?" I asked Jeanne.

"Your word, swell, expresses it, darling. I would not have missed it for anything. I think they make a grand pair."

Mac looked at us with a grin, his eyes atwinkle.

"Look out, Jeanne. Mac's getting an idea," I warned her.

"A very interesting one, to judge by his expression. What is it, sergeant? You'd better share your idea before you burst with it."

"Oh, I was just thinkin'," said Mac.

"I believe you were," she laughed. "The indications all pointed that way. But what?"

"That if Judy had a little nerve and would ask you a certain question, what an elegant wedding party could be staged in Paris."

A thoughtful look passed over Jeanne's face before she smiled. "But he *has* asked that question, Sergeant, and I have been delighted to accept, but our party must be deferred until a later date." She looked to me for corroboration.

"Yeah, that's right, Mac. I did, and she did, but we have a war to fix up before we can do our marrying."

The wedding party returned amid much hilarity and a cloud of steam from the Ford. We returned to the house, where Jeanne and I took advantage of a lull in the festivities to pay our respects to Yvette and Tony before leaving.

We walked back to the hotel, thoughtful on this, our last night together. The past few days had been unbelievably short. I wondered what the future held for us—if, indeed, there would be any future. I'd seen so many lives snuffed out in the wink of an eye that I didn't hold much hope for myself.

I glanced sideways at Jeanne. Occupied with her own thoughts, she drew a long breath and squeezed my hand.

"Well, darling, it's been wonderful, has it not?"

"All of that," I agreed. "But all too short. Why must we always snatch a moment here and there from the hell and heartache?"

"I have often wondered the same thing, Judy dear. I think it's because the hard things in life give value to the precious moments."

"Well, you may be right, but I think it's a damn lousy shame this can't go on for a few more days."

My mood was angry, ready to curse and revile the way things were, but Jeanne put her hand over my mouth. "Hush, Judy, please. My work has its dangers and risks, too, but I don't want to think about them now. Besides, I do not want to remember you as a hard, venomous, cursing soldier. You have been so nice. Let me remember you that way."

I regretted my outburst. "I'm sorry, darling."

"I know, sweetheart. I know. We must bear it like soldiers. Smile for me, Judy."

I tried to summon a grin, but the best I could do was a weak attempt as we turned in at the hotel entrance. The night passed all too quickly as we lay clasped in each others' arms. We talked far into the early morning. For some time we lay silent, then she asked, "Judy, how soon will you have to go to the front again?"

"I don't know for sure. There's been talk of making us an assault division. If that happens we'll probably have to go to the front more often, but we won't have to stay so long as we've had to before."

"Well, promise me, darling, that you will always be careful. Remember that I am waiting for you to come through and please, please do not take any unnecessary risks."

"No fear, dearest," I assured her. "I am naturally the most cautious guy you ever saw. I'll be twice as cautious now."

"And Judy," she continued . . .

"Yes, dear."

"Be careful of your drinking. I know you do it to numb your feelings to the hardships and horrors of the front, but you don't know how a few drinks change you. You are not the same person when you are drinking. You take on a hard, determined manner that changes you and makes me afraid. You will watch this for me, will you not?"

It was touching, having someone who cared so much about my welfare. I promised her faithfully to cut back on my drinking. After a little more talk we drifted back into slumber wrapped in each others' arms.

Morning found us headed to the station for Jeanne to catch her train. As she was strong the night before, now it was my turn to be strong. We embraced when the train arrived and as she wept on my shoulder, I tried to soothe her. She kissed me time after time. I boarded the train with her, and as it started to move I gave her a long lingering kiss and leaped to the platform, just in time. I stood alone in the early morning light watching the train disappear, a disconsolate figure of a soldier.

I stood there after the train had ceased to be any more than a puff of smoke on the horizon. It felt like the events of the last few days never really happened—all a dream, too wonderful to be true. Still, the wedding must have happened, but the reality of it evaded me. I turned and walked slowly down the street toward Yvette's house to join the gang for the trip back.

I arrived to a subdued household. My parting with Jeanne was not the only sad separation that day. Yvette and Tony greeted me quietly, holding close to one another, intending not to part until the last possible moment. My feelings must have shown, for John Gallagher poured a glass of brandy and brought it to me, an act of kindness from a guy who cared more than he disapproved of liquor.

"Here, Sergeant. Maybe this will make you feel better."

The drink warmed me and sent a glow that would soon deaden the pain. To hurry the reaction, I tossed off another one.

Red sat down beside me, he and Mac least affected by the termination of our holiday. "How's everything, Judy?"

"Okay, I guess. Has anything been done about getting back to the outfit?"

"Sure. We're going back in the Ford and the Cadillac. Take your pick. Plenty of room."

Since I had my doubts about the reliability of the Ford, I picked the Cadillac.

"Where'd that Ford relic come from?" I asked.

"Mac and I resurrected it from a French salvage pile up near Beaumarchaise, and John coaxed it into running." Red was proud of his contribution.

"Beaumarchaise?"

"That's the name of the town where the company's stationed, dumbbell. Don't you ever look at the names of the towns you're in?"

"Oh, sometimes. Anyhow, what the hell difference does a name make?"

"Jesus, you're down, ain'tcha? Hey, John, bring us over a drink."

John looked up with a grin. "Nothin' doin,' Red. You're big enough and ugly enough to get yourself a drink if you want one."

Mac appeared in the doorway. "Come on, John. Get that gondola rattlin.' It's time for us to take off." He threw me a glance. "How are ya, Judy? You ready to go back up and do your stuff again? Come on, let's get this show on the road."

Everyone traveled light, so we didn't have much stuff to look out for. In a few minutes, all of our effects were piled outside the door and John rattled up in the ambulance, followed by Harris in the Cadillac, as Tony and Yvette came to the door, and we all bid Yvette goodbye.

I took her hand and slipped her couple of hundred franc notes as a wedding present. "Au 'voir, Yvette. Be a good girl."

She looked at me with shining eyes. "Au 'voir, Judee. You will be so careful, no? But you must. Also you must be so careful for Tony." Her lips trembled, her voice quivering.

I patted her shoulder to reassure her, but before I could turn away, big tears rolled down her cheeks. A lump rose in my own throat as I climbed up in the Cadillac beside Preacher.

Tony and Yvette reentered the house, closing the door. In a few minutes, Tony reappeared, his expression bleak. He strode straight to the Ford and climbed in without a word. John let in the clutch and we rolled slowly back along the road to war.

CHAPTER XXVIII

BEAUMARCHAISE
JULY-AUGUST, 1918

After a tiresome and bumpy ride, we clattered into the village of Beaumarchaise at about ten o'clock. Captain Weyandt greeted us in his billet, his leg greatly improved. Lt. Courland, just returned from the hospital, helped him give us a warm welcome.

"I wasn't looking for you men back until tomorrow," the captain smiled. "What happened? Did you run out of money?"

"No, sir. We just gave ourselves a day's leeway in case something happened," Mac explained.

"Good idea. You all had a good time, I hope."

"Good time! That ain't the word for it. We had ourselves a wedding!" Mac was still joyful about the nuptials.

"A wedding! For Christ's sake, who got married, and why?" The captain found this revelation surprising, if not unbelievable.

"Well, Tony and his girl thought it would be a good idea, so we just fixed them up with an 'A-Number-One' ceremony. Champagne, lobster salad, everything."

The skipper rose with a grin and reached for Tony. "Come here, Corporal. Let's look at you. How's it feel to be a bridegroom?"

Tony emerged from the shadows, grinning sheepishly with nothing to say.

"Well, Corporal, let me add my congratulations, belated though they may be." The captain extended his hand. "This comes as a surprise, but I do wish you and the lady all the happiness in the world."

"Thank you, sir. I think we'll have our share."

Lt. Courland came forward with a bottle of Hennessey. "I was saving this for some sort of special occasion, but I don't know of any occasion more special than a wedding. If you men will just be patient for a minute, we can drink one to the bride and groom."

We drank the toast and turned to take our leave, but the captain put a detaining hand on my arm. After the others had gone, he turned to me. "Sit down, sergeant, and tell me about this. Why did you let him do it?"

"There wasn't much that I could do or that I wanted to do, sir. It's been arranged for a couple of months—first chance Tony had to get away. To tell the truth, that's why we went to Vitry le Francois."

"Oho, sergeant. So that's the way it was."

"Tony's been crazy about the girl ever since we were in the Bathlemont sector, but after we left he never had a chance to see her."

The skipper turned an intent gaze on me.

"Remember, sir, when you sent me to Saint-Nazaire to get the ambulances?"

He nodded. "Day after I took command of the company."

"That's right, sir. Well, we stopped in Vitry on that trip and she and Tony had quite a visit. When we left, it was all fixed up."

Captain Weyandt sat motionless, gazing intently at the floor. He raised his head and gave me a long look. "What do you think about it, Sergeant?"

"What is there to think, sir? If they wanted to get married, it's their business. I think it's a damn swell idea. I'd like to do it myself."

He grinned. "I wouldn't have been surprised if it'd been you. I heard you had the habit. Why don't *you* get married, Sergeant?"

"I asked her, and she said no," I replied, laughing.

"Well, I'm sorry Tony's girl didn't say no. None of us has any great expectation of survival, and Corporal Lambert has had more than his share of luck."

Startled at the captain's ominous words, I reached for the Hennessey bottle and took a good stiff drink, in which the skipper even joined me. His eyes followed me to the door as I left. "We move in a day or so, sergeant. Keep the men close."

"Yes, sir. I'll do that. Does the captain know where we're going?"

Somewhere in the vicinity of Toul, I think." He smiled, adding, "Old stomping grounds for us, eh, what, sergeant?"

"Yes, sir. Good night, sir."

In the morning, I met a new crop of smiling faced youngsters whose idea of war was a frolic in the woods with free fireworks. After breakfast I formed my section to check their equipment and look them over. These replacements brought us up to about two-thirds of full strength. We were fortunate enough to have nine of our old men returned to duty. Bruce was back, as was Scotty Baugh, Pittles Hanks and Jack McCardy. I was more than glad to see them.

I looked at the wound that sent Hanks to the hospital the last time, his third, a machine gun bullet through the nose. "They sort of ruined your beauty that time, Pittles, Old Boy."

"I still get by," he grinned.

"With a face like that, I don't know how you do it." I shook my head.

"By God, listen, Judy. We wounded heroes got it all over you guys when it comes to women. Don't you forget that."

"I'll try not to,"

The new men were all ears and smiles. As soon as they were dismissed, some came up with questions about this, that and the other.

"How far to the front?"

"Is that artillery we hear?"

"Is it true that machine guns are that deadly?"

I answered them as honestly as I could. "Yes, that's artillery. It's about thirty miles to the front. No, machine guns aren't dangerous unless they hit you. Women and liquor are your greatest dangers."

They laughed and I warned them to stick around the company area. I leaned against a tree, watching them go over their equipment and talking among themselves, when John joined me. "Why don't you tell them something instead of kidding them like that, Sergeant?"

"That's the trouble. They've been told too much already. I can't tell them anything that'll do them any good. I can describe the sound a shell makes when it's close—tell them what it sounds like to me, but they'll have to hear it before they know what it really sounds like. They'll learn the same way we did— by experience, instinct and observation of the old timers."

John listened in silence. "I guess there's some truth in that. Talking really doesn't do much good."

Dave Evans came down the street—my first chance to talk to him since he got back from the hospital. We shook hands. "How ya feeling, Dave?"

"Oh, I'm okay," he grinned. "Thanks to the doctors back at the hospital, I'm pretty well fixed up."

"So, did you bring anything back with you?"

"Yeah, but Mac drank it all."

"Sure, that's what I'd expect."

"There's more in the café," suggested Dave, smiling.

"Well, what are we waiting for?" We moved up the street toward the café, collecting Tony, Mac and Jack McCardy on the way.

We engaged in aimless conversation until Tony asked, "You guys heard any news?"

Jack put down his beer and turned to him. "What kind of news? I heard you were married, if that's what you mean."

"That's not what I mean. I heard a rumor about a big concentration of American troops near Toul. Sometime in the late summer we're gonna take a shot at the St. Mihiel salient."

We digested the news in silence. The St. Mihiel salient was a series of fortified hills and ridges — one hard spot to crack.

"Well, by God," Mac said, "if they expect us to do it with all these green men, they're crazy."

"What the hell do they care?" asked Tony. "How many men we lose is no skin off their noses. If we reach our objective, the big ginks get the newspaper story and we get the casualties. What the hell is a few dead men to them?"

"Nothing. Not a damn thing." Jack McCardy backed Tony. "You should see some of the cemeteries back in the rear if you think dead men mean anything in this war."

"When is this supposed to come off?" I asked.

"Late summer or early fall."

"Hell. Who wants to worry that long? Now, if you said tomorrow, I'd start to worry right away, but if it's not for another month, that's just as good as never for some of us. How about another shot of cognac here?"

In a few minutes, first call sounded and we went out in the street, where the skipper told me to form the company. Since he hadn't appointed a First Sergeant to take Stubby's place, I fell the outfit in, took the report from each platoon sergeant, and reported the company formed to the captain.

The skipper directed us to form the company at three o'clock with full equipment for the march to Dammartin, where a train awaited. He told me to dismiss the company and have each platoon commander detail a squad to police its area before we moved.

After dismissing the outfit, I helped the new men make their packs and tended to the little details necessary before moving on.

Evening found Tony, Mac, John, Harris, Red and me comfortably situated in a caboose at the rear of the train by virtue of a half a jug of beer and two packs of cigarettes. We headed off into the night in an easterly direction, close to another part of the front.

"How's old Heartbroken?" Mac kidded Tony, grinning. But Tony was in no mood to be twitted about parting with his bride of a few hours.

"Go to hell," he replied.

"Okay boy, if that's the way you feel. But I ain't goin' just because you tell me to."

This was all fun to me, but Tony was inclined to take it to heart. "Don't mind him, Tony. The boy's a little jealous."

"There's the other one." Red fairly bellowed from a comfortable seat in the corner of the car where he nursed a bottle of beer. "What's that old sayin'? Birds of a feather gather no worms, or save nine or somethin' like that? Well, just look at these super lovers stickin' up for each other."

As the wheels clicked over the rails I wondered what destination their clickety-clack was hurrying us toward. The same thought must have occupied other minds, for Red spoke again. "Now that we got these two extra special heart-busters disposed of, there oughta be a chance for us, wherever we're goin.' Whaddya think, Mac?"

"You'll have to change your style if there is," I told him before Mac could answer.

"Speak when you're spoken to, Wetnose," growled Mac. Then to Red: "These guys never cramped my style any. I just hated to take their playthings away from them."

"Yeah? Listen, you big ape, I'll beat you at anything you wanna do—lovin,' fightin' or footracin' for money, marbles or chalk. What d'ya know about that?" I was half in the bag and feeling a little feisty.

"You're nuts, Scissorbill. Just plain nuts," Mac replied. "Don't forget, when I was a kid in Sout' Boston, I was a pretty popular guy!"

"With who?" Tony snorted in disbelief.

"With the women, Snipe Dung! Who'd you think?"

"Yeah, I betcha," I jeered.

"Listen, boy. It wasn't nothin' to see from five to fourteen women following me down the street."

"Each with a mattress on her back," jibed Tony.

Mac turned a scornful stare. "Mattress? Mattress, hell! With the keys to their apartment dangling from their fingertips!"

"Next liar stand up!" We looked around in surprise. Harris, the quiet one, the guy who held the world's record for not talking opened up. We shouted with delight.

"What the hell's come over him?" asked Red.

"I don't know, but I do feel kind of good," smiled Harris. "I could stand a bottle of that beer if there's any more left."

Mac scowled. "Nothing doin,' soldier. You're too damn good without any beer!" But he flipped Harris a bottle anyway.

We moved out to the platform of our super-special coach and sat with our legs dangling over the rail bed, watching the stars. Harris drew a deep sigh. "Funny world, isn't it?"

"How d'you mean funny?" asked Tony.

"Well, take us, for instance. Here we are on our way to we know not where, to do we know not what. We fight and kill or are killed by men with whom we have no quarrel. Men we've never even seen before. And for what?"

"Hell, don't ask me why," growled Mac. "That ain't my business. My business is carryin' out orders. Let the other guy figure out why."

"Yes." Harris nodded. "That's what makes you a good soldier. You close your mind to the why of things. Your philosophy is summed up in one word: do."

"There's no reason to worry about the other stuff, is there?" asked Tony. "Take where, for instance. We never know where we're going. Why, Hell's Fire! Nine times out of ten we don't even know where we are after we've got there!"

"That's life," Preacher told him. "We grope our way on and on, looking for the light. The farther we go, the deeper we search, the dimmer the light. Maybe man was never meant to fathom the darkness."

I pricked up my ears, always curious about Harris. Up to now, respect for his privacy had restrained me, but tonight curiosity led me on. "What happened between you and the church, Harris? If it's not too personal, that is."

He gave a short laugh. "Nothing. Nothing at all. I just wanted too many answers—Maybe some questions just don't have answers—at least any we've been able to fathom so far. Anyway, the whole structure gave way for me—seemed built on sand. A man can't teach what he doesn't believe. Once I'd reached that point, I decided I'd better throw it all up."

We rode along in silence for a while. Then Red Conlon snorted. "Hell, I thought we were gonna get a nice juicy piece of scandal. What the hell, Harris? No women?"

"Well, that might have been a minor factor, but not enough to destroy a man's faith." After that, he reverted back to character—quiet and reserved.

As the night train carried us into the unknown, one by one we sought our bunks. I stayed outside by myself, thinking of

Jeanne, wondering about her in the same old way. I leaned back and let the cool night breeze ruffle my hair. No answers except her vague explanation—not enough. Finally, I followed the others and climbed into my bunk, lulled to sleep by the click, clickety, click of the wheels over the rail joints.

Our train stopped at a small town called Rimaucourt, not far from Toul. The men disembarked and stood around waiting for someone to tell them what to do. Next thing I knew, the captain called upon me to act as first sergeant. I formed the company and marched them up the hill into the village, found billets for them, and returned to the company office, where the captain awaited.

"Hello, sergeant. Got 'em all billeted?"

"Yes, sir. The cooks have a meal started and our wagons and animals are corralled at the lower end of town."

"Good. Now bring your stuff up here where it'll be handy."

I looked at him in surprise. "What, sir?"

He grinned. "I forgot to mention it, but the order is gone in making you First Sergeant."

The news didn't please me. I'd rather stay with my section. "Is this required, sir?"

"Yes, it is. I know you aren't pleased with the arrangement, but we need an old man in the job. I promise as soon as Sergeant Stubblefield gets back from the hospital, you can go back to your section. Now come in the office. We have some business."

I followed him to a couple of field desks set up across from each other in the canvas tent. "We have vacancies for eleven new sergeants. Who would you suggest, sergeant?"

"Corporals Lambert, Gallagher, Conlon and Harris," I replied without hesitation.

"I already have them down." His eyes twinkled. "Now, who else?"

We worked on the list until supper time before it met the captain's approval.

Two more days in Rimaucourt, and on the evening of the third day, we were moved again to a quiet sector near Pont-A-Mousson.

CHAPTER XXIX

GONDRECOURT—SAIZERAIS
AUGUST, 1918

In this sector, we had absolutely the best war I'd seen yet—practically no war at all. At night there was sporadic shelling of the roads by both sides, but aside from that there was little to remind us we were at war. High, steep ridges and deep valleys alternated with heavy woods and hillside meadows. Shell holes were few, and after the experiences of the last six months, I couldn't wish for a better place to spend the war.

As First Sergeant I spent my time in the HQ dugout making fatigue details and working parties. Rations were on time every night, no lapses between meals. We were here to give the new men a little breaking in before we introduced them to the real war.

When the mail arrived I got more than my share. A newspaper clipping from home announced the marriage of my old girl, Claire, to her butcher boy. My mother's letter cautioned me to do nothing rash on receiving the news. I laughed to myself for I had all but forgotten Claire.

Two letters from Jeanne. In one she wrote that her brother was wounded and in a base hospital at Toul. She asked me to go see him when I got a chance as he had something to tell me. Well, I'd certainly do that. Her other letter was just a note that she was leaving Paris—to be gone for some time. I wasn't to worry at not hearing from her, for she wouldn't be able to write while she was away. That was funny. Surely she could find time to write just a note, at least.

The days passed quickly in this aura of warfare deluxe and before I realized it a week was gone. Then, one afternoon, the skipper chugged down the dugout steps smiling. "Ah, there, sergeant, pack up, we're leaving."

"Leaving? When?"

"Tonight."

"Gee! Pretty short stay."

"Yes, it is, rather, but we'll be relieved tonight by the 90th Division.

So we got ready to leave, but in typical Army fashion, the relief wasn't completed till daybreak, and the sun was peeping over the hills when we moved out of the sector. I stood aside as the company filed past. When the second platoon reached me I had to take a little sass from the men.

"Eyes right," shouted some wag.

"Jigadier Brindle Redding," cried another.

"What price to speak to a first sergeant?" yelled Tony.

"You'll draw a wiring party for that!" I shouted in return.

Happy as a gang of schoolboys. Why shouldn't they be? Hadn't they just completed a tour of the front without losing a man? That would make any soldier happy. We marched for an hour and were well back among the heavy artillery before we took our first ten-minute rest. The men sprawled along the side of the road. Some smoked, some took a drink, but all were grateful for the rest and made the most of it.

We'd scarcely resumed our march when a shell came over. There was no military target in the vicinity, so what the hell? We weren't under observation by the enemy, so there was no logical reason why it should ever have been fired. We heard its warning whistle a long way off. It grew louder, shriller until it was a piercing shriek.

"Down!" I shouted and dived into the ditch beside the road. The shell landed with a thundering crash just off to the left. The stench of explosive was strong as I rose to my feet, looking around for damage. Someone had been hit. I made tracks for the knot of men gathered around one still figure lying on the edge of the road.

"Who is it?"

Pittles Hanks looked at me and turned away without answering.

"What the hell?" I shouted, running up. "What's the matter? Who's hit?"

Someone took me by the arm. I turned. Harris. "Steady, sergeant," he said quietly. "It's Tony."

Oh, my God. Tony? It can't be, not Tony! All the strength went out of my body, my knees buckled, but I caught myself. I ran, shouting, to where the still figure had been moved to a grassy patch beside the road, my voice catching in my throat. It was Tony, his black hair glistening damp against his forehead, his eyes closed. Red Conlon knelt beside him, cradling his head. He surrendered his place to me and I knelt, searching frantically for signs of life.

"Tony, Tony, answer me. It ain't bad, is it, Tony?"

I shook him gently. His eyes blinked open, and he recognized me. He smiled weakly as I leaned down to catch his faint whisper. "Hello, Damn Yank. Look out for Yvette." His head rolled and I thought he was gone, but no, his eyes fluttered and his lips started to move again. I barely caught the words, "Stay with 'em, Judy. See ya later." He let go a weak sigh, then went limp in my arms. Dead.

Hot tears ran down my cheeks, uncontrolled. Red, John and Harris formed a human hedge around me as I held my best friend and sobbed. The rest of the company moved on up the road. Lost in grief, I had to be lifted to my feet and led away from Tony's body.

I stood with my guys a few feet away, watching other companies file up the road. As each passed, the men came to attention and saluted the dead body lying there in the ditch. I couldn't bring myself to leave. Tony—gone. He couldn't be gone! Didn't he just yell at me a few minutes ago? But the desolate fact remained unchanged. There was his waxen face and his blood, bright red in the early morning sunlight. I picked up my pack and staggered away. Regardless of direction, I had to move.

Harris stayed with me, more comfort than a woman at such a time. After we'd walked some distance, he asked, "Judy, would you like us to carry his body back and bury him in the first cemetery we come to?"

I tried to answer, but words wouldn't come. I could only nod. Harris called for a stretcher, and I watched from a distance as they placed Tony's poor, broken body on it and we moved up the road in silence. Red fell back, walking by my side.

I kept looking back at Tony, his black hair showing under the end of the blanket. Sorrow engulfed me and, against my will, tears flowed unabated down my cheeks. I walked along, grief-stricken, a dull ache in my chest, trying to take comfort from the fact that he hadn't suffered much.

I voiced this thought to Red, who was trudging heavily beside me. "He seemed to die easy, didn't he, Red?"

"The shock numbed him."

"Where was he hit?" I asked.

"Big piece broke his back," was the terse reply.

We made our sorrowful way up the road to the rear for about three hours, marching along, numb and staring. At a village called Saizerais we gently deposited our burden on the roadside.

Captain Weyandt came back and put his hand on my shoulder. "I'm sorry, sergeant," was all he said. Then he turned to Mac. "If you men want to bury Sgt. Lambert's body in the cemetery here, I'll see the town mayor."

"Thanks, sir," returned Mac. "That'd be a big help."

"Move over under those trees." The captain, indicated a small orchard across the street. "Wait there until I come back."

Our little procession had attracted attention and a crowd had collected, standing around, whispering in awestruck tones. These were mostly men from the division that relieved us and death was still new and unfamiliar to them. They were little better than uniformed civilians as yet.

Two YMCA women paused in passing and murmured their sympathy, as did a nurse from a nearby hospital. One of the YMCA girls addressed Red. "Are you the men with this body?" she asked.

"Yeah, we are," answered Red, glancing at me.

"Are you going to bury him here?"

"That's our idea if we can arrange it."

"Well, it's a lovely, fitting resting place, I think." She moved away, head down, as though she'd known him.

Mac sat down beside me, too stunned to speak. He, too, felt the loss of a good and dependable friend. "It's near noon, Judy. I think we'd better eat something."

"I don't want anything to eat." I downed a big slug of brandy from my canteen.

Then a group of civilians headed by a YMCA man strode briskly down the road—welfare workers, YMCA, Salvation Army, general do-gooders. I watched them closely, for I had no love for civilians looking for a chance to experience war without the dangers and hardships. It was for apes like these that good men like Tony had to die.

The foremost YMCA man strode boldly up to Tony's body, raised a corner of the blanket and looked under. Then he straightened up and glanced around. "Here, a couple of you men, lay hold of this stretcher and carry it up to the cemetery."

Infuriated, I leaped forward, but Mac was ahead of me. He placed his hand on the Y man's arm. "What're you gonna do?" he asked, his tone warning of peril.

"Well, I'm going to take this poor boy's body up to the cemetery and give him a Christian burial."

"Listen, brother." Red joined Mac and me, his voice hard and brittle. "That's the body of no boy. That's Sergeant Tony Lambert, who was all man. He lived with us and fought with us. It was tough that he had to die, but now that he's gone, *we're* gonna bury him. Not you, *us.*"

The Y man, probably some small town minister whose opinion had been deferred to for so long he couldn't imagine any other response, pulled back his head in obvious consternation. It was also probably the first time he'd ever met a real, genuine front-line fighting man who carried no respect or deference for him or his calling.

"But I am a minister," he humphed.

"That's okay," said Mac. "We're soldiers. This man was a soldier. We can bury him better than you can."

The preacher, flustered and at a loss for an answer, fell back on the timeworn 'holier than thou' attitude. "Why, it is doubtful if some of you men have ever even been saved."

Red's laugh was short and bitter. "Yeah, that's right, I guess, but there's times when we do a hell of a lot of savin' of you guys back in the rear. But that's not the point. The point is that *we're* gonna bury our friend."

The Y man, sensing defeat but still bent on saving face in front of his friends turned away, saying, "Well, I've done all I could. You men are not very righteous or patriotic to refuse this man a Christian burial."

"Why, you son of a bitch," I shouted, jumping for him. These flop-mouthed war dodgers drooling about patriotism made me see red. I'd break that bastard's neck.

Harris grabbed me from the rear. "Let me handle this, Judy."

He slipped past me and confronted the thoroughly startled Y man, lay a detaining hand on his arm and spoke in a firm, well-modulated voice.

"Listen. There's a lot you don't understand. I used to be a minister, too, so I know your point of view. Now I'm a soldier, so I also know their point of view. You deal in words. They deal in deeds. You're a man of talk. They're men of action. None of them are boys. They are men — in every sense of the word except years. Experience has made them men in ways you can only imagine. Do you think talking about patriotism can compare to the patriotism they live? These men know what patriotism is. They've seen it acted out to the bitter end a thousand times on a dozen different fields of battle. It's not something they talk about because they've lived it. It's the strength to endure filth and slime, blood, torture, scraps of bodies strewn across the landscape. Patriotism for them means stark heroism, dogged courage and faithfulness — even unto death."

He stopped abruptly and looked around, bewildered, as though he hadn't meant to go on so long. He smiled an apologetic half-smile, glanced in my direction, and came slowly toward me, still lost in his words. I heard a hand clap, slow and deliberate. I looked up to see Captain Weyandt standing on the edge of the crowd, admiration on his face. A storm of applause broke out as Harris effaced himself in the crowd.

As the gathering slowly dispersed, the captain joined Red, Mac, John and me. "The grave diggers are here, and I found a French carpenter to make a coffin. You men can take the body up any time. I'll have the company march up in formation."

The four of us took the stretcher and moved slowly toward the grassy slope of the cemetery with our burden. Soldiers all along the way came to attention and saluted as we passed. Halfway up the village street, two little girls ran alongside with a large bouquet of wild flowers. We stopped and lowered our burden so they could lay their offering on his chest. By the time we reached the cemetery and turned in at the gate, a crowd had fallen in behind us, following across to where fresh dirt marked the new grave in one corner of the churchyard. The box was already there, and we gently raised Tony off the stretcher and placed him in it. Oh, God. Not Tony. Once again I was overwhelmed with grief. Not Tony.

Mac beckoned to Harris to join us from the edge of the crowd and asked him to say something for Tony. I went to stand by the box and looked at Tony for the last time as the old Frenchman prepared to fasten down the lid. A group of soldiers slowly lowered the box as Harris stepped to the head of the grave. He stood there, his shirt open at the throat, the breeze ruffling his light hair, manhood written in every line of him. He looked beyond his surroundings into the distance before speaking, quietly and distinctly.

"Men, this man was my friend — the friend of all of us. Just a simple soldier, he aspired to no high rank. Satisfaction for him came from knowing he did his duty. With his comrades he was cheerful and helpful, one of the most loved men in the company. We feel his loss. No matter how many men may come to take his place, or how fine they may be, his particular niche will never be filled. This is proof of a life well-lived. Sergeant Lambert was admired, respected and loved by all of us. Nothing more need be said."

He stood silent, his head bowed for a moment, and then turned and stepped over to where we stood. Mac and I each grasped one of his hands. The Frenchmen lifted their shovels and filled in the grave. Listening to the clods fall on the box, I thought of Yvette. War's terrible finality touched me more forcefully at that moment than at any other time. We turned and walked slowly down the slope to the village.

When we got there, the captain told me to fall the company in at nine p.m. We had orders to move farther back. As we departed, depressed about Tony, I forgot to arrange for a ride on the driver's seat and found myself riding in a crowded truck, lost in thoughts of nothing but Tony—alive and happy this morning, now dead and buried. The finality of it made my heart ache. For him. For Yvette. For all of the young lives snuffed out in an instant or over agonizing days, weeks or months. For what? God, I hated war.

CHAPTER XXX

GONDRECOURT
AUGUST, 1918

As our trucks rolled along, the country was beginning to look familiar. We rolled through Vaucouleurs, De Luge and Abainville, all villages we'd known in the Gondrecourt Sector almost a year ago. When we finally pulled into Gondrecourt itself at eight o'clock in the morning we found billets and let the men turn in for some sleep. As I was setting up a desk in the company office near the town square, Captain Weyandt came in.

"Well, sergeant, here we are again, eh, what?"

"Yes, here we are, sir," I answered listlessly, "What there is of us."

"I'm sorry about Tony, but I was afraid of something like this. Ever since he got married I had a premonition he was in for it. I can't explain it, but the feeling seemed fixed in my head."

"I've heard of that before, sir."

"Yes, so have I, but I hope I never experience it again."

We organized the office and made up details for various jobs. Lt. Courland stepped in and he and the captain talked for a while, then left together. Then Mac came in looking like there was something on his mind.

"Say, Judy, what the hell do you think?" he burst as soon as the door was closed. "I was just down to see Georgette and her mother, and by God, there's a couple of recruits hanging out down there now. What the hell are we gonna do?"

"Well, what'd you expect?" I asked, amused. Mac was old enough to know better. "You didn't expect a couple of women like them to sleep alone just because you weren't here, did you?"

He scratched his head and sat down at the captain's desk. "Well, I guess I didn't, if I thought about it at all, but it was a hell of a shock to walk right into a couple of wet-behind-the-ears punks occupying our old space."

The idea of Mac being taken aback by any circumstances gave me a chuckle. 'His Pugnacity' was always more than capable of dealing with any kind of situation.

"A couple of punches in the nose should have fixed everything up. What's wrong with you? Gettin' old?"

"Hell, Judy, there's too damn many MPs around here for that." He shook his head plaintively. "The minute you'd slug a guy, there'd be at least a dozen of them grab you. Hell, there must be three MPs for every soldier in this town."

Since I'd met Jeanne, I'd forgotten about Georgette and her mother. It was plain that Mac wanted to stay at their place while we were there, but he wasn't sure where I stood on the matter. Other women had lost their appeal for me. I'd have liked the comforts at Georgette's, but Jeanne was a new part of the equation. Mac watched me intently, anxiously awaiting my decision. I decided to humor him — for a while at least.

"Come on," I said, starting for the door. "I'll give you a practical lesson in ousting intruders."

As we passed along the street, everything about the place reminded me of Tony. The community laundry pool where he went swimming. The cafe where he shaved the proprietor's head while he slept. There on the horse trough at the pump was painted in red letters: Tony Lambert, Spartanburg, S.Carolina, U.S.A. Engulfed in a wave of sorrow and loneliness, my eyes grew moist and a lump rose in my throat. God, but I missed him.

Mac noticed my silence and turned to me. "What's the matter?"

"Oh, just thinking about Tony."

"Yeah, I miss him too, but there's not much we can do about it."

Mac's response came after a long silence. I wondered if his thoughts were the same as mine. "No, that's the trouble."

"Well, hell, let's get a drink."

We stopped at a café a few doors away from Georgette's shop and downed a couple of drinks of rum. After it took hold, I felt a little better. Liquor was great for numbing the sensibilities. It'd dull pain, deaden sorrow and take the sting out of unhappiness. True, the relief was temporary but after all, the life of a soldier at the front was temporary, too.

We left the café and went on to the little coffee shop. The sign, "English Spoken" was still in the window, and we entered to find everything unchanged. The same little bell tinkled as we opened the door. Tables and chairs occupied the same positions. There was no reason why things shouldn't be the same, but we'd been through so much in the intervening months, it seemed as though everything should be different. Two soldiers sat at a rear table looking very much at home and somewhat proprietary.

"You here again," said the older of the two, looking at Mac with hostility.

Mac started to answer but was interrupted by Georgette, who had emerged from the back room to serve what she thought were just a couple of ordinary customers. On seeing us she ran to me with outstretched hands. "Ah, Judee," she cried, "I am so glad to see you. You are not wounded, no?"

"What the hell goes on here?" asked the soldier who spoke before, rising and knocking his chair over. He moved in my direction, menace written all over him.

Mac stepped up to meet him. I released Georgette's hands and stepped to the side. Now, trouble was the last thing I wanted if there was any possibility of avoiding it. I moved toward the younger of the two, still seated, and demanded in my sternest drill ground manner, "Just what the hell do you boys mean by messin' around my wife? Are you tryin' to get in trouble?"

The man in the chair looked up, fear in his eyes. "Your wife?" he gasped. "My God, sergeant, I didn't know she was your wife!"

"Well, she is," I thundered. "If you don't want me to turn you over to the MPs you'll get out of here just as damn quick as you can."

He rose and started for the door, but his companion wasn't so quick to give in. "Yeah?" he snarled. "Who says she's your wife? They ain't both your wife, anyway."

"One's my mother-in-law," I growled, starting for him. He was considerably heavier than I, but not so sure of himself. I just might be telling the truth. The advantage was all mine.

"Call the MPs while I hold this bastard." I lunged at him.

"Not me, you ain't gonna hold," he cried and joined his buddy in a rush for the door. I followed and watched them tear down the street. Then I turned to face Mac and Georgette, both doubled up with laughter. I had to smile myself at the ludicrous spectacle.

"Well, see how it's done?" I gave Mac the eye.

"I'll tell the cock-eyed world, boy, that was all right."

Georgette's mother, coming in from the street, stared in surprise when she saw us. She ran over and embraced Mac and clucked over him like a mother hen over a lost chick. Finally, she greeted me. "Sarjong Judee," she said, "you look very well, but you are much older, no?"

"Just a year."

"Ah, but the hair. It is gray here." She reached up and caressed my temples.

I'd have never given it a thought, but as I studied it in a glass on the wall, I saw that she was right. A slight tinge of gray had crept over my temples.

Georgette came up and touched the gray. "I think it looks very nice, Judee."

"Well, it beats getting bald."

After we'd sat around for a while, I took my leave, pleading work at the company office. I plodded along the street, wondering what kind of fool I must be. I'd gotten myself into a predicament for no reason at all. What would Jeanne think? The girl, Georgette, awakened absolutely no response in me. In fact, the thought of intimacies was distasteful. Now how could I get out of this mess without upsetting Mac's plans or insulting Georgette? When Mac first mentioned the idea, I thought it might work for comfort's sake, if nothing else. But seeing and talking with Georgette brought up the inevitable comparison with Jeanne. Put simply, Georgette held no charm for me. Now, how could I get out of this mess without offending everyone involved? Still in a quandary, I entered the company office.

Captain Weyandt, seated at his desk, sealed an envelope and placed it in the outgoing mail.

"Where've you been, sergeant?"

"Oh, finding myself a billet," I answered.

"Why, I thought you had a billet." He looked up, questioning.

"Well, sir, you know when we were here before I had what was considered a pretty extra special billet with Mac. So when we happened to hit this town again he thought it'd be a good idea to prospect around and see if we could get that same one again."

"Oh, that kind of billet? Well, did you get it?"

"Yes, sir, we got it."

"Humph, you don't sound very enthusiastic, sergeant. What seems to be the trouble?"

"Oh, Christ Almighty, captain, Tony's dead and everything's haywire. What the hell's it all about anyhow?"

He rose and stood in front of me. "You cared a lot about Tony, didn't you, sergeant?"

"Yeah, sir. I did. More than I ever realized 'til now that he's gone."

"You knew his wife, too."

"Yes, sir, I did."

"Well, I think you need a little change, so I'm going to get you a few days leave to go visit Sgt. Lambert's widow. Some of the men brought me some money to send her. I'll let you take it and extend the sympathy of the company in person. Can you be ready to leave tomorrow?"

A way out of my predicament!

"Yes, sir! But could you have that leave ready for me by this evening?"

"Well, I guess so, sergeant, but what's the hurry?"

"Well, sir, if the captain must know, I have no intention of sleeping with the young lady I'm hooked up with tonight."

"Why sergeant." He looked at me in mock astonishment. "I never heard of such a thing. You must be off your feed to turn down a good bed and a marvelous chance to improve your French."

I felt my face redden under Captain Weyandt's pointed wit, and we both had a good laugh.

"It's all right, sergeant. Whatever your reason, it's all right with me. I'll have your leave for you tonight."

After clearing up what little work was to be done, I went looking for Red Conlon. I only had to explore a few cafés before I found him alone at a table with a bottle of cognac.

"Hey, Red, want a long-haired Bunkie?"

He looked up in surprise. "Get away, Snipe Dung. Who're you tryin' to kid?"

"I'm not kidding. I've got a swell billet up the street with Mac, but the skipper's sending me away on an errand and I can't use it. You might as well step in."

"Where is it?" he asked, eyeing me suspiciously.

"Up the street at Georgette's coffee shop."

"Oh, boy, am I stepping into something?"

"Well, now, listen. You go up there and tell Mac that the company commander's sending me away for a couple of days. Georgette'll be there, and it's up to you to make yourself solid. Mac'll put in a good word for you, and with that charming mug of yours, you should get along all right."

"Okay, Jude. I'll go right up." He was so pleased with his good fortune he bought me a drink. "Where are you goin'?" he asked.

"Never mind that, Dish Face. Just be glad I'm goin'."

About five o'clock that evening, the captain stepped into the office and handed me an envelope. "There are your leave papers and travel orders, sergeant. You can leave any time you feel like it. You've got four days, so I hope you'll be out of the doldrums by the time you get back."

Tucking the papers into my breast pocket, I took the billfold with the gift for Yvette and stepped out into the late afternoon sun. I hoped to take advantage of this opportunity to visit René Trevost in the hospital at Toul, so I struck out on the road toward Vaucouleurs, where I got a quick ride on a truck all the way to Toul. It wasn't even dark when I arranged for a room at the Hotel Villa Lorraine inside the walled city.

CHAPTER XXXI

TOUL/VITRY LE FRANCOIS
AUGUST, 1918

In the morning after an early breakfast I started on a canvas of the French hospitals in search of René Trevost. Luckily, I located him on the third attempt. Visitors were not admitted until ten a.m., so I passed the intervening time walking the streets, enjoying the sights of the historic city. I stopped and gazed at the Gothic cathedral and visited some of the shops. I even bought a guidebook to learn some history of the place. In another world, I would have spent days here, absorbing the history and lore of medieval France. Today my time was limited, so I returned to the hospital promptly at ten.

Escorted to René's ward I found him sitting up in bed. He smiled and extended his hand in greeting.

"Good morning, sergeant. I'm glad to see you. Jeanne wrote that you were coming."

"Yes. She wrote and told me where to find you. How bad is it?"

"Not bad, sergeant. Just a couple of machine gun bullets in the shoulder. Painful, but not serious."

"I'm glad for that. Jeanne's worried about you."

"Yes, I imagine she is." He smiled lazily. "You know, sergeant, it is about her that we must talk."

"That's what I understood from her letter."

He hesitated for a moment, then said, "You care a great deal for my sister Jeanne, is it not so, sergeant?"

Impressed by his sober demeanor, I responded. "Yes sir, I do think a great deal of her."

"So much that you contemplate marriage?"

"Yes. Yes, I do."

"I am sorry, sergeant." He spoke so slowly and earnestly that I had to lean closer to understand. "What I have to tell you is not pleasant for me. But the fact is that Jeanne has been betrothed since childhood. Her marriage has long been arranged to the son of an old friend of our family. You perhaps are aware that this is an ancient custom in our country and is still followed by some families. Jeanne, it seems, reciprocates your feeling. She wrote to our father who is at present in your country on government business. She told him of her feeling for you and requested that she be released from the alliance."

"My father communicated with her fiancé, asking his pleasure in the matter, and he refused to relinquish his rights. Upon receiving this news, my father directed me to have an interview with you. It is his opinion that, knowing conditions for what they are, it is only proper that you should withdraw your attentions."

He paused, watching my reaction and then went on. "Believe me, sergeant, I do not like to have to tell you this, but as Jeanne's elder brother, it is my duty. Personally I have a high regard for you, but our personal feelings do not enter into this matter and, as I said before, I am sorry." He stopped and reached for a cigarette, lit it and offered one to me.

Astonished, I could scarcely believe my ears. I didn't know what to say. I sat there like a fighter knocked senseless by a powerful blow, Captain Trevost, watching my reaction with a serious gaze, continued, "It is all very lamentable. I think I know something of what you feel."

I raised my head to look at him, still bewildered beyond words. "Who is this other man?"

"That I cannot divulge."

"Is he a soldier?"

"Yes, he is a member of the French Air Service."

There didn't seem to be much to say or do. All along, I'd thought this was too good to be true. Turned out, it was. René reached over to the little stand beside his bed and handed me a glass.

"If you would be so kind, sergeant, there is a bottle of brandy under the stand. A drink would do us both good."

I picked up the bottle and filled the glasses, and as we drank I turned the glass in my hands. What should I say? What could I do? Finally, I addressed him, my eyes level. "Captain, what would you do in my position?"

He gave me a rare smile. "Sergeant, I have delivered my message as I was instructed. Now you ask me what I would do were I in your place. I don't believe I would be violating any trust by saying that, were I in your place, I should not give up."

He was still smiling. I was relieved. Not elated, but at least it felt good to know Rene sympathized and would help me if he could.

"Have you spoken to Jeanne?" I asked.

"No. I have not seen her since before the big drive. She has written to me several times, though."

"What's she got to say about it?' Recovered from the shock, I was determined to dig to the bottom of this from every angle.

"Oh, she is bound not to allow anything to come between you two. She even threatens to join you in an illegitimate union if our father tries to force her to carry out the family plan."

"That's encouraging! Looks like I still have a chance, then."

"Yes, as far as she is concerned, you have a very good chance. But should you go ahead and be married, I'm afraid trouble would result. There is money involved, and, of course, honor. This other gentleman has some rights in the matter and could make things unpleasant for you."

I wasn't anxious to make trouble for Jeanne or her people, but I still couldn't entertain the thought of giving her up without a fight.

"I'll tell you what, sergeant," René suggested. "Wait until Jeanne returns and we three can talk it over. I'm on your side, and if there is any satisfactory solution, we should be able to find it."

"How soon do you think she'll be back?" I asked, pleased with the idea of a three-way meeting.

"That I can not say, but as soon as she does I will get in touch with you."

"Where is she now?"

His glance let me know his willingness to talk about his sister's activities had reached its limits. He continued in his impeccably formal manner. "We do not know exactly, but if we did, it would not be possible to divulge the information."

Christ, I thought. More mystery. What was this, anyway? She couldn't write to me, and he couldn't tell me where she was. Who was crazy — them or me?

Rene caught my mystification and moved to soothe my curiosity. "You are a soldier, sergeant. Surely you realize that war places people in strange situations. Jeanne is engaged in work very important to the nation and for which she seems to show a remarkable aptitude. More than this I can not tell you at present."

I was about to question him further, when the door to the ward was flung back and trays of food were wheeled into the room. A nurse built like a wrestler and wearing a frown of fearful aspect notified me that visitors were not allowed in the ward during meal times. Even though completely dissatisfied, I had no choice but to leave. I shook hands with René and bade him good-bye.

"Come and see me again, sergeant. You are always welcome."

"I'll be glad to, captain. Any time I can arrange it. Take care of yourself."

He waved as I left the ward to continue on my errand to Vitry Le Francois. My train left in a half hour, so I ate a hurried lunch and boarded just as it departed. When I arrived at Vitry, near dusk, I walked alone up the darkening street, haunted by memories of my last visit here, listening to the echoes of toasts and laughter and Tony's rapture at having found the love of his life. As I lifted the old-fashioned knocker I girded myself for my task. Yvette opened the door, dressed in a light wrapper, her hair let down and brushed to glistening.

She gazed at me in surprise. "Why, Judee. I do not think it is you. Why are you here?"

"You haven't heard anything, then?"

"Hear anything? What you mean, do I hear anything? What is it, Judee? Tony, he is hurt?"

"Yes, Yvette, he is hurt. I thought you would have heard by now."

"I know nothing, sarjong. Tell me, is he keel?"

She knew without being told and there was nothing to gain by prolonging the moment. I nodded. "Yes, Yvette, he is killed."

I expected her to lose control, but she sat down on a chair very calm. "Tell me about it, sarjong."

As I told her how Tony died, she sat quiet, with no visible reaction. When I finished, she looked at the floor, her eyes steady, without a word. I gave her the money from the men, and she held it to her breast and lowered her head in gratitude. Then she placed the pile of bills on the table and stood looking at it like she was wondering where it came from. I sat on the seat by the window, watching her, puzzled. She seemed more in a pensive mood than stricken by uncontrollable grief.

She rose and came over to sit by me on the window seat. "You like Tony very much, is it not so, sarjong?" she asked, looking up at me.

"Yeah, I did."

"You like him so much that you want for him to marry with me because he want to marry with me?"

"That's right."

"You did not want to marry?"

"No, I don't want to marry with anyone."

"Oh, yes, sarjong. That very nice lady you have here for our marriage. You want to marry with her."

"Yes, I would like to marry her, but it seems that is impossible."

Yvette got up and crossed the room to a cupboard built in the wall and reached in for a bottle of brandy and a glass. Returning to where I sat, she said, "You will eat with me, please, sarjong?"

"Why, yes, if you want me to."

She set the bottle and glass down convenient to my hand. "I must prepare something to eat. You must have something to drink while I am occupied."

I poured out a drink and watched her busy herself at the fire. In a short time, she'd cooked up an omelet, fried potatoes, bread, butter and coffee. I took another drink—good brandy that took hold without hesitation. Merciful relief. We sat down to eat, and I felt better than I'd felt for days.

"When must you return?" she asked, pouring coffee.

"Oh, in a day or so,"

"Then you will be here for a little while?"

"No. I expect to return to Toul in the morning."

After drinking my coffee I excused myself and went outside to sit on a bench by the doorstep while Yvette cleaned up the dishes. The night was warm and pleasant. Inevitably, I thought back over the events of the last few days, Tony's death and Capt. Trevost's disclosure uppermost in my mind. The captain's message was disheartening, but his personal attitude still encouraged me. I wondered if he was just trying to let me let me down easy or if he really sympathized with Jeanne and me. My thoughts returned to Yvette, so young and sad, with little hope for the future now. I still felt affection and sympathy toward her. Poor kid. Her entire life had been mostly trouble. Father killed, mother dead. She herself the plaything of passing soldiers, then her marriage to Tony and now a widow already. What was in store for her? I was surprised and inclined to wonder at her stoicism at the news of Tony's death. French women were supposed to be very emotional, but so far she was the exact opposite.

Passers-by greeted me with the customary 'Bon Soir, m'sieur'. which I returned in kind. The night became hazy as a slight chill descended. I threw my cigarette away and entered the house with the intention of drinking a nightcap before going to the hotel. I didn't see Yvette at first, then I spied her lying down on a couch, her back to me, her shoulders shaking, weeping in silent grief. I picked up the brandy and tiptoed out the door.

When morning arrived I couldn't decide whether to stay in Vitry for another night or go back to Toul. Since I wanted another talk with René, I decided on Toul. I returned to Yvette's house where I found her red-eyed, but composed. "Judee, why did you go off last night?" she chided me. "You know you are welcome here."

"I thought it best. You know, people do talk."

"Oh, let them talk. Your were Tony's friend and you are my friend. What can people say that will hurt me more than I have been hurt already?"

"You talk like a soldier, Yvette."

"I have known nothing but soldiers all my life." She smiled thoughtfully. "Perhaps that is the reason. But you are hungry, sarjong. Come eat."

As we ate I told her I'd return to Toul in the evening to finish a few things.

"Oh, I know you think about something," she said. "I can see last night. You think and think."

I decided to tell her about my problem. She was sympathetic but not much help, for her idea of a solution was for me and Jeanne to run away and get married. I thought it might be a good idea but dismissed it as too complicated. The day passed, and toward evening I bade Yvette farewell.

As I turned to leave, she asked, "You will come back and see me sometime?" loneliness in her voice.

"Sure, I'll try. Later on toward winter the fighting should die down and I may be able to come and see you then."

"You will try very hard, please." Her lip quivered as she tried to hold back tears. She was so plaintive standing there struggling for control that I gathered her in my arms and kissed her forehead.

Just then motorcycle turned the corner, chugging toward us—an American machine with a man in the sidecar. It stopped in front of the house and the sidecar man got out and approached. I saw an MP band on his arm and my gorge began to rise. One wrong word from him and we'd clash. As he took in my stripes and the insignia denoting my outfit, his demeanor softened.

"Are you on leave, sergeant?" He was cautious with the question.

"Yes."

"May I see your papers?"

I surrendered them and he looked them over closely. Then, looking at his watch, he made note of the time and date on the papers. He handed them back and looked up. "I'm sorry, sergeant, but all Americans separated from their outfits are ordered to report back immediately. I have marked the time and date that I delivered those orders on your papers. You're an old soldier, so you know what to do."

"Okay, buddy," I answered. "You seem pretty decent for an MP. How 'bout a drink?"

He smiled. "I ain't an MP because I want to be, and I could stand two drinks."

"Call your buddy," I told him. Yvette turned to me as I entered the house for the bottle.

"What is it?" she asked.

"Seems like there's a war on. I've got to go right away."

She didn't try to hide her disappointment, even though she knew there was nothing to be done. While the two MPs lowered the level of the brandy bottle, I bade her good-bye. She clung to me for a moment. "But you will come back?"

"Sure I'll come back."

"You come back."

I turned to the MPs. "Where you fellows from?"

"Toul," they answered in unison.

"When are you going back?"

"Right now."

"Is there room in that contraption for another passenger?"

"Sure," answered the driver. "Get on behind me."

We rattled out of Vitry for the long, bumpy ride back to Toul, where we arrived in the middle of the night and, according to instructions from my guides, I checked in at the MP station.

"There's a truck leaving for Gondrecourt in a few minutes, sergeant," the lieutenant of MPs told me. "You'll have to catch it."

This precluded any chance of visiting René again, so I gathered my gear and headed for the truck, climbed aboard, and we were soon on our way to Gondrecourt.

For some unknown reason I'd had a feeling of elation since the orders came to return to the outfit. I couldn't figure out why. Jeanne may have been right when she said that after some time away from the front a soldier would get restless and long for action. Whatever the cause, as we rumbled into Gondrecourt I felt much better than I had for a long time.

CHAPTER XXXII

ST MIHIEL
SEPTEMBER, 1918

When I got back to Gondrecourt I found that Stubby had rejoined the company, so he resumed his duties as first sergeant and I went back to my section. Glad to be back with the old gang again, I met up with Mac at the first formation.

"What's goin' on?" I asked.

"Nobody seems to know for sure, but something's up. Hundreds of guns and ammunition trucks pass through every night. Big drive scheduled for somewhere, and it's not far off."

"Any idea where?"

"Your guess is as good as mine. Must be somewhere pretty close around here, though."

"St Mihiel." I guessed.

"St Mihiel." He nodded emphatically.

"Well, I hope we're not in front of Montsec."

As we sauntered down the street we met Tommy Connors, another late arrival from the hospital. We slipped into a café and found a table for three.

"How many old men have come back to the outfit?" I asked, sipping a beer.

"I don't know." Tommy wrinkled his brow. "There's quite a few sprinkled around in each platoon, though."

Mac tallied on his fingers, frowning. "We've got sixteen in the second platoon, so I guess the rest would run about the same."

Sixteen old men out of fifty, nearly a third. The rest were recruits who'd spent but one week at the front. Well, we could be worse off. Maybe.

My third day back, we left Gondrecourt on foot, hiked for three days and stopped in the Bois du Sanzey, a great forest, teeming with troops. Guns were everywhere—great, large calibers that a man could crawl through with no trouble. Long barreled rifles, shorter barreled howitzers and stubby looking mortars. There must have been thousands of them. Many had never been fired except for a few ranging shots to tape enemy targets. The place had an ominous look.

I met John Gallagher after supper one evening, and we sat on the grass in the waning sunlight. Except for the artillery, this place would have been a serene retreat for a troubled mind. As it was, it was anything but.

Taking it all in, John gave voice to his thoughts. "Well, it looks like we're going to get a chance to do what we've always dreaded."

"What?"

"Run up the side of Montsec under machine gun fire," he replied.

"Well, you might run up." I told him. "But if I ever reach the top, I'll be crawling on my belly like a damn snake." We laughed to ease the tension.

The company lay in this position day after day. At night, working parties went out to unload material and ammunition at strategic points along the front, and every day new outfits moved into the woods until it seemed they couldn't hold another man.

The new men amused us with their continuous talk about the horrors of a war they hadn't experienced yet. They complained about the hardships. What hardships? The weather was good and we were getting regular meals and rest, more like a picnic than a war. If this was what these boys called hardships I shuddered at how they'd react to the real thing. When I heard men who hadn't even been in combat yet wish the war were over, I didn't get it. All they wanted was to be home. Well, when they'd get home they'd probably find a job in some factory where they'd drudge the rest of their lives away, watching some woman grow fat on the proceeds of their slavery. Hell, I'd take a short, exciting life over that any day.

As the fair weather gave way to rain, the new men needed some lessons in arranging their pup tents to keep them dry. John and I chuckled at two new men who pitched their pup tent in a depression that soon turned into a miniature lake. Their frantic efforts to keep their equipment dry entertained us until they finally admitted defeat and moved to higher ground.

One afternoon I went looking for the captain. "Can the outfit get along without me for a couple of hours?" I asked.

"Why? What do you want to do?"

"I have a little business over in Menil-La-Tour."

"Can you keep a secret, sergeant?"

"Oh, yes, sir. I kept one once."

He grinned. "Keep this one, then. I think tomorrow is the day."

"Uh oh. Montsec, eh, what, sir?"

"Yes." His expression changed from smiling to grim. "If you'll promise to be back by evening, you can go. Have some fun, 'cause tomorrow's probably the day."

I slogged along the muddy road thumbing a ride. An empty ambulance came to my rescue, and in a few minutes deposited me in Menil-La-Tour. I searched the shops and compared prices before buying a bottle each of cherry brandy, Benedictine and cognac. Then I found a restaurant for a good meal before heading back to the outfit. I figured it might be the last one for a while.

As soon as I got back I wrote a short letter to Jeanne telling her we expected to go over in the morning. I wrote that I'd met with her brother and asked what we should do about this complication in our lives.

At the company office a bunch of men stood around talking to the captain. One detached himself from the group and greeted me. It was Morrie Muller, back from the hospital. Good to see him in fighting form again. After I mailed my letter, we moved toward the company area, clapping each other on the back and catching up.

"Well, kid, you sure came back at a hell of a time," I told him.

"Looks that way, but bein' back in the rear ain't what it's cracked up to be. Up here we live rough and have to take our chances with 'old Jerry'. Back there, with the reformers, welfare workers and MPs all on your tail, a soldier leads a dog's life. It's all talk back there, Judy. More damn war dodgers shooting off their mouths than could patch hell a mile. Christ, I'm glad to be back."

"Maybe this time tomorrow you won't be so glad. You'll be wishing for someone to save your soul or offer you a cookie."

"Maybe," he laughed. "Say, Judy. How's chances of finding a drink?"

"Chances are good." We went to my pup tent and I dug the bottle of cognac out from under my bed roll. Mac wandered in, cursing as he stumbled into a puddle of water in the dark. Morrie laughed. "Same old Mac."

"Who the hell is that?" Mac growled. "That sounded like Muller."

"It is Muller."

"The hell it is. Welcome home boy, welcome home. You're just in time to get your head shot off. Gimme that bottle."

Once the rain had slackened we tore down our pup tent, threw all our blankets together and lay talking and pulling at the bottle of cognac until it was empty. Mac went to sleep, snoring lustily. Soon Morrie's steady breathing testified that he'd followed suit.

I was left awake with my thoughts, and a wave of bitterness swept over me. Jeannie, who professed to care so much seemed to have deserted me without a word. She knew how I felt. If I were in her place, nothing could have kept us apart. She who loved me so deeply dropped it all at a word from her family. Well, to hell with her. God damn her; damn all women. I hoped she'd rot in hell. No, I didn't. I loved her, and no matter how she treated me, I'd always love her. I'd die before I'd let any harm come to her. God, why couldn't she just write me a note? I lay there struggling with my thoughts until I finally dropped off to sleep.

A crashing roar and the night was made hideous by a gigantic deluge of sound—our guns. They'd started the preparatory bombardment, the prelude to our attack. I looked at my watch—near midnight. The noise of the guns guaranteed no one would get any more sleep. The replacements looked at each other, alarmed. If friendly artillery sounded like this, what must enemy shellfire be like?

The captain approached, a shadowy form in the darkness. "Have the men make combat packs and be ready to fall in in half an hour."

We were going over light, so we'd leave our blanket rolls here. The men stumbled and fell over each other preparing to move, partly because of the darkness and partly because the concussions of the guns rattled their brains and disoriented them. With the gun flashes so bright and so close together it was like someone opening and closing a gigantic shutter against the sun. Everyone was half blinded. Mac stumbled into me and grabbed my arm to keep from falling.

"How much bombardment do we get?" I asked.

"I dunno, Judy. Five or six hours, I guess, but it won't be so bad after we get out on the road."

"I hope not. In these woods it's just about like sitting on the gun carriage."

The captain's whistle sounded, we fell in and were once again on our way to battle. As we emerged from the woods and gained the open country, the artillery fire seemed less disturbing. A brisk shower pelted down upon us, and we were soon well spattered with the gray mud of the road.

A couple hours' march brought us to the town of Beaumont. We turned to the right, proceeded a few hundred yards, and fell out along the road. The mouth of the communication trench showed, a deeper shadow than the surrounding blackness. Those of us familiar with the sector exchanged knowing glances. This trench joined the front line at Seicheprey, directly in front of Montsec, a gentle looking hill a little over twelve hundred feet high. That may not sound like much, but trying to scale it with machine guns bearing down on you made all the difference.

We lay along the road in the rain and watched the shells burst high on the side of the mountain, twinkling and winking like fireflies. The flashes showed singly or by twos and threes, at times a flurry of perhaps a half dozen or more. Lucky for us, not a single enemy shell had come over yet.

The skipper came along to remind us to look to the men's equipment. We wouldn't have much chance to see to anything after we left here. We inspected each man's ammunition, looked for full canteens, and repeated oft-given instructions. I looked over the new men in particular, noting the look of fear in their eyes. I was inclined to give them some friendly advice, but I changed my mind. Better to make them angry. Get them sore. That was the thing. I strutted up and down in front of the section and in a voice full of arrogant sarcasm, I growled, "You better suck up your guts, you guys. You gotta wipe your own noses today. Your mamas ain't gonna be with you, and I'm gonna be busy." Growls and curses let me know I'd hit the right nerve. I smiled.

Mac sidled up to me. "Smart, ain'tcha?"

"Like a carload of foxes."

The first platoon moved out, and we rose and followed in single file. We entered the communications trench and moved through the inky black darkness. Thousands of men moved in the same direction, all bent on the same objective. But to what end? Some to death, some to mutilation, some to glory, and some just going to work.

An hour later, I sat on the bottom of the front line trench smoking a cigarette. Over our parapet shells passed with a continual swish and howl. I took a big drink from my canteen and leaned over on my elbow. God damn it. Water up to my shoulder. I stood up in the trench. A slight lull in the shellfire preceded a sudden, steady rolling crash. Fountains of earth spurted up in front of our wire. The barrage had begun. Now we would go. I looked up and down the line to make sure everyone was out before I went. This wasn't the old outfit. This was the flower of the nation, so we had to watch out that none of the posies wilted and dropped off. A whistle. Over we went. I looked down the section and saw a man hanging back. He caught my eye and crawled out. Another who'd turned back saw me and turned about. Mac collared him, and I climbed out of the trench.

Our barrage was so thick it was like a solid mass of earth being thrown up by the shells instead of separate shell bursts. This was the thickest barrage I'd ever seen, lovely in its promise of protection and security to those who followed. Smoke shells started to fall, and quickly a solid white wall of vapor shielded us from enemy eyes. We moved steadily forward, the white wall nearly solid red at the bottom from shell bursts. Artillery markers, like sky rockets, burst at the crest of the smoke screen. The whole spectacle stretched as far as the eye could see. I watched the horribly beautiful scene with admiration, thrilled to my soul by the gigantic might of it. Ah. True enough. We damn war lovers did have our high moments.

"Keep moving. Don't gang up. Close over to the right a little there, not too fast now, not too fast." I herded my section along, lucky so far not to have heard a hostile shot. The drizzle continued. Mac abruptly cut off at an angle to the left with a squad of men. I watched as an enemy figure appeared at the rim of a shell hole, hands high, then another and another. Finally a whole section emerged to be taken prisoner and sent to the rear. We continued to move ahead behind that magnificent barrage. Nothing happened except Red Conlon fell in a shell hole full of water and came out cursing and shivering. I fished in my gas mask bag and gave him the cherry brandy left over from filling my canteen. He took a big drink and handed the bottle back for me to take a drink.

"Thanks, Judy." His eyes twinkled. "I've got a canteen full myself."

"Why you son-of-a-bitch. You get to take the first machine gun we see, just for that."

We advanced almost a half mile with no opposition, the tension increasing with every step. I was sure we'd get it when they did open up.

We climbed a slight rise with our barrage still thundering ahead of us, the ground slippery from the rain. What was that? I thought I saw movement on the edge of a shell hole ahead. There it was again. Ah, a hand waving a handkerchief. Two hands appeared, followed by the figure of a man. Red looked my way.

"That's my meat, Judy. You said the first one."

Another figure appeared as Red covered the hole with his chau-chau. Soon there were nine of them standing on the lip of the hole with their hands up, two badly wounded. Five others lay in the bottom of the hole, the result of our barrage. I felt over the live ones for concealed weapons.

"Parlez-vous Anglais?" I asked.

"I speak a leetle bit," answered a tall, good looking Deutschlander.

I motioned to the figures in the hole. "Any of them alive?"

"No. Alles tot."

"What's wrong here that you aren't shooting at us?"

"All have gone but us," he answered. "We they leave behind with machine guns to stop you. You are too many. Your barrage is too thick. We shoot, you kill us. Maybe we not shoot, you not kill us. We not shoot."

"That's logical. You no shoot, we no kill."

They gathered around and gave us their watches, rings and money. We cut the suspender buttons off their pants and sent them back with one man, not so much to guard them as to keep anyone from shooting them. The information they gave us was encouraging. We topped a slight incline and descended a steep bank to the edge of a creek known as the Rupt de Mad.

On the far side lay rubble piles marking the site of the ruined village of Richecourt. Overgrown with weeds and bushes, it was an ideal place for a machine gun emplacement. Sure enough, as we started to ford the stream a light fire crackled from the other side — very thin. No one was hit yet. We fired a few bursts from our automatic rifles at suspicious looking spots and waited. Mac sent a flanking party out to draw their fire so we could locate the guns. We waited a few minutes, but nothing happened, then a shout from the ruins, "Hello, Americans!"

"Hello yourself," shouted Mac.

"We give up," cried the voice from across the creek.

"Come out with your hands up," Mac yelled

They filed out until thirty-six prisoners stood on the other side of the stream. We moved across the creek, and they showed us where their six guns were. The normal procedure was followed before we sent them back.

Captain Weyandt, coming from the right, probably saw us with the prisoners and purposely delayed his arrival until we had them properly looted, then sent us on an oblique cut to the right. We were right on the bottom slope of Montsec now. Cutting to the right would take us around the base of the hill instead of climbing directly up.

We followed instructions, altering our course. The barrage stopped. We were past the extreme range of the 75s now and only the most advanced of our guns could reach us. This would be Indian style fighting if there was any. We encountered a few enemy groups, but most gave up without any resistance. Here and there was some thin ineffective fire, but in only one case did we have to fight to subdue them. Our section had only lost one man.

After climbing a gentle slope, we entered the remains of the village of Montsec at the bottom of the right slope of the hill. Orders were to stand fast and let the next wave push past us. Once that happened, we formed the reserve. Instead of advancing in combat formation, we moved along a road in columns of squads, marching and resting at intervals. A column of cavalry dashed past, spattering us with mud.

"Lie down, doughboy, and rest your feet," they shouted. "This is our war now."

"Go ahead," cried someone. "We loosened 'em up. You chase 'em."

All through the night we advanced in the same way. Some time early in the morning we deployed in a line and started to dig in, having advanced a good many miles and pinched the St Mihiel salient completely out of existence. The company lost only fourteen men and, to our good fortune, the enemy had pulled out of the sector with practically no resistance, leaving us in undisputed possession. Along with the outfits on both flanks, our men dug all day so that by nightfall we had a fairly respectable front line. Tonight barbed wire would go up, and for many nights thereafter.

CHAPTER XXXIII

NONSARD WOODS
SEPTEMBER, 1918

We weren't to be bothered working on the barbed wire, though. About midnight, we were relieved and marched back to take up reserve positions deep in the Nonsard Woods.

Mac looked the platoon over as we settled in to whatever comfort we could find.

"Boy, that's what I call a nice war. Two days driving and we only lost three men." That was Morrie Muller.

Red Conlon lay on the ground with his pack for a pillow. "I'll say. I never looked for anything like that. I was set for a hell of a flight."

"Me, too. I never dreaded anything like I did this. My God, with the fortifications they had! And those hills! Hell, those babies could have held us off for a month." I took off my boots, stripped my worn out socks, and reached in my pack for a spare. "I figured Montsec would be my dying place."

"What're you guys squallin' about?" demanded Mac. "I'm damn well satisfied."

The four of us started a stud game, which soon expanded to eight hands. Nearly everyone had fared well with the prisoners. I was over twelve hundred francs richer as a result of the advance, not to mention several watches, half a dozen rings and three iron crosses. We played cards and lay in our pup tents during the day and sent working parties out at night.

One afternoon a few days later, I wandered back along a road toward the rear. The rain had stopped and the day was intermittently bright and cloudy. During a bright spell I sat down beside the road, enjoying the sunshine. Across the way was a little shack, just a thrown-up pile of boards and two-by-fours. As I watched, the door swung open and a YMCA girl set up a table in front. She put out packages of cookies on one end and a pile of cups on the other. Pretty soon men begin to gather around for cookies and chocolate, mostly replacements, homesick kids for whom the past operation was a great battle instead of something like a marathon race. I smiled at their naïveté.

I watched the young woman taking care of these poor lost boys—not too bad looking, probably reminded the recruits of the girl back home. A chill breeze stirred the trees as I regarded the scene, taking an occasional drink from my canteen. Then I rose and moved along the road for about a mile, but it looked like it led to nowhere, so I turned and retraced my steps. When I got back to the hut, the troops were all gone and the girl, sitting in the doorway, looked up as I approached.

"Would you care for some hot chocolate, sergeant?" she asked. Chocolate wasn't much in my line, but I stepped closer and made myself comfortable, sitting on the other end of the table. "Where're all the heroes?"

She gave me a shy grin. "They've all gone for supper, I think. Won't you have a cup of chocolate?"

"Well, just a wee drop if you have any left."

"I'm sure I have a little."

As I followed her into the shack, she looked around in dismay. "Oh, sergeant, you're not allowed to come in here. Don't you know that?"

"Yes," I replied smiling at her alarm. "I have heard of that, but it doesn't apply to me. It only applies to those who comply with it."

She handed me the cup of chocolate. "Don't you obey orders? I thought all sergeants obeyed orders."

"We do in line of duty. This order deals with my personal liberty. I only obey orders like that when they can be enforced."

"Well, can't this one be enforced?" She looked a little scared.

"Not very well."

"Why not?"

"Well, suppose I sit down in here with you and someone reports me. What can be done about it?"

"You could be court martialed."

"Yes, yes. Go on. And?"

"And put in the guard house."

"Which would be a welcome improvement over the front."

She hesitated as the irony dawned. "Yes, I guess it would."

"You needn't be alarmed, though. I just stepped in to save you the job of bringing the chocolate out."

"It's nice to have company," she said quietly, "but it could cause trouble."

"You had plenty of company a little while ago."

"Oh, yes. Yes, too much—all talking at once."

"Yeah, I noticed. And all killing the enemy by the thousands for your benefit."

She laughed. "How many thousands have you killed, sergeant?"

I held up my hand and counted on my fingers. "Aracourt sector, Toul sector, Montdidier sector, Cantigny attack, Soissons-Saizerais sector attack and now this farce. I leave the war at the front, my lady. In the rear I like to talk to pretty girls, drink good brandy, eat good food, rest and relax. The heroes who talk loudest in the rear have seldom been near the front."

"My, you really have been to the wars," she said, getting up and moving out the door toward the edge of the road. She looked down the road in both directions. I took advantage of her absence to down a big drink of brandy and followed her to the roadside.

"How far up the road were you?" she asked.

"About a mile."

"Did you see a YMCA truck anywhere?"

"No."

"A truck is supposed to come and take me back to Toul before dark. I wish they'd come soon. I wouldn't want to spend the night here."

"I can think of more pleasant places. But still you have a good roof, and with plenty of blankets, you shouldn't be so bad off."

We moved back and sat down in the doorway of the hut. Soldiers passing along the road glanced at us from time to time, probably wondering how I got so lucky.

"How long have you been in France?" she asked.

"Over thirteen months."

"Goodness! I didn't know anyone had been over here that long yet. Don't you ever get homesick?"

"Not me, lady. I'm at home wherever I am. I like France. I like the people. I like the customs. In short, I like everything about the place."

"But you wouldn't want to live here, would you?"

"Why not?"

"Why, because you're an American. Surely that means something to you."

"Nationalities don't mean anything. I can have a good time in any language. I can't see that an American is any happier than a Frenchman or that either is happier than a Dutchman or a Brit."

"You're not very loyal to your country then, are you?" I caught a tone of reproof.

"Everyone is more or less loyal to their native country, because that's what we're taught from childhood. It's not that our country treats us any better than any other country treats its people. If a person has any talent or ability to sell, he can sell it in any country in the world and maybe receive better treatment from a foreign nation than from his own."

"Why, sergeant, you sound almost treasonable!" She was clearly shocked at my sentiments.

"It's not treason to see things as they really are. I've just been around a little bit and have learned to see though the pretty lies people tell. Politicians are the biggest liars in the world."

"If that's how you feel, why do you fight for your country?."

I laughed. "I don't fight for my country. I fight to keep from being killed."

"I know, but why did you enlist in the first place?"

"Because it offered a chance to see new things and places, a chance to get around. I don't want to slave my life away in some factory just to retire on a pension with a stoop to my shoulders and a hump on my back."

She digested this in silence for a few minutes, then looked up and asked, "How old are you, sergeant?"

"I'll be twenty-three next January."

"Well for goodness sake. Here I am listening to a lecture by a man two years younger than I. I took you for much older."

"How much older?"

"Oh, at least forty."

"Yugh! I've been told that before."

It was growing dark and I got up to leave. The young woman didn't say anything, but I knew she wasn't anxious to be left alone.

"Well, I'll have to shove off. If I see any YMCA people, I'll tell them about you."

"I wish you would," she answered. "Good-bye."

"So long. If you're still here, I'll see that you get some blankets later."

As I moved along the road I reflected on how tough it'd be for her to have to spend the night alone in that shack. In fact, I didn't think I should let that happen. How would I feel if that were Jeanne? I figured to check on her later and see what I could do to make her comfortable.

Supper was in full swing when I got back to the outfit so I got my mess kit and took my place at the end of the line.

"Where you been?" Mac asked as I sat down beside him.

"Back the road a piece."

"What's back there, anything?"

"Not a damn thing. What's on tonight? Any working parties?"

"Yeah, several. You're gonna take a party out with two truckloads of barbed wire if that's what you want to know."

That was what I wanted to know all right, but it was not what I wanted to hear. I stalled around for a while, hoping the night's plans might change but I was doomed to disappointment.

At the appointed time I went to the company headquarters tent, where a squad waited for me. Stubby gave me my instructions. "Take these men and meet two trucks of barbed wiah at the crossroads near Nonsard. The truck drivers know where to go. Your detail will unload the wiah and the trucks will bring you back."

"Okay." I turned to the men. "Come on, soldiers. Let's go."

As we marched single file to the road, I kept a sharp lookout for Red Conlon or Morrie Muller. I finally spied Red lolling at the edge of the road, apparently nothing on his mind, as usual, so I called him over.

He saw me coming and growled, "No, I won't take your detail tonight. Outside of that, what do you want?"

"Go to hell. I wasn't gonna ask you to take my detail. I was gonna put you wise to something."

"I bet it's good if you're gonna tell me about it." Always the skeptic, Red.

"Well, shut up and listen. I haven't got much time."

"Go ahead. I'm all ears."

I took his arm and moved out of earshot of my working party. "D'you know where that shack is that stands along the road about a half mile to the rear?"

"Yeah, I know the place. What about it?"

"Well, I was back there this afternoon. There was a YMCA girl still there when I left at dark. Her truck hadn't come for her yet. Probably hasn't come at all. I told her I'd see that she got some blankets and now I get screwed into this working party. It'd be pretty risky for her to spend the night alone back there, wouldn't it?"

"I'll tell the world it would."

"Well, just grab a couple of blankets and slide back there. This damn working party has me tied up or I'd take care of it myself."

He laughed. "I'll see what I can do to comfort her. Hooray for working parties!"

"Oh, you go to hell," I told him as I moved away and joined my detail.

He disappeared into the dark woods and in a short time our trucks rumbled up the road and stopped.

CHAPTER XXXIV

MEUSE-ARGONNE
SEPTEMBER-OCTOBER, 1918

The next morning, somewhere far to the west we rattled along the road in empty trucks. The barbed wire unloaded, we arrived back at the company area in time for breakfast. The sun wasn't up yet, but a glow in the east foretold its early appearance as we de-trucked. I went to my hole, picked up soap and a towel, and followed a path to a small creek to freshen up before breakfast. As I approached the stream, someone was there ahead of me, stripped to the waist, scrubbing himself vigorously—Red Conlon, his face and neck a mass of scratches. Some of his wounds looked like teeth marks.

"Where the hell have you been? To an earthquake or something?"

He looked at me, terror in his eyes, like a child caught in a lie.

"I was back to that shack," he said.

"Was she still there?"

He nodded soberly. Then awash in remorse, he burst out, "My God, Judy, I'm sorry! I shouldn't have done it. Why didn't I leave her alone? I went back there to help her, but the longer I stayed, the less control I had. It just happened, Judy! It just happened."

Jesus Christ! Rape! I took a step back, feeling sorry for this shaking mass of regret standing in front of me. The MPs would

278

probably be here before noon. I tried to offer comfort but was overcome by the gravity of what I knew must have happened.

"What's the matter? I mean, did she go along—at least a little bit?"

"No. She fought so hard and was so scared. God, I wish I'd never gone back there."

Touched by his regret and horrified that I'd had any part in it, I tried to soothe him. "Well, you know these girls who come over here trying to do good should have some idea of the risks they take. Makes you wonder what the organizers of these do-gooders are thinking. There's not much can be done about it now. War is hell, and it makes monsters of us. "

He regarded me in silence before returning to his washing. I took off my shirt and rolled up my sleeves. Red suddenly straightened up.

"Listen, Judy, you know it was rape, don't you? My God. I raped that girl."

The anguish in his voice tore at my heart, and I pictured the girl—God knew where now—curled up crying in a corner somewhere.

I did realize it was rape, and I felt partly to blame for setting Red up, but I didn't see how heaping guilt on him now would change anything. I hoped the young woman had the strength to get over this, but Red beating himself up over it wouldn't change a thing.

"Look, Red, you just got carried away. It's been a long time since you. . . . I know. War messes up your mind—makes you do things you never thought you'd do."

He refused to be comforted, lost in remorse, so we dried ourselves in silence.

"Here, roll some of this over your tonsils. It'll make you feel better." I offered my canteen. As he drank, I continued. "She came over of her own free will, didn't she?"

He nodded, handing the canteen back.

"Well, by God, I guess if you want to go visit war, you'd better be ready to see the awful side of it, too. Hell's fire, giving recruits chocolate and cookies ain't worth nothin.' She put herself in harm's way, that's all. I'm not saying it was right, but she had something to do with it, too. I wonder why the YMCA sets a girl up like that. They left her there, didn't they? They should take better care of people in their charge."

All the while I tried not to think of the girl—well-meaning though she was—being overpowered by someone as big and burly as Red. God help her. I liked Red, relied on him in a fight, but this was way more than I could understand. Still, I was pretty sure the Germans would exact their toll when the time came.

I followed him as he walked back through the woods, head down, almost running into Mac on the path near the kitchen. Red merely nodded, engrossed in regret. Mac looked questioningly at me and jerked his thumb in Red's direction.

"What the hell's wrong with him? Who stepped on his face?"

"We were tusslin' down at the creek and he slipped and fell down the bank on his mug." It was a half-way plausible answer. "Slid the whole way down. Don't think he missed a stone on the way."

My explanation satisfied Mac for the moment, so that story would go the rounds of the company. But Red'd have to lie low for a few days in case the MPs got wind of his adventures. Later on, I strolled up the road to the hut and found it deserted. If the woman did talk, it'd take time for an investigation to get under way. Besides, in a few days anything could happen in a war.

We were soon relieved and moved out of our position in the woods. Glad to put that shack by the side of the road in my dust, I knew I shared the guilt, but I also knew I had to get on with whatever was left of my life. The night we left the roads in the back area were heavily bombed. Gothas and Taubes came over in droves, drenching dumps and heavily traveled roads with their loads of explosives. Anti-aircraft batteries blasted away at full speed. Occasionally, a searchlight picked out a plane moving high in the air. It made a beautiful spectacle, like a gigantic silver fish twisting and turning to escape the beam of light into the protective darkness.

We bivouacked in a forest not far from Toul, and all I wanted was to get away long enough to pay René Trevost another visit. "How long are we gonna be here, d'you know, Stub?"

"I don't know exactly, sawjint. Why?"

"Well, I need to see a guy over at one of the hospitals if we'll be here long enough." Stubby and I were old friends, so I wasn't shy about telling him what was on my mind.

"We won't leave befo' tonight, ah'm sure of that. Is that long enough?"

"Plenty."

"Well, watch the MPs, and bring me back a bottle of Three Star."

"Okay." I gave him a wave and hurried back to my tent to gather my gear for the trip. Toul wasn't more than four miles away, and in less than an hour I was escorted into René's room at the hospital. My guide was a smiling nurse on whom I practiced my French as we walked down the long avenue between the buildings which housed the wards. We found the convalescent René propped up in a wheel chair, allowed to wander around wherever his interests might take him. Obviously glad to see me, he extended a cordial hand.

"Ah, sergeant," he smiled, "I am glad you received my letter."

"What letter? I didn't get any letter."

"Why, I wrote you over a week past requesting that you visit me as soon as possible. Naturally when I saw you, I thought you had come in response to my request."

"Well I haven't gotten it yet, but you know how it is, moving around like we do."

"Yes, yes. It is to be wondered at that mail ever overtakes us." He paused, then continued. "I suppose you are preparing for the big drive."

"What big drive?" I haven't heard of any proposed drive since the one at St Mihiel.

"Oh, you Americans are going to make another big attack late this month. Haven't you heard about it? Everyone else seems to know."

"Does the enemy know about it yet?"

"Oh yes, very likely he does. He generally gets wind of these things before anyone else."

We shared a laugh before he got serious. "Have you heard from Jeanne?" he asked.

"Not a word. I was hoping you'd heard from her."

He produced a bottle from under his lap robe. "You see, I have expected you, sergeant. We may as well be comfortable."

He poured me a drink and filled his own glass. I watched him with impatience, for it was obvious he had news. I downed my drink in silence. He sat gazing at the glass of whiskey, turning it absently in his fingers as if measuring what he would say.

Finally, he began to speak. "Sergeant, what would you say if I were to tell you that Jeanne is dead?"

"Oh, my God!" I jumped to my feet. "She can't be dead!"

"No." His countenance was sober. "She is not dead, but we are afraid that she is the same as dead as far as we are concerned."

"Why? She was perfectly healthy the last time I saw her. What's wrong? Where is she?"

"Well, sergeant, it's this way. In this war people are called upon to play strange roles. The women of my country do not hold themselves aloof when an occasion arises for them to render service. Such an occasion arose for Jeanne and she volunteered her services without hesitation. As time passed she grew more and more proficient in her work and was entrusted with missions of great importance. Jeanne is a very intelligent and resourceful woman and she has developed into a full fledged operative. Her work is very dangerous, and for that reason we are afraid that she is at present in danger of death."

"What sort of work?" I asked, weary of formality and circumspection. "Is she a spy?"

"Ah, sergeant, the very nature of it makes me hesitate to tell even you, tried soldier though I know you to be."

He pondered for a moment. I got up and paced in front of his chair, then returned to my seat, as with a gesture, he continued.

"Remember, sergeant, what I am about to disclose to you is strictly confidential. You must promise it will never be repeated to anyone. Not even to your most trusted superior officers. Not now or ever. Even after this war is over, these things could still have repercussions. It is for Jeanne's safety that I demand this secrecy of you. Do you promise?"

"With all my heart," I assured him.

"Yes? That is good. Now I will tell you. My little sister, Jeanne, is an espionage agent in the service of France. For the past eighteen months she has been detailed on work of great importance and unusual danger. She has been very successful in obtaining information. Her work has dealt generally with political and other than military information. In the past year and a half, she has traveled to Germany, Switzerland, Spain, Belgium, and Italy. Her latest assignment took her into Luxembourg."

My God, my Jeanne, a spy! The gentle, refined, cheerful girl I'd fallen in love with—a full-fledged espionage agent! Unbelievable. No government could be so callous as to send a defenseless creature like her on dangerous, death defying missions. Suddenly, in my mind's eye I saw the half-forgotten picture of the front. Dead piled in heaps and lying in rows, blood tinted mud, the screaming wounded and the dying, beating, kicking and biting the ground in their agony. Governments would stop at nothing to achieve their objectives. That was war. I looked at Rene, my feelings written all over my face.

"Oh, yes, sergeant," said René quietly. "That is war."

"But where is she now? What have you heard from her? Doesn't anybody know anything?"

"As I said," Rene continued with irritating calm, "her last mission was to Luxembourg. It has long been thought that the Grand Duchess holds pro-German sympathies and that she allows the movement of troops and supplies across a state that heretofore we have considered neutral. If this were proven to be true, Luxembourg's neutrality would be at an end and we could do something about it openly. Jeanne's mission is to secure information to prove these rumors. She left France seven weeks ago. Three weeks ago, her last carrier pigeon arrived, bearing the message that she'd been successful and was even then coming home. Ten days ago, my father returned home and received a message from the chief of her service stating that she had been captured and was being held prisoner. You know what that means."

Yes, I knew what that meant, but surely they wouldn't shoot a woman. Like hell they wouldn't. Didn't they shoot Edith Cavell? Didn't the allies shoot Mata Hari? Some had even been shot by their own divisions. As usual, when deeply disturbed I jumped to my feet and started pacing. Christ, we had to do something.

"Where've they got her? Do you know?"

My French broke down under the stress and I reverted to American slang.

"Hell's Fire," I fumed, "we gotta do something. We can't just sit here like frogs on a log."

He waved a weak hand. "Sit down, sergeant, sit down. You are like a caged tiger pacing back and forth. You would frighten the devil himself."

So wrought up, I refused to sit, but I did stop pacing and stood leaning on the back of my chair.

"Now sergeant," he said, "my father instructed me to tell you that in view of what has happened he has decided to accede to Jeanne's request that her betrothal be terminated. We now regard you as her chosen fiancé, and as such you will be informed of any new developments as they take place. Now, as to what has been done. My father, as a government official, is not without influence. We had many friends in Germany before the war, some in government circles. My father has appealed to these friends to use their influence to save Jeanne's life."

"Several answers have been received, all couched in the most cordial terms, all promising to do everything possible. But none have held out much hope. You see, the information which Jeanne has secured is of such a nature that if it is made public the enemy will be further discredited among neutral nations. This is something Germany cannot stand, and while I hope with all my soul that I am wrong, I am afraid that they will take the one sure method of suppressing Jeanne's information."

As René finished speaking I stood in silence, a hundred plans flashing through my mind, all of them futile. There was nothing we could do. I had wild thoughts of slipping over behind the enemy lines and rescuing Jeanne. That's how it would happen in the movies, but unfortunately this wasn't a movie. Then there was the fact that no one had the slightest idea where she was. I pictured her in irons in some dungeon. Then I saw her pacing the floor in a bare, cold room at some military headquarters, half starved and brutally treated by her captors. As these things passed through my mind, I reached a frenzy of rage at my helplessness.

Rene watched me, sympathy in his eyes. "Sergeant," he said at length, "I know how you feel, but everything that can be done is being done. My father is nearly mad with anxiety. He has lost two sons in the war and now is in danger of losing his only daughter. We have had to learn to bear our sorrows, we Trevosts, but this is too much."

I rose and placed my hand on his shoulder. He looked up with a sorrowful smile. I wanted to say something to express my feelings but there was nothing to say.

Finally, Rene broke the silence. "You know, Sergeant Judee, you and Jeanne have had my sympathy all the time. I had hoped that something would happen to break up that old arrangement. I need not tell you that I have never hoped for anything like this, though. I can assure you that if she does come through, the way is cleared for the two of you. My father gave his word to that effect when her fiancé did not respond to his summons to come see him when he first got this news."

Under any other circumstances such a revelation would have made me extremely happy. As it was, I could only nod dumbly. It was getting late and I had to think about getting back to the outfit. I hated to leave. With Jeanne in danger I needed to be with her people in their distress. I felt bound to them by common grief, but the war had no respect for personal feelings, and I either had to rejoin my outfit or desert. I would have done that willingly if it could have benefited Jeanne.

René poured drinks for us both. "It is growing late, sergeant. Have you far to go?"

"Not very far. Are you sure there's nothing I can do?"

"Nothing, sergeant. Nothing. Go back to your regiment. You are helpless here. I will try to inform you of every development.

Come and see me when you can." We shook hands as I left. "Good-bye, sergeant, and take care of yourself."

CHAPTER XXXV

MEUSE-ARGONNE
OCTOBER, 1918

René's parting words echoed as I moved down the hall. I walked along the road back to camp in a daze, my mind numb from the shock. I wondered about Jeanne, my mind conjuring horrible scenes. Would she get a trial? A fair trial? Even at that moment she could be sitting accused before some military court on the other side of the lines. Even then she could be marching out between two guards to face a firing squad. Torn by anxiety, I made my way along the road, insensible to all that passed. In this condition, I nearly bumped into two soldiers walking in the opposite direction.

"Christ, he's drunk as a boiled owl. Hey, Judy, wake up!"

I looked up to find Mac and Morrie Muller gazing at me, questioning.

"What the hell's the matter, Judy? You look like you've seen a ghost." Mac asked. "I thought you were drunk."

"No. I've just been to see Jeanne's brother. She's very sick. Not expected to live."

"Well, you don't say. No damn wonder you act like a sleep walker."

They teemed with sympathy. Morrie hadn't met Jeanne, but the story of our love affair had spread all over the company, so he knew about her.

"Where you guys goin'?" I asked, more to change the subject than for information.

"Oh, just down the road to get a few drinks," answered Morrie. "Come along and drown your troubles."

I suddenly remembered that bottle of cognac I'd promised Stubby, so I turned and headed off down the road with them.

The company stayed in the same location—no orders to move. We spent the time practicing with machine guns and automatic rifles and drilling the men in combat formations. I was getting to know the new men pretty well. At first I resented their naïve disrespect, but now I understood a little better. All they asked was to be allowed to live a peaceful life. They were mostly salt of the earth types—willing to earn their living by the sweat of their brow. For them, this war was a catastrophe, an interruption in their lives. A few were inclined to be contrary, questioning every aspect of military life, but most of them cooperated and tried to be good soldiers. They weren't a bad lot once you got to know them. Take Mr. Spence, with whom I'd had a slight disagreement before the St Mihiel drive—now a corporal in my section. I smiled as I watched him make his squad toe the line.

The weather was cold and the rains set in, so—of course—we got orders to move. We loaded our trucks, and in about four hours unloaded near a village called Rignaucourt, not far from Verdun. As the dawn broke, cold, wet and cheerless, I surveyed our surroundings. From the sound of the guns and the amount of traffic on the roads, we were still quite a ways in the rear. It looked like an enormous concentration of troops, probably the offensive Rene spoke of.

The supply service was hard put to distribute rations to so great a number, so meals were late and in some cases missed all together. The countryside was saturated, everything soaked by the rain. Our blankets were a sodden mass, and the ground where we tried to sleep was cold and wet. Misery was written on every face. My state of mind, coupled with the physical hardships, deepened into depression.

Jeanne and her plight were always on my mind. No matter what task I was engaged in or how engrossed I was in getting something done, my brain was preoccupied with her. At night, as I lay in my soggy blankets, I closed my eyes and she invaded my consciousness, and concern for her safety pushed me to rise and pace up and down in the rain. If only there were some news! But no. Such prisoners couldn't communicate with anyone. Unless she escaped, nothing would ever be heard from her again until we learned of her execution from some of our agents.

Such thoughts filled my mind with uncontrollable rage. I longed for something to fight—to rip and tear and beat down. To me, the enemy became monsters bent on destroying the one thing in the world I treasured. Now my personal enemies, I wanted to rend and kill—do bodily harm—to see their blood run and hear their cries of anguish. Beside myself with fury, I realized it did no good. It only left me weak and spent and accomplished nothing.

After one such sleepless night, I went for a walk along the road toward the front sometime after daybreak. I walked about two miles from camp and as I retraced my steps I came upon a dejected-looking figure, one of the new men, sitting along the road.

"Hello, sergeant."

"Hello, son. What are you doing way over here?"

"There's no breakfast this morning, and I thought I might find a few potatoes in one of these fields." His demeanor spoke of wretched homesickness.

"So there was no breakfast," I said, half to myself. I'd forgotten that I hadn't eaten yet this morning.

Poor kid, sitting there sad and alone. Since I had troubles of my own, it was easier to sympathize with him. "Well, what do you say we have a little breakfast?"

His face brightened immediately. "Swell, sergeant, but how?"

"Just follow me, my boy. I'll show you how these things are done. It's a soldier's first duty to keep his belly full. We can't lick the friend across the way on an empty stomach."

We walked up the road to where one fork led to the village of Rignaucourt and the other kept straight on past to where the outfit was camped. We took the fork into the village.

"Your name's Kennedy isn't it?" I asked.

"That's right, sir"

"Don't call me sir. I work for a living."

He laughed and I saw he was just a kid — fresh off the farm, probably.

"Well, Kennedy, just pick up an empty sand bag from the first pile you see, and I'll show you what can be done about food."

As we approached the first house in the village I maneuvered to keep the outhouses in line between us and the house. I cocked my head to listen and was rewarded by the sound of chickens clucking as they foraged for bugs in the barnyard. I made a clucking sound as I'd so often heard the French women do when they called the chickens to feed. We didn't have long to wait. The chickens came trooping around the corner of the outhouse where I waited until three or four came within easy reach, then grabbed one, swung her by the neck and felt it give. I stuffed her hurriedly into the empty sand bag, threw it over my shoulder, and we went sedately on our way. As we passed the house, a buxom madam stood framed in the doorway, seeing nothing more suspicious than a couple of soldiers making their way unhurriedly up the road.

"Bonjour, madame," I called. "What price chickens?" I said under my breath. Kennedy nearly gave the show away with laughter but kept it in until we were out of earshot.

Taking a roundabout route out of the village, we hurried to the company, where we dug out our mess kits. I wangled a chunk of bread and a lump of butter from the mess sergeant and we wandered out to a little valley opposite camp and had a breakfast of fried chicken. After we'd eaten our fill and sat back to have a smoke, I gave the boy some excellent military advice. "Now that you see how it's done, don't ever let me see you going hungry again."

He grinned. "I'll try not to, but ain't a fellow liable to get in trouble?"

"Hell," I replied, "if you know of any worse trouble than soldiering on an empty stomach, bring it on." Then I thought to myself, 'Yes, I know a far worse trouble than an empty stomach, but he'll have to find that out for himself.'

Sometime after noon, I encountered the skipper striding down the muddy path in camp. "Keep the men close. Things are due to happen soon. By the way, sergeant, how do you like being shock troops?"

"Is that what we are, sir?"

"Why sure. Haven't you noticed? We haven't been to the front since July, except to take part in a big attack."

"Well, I guess it's all right, sir, as long as we don't get shocked too much. I can't say much for the present accommodations, though."

"Neither can I." He laughed, giving me a pat on the shoulder as he moved away.

During the night, anyone lucky enough to be able to sleep was awakened by a terrific bombardment. It rolled, rumbled and crashed with great intensity, and the horizon lit with flickering gun flashes as far as the eye could see. The great offensive had started.

We lay awake most of the night, smoking and talking. Some of the men built fires and we huddled around them in the rain, listening to the gunfire amid idle speculation about how soon we'd move up. Along about daybreak, the note of the guns changed. We recognized it as barrage fire and knew that upwards of a million men were climbing out of their trenches and advancing to the assault at this moment.

On orders to move up, we broke camp at dusk and hiked forever along the windswept, rain-drenched road. Time after time I pulled at my canteen, but the chill of the night dissipated only to return with twice as much force. I cursed as a gust of wind blew rain in my face and plastered my sodden slicker against my body. The sky had grayed to the east when we finally stopped in a sea of mud just beyond the village of Esnes. We were on the edge of the famous 'Dead Man's Hill', known for the furious fighting that happened there in the assault on Verdun.

Word got around that we were in support of the Fourth Division, but no one was interested. What we wanted to hear about was food. Anxious eyes watch the road for a first glimpse of the rolling kitchen, but no. Probably got caught in traffic, and chances were it was stuck miles in the rear. The road was a solid mass of wagons, trucks, carts and ambulances. They moved but a few yards at a time 'til the whole line was held up and everything stood and waited until they moved again for a rod or so.

Suddenly I heard shells approaching. I recognized the peculiar sound of several coming at once and they landed with a deafening crash up the road about two hundred yards. I saw animals kicking and struggling in the throes of death. Here came another salvo to land in almost the same place. I waited for the next one, but no more came over, so I slogged up the muddy road, trench knife in hand. At the body of the first fallen horse, I knelt down, skinned the nearest hip and cut a big steak off of it. As I carried my prize back to the company, I looked over my shoulder. The body of the horse was completely hidden from sight by screaming figures fighting for food.

The powers that be had evidently decided that the Fourth Division was not in much need of immediate relief so we were sent off to a new destination. Rumor had it that we were moving up behind a division that had made nice initial gains in the assault but couldn't hang on in the face of the smashing enemy counter-attacks. Now they were losing all they'd gained in their first assault.

The sun came out and its warmth raised the men's spirits, to say nothing of drying our clothes. Someone remarked that this date should be marked on the calendar as the first sunny day in weeks. "What date is it, anyway?" asked another.

After much discussion a calendar was secured and it was decided the date was October first.

About mid afternoon we bivouacked near the Cheppy crossroads, instantly welcomed by desultory shellfire from the enemy's 77s, which meant we were getting pretty close to the front.

Mac came by. "How you doin,' Judy?"

"Okay, Mac. What do you know?"

"Not much. I was just talking to the skipper. We're in support here. Nothin' to do unless the outfit that's in there needs help."

"I guess we'll all go over again shortly, though."

Mac nodded. "Oh, no doubt. No doubt. We generally do."

CHAPTER XXXVI

MEUSE-ARGONNE
OCTOBER, 1918

Jeanne

The light of a cold, gray dawn seeped through the windows of a small, barren room. While the faint glow of the coming day dissipated the shadows and brought the meager furnishings into view, it did nothing to dispel the chill. Fog and mist covered the surrounding country, adding to the clammy cold. Apprehension filled the room's lone occupant, a slight form moving restlessly on the bed. She sat up and stared anxiously about, as though afraid she was not alone. The room was empty, a relief. She pulled herself up to the head of the bed and leaned back against the headboard, still wary. She wrapped herself tightly in the bedclothes to keep out the cold and sat staring straight ahead, as though waiting for someone.

She'd been confined to this bare room for weeks, ever since being transported from Luxembourg, her only clothing a nightgown, robe and slippers, while outside her door two booted, helmeted soldiers stood guard with loaded rifles. Under her window stood two more. Her needs were attended to by an aged French peasant woman who was searched before she entered and after she left the room. This old matron cleaned the room, made her bed, tended to her toilet and served her meals. At any moment of the day or night her door might swing open and admit a cadre of German officers, resplendent in their gray uniforms, glittering spurs and shining boots. They fired questions at her singly and in groups until her head spun so that she couldn't have given correct answers if she wanted to. So far she gave only one answer to all the thousands of questions. "I do not know."

She hadn't been physically abused, but the mental strain was intense. Pale and wan, she looked unutterably weary as she leaned back, waiting for her aged attendant. Muddled thoughts raced through her mind. If she could just get one small note out through the lines. If only word could be gotten to her father, René or Judy. She thought of him with a gentle smile, and her expression changed from despair to child-like hope, her lips slightly parted, a look of longing on her face. But as reality intruded, hope faded and a tear made its way down her cheek. Despairing thoughts raced through her mind of the many others of her craft who had silently disappeared, leaving no trace. Would her fate be the same? She'd been offered an alternative, but she was loath to take advantage of it. No. She would let the court martial pronounce its verdict and face the firing squad in the same manner as Jean d'Arc, her namesake and the idol of all French women.

The thought of her young body lying blood-smeared and broken in the cold ground brought a flood of self-pity, and she broke down in quiet sobs. When she regained control she sat up and wiped her eyes on the hem of her nightgown. A key rattled in the door and her aged lady-in-waiting entered.

"Ah, my little chickadee. And how is it this morning? So, you've been weeping. You mustn't weep. If you do, I cannot make you beautiful, and we must have you beautiful for the colonel. He comes again this morning."

"I don't want to see the colonel." Jeanne cut her off short.

"Ah, yes, you must see the colonel. Why, he can save your life."

"Yes. Yes, I know, but at what price?"

"Oh, I don't know. A great many girls would jump at the chance to marry a colonel and here you hesitate about marrying one when it is the only thing that can save you. In my day a girl was not so crazy."

"But mother, he is an enemy, and besides that, I love another."

"Bosh. A man's a man, no matter what his nationality, and I tell you, I could soon learn to love any man that saved my life. There now, let me comb your hair and we'll be ready for breakfast."

Jeanne submitted to the ministrations of the old woman in silence, but the words lingered in her mind. Truly, Colonel Von Boehm could save her from the firing squad. Before the war he was a friend of her family and an ardent, if hopeless, suitor. At about thirty, the eldest son of a proud old German family, he was in command of an intelligence section of the army — proof in itself that his family had abundant influence. A word from him in the proper quarters would unlock the door that confined her. He would not hesitate to say that word if she promised to marry him — he'd assured her of that. Oh, if there were only someone she could turn to for advice. Should she give that promise to save her life?

She thought of Judy and their dreams of a life together. But would he still love her after the war or would he go back home and take up his old life without her? In reality, she hardly knew him. All the time they'd spent together wouldn't amount to more than a week at the most, while she'd known Colonel Von Boehm since childhood.

The old woman gave a final stroke to her hair and stood back, surveying her handiwork. "My, but it shines, ma enfant. The colonel will be more impressed than ever. Now you just wait, child. I'll be back with your food in a wink."

As she left the room, the roll and thunder of the guns sounded louder. Always there in the background, today it sounded even closer than yesterday. The old woman kept bringing rumors that a great American offensive was under way. Jeanne's thoughts turned again to Judy. Was his regiment engaged? Might he even be near? This Army Headquarters was well back from the front, but if she was any judge, the sound of the guns was more distinct this morning than it had been for days. A faint hope sprung in her breast, only to be instantly dispelled. This headquarters would move to the rear long before the assaulting troops came near enough to offer any chance of escape.

The door swung back to admit the old lady, bearing a tray with a few slices of brown bread and a pot of weak coffee. Jeanne didn't feel like eating, but as the tray was placed on her bed, she made a half-hearted effort.

The old one stood by watching, then croaked, "My, the pigs are excited. The battle must be going against them. Well, it's soon time, and I, for one, won't be sorry to see the last of them." She finished with a vehemence common among her countrywomen.

Jeanne gave a little cry of hope at the news. "What is it? What is the news?" she asked, excited.

"There is no news. The dogs don't tell me anything, but they're excited about something. There is a steady stream running in and out of the headquarters building, and last night fresh troops kept passing through on their way to the front."

"But, mother, don't troops often pass through here on the way to the front?"

"Yes, but always there are the worn out men coming back. Last night none came back. Ah, my little robin, and that is not all. Listen."

She cocked her head sideways and held up her finger for silence. Jeanne listened so intently she feared the ringing in her ears would deafen her. The roar of the cannonading was her only reward. But wait! What was that faint insistent hammering, strangely reminiscent of a woodpecker a long way off? There it was again. There was no missing it this time. The rat-tat-tat of machine guns! Faint, but unmistakable.

The old woman's haggard face lit up with venomous glee. She clenched her hands and spit in delight. "Wait, you dogs. Wait just a few hours more. You'll see what you are. For four years I've licked your boots and been your slave. But wait. My time is coming, and it's not far off."

Jeanne, confused by the outburst, asked. "But, mother, I thought you liked these people. You seem to get along so well with them. Just this morning you urged me to marry the colonel."

"Like them?" The old eyes flashed with venom. "I hate them. True, I get along. I urged you, and I still urge you to marry the colonel. To save your life. They will leave before the battle reaches here and take you with them. You have hopes of a trial? Well let me tell you, you've already been tried. If you ever face a court martial, it will be nothing but a sham. You are already tried and sentenced."

Jeanne's heart sank at this pronouncement and she feverishly tried to think of some way out other than marrying a man she didn't love.

Her thoughts were interrupted by the clatter and clump of boots in the hall. The door swung open and one of the sentries stalked into her room, came to a halt with a click of his heels, stood at stiff attention, and announced, "Colonel Ludwig Von Boehm!" He did an about face and strode from the room in the same accentuated military manner.

The colonel was a tall, blond, pleasant-looking man, his uniform immaculate—boots, spurs and accessories shined to perfection. But as he advanced to the side of the bed to greet Jeanne there emerged a human quality not concealed by military formality.

"Well, my dear lady, I trust you've had a good night, considering everything."

He was friendly and solicitous of her comfort, even though he couldn't deny her role as an agent against his country.

"Yes, a good night, considering everything."

He glanced around the room and his eye lit on Jeanne's elderly maid. "Here, grandma." He handed her a folded paper. "Take this to one of the kitchens. You look as though food might interest you."

The woman took the paper, unfolded it and looked at it with suspicion. She folded it again and stalked out the door, a picture of ancient and unbending dignity.

The colonel laughed quietly. "Ah, the nearness of the battle seems to have its affect on her. I've never seen her so independent before."

Jeanne was quick to support her old friend. "Were you in her place, would you not be glad to see the invader driven from your home?"

"Oh, doubtless," he agreed. "But really, we are not going to be driven out. We may fall back here and there to shorten our line and facilitate our defense, but our positions are too strong to collapse."

His confidence gave Jeanne pause and she lowered her head, disappointed. The colonel noticed. "No, my dear, I am afraid help for you from that quarter is impossible. True, the Americans are advancing, but they will only advance as far as we allow them to. Once in the position we ordain, we will snuff out their advance as one snuffs out a candle flame."

"Are they such poor fighters, then that you'll be able to stop them at your pleasure?"

The Colonel smiled a superior smile. "They are fresh. Fresh troops are always keen and successful at first, but once the weariness of war grips them, they'll be easily crushed by our

Imperial Army. But enough of that. I have other news that will be of more interest to you."

Jeanne looked up expectantly. "Such as what? Am I to be tried soon?"

"First, you are to be moved. This Army Headquarters is moving to the rear immediately. Your trial had been set for this afternoon, but due to the change of location, it will probably be postponed until tomorrow."

"Where are we going?"

"That I cannot disclose, but I have arranged for you to be placed under my personal custody, so now I will leave and have your clothes sent to you. I will have transportation here at eleven, and you must be ready."

He bowed over her hand as he took his leave. In a few minutes the old French woman brought in her clothes. The door had no sooner closed behind her than she burst out volubly, "See, what did I tell you? They're leaving. Already some of their guns are moving through the town toward the rear."

"Will you go with us?" Jeanne asked. She'd become attached to the old soul and was genuinely apprehensive for her.

"I will do nothing of the kind. I will stay right here and be the first to grasp the hands of our troops when they enter the village. Leave here now? I should say not!"

As Jeanne dressed she noticed that the seams of her clothing had been ripped apart in a search for more evidence to be used against her. They'd been sewed up again, but clumsily.

"Where am I to be taken, have you heard?"

"Back. That is all I know. But if you would save yourself, you will listen to the colonel."

"But, mother, I don't love him." Anguish filled her voice.

"What's the difference?" cried the old woman. "Let me tell you this. When the firing squad gets through with you, you won't be alive to love anyone. Don't forget, while there's life, there's hope."

A harsh rap on the door interrupted the conversation.

"Who is it?" The old attendant waddled toward the door.

"The colonel waits below. Come."

Jeanne turned to the old lady. "Good-bye, mother, good-bye!" Tears filled the eyes of both as they embraced. "Are you sure you'll be safe?" Even now Jeanne was concerned with the welfare of her aged friend.

"Oh, yes." The old eyes twinkled in reassurance. "I shall hide in the deep wine cellars until the pigs are chased out. But you. You must marry the colonel. It will only be for a time. You can divorce him when the peace is declared."

"Come, please." The call from the hall was insistent. Jeanne hurriedly embraced the old lady for the last time. "Good-bye, mother. Good-bye."

As she stepped out into the hall the two guards fell in on either side of her, keeping step until she got into the back seat of the automobile where the colonel sat waiting. The driver and another guard occupied the front. No chance for escape.

As the car rolled slowly through the only street of the village, neither Jeanne nor the Colonel spoke. Jeanne noticed an abnormal amount of traffic, while here and there columns of smoke from burning supplies appeared on the horizon. The retreating Army was destroying them rather than let them fall into the hands of the Americans. Once clear of the village, the colonel turned to her with an intimate glance. "Comfortable?" he asked.

"Yes, thank you," she replied. "As comfortable as possible under the circumstances."

"My dear Jeanne, you know I want to help you. Have I not already offered to save you from the firing squad?" He spoke barely above a whisper so that the occupants of the front seat couldn't hear him over the noise of the motor.

"Yes, you have, but only on your conditions."

"Ah, that is true, but you understand that the conditions are necessary. I can have your court martial squashed immediately by saying that you are a double agent operating directly under my orders. If we are later to be married, the facts would then bear out my statement. But if I made such an avowal and you were to be freed and subsequently disappeared, never to return, then I would be discredited and probably tried for aiding a known spy to escape custody."

"Oh, but Ludwig." The words came with a rush. "I'm not a known spy. Nothing has been proven against me."

The colonel suppressed a well-bred smile. "My dear, my dear. For a successful espionage agent, you retain a surprising amount of artlessness. Surely you must realize that your movements have been watched for some time. For the past year, you have been the subject of unremitting surveillance on the part of our counter-espionage department."

The girl looked at him, shocked to learn she wasn't as successful at evading detection as she'd thought. True, she knew of hundreds of cases where spies were set to watch other spies. It'd never occurred to her, though, that she might be the object of such scrutiny.

He read her look and continued. "To prove my statement, I should tell you just where you were and what you did while under surveillance."

He produced a notebook from his pocket. "These notes were just taken at random from my files. Shall I read them to you, or would you rather read them yourself?"

"Let me read it myself." She reached for the book.

"There will be no point in destroying it. This is just what I copied in order to assure you that you have no chance with a court martial."

Dismayed, she perused the pages. Sure enough, the facts were there. Enough to prove her guilty in the eyes of even the most favorable of courts. She hadn't a chance. Every damning detail was here. One entry to the effect that she'd met and become intimate with a Sergeant Redding of the 1st Engineers, First American Division was particularly poignant. She closed the book with a sigh and sat watching the landscape slide through tear-blurred eyes for ten or fifteen minutes before she spoke again. Out of respect, the colonel kept silent. Finally she turned and addressed him seriously.

"And you wish to marry me, Ludwig?"

"Yes," he answered simply.

"Why?"

"Ah, Jeanne, have you forgotten the summer we spent together in Switzerland before this awful war? Surely you remember those glorious days and nights. I told you then that I loved you. A thousand times and in a thousand ways I told you. Now I tell you again that I love you and want you for my wife. Love, is that not reason enough?"

Moved by his declaration, she whispered with bowed head, "Yes, it is. Love is reason enough."

"Then why do you hesitate? Your life is at stake. Surely you realize that now, even if you did not before I showed you the book. Darling, don't make this any harder for both of us. Do you think I could stand to see you executed? It would be the end for me, too,"

"What do you mean?

"I mean that I could not bear to live, knowing it was in my power to save you and I did not do it."

"Oh," she cried.

He silenced her with a meaningful look at the guard and chauffeur.

"But you will," she continued eagerly. "You will help me to escape."

"You misunderstand me, darling. What you ask would be the act of a traitor. I have not asked you to betray your country. It is not fair that you should ask me to betray mine. No, I ask that you become my wife because I love you. Then, as my affianced bride, I will be in a position to stop the court martial proceedings. If you persist in refusing, matters will just have to take their course. After the inevitable end, I shall simply take the easiest way out."

Rebuked by his refusal to betray his country, Jeanne pondered his offer. She respected that loyalty and honor occupied as high a place in his mind as did personal emotions. She was almost ready to give in to his offer, but her thoughts still turned to Judy, and a little cry escaped her.

"What is it, my dear?" The colonel was instantly solicitous.

"Suppose," she faltered. "Suppose I don't love you. Suppose I love another."

"Ah, my dear, I've expected that. Who is it, this American? This Sergeant Redding, whose name appears so often in our files?"

"Yes. Sergeant Redding. Could you accept me as a wife, knowing that I loved another man?"

"Jeanne, dear, I could be happy with you as a wife under any conditions. This Sergeant Redding may be a very estimable fellow. No doubt he is. But he is a soldier, and soldiers are notoriously unfaithful, much like the sailor with a girl in every port. How do you know he hasn't loved a dozen girls since you last saw him? Who is he? Who are his people? Has he any background? Could he move among your friends? In short, would he make a suitable husband for you?"

The girl smiled ruefully. "I don't know. I've asked myself the same questions. I only know that, regardless of the answers, I love him. I'm sure he loves me, and as you said a while ago, what else matters?"

The colonel tapped his finger reflectively on the shining heel of his boot before speaking. "Yes, that is exactly the way I feel about you. Perhaps I shouldn't tell you this, but the First American Division attacked this sector yesterday morning. Last evening they had the town of Exermont and this morning they resumed their advance."

Jeanne digested this news in silence. "And he may be near at this very moment," she whispered softly.

"Yes, he may be near." The colonel eyed her intently. "Or he may be among the fallen," he added softly. "Who knows?"

"Yes," she agreed. "Who knows?" She dabbed at her moist eyes with her handkerchief. "It would be terrible."

"Many terrible things happen in war. The American casualties were very heavy yesterday."

Jeanne sat in silence, considering her alternatives—which were but one. "Ludwig, I've always liked you, but you know that I love Sgt Redding. Suppose I were to marry you and the memory of him came between us. What would we do? I couldn't stand a life of petty bickering and quarrels."

"Oh, my dear girl, if you accept my proposition and at the end of a year of married life you wish it, I will grant you a divorce."

"Do you really mean that?"

"My dear, I will put it in writing if you wish."

"No, that's not necessary. Your word is all I need. On those terms, then, Ludwig, I will marry you."

"Thank you, my darling. Thank you." He wrapped her in his arms, ignoring the two soldiers in the front seat.

The rumble of the guns interspersed with the faint crackle of small arms fire floated in on the breeze. For one whose life had just been saved, Jeanne felt little relief or joy. Back somewhere in that roar and rattle was a presence she could not forget.

CHAPTER XXXVII

MEUSE-ARGONNE
OCTOBER, 1918

Night, black as pitch. No sign of moon or stars to guide us as we staggered and stumbled our way along the rough, muddy road. For three days we'd been held in reserve at the Cheppy Crossroads. Now, in the dead of night, we moved up to hit the enemy again at daybreak. Fit and well rested, the men were hard as nails, and food was just scarce enough to put them in a vile temper, the spleen of which would be vented on our adversaries in the morning. The road, in bad shape from continued use and heavy rains, was filled with stalled traffic, mired trucks and wagons. We hiked in single file along the edge, no talking except for a muttered oath as a man slipped into a rut or turned an ankle on a stone. Sometimes during the frequent halts one man would bump into the man in front of him and be roundly cursed for his clumsiness, another indication that the outfit was at fighting pitch, whether with the enemy or among themselves didn't appear to make much difference.

I slipped and slid along with the rest, but in spite of the chill temperature and misty rain I was sweating profusely. When the outfit halted I took advantage of the stop to try to locate Mac or Red. I might as well have tried to pick out one particular drop in a bottle of ink. I lit a cigarette as the column moved forward again. We climbed a steep hill that seemed to go up and up forever.

"Hey, Judy." A voice reached me out of the darkness. "Where the hell are you?"

"Back here, Mac." As we moved along I felt a figure brush my side, invisible in the darkness but I could feel his presence and hear his heavy breathing.

"That you, Mac?"

"Yeah. How're we doin'? Are many of 'em falling out?"

"I haven't noticed any yet. How far've we got to go?"

"Four or five kilometers, I guess. It won't be bad after we get over this hill."

Mac had been up here yesterday to reconnoiter our position so he had some idea where we were.

"This sure is a bastard of a hike," he remarked.

"Boy, howdy, I'll tell a man." As we staggered on in silence I found the grade a little less steep and progress a little easier.

"Say, Judy, have you had any news of your girl friend lately? Is she still sick?"

"No, I haven't heard anything since we left Toul. I don't know whether she's better or not." A wave of misery swept over me when I thought of how much I did know and yet how little. "Christ, I don't know a damn thing. She may even be dead for all I know."

"It's tough going into a drive and her sick and you not knowing how she is." Mac waxed sympathetic, a rare role for him.

"Yeah, you'll never know how damn tough it really is."

We halted again and I heard a gurgle as Mac took a pull from his canteen. I felt him groping for me as he pushed the canteen into my hand. I took a long swallow of the fiery brandy and returned it.

"Well," he grunted, "I'll look over the rest of the platoon."

As he moved back along the column I noted that the darkness was becoming less opaque, taking on a gray tinge as we descended into a deep valley. We traversed the floor for perhaps two kilometers and started up the ridge at our right. In the dim gray light we could see the ruins of a small village crowning the crest of the hill. The outfit halted, and we proceeded by sections with an interval of about a hundred yards between us, to within firing range of the enemy. We moved through the town, the village of Baulny, and out the other side onto a wide plateau.

As we emerged from the village an enemy plane thundered overhead, flying low. We could see him dimly through the mist. I hoped he didn't see us, but the hope was in vain, for he wheeled and dived — rat-tat-tat. Machine gun bullets kicked up the dirt ten feet to our left. As he continued on his original course, a colored rocket burst over the side of his plane. We continued to follow the dirt road across the plateau, but in a few minutes the results of his rocket brought a shell whistling over, then another, then two more. Then we were smothered under a perfect rain of 77s.

I dropped flat on my belly and lay inert. This couldn't last long. It was harassing fire meant to disorganize and cripple us before we could get into position. They always did this when they caught troops in the open. Curiously enough, as I lay there waiting for the shelling to stop, my mind wasn't on my own safety. I was thinking of Jeanne. Would I ever see her again? Was she even now beyond help? Would I survive this attack and get news of her? Depression overwhelmed me, and suddenly I got up and ran blindly up the road as the shells still fell. I didn't much care what happened to me. Red Conlon, from where he lay in a ditch along the roadside, cursed me for my folly.

"Judy, you goddamn fool, get down! You'll be killed," he shouted.

I looked at him dumbly, then stopped, turned and crawled into the ditch beside him.

"What the hell's the matter with you, anyhow?" he berated me. "Tryin' to get yourself killed?"

"It doesn't make a hell of a lot of difference, does it?"

"Maybe not to a damn fool like you, but it does to your friends. You better pull up your guts. Remember, we got a fight ahead of us."

After the shelling died down we cared for the wounded and moved on up the road. Captain Weyandt came back along the column, furious.

"What's the matter with you sergeant? Are you getting cold feet?"

His reproof hurt. "I guess I must have lost my head for a minute, sir."

"Well, don't lose it again, damn it. It might be permanent the next time."

The edge of the plateau terminated above the steep slope of a deep, narrow valley. A line of foxholes, probably made by the enemy, embroidered the crest of the hill. Regardless of who dug them, we gladly took advantage of the shelter they offered. After we were settled in, I hunted down Mac for orders. As I moved toward the end of the platoon, I took in the scene in front of us, where a fairly heavy bombardment was going on down in the valley. The smoke from the shell bursts mingled with the fog forming a mist that completely hid the valley floor. It seemed as though we were on the edge of a giant kettle partially filled with boiling water. We could hear it bubbling and gurgling far below but could see nothing beyond the impenetrable curtain of steam and vapor rising from it. We'd soon be moving down into that seething inferno. The phrase 'the valley of death' came to mind. It seemed most appropriate just then.

I spied Mac's familiar form just a few holes farther on, Lt. Courland with him. The lieutenant looked up as I approached. "Good morning, sergeant. I was just going to send for you."

Mac gave me a nod and a wink as I slid into the hole. Dave Evans was already there. The four of us made an uncomfortable crowd in the small space, so Lt Courland wasted no time in giving us our instructions.

"We're in reserve today. You men know what to do. Keep an extra sharp lookout for machine guns or for groups that've been overlooked by the assaulting waves."

The country below was low bushes and grass, so there'd be plenty of places to hide machine guns. Lots of luck, boys.

"Be sure to investigate every possible hiding place before you pass on. Keep the prisoners moving, and leave the wounded for the first aid men." He looked around for questions. When none arose he shook hands with each one of us. "Good luck, men. Go back to your sections."

I crawled into my hole with John Gallagher and Klein. "We're in reserve today. Lucky. Nothing to do but mop up and chase prisoners back."

"Yeah," growled Klein, "and catch the heaviest part of the shell fire." He joined the outfit before Cantigny, so he knew what he was talking about.

John gave a little laugh. "Well, I guess we *are* lucky. We'll probably get some shell fire, but it won't be as bad as routing machine guns out of those woods. Gosh, some places they're so thick you'll never be able to find a gun until after he's found you."

We stayed in our holes during some intermittent shelling. Then a whistle blast signaled the start of our descent into the valley. I shivered with a chill as we moved slowly down into that all enveloping, smoky fog.

We moved down slowly, in single file. The enemy had been fairly well routed by the assault group, and apparently the support had done a thorough job of mopping up. Shells came over at frequent intervals, causing us to drop flat on the muddy slopes to escape the flying fragments. We were about two thirds of the way to the bottom when a strange sound drifted up from below. It sounded like singing. It *was* singing. A couple of wags up at the head of the platoon lustily sang the song, 'We Are Going Down the Valley One by One.' The humor of the situation struck the entire company. A trickle of laughter rippled along the line, then burst into a roar. The column moved steadily down, laughing as we moved, and in their laughter, the men forgot their fears.

As we reached the floor of the valley we met an awesome spectacle. Bodies everywhere, lying in grotesque positions, dotted the fields in every direction. Here lay a heap piled up where a machine gun caught a group fair in the open. The wounded groaned and thrashed around. Some lay motionless, their groans alone giving evidence that life still clung to their bloody, shattered bodies. We passed through the courtyard of Chandion Farm, a blood-soaked shamble, bodies littering the place.

Bodies of the enemy and those of our comrades lost their identity once they were down and helpless. There was no distinction in our minds as we viewed them in passing. To us they were all wounded or dead. The uniform they wore made no difference now. Struck by my own lack of emotion looking at the carnage I remembered how in the beginning, this would have set me to vomiting or worse, but now it was just the way of war. I wasn't sure whether my callousness was right or wrong, but I knew it was the only way to get through this carnage. It just was.

We moved slowly up the farther slope, stopping often. Near mid-morning we reached the edge of a wood crowning a rise and dug in. We'd lost some men from the shell fire, but I didn't know how many. Muller seated himself on the edge of my hole and offered me his canteen. I accepted a drink, and as I handed it back I watched him take inventory of the contents of his pockets.

"How do you like this for an iron cross?" He held out a medal for my inspection, a beautiful bauble, the center gold with four silver wings. There was an inscription on the back which we couldn't decipher, so we called Harris over to read it. "Personally awarded by Kaiser Wilhelm II for extraordinary heroism in action. July 15, 1916," he translated for us. I reflected on what great deed or series of deeds it must have taken to earn such an award, only to have it seized as spoils of war by a common soldier.

About mid-afternoon we resumed our progress through diminished shelling. We had little to do as we plodded through the mud, except to keep scattered groups of prisoners moving toward the rear. Occasionally we disregarded instructions and bandaged a wounded man or helped one into a more comfortable position.

Near evening, we dug in on the slope of a steep hill. To our left front we could see the buildings of a town nestled into one of the innumerable valleys. We learned through the grapevine that it was the village of Exermont. I started making the rounds to check up on my section when the captain appeared.

"How many have you lost, sergeant?"

"Four, sir."

"How do you feel now, sergeant?"

"All right, sir. Why?"

"Well, you had me worried this morning. I was afraid you might be reaching the breaking point."

"Oh, nothing like that, sir. I was just thinking about something else, and sort of forgot about those shells."

"I see," he said, giving me a calculated look. "You've been thinking about something else a good deal during the last few months, haven't you?"

I looked at him in surprise. I thought I'd kept my secret pretty well hidden.

"There's no use evading me, sergeant. You've been worrying about something for some time. We're old friends, you know, so don't hesitate to come to me for help if I can do anything."

Good old Capt. Weyandt—a leader in every respect. I was more than grateful for his offer, futile though it may be. "Thanks, Captain. You know how much I appreciate that offer, but there's nothing you can do."

"Well, don't hesitate if there is." Then his demeanor changed to all business. "Now, in the morning, sergeant, we take the assault. We will have no barrage. You know what to do, so there's no use in my talking to you. In this broken country we must be very careful about maintaining contact. Keep in touch with the elements on either flank at all times. Don't let your section get ahead or behind. Each group is going to need the support of neighboring groups, so we can't lose touch. If we do, it will be practically impossible to regain contact in those woods."

He hesitated, as though making sure he hadn't forgotten anything, then went on. "Tell the men to make coffee from their reserve ration. We're far enough to the rear that we can build small fires in the holes, and it'll probably be the last chance for them to get something warm for a while.

"Good idea, sir."

He extended his hand. "Well, good luck, sergeant. Get a good night's sleep if you can."

"Thanks, sir, and good luck to you, sir. Don't worry about the sleep. I'll get that, sir."

He moved on down the line, where I saw him talking to Mac. I gave the men all the information and, as the night fell dark and impenetrable, they turned in to their holes to make coffee.

A dark and misty morning dawned as the company moved forward to the attack, divided into combat groups. No sound was uttered as we moved ahead in the gloom. We'd already passed through the supports and were approaching our front line, the trees and bushes, wet from the heavy mist which lay over everything like a blanket. We passed out of the woods and crossed a section of meadowland where the dead grass reached halfway to our knees. Something moved ahead, and we distinguished yesterday's assaulting outfits, dug in. They gave us words of advice as we passed over and between their holes.

"Boys, this one's a bastard. Just like Soissons."

"Much artillery?"

"Nope, but the damn machine guns grow on trees."

"Okay. We'll watch for 'em."

"So long, buddy. Good luck."

"So long."

We moved on across the meadow. From the edge of the wood on the far side came a burst of fire on our left. A chorus of shouts intermingled with screams and groans. Then silence. Then another burst. This time it had a different sound. One of our automatic rifles sprang into action, joined by another. The machine guns entered the fray again. The automatics continued to hammer. Rifle fire and grenade explosions added to the din. I couldn't see what was happening in the dim light; I only knew the enemy'd been engaged.

Movement in the bushes directly ahead. "Down!" I signaled and dropped flat. A crackling fire burst out, not at us but to our left. We fired our automatics and the fire from the bushes slackened. We crawled forward through the grass. Then, without warning bullets started to clip the grass over our heads. We kept crawling, even as I heard bullets hit flesh and moans come from behind me. I didn't think they could see us. We were well concealed in the grass, and the light was too dim. They were firing at the sound of our guns.

I signaled to cease firing and kept on crawling forward. We were close to the edge of the wood now — so close I could see the twigs of the bushes that concealed the enemy guns. Their fire to our left showed they hadn't located us yet. I looked to my right to Klein and Swartz, crawling near me, and motioned to them with a grenade. They followed suit, each with a grenade in hand, and we threw them together. When I blew my whistle, the entire section rose and rushed forward. We burst through the bushes, ready to engage them hand to hand, but they offered no resistance, just stood there with their hands raised. We disarmed and plundered them before sending them back.

Mindful of the skipper's warning, I held the section in the shelter of the gun emplacements while I sent out men on either flank to contact our neighboring groups. I took advantage of this pause to count faces. Five missing. Our man on the right flank returned with the news that the third platoon was in the woods a little ahead of us. We resumed the advance, but as the day grew lighter, snipers in trees took advantage of the increasing visibility and, harassed us continually.

Bullets zipped and whined around us as we encountered heavy fire from our left. The first burst caught us upright, creating havoc. We dropped flat on the ground and crawled to shelter behind trees and stumps. The source of the fire couldn't be located, but as soon as a man exposed any part of his anatomy, he drew a rush of bullets. Those damn snipers did everything they could to add to the precariousness of our situation. It was impossible to move or change position enough to locate them because of the everlasting machine gun fire.

Our location rapidly became untenable. To fall back would be to leave a gap in the line, exposing and losing contact with the groups on either flank. Lt. Courland started to crawl diagonally forward through the heavy growth, motioning for the rest of the section to follow. The entire group obeyed his command, and we moved forward slowly and painfully. The enemy observed the maneuver and redoubled his fire. A new note added to the clamor; the first section had located the guns. The lieutenant signaled again, and we resumed our original direction. Bomb explosions from hand grenades silenced the enemy guns. Shouts and screams told us that the first section was engaging them hand-to-hand. We rose to our feet and continued our slow advance, with the enemy putting up a dogged resistance. I heard a bump and Benson, on my right, turned halfway around, a blank expression on his face, and sagged slowly to the ground. We moved ahead warily, trying to anticipate Heinie's fire. A man approached from the first section. "Where's Lt. Courland?"

"Over there on the right." I pointed to the lieutenant, partially concealed by the heavy undergrowth.

"What's the dope?" I asked as he moved away.

"We're to dig in when we reach the edge of the woods." He gave Lt. Courland the word and moved on to the third platoon.

Lt. Courland motioned for me. "Send a man back to the supports as soon as we reach the edge of the wood, sergeant. Have him notify them of our location and tell them we're digging in."

"Yes, sir."

"And, sergeant."

"Yes, sir?"

"Tell the men to be careful of their ammunition. We'll probably have to fight off counter attacks shortly after we start to dig, so we can't afford to waste any.",

I passed on the instructions, and we took up our cautious advance once more. To my surprise, we moved some distance without encountering any resistance, but suddenly the enemy opened up on the woods with his artillery, their aim excellent. Shells landed just to the rear of us. As the fire increased in intensity, trees fell with a roar. Shells burst up among the limbs, sending branches crashing down upon us to add to the danger of flying shell fragments.

Lt Courland jumped to his feet and blew his whistle. He waved his arms and started to run forward at full speed. We followed – like trying to run on a platform, shifting first one way, then another. Our lives depended on speed now. The quicker we left that zone of deadly shell fire, the safer we'd be. Figures ran to the right and left of me. Twisting my head, I saw Mac, on my left, his short legs pumping. He stumbled and almost fell. I went flat on my face in the mud. Shell bursts, falling trees, crashing limbs all added to the indescribable confusion. I picked myself up, spit the mud from my mouth and resumed the mad gallop. Ah, at last, the edge of the wood. Men were already there, unlimbering their entrenching tools. I went to report to Lt. Courland, but we were both panting too violently to speak.

The bombardment increased and spread over a wider area. Falling shells burst closer and closer to us. Finally, the space where we'd started to dig in was overwhelmed by the roaring shattering blast of exploding shells. Clearly this was not just a harassing bombardment—too prolonged and covering too large an area not to be the part of some definite plan. The men cowered in the shell holes they'd started, hoping against hope that their meager protection would help them weather the fury of shell fire. I squatted with Harris in a natural depression in the ground—not very deep, but a small measure of protection, anyway. The shells—good sized ones: 210s and 155s—lifted a great mass of earth high into the air where it disintegrated and fell back in clods and stones and dirt. I took a big drink from my canteen and offered it to Harris. He shook his head but smiled anyway. I scanned our line of holes through the smoke and dust of the explosions and saw nothing but motionless figures. It was impossible to differentiate the dead from the living. All lay inert.

I saw an arm waving away down the line. A figure sprang up and motioned to the grassy hillside beyond the edge of the wood, his meaning plain. We were to move forward, out of the zone of falling shells. To remain where we were meant annihilation. If we moved back, we'd lose the advantage of observation we'd gained by reaching the edge of the forest. The men saw and interpreted the signal, and in a few seconds of concerted rush, we'd formed a line of resistance a couple hundred yards in advance of the timber, well concealed in the tall grass, which, while it afforded no actual protection, made enemy marksmanship a matter of guesswork.

As I moved about with Lt. Courland, helping organize the position, I counted noses and found we had fourteen men still with us. We'd lost thirteen since yesterday morning. I flopped down on my belly beside Harris and watched the shells burst in the wood to our rear, nothing but a tangle of fallen trees and branches. God pity any wounded lying back there.

"How do you like the war?" Harris's voice drew me from contemplation of the desolate scene. So placid and self-possessed, he might have been sitting in a field miles away from the spectacle rather than directly in the heart of it.

"I don't like it a damn bit."

"Neither do I, but it's better than Cantigny or Soissons."

"How do you figure?"

"Because there, it was a continual hammer, hammer and pound. This resistance is intermittent. We advance for a while against light opposition, then hit a tough spot like this one. We'll get over it, and then the going'll probably be fairly easy again."

I had to admit he was right. We had artillery fire here, and while it was heavy, it wasn't as prolonged as in other battles. Then, too, there seemed to be more of us than the enemy. His strong points weren't manned with forty or fifty men to half a dozen machine guns like they used to be. The largest strong point we'd encountered had five guns and seventeen men. I was inclined to agree with Harris when I noticed the shell fire had slackened. As I gazed toward the forest where shells still fell at a much reduced rate, Mac loped casually toward us, wearing that dumb grin of his. Farther on, Red Conlon sat in a depression, wiping his rifle with a piece of rag. Mac screwed into position between Harris and me.

"Well, how you doin'? How many men you got left?" he asked.

"Eleven men, two sergeants and a lieutenant. Where do we go from here?"

"We don't go for a while. We'll be damn lucky if we can stay here. Now listen, you guys, as soon as the bombardment on those woods stops, take your section back there. Establish a line at the edge of the woods and wait for orders. That shell fire knocked enough trees down so that we can have plenty of protection. You got that straight?"

"Okay, I got it." Then as an afterthought: "Hey, Mac. Seen John Gallagher lately?"

Mac paused and looked around. "He's out in front with an outpost. Lt Courland just went out to give him his orders about coming back to the woods."

Mac disappeared in the grass. I took a drink from my canteen and looked over the section. Some shells were still coming over, but not many, and they landed deep in the forest, falling on the support outfits. I bet the supports caught merry hell in that bombardment.

I stood up and told the men to get their stuff together, we were moving back to the woods.

"Hell, that suits me all right," growled Klein. "I'd just as soon go clear back to Hoboken."

"Don't worry, you will." Corporal Spence told him. "In a box."

As we moved toward the timber, the men indulged in a running banter, spiced with cryptic remarks and haughty retorts, a sure sign that their spirit was still intact. At the sound of scattered rifle fire to our rear, we broke into a run and hurriedly established ourselves behind fallen trees and stumps just inside the heavy growth.

As we turned to fight, the enemy launched his counter-attack. They'd emerged from the woodland on the next hill and had already engaged our outpost. They advanced by rotating groups without a barrage. One group protected the advance with machine gun fire until they reached a certain point. Then they stopped and the next group continued the protective fire while the first group advanced.

They couldn't locate our outpost, and each time one of their groups tried to move, a withering fire from our advanced post stopped them. The range for us was about four hundred yards, and we immediately joined in the fire. The enemy kept well concealed in the grass, but here and there a helmet or a piece of equipment showed. As each appeared, it drew a storm of rifle and machine gun fire to sink and rise no more.

Still, the enemy would not be denied. Repeated bursts of fire from our outpost let us know that they hadn't given up trying to locate and overrun their position.

Capt. Weyandt came down the line. "Forward, men. We've got to meet them in the open. Form a line of skirmishers and crawl through the grass. All second sections go first. First sections form support."

We crawled out into the grass, awaiting the word to go. I caught a whisper from the left, and a hand waved. We crawled forward on hands and knees as the firing ahead increased in volume and rapidity. I rose to my knees and saw booted and helmeted figures running through the grass. They'd located our outpost and were pouring heavy fire into it. I fired from a kneeling position. A figure dropped. I fired at another. He stumbled a few steps and fell. Surprising how easy it was. Just like on the range—front sight even with the shoulders of the rear sight. The target standing on the front sight. Squeeze the trigger. Wham! A bull's eye. Instead of a white marker here, a bull's eye was marked by a falling body. This didn't seem real. I felt detached, watching a performance with disinterest and yet I was one of the chief actors.

Abandoning any attempt at concealment, we advanced straight up. We ran a few steps, dropped to our knees and fired, then jumped to our feet and ran a few more steps. The enemy, aware of our presence, was still preoccupied with our outpost.

Within a hundred yards of them now, they seemed uncertain whether to advance or fall back. We slowed our advance, trying to keep our organization. The fire from our outpost stopped. No. Not quite. A single rifle still fired. It sounded like it'd moved forward from the outpost.

A whistle blast on my right, and a line of men advanced on the run.

"Come on, guys!" I ran forward, the section at my heels. It was too much for the enemy. After the punishing fire he took from the outpost and the company, facing this horde of yowling maniacs made him turn and flee in confusion for the shelter of the wood from which he'd emerged.

Now, in a decidedly precarious position with the enemy hiding in the timber, we were in plain sight in the open fields. To protect our position and in hopes of trapping a large force of the enemy, the captain called for artillery fire in the woods. His message was answered unbelievably soon and shell after shell hurtled into the forest.

I moved over to our outpost where some of the fourth platoon were engaged, and as I approached, I saw four bodies laid out in a row. Lt Courland, minus his shoes, Herman, Golden and Moore.

"Where's John Gallagher?" I asked.

"Come, I'll show you." I looked around. Morrie Muller wore a bloody bandage around his head where a bullet went through the top of one ear. I followed him forward about fifty feet. There in the tall grass, curled up as though sleeping, lay the body of John Gallagher, a neat hole between his eyes. A short distance beyond lay the bodies of six enemy soldiers, mute testimony to the steadfast loyalty and courage of my bunkie. I stood saddened by his death, but so much death and dying had numbed my soul. I stood looking at him — so like a child. Strange that this innocent looking boy could have snuffed out six lives in his dying seconds. The captain, come over to look at the outpost and what remained of his friend, Lt Courland, stood beside me.

"Well, sergeant, we lose our friends, it seems."

"Yes," I nodded, then shook my head. "Tony and now John. Who'll be next?"

He sighed. "Hard to tell. There aren't many of the originals left."

"That's right. Less than a dozen."

"Yes, and they've all been wounded at least once, except for you and Mac."

"Yeah, and I'm looking for mine any time now."

"Well, let's hope you never get it. You might get through the whole damn war without even a scratch. I hope so, anyway."

"Thanks, Captain. The hope is mutual."

"Oh, I don't know." Deep sadness filled his voice. "When I think of all the good fellows who've gone before, sometimes I think we'd be better off if we just followed them. Anyone who survives this war is going to live in a new and strange world when it's over. There'll be those who'll disrespect us and make light of our achievements before the sound of the guns has died away. It's not what you did, but what you have that counts. God knows, damn few soldiers are ever going to have anything except memories of incredible accomplishments against impossible odds and inconceivable hardships.

"By God, I'll drink to that, Captain." Mac had joined us unnoticed.

The captain turned to face him. "Were you looking for me, sergeant?"

"Yes, sir. There's a runner from battalion headquarters wants you, sir. He has some orders, I think."

"God, I was hoping for orders from someplace." Before he turned to go, he swung around facing John's body, stood at attention and saluted. Mac and I did, too .

As he moved away, Mac said, "By God, there's a soldier." Whether he meant John or the skipper, I didn't know, probably both.

We settled into a line of fox holes which just a few short hours ago protected the enemy. I looked at my watch — nearly 3:00 pm. We sat in our holes, watching the shells crash into the timber ahead.

"This damn country is just one woods after another." I looked up in surprise to hear my thoughts so neatly voiced. Red Conlon stood at the edge of my hole. "Well, don't you invite a guy in when he comes calling?"

I was amazed that he could still kid after the hell we'd been through.

"Sure. Sure. Sit down. Make yourself at home." I moved over to let him in. "How're you making out? I haven't seen much of you today."

"I'm doin' all right, I guess. Too bad about John, ain't it?"

"Yeah, it's too bad. It's been too bad for a hell of a lot of guys in the last year, if you ask me."

"You're damn right, and what good is it? What's it all for, anyway?"

Katovich, a new man, voiced his thoughts from the adjoining hole. He crawled out and joined the group, followed by Harris from the hole next to us.

"What's all what for?" Harris repeated the question.

"Why all this damn fighting and killing? What's the difference who wins the war? What the hell do we care what kind of a government we live under, just so we live?"

"Damifino," Red mumbled. "I don't know anything about it. All I know is that we go forward when we're told. When we meet the other guy, we fight. If we don't fight, we'll be killed. Sometimes we're killed anyhow. Why? I don't know. I never did anything to those Jerries to make them want to kill me. They never did anything to me. I guess we just fight to show them they can't lick us."

"Is that a good reason?" Katovich asked.

Harris raised his head and looked around. "Good question," he said quietly. "Too big to decide off hand. Wanna know my view on it?"

"Go ahead," I said. "The war seems to be at a standstill for a while."

We had men on post alert for any movement by the enemy, and until the artillery got through with those woods, our time would be our own. We leaned back in the hole listening to Harris.

"First, America was settled by people who weren't satisfied with conditions in Europe. They went to America to establish a country based on principles of freedom. Freedom of speech, religion, freedom to criticize, to pursue wealth, to live and do as one pleased as long as it didn't infringe on the rights of others. But our forebears had to fight for it. First the Indians, then the French, then the British. Then came the Civil War, fought to preserve and protect the nation they'd created. Throughout history, wars have been the rule, not the exception. Out of all this has emerged a nation where every man has opportunity. Freedom, a chance to live his life as he sees fit."

He turned to Katovich. "Where were you born?"

"In Lithuania."

"How did you come to America?"

"My father brought me over."

"Why?"

"Because there was more chance to work in America, wages were higher, living was better."

"Exactly," said Harris. "Now suppose the enemy won this war. We'd end up with the same conditions in America as those your father fled Europe to escape. Isn't that right?"

"Yes, but we had no business . . ."

"Wait." Harris cut him off short. "You say we had no business getting in this war. You're not a diplomat. You're a soldier. Whether the statesmen were right or wrong in getting us into the war, it's our duty to get us out of it with our creeds and institutions intact. If immigrants come over anxious to share the advantages our country offers, they have to be ready to fight and bleed and die for the institutions our forefathers fought and bled and died to establish. Otherwise, they might as well stay home and watch conditions in America turn into the same ones they left Europe to escape."

"Hear! Hear!" Red clasped his hands above his head with admiration. "That son sure knows a lot of words."

Mac headed for us through the grass, and I could tell by his manner we were about to move again. He slid down into our hole.

"What the hell goes on here?" he asked, displeased to find so large a group in one hole. "Don't you know any better than to gang up like this?"

"Yeah, we know better, Mac, but there ain't enough holes to go round." Red always had a come-back.

Mac grunted his displeasure. "Well, get to your places. We're going forward at 4:20. The other side of that woods is the day's objective. We'll dig in there. Judy, you'll be platoon leader. I'm takin' Lt. Courland's place."

Harris replaced me as section leader as I moved away with Mac. My watch said 4:12. Not long to wait. Shells still fell on the forest ahead.

"Where are we, Mac? Do you know?" I asked.

"Hell, no. All I know is we're somewhere between Exermont and Berlin. The map shows a little town ahead, but I don't know its name or how far it is. There was an enemy headquarters there until this morning, but they pulled out. How's your canteen?"

"Okay." I offered it and we each took a big drink.

"I don't think we'll have much trouble with these woods," Mac stated confidently. "The guns have pretty well cleaned them out."

"I hope you're right." I didn't share his confidence. Generally trouble hit us when least expected.

Mac rose and looked at his watch. I looked at mine just in time to catch a signal from the left.

"Get 'em goin'," Mac ordered. I signaled the section leaders and the platoon moved forward.

Our progress through the wood was relatively swift—no resistance whatever. Overturned guns, discarded equipment, scraps of clothing, blankets and bodies all bore witness to the effectiveness of our artillery fire. The advance was impeded only by fallen trees and the tangle of broken limbs and bushes. I heard a moan. At first I couldn't locate the source, but then I heard it again and investigated closer. Ah, there under a fallen tree—a wounded enemy. Using my rifle as a lever I swung the small tree enough to free him. "Danke." He gave me a grateful look and I moved on. War was so ridiculous.

After about a half hour we reached a clearing in the middle of the wood, where we halted while the skipper conferred with the remaining lieutenants. The place had an ominous look—a clearing about four hundred yards long and near two hundred yards wide.

Morrie Muller sidled up to me. "Pretty easy, eh, what, Judy?"

"Too damn easy," I replied. "There should have been some resistance. They're probably ganged up some place to make a stand. I don't like the looks of that open space."

Mac beckoned and I joined him. "We're gonna leave two squads here with rifle grenades. If anything turns up, take cover wherever you can and stay put till the grenade barrage is under way."

The whistle blew and we started forward again, every man tensely alert. Grimly silent, the men sensed trouble. We moved ahead ten yards, twenty yards, fifty, seventy-five. Once we were halfway across the danger zone my fears subsided. I expelled my pent up breath in a long, whistling sigh. Bushes and stumps here and there would provide good cover in case we needed it. It didn't look like we'd need any cover, though. It appeared our fears had been groundless.

Two thirds of the way across I spied a stump directly in front of me and altered my course to go around it. Suddenly hell broke loose in all its fury—a deafening crash of machine gun fire. I dove forward behind the stump but before I could move, bullets zipped past at a furious rate. From my makeshift shelter I twisted around to view the platoon, so well concealed I couldn't see a one of them.

Our rifle grenades landed at the far edge of the glade in a storm of explosions. They kept up a steady fire, but the machine gun fire did not abate. I heard a whistle blast. To the left, Captain Weyandt on his knees behind a stump, waved us forward. I crawled through the grass until I spotted movement at the edge of the undergrowth. Lying flat, I took steady aim and squeezed the trigger. The movement ceased. Rifle fire all around. We'd located the gun positions. I picked out another figure, fired and missed. I looked to the right, moved to admiration by the heroic actions of my men. But the enemy fire was taking a ghastly toll; they had our range to a hair.

Annihilation faced us in just a matter of minutes if we didn't do something right then. I heard that soft p-lup of bullets hitting flesh, groans and cries, and still those guns fried and crackled away, firing in relays. There must have been at least a dozen. We kept crawling till we weren't more than twelve yards away. A sudden shriek from a whistle. Figures jumped to their feet. I jumped up and started running.

Red Conlon on my right stumbled and turned partly toward me. Even as I looked his face disappeared in a bloody welter. I pushed on, the section all around me. We leaped over a fallen tree directly into a gun emplacement. Fighting with bayonets, fists, gun butts, even teeth, figures floated in and out of my vision, taking on distorted shapes then returning to normal. The frenzy lasted only a minute, and then, that quick, it was over. Five prisoners cowered against the side of the hole with their hands up.

Klein, the heat of the moment still on him, started to shoot the wounded. I tried to stop him, but he looked at me vacantly and pointed his pistol at me, drooling and glassy eyed. I swung my pistol, catching him fair in the jaw with the barrel, and he dropped like a pole-axed steer. Kennet had a minor leg wound, so I put him in charge of the prisoners. The emplacement contained three guns, and fourteen inert enemy figures lay in the hole, along with three of ours. I marshaled the rest of the section together and moved to help other groups. We were too late; the position had already been subdued. There were five emplacements, totaling sixteen guns and I didn't know how many men. We sent thirty-six prisoners to the rear.

. Captain Weyandt arrived. "Good work, men. I see you've been in the fight, sergeant." He indicated my bayonet, covered with blood. I dimly remembered having used it, but I didn't recall anything from the time we started to rush the position until we counted faces in the machine gun emplacement.

The captain continued, all business. "Send a man back to have the rifle grenadiers move up and join us, sergeant."

"Yes, sir. Will we wait for them?"

"Yes, we'll wait here for them."

I called Muller, who'd escaped unscathed, and gave him the instruction. I trudged along with him a little way, then left him to start searching. Finally, I found Red's body, beyond help. At least thirty bullets must have hit him in the face, a red pulp. I gazed dumbly at him unable to feel or comprehend anything anymore. I guessed the girl in the shack had her revenge.

I heard Muller coming up with the grenadiers. I joined them and we made our way back to the company in silence. Mostly new men, the sights they'd witnessed that day would leave ugly scars on their minds.

The company reformed again to continue the advance. Here and there, scattered machine gun ports and light artillery fire impeded our progress. We fought our way doggedly onward and at last were rewarded by the sight of open fields ahead. When we finally reached the edge of the forest, we got orders to dig in and consolidate our position.

As we labored to make ourselves secure against enemy counter-attacks, I surveyed the country ahead. Rolling fields dropped away in front of us. A road, like a white ribbon, ran diagonally ahead, appearing on our left and sinking from sight in a shallow valley about a half mile away on our right front. In the distance a cluster of roof spines marked the site of a small village. That must be the place Mac told me about where the enemy headquarters had left this morning.

Dusk deepened into full dark by the time we had the position fully organized, and the company was called upon to furnish a patrol. Luckily, we weren't required to man any outposts, a detail taken care of by the companies on either flank. We had hard tack, corned beef, coffee, salt and sugar in our combat packs. I still had a can of heat and a small piece of bacon, so after darkness fell, I took off my slicker and hung it in front of my hole. Behind this improvised curtain I lit my canned fire and fried some hard tack in bacon grease. While I was engaged in my culinary endeavors, Mac slid into my hole.

"Hello, soldier," I greeted him.

He sniffed my frying hard tack. "Aha, war deluxe," he smiled. "Just dish up a double order of that while you're at it, Judy. Save me dirtying up my mess kit."

"There's the fire. Also the bacon and the mess kit, but you do your own damn cooking."

"Okay, okay. This'll do me fine." He calmly appropriated the portion I'd cooked for myself and, leaning back comfortably against the side of the hole, proceeded to eat.

"Why you son of a bitch, you. You've got more nerve than a brass monkey."

"I'm a damn site hungrier, too. Here, take a jolt of this and shut up."

I accepted the canteen and took a big drink. Groping around in the dark, I pulled the cork from my own canteen and replenished its contents with a good measure from Mac's.

"Hey, hey! What the hell you doin'?" he yowled. "You bastard. I should've known you'd do that. Well, that makes us even, doesn't it?"

"More or less," I agreed as I continued cooking.

While I was eating we had another visitor, Tommy Connors from the fourth platoon. He'd just been talking to the captain.

"Did you hear the dope for tomorrow?" he asked.

"No, is there any?"

"None except that we continue the assault."

"Why, what the hell's the idea?" I asked. "Where's the reserve?"

"Well, it seems they had to send them over to help some other outfit, so we stay in front till noon tomorrow. At noon, the outfit behind us will take over and we'll drop back."

Unwelcome news, to say the least, but there was nothing we could do about it. If that was the way it was, that's all there was to it and nothing we did or said would change it.

I spent the night going from hole to hole, making sure there was at least one man awake in each. After midnight, Mac relieved me and I caught a few hours of sleep before morning.

I awakened before dawn to a steady downpour, took a stiff drink, and ate some hard tack and cold corned bill. At the captain's summons we gathered round in his hole.

"Well, men," he began, "I'm sorry we're not to be leap-frogged this morning, but I do have a little good news for you. We'll get a barrage for our advance today. It'll be with us until we pass beyond that little town. There'll also be some light tanks. Go back to your holes and wait for it."

The rain continued as we returned to our sections. After a wait of maybe twenty minutes, light tanks came clanking up through the woods, and as soon as they were in position the barrage was put down—not a very thick barrage, but in this style of advance, it'd be protective enough.

We started to move forward, with the tanks in the lead, not encountering much resistance. Scattered machine guns opened a half-hearted fire, only to give up almost immediately as a tank bore down on them. In not more than twenty minutes, we'd reached the town. This village hadn't suffered greatly from artillery. Most of the houses were intact. Our barrage ended as we entered the place. With some sporadic fighting in the streets, the tanks were a great help. There weren't many defending troops left, and those, knowing they'd been left behind as a sacrifice to impede our progress, appeared to have little heart for the job. In a very short time the place was safely in our hands.

As we re-formed at the edge of the town to continue our advance, I noticed the figure of an old woman emerge from one of the cellars. She looked around, bewildered, then raised her hands over her head and clasped them. A torrent of French poured from her lips as she rushed over and embraced the men. She kissed one on the cheek—much to his embarrassment—jumping with joy, tears glistening in her eyes. Suddenly she spied a group of prisoners bunched together under guard. She dashed over in front of them and reviled them with every manner of French invective. They understood enough to laugh at her antics. She left them and returned to heap praise upon us. I wondered if she had any food. The same thought must have been in the minds of many. A box of hard tack fell at her feet, then a can of corned willie, followed by another one. Soon she was surrounded by corned beef and hard tack. The last sound I heard as we moved off in answer to the whistle was her "Merci, mes amis. Merci bien."

Beyond the village, resistance stiffened up again. The enemy had his guns concealed at the edge of the next wood, about five hundred yards ahead. They worked on us in short bursts, and we dropped to our bellies in the grass and threw it right back. Concealed in the woods, they had the advantage of cover, while we lay in the open fields. We crawled forward, then rose to our knees and fired, dropped, and crawled some more. Slowly but surely we shortened the distance between us. I paused for a good look. The forest was about two hundred yards away and the fire was getting heavier. I scanned the position ahead for a sure target. Ah, there was movement. I rose to my knees and took good aim. Bullets clipped the grass to my left.

I heard a blast of automatic rifle fire on my right. Bullets kicked up dirt where I aimed and the movement ceased. Someone beat me to it. I crawled forward a little farther and rose to my knees again. I saw Muller fire and drop down. Dirt flew up on my left rear. I couldn't see anything to shoot at. There was Mac on his knees shouting at someone. A sudden smashing shock, ripping, tearing pain high in my left breast, burned through me. Again, lower down. Yet again. I fell through a red haze in searing pain. Choking. Blood in my mouth. Blackness.

CHAPTER XXXVIII

EXERMONT
DECEMBER, 1918

Sergeants MacCarthy and Harris

Peace had come to the land. The warring armies had withdrawn from the ridges and valleys desecrated by their chaos and destruction. The hills no longer trembled under the concussion of shattering blasts. The deadly chatter of machine guns no longer awakened echoes in the woodland and valleys. The countryside had been given over wholly to the dead, many of whom still lay unburied in the fields and forests, evidence of the gigantic strife still visible on every hand. Thousands of rifles, bayonets, machine guns, even pieces of field artillery lay scattered about. Here and there a tank sat useless, passively awaiting the salvage squads that would eventually gather them up and ship them away.

The day was warm for early December. Bright sunlight touched the slopes and fields like a benediction on the fallen. The scene evoked an awesome reverence. Here men who had fought and died by the thousands ceased to struggle. Silence held sway as they rested. "Now may the God of peace be brought again from the dead—Peace, yes, everlasting peace for those who lie in these shallow graves."

Peace for the two figures that made their way slowly along the muddy road beyond Exermont, walking at a leisurely pace scanning the countryside—not strangers here.

One of them, stocky and rotund, threatening to burst his olive drab uniform at the seams, commented on the unfamiliar quiet. "By God, it don't seem right for us to be walking along this road like this. I want to get down and crawl."

His companion laughed. "You, too? I feel the same way. It seems like a shell's gonna come over any second now, and I'm lookin' for cover."

The rotund man stopped and shaded his eyes. "Down there is Gisnes. Now we'll have to leave the road about there, at that low place." He pointed to a dip in the hills slightly beyond and to the right. "What do you think, Preacher?"

"That looks about right. If we follow the path of the outfit we'll find the graves."

"Well, that won't be hard," Mac replied. "I don't think I'll ever forget the place. Will you?"

"Never—as long as I live," Harris answered, his face grave.

They moved along the road a little bit faster, stimulated by the realization that they were getting close. As they reached the slight depression they turned abruptly to the right and scrambled up the low bank at the side of the road. After some distance they stopped, and Mac looked around. "See anything that looks familiar?" he asked.

"Not yet." Harris gazed toward the ridges on the left. "Seems to me, though, that I recognize those hills. Look, that one with the three peaks. That looks like hill 269. Then that one, farther over, isn't that hill 240 where the 18th Infantry had such a hell of a fight? Sure it is. Let's just keep on in the same direction so we'll cut across the route the outfit took in the advance."

Harris wandered on some distance ahead. He stopped and examined the crosses on a cluster of graves near the edge of a wood, then straightened up and waved to Mac. "Remember Benson?"

"Sure, he was in Judy's section."

"That's his grave, so we must be close."

Mac produced a notebook from his pocket and marked the location of the grave. "Yeah. We're on the right track. All we have to do is turn left and follow our noses."

A few yards away they found more graves, and Mac made a careful notation for each in his little book. This expedition was undertaken voluntarily to find the graves of their buddies and let the next of kin know where they were. They made a note of every grave, even those of the enemy, when they could be identified.

Harris approved of marking the enemy graves. "You'd want someone to do that for you."

"Well, they were soldiers, too," Mac agreed. "Their people will probably be just as glad to learn where they are as our people will. I'll put 'em down. It won't do any harm."

"Kind of tender-hearted for a tough guy, aren't you, Mac?" Harris spoke in an undertone.

"Tough guys always are."

The list in the book grew longer, taking up page after page. Wagner, Klein, Benson, Haggerty, Kaufman, Herman, Evans, Wayne, Morse, Muller and then the dog tag on the cross read Conlon, Elmer. "One of our very own," Harris noted.

"Yep. One of the family."

Touched by the grave of one so close, they stood motionless. Mac broke the silence. "A soldier he was, and he died a soldier's death." He straightened and looked around, as though embarrassed by the show of the sentiment. "Come on," he said gruffly. "We got more to look up."

As they came to the edge of the woodland, Harris wandered about, searching. He stopped on the edge of a hole and called to Mac. "Remember this spot?"

Mac surveyed the surroundings and hesitated for a minute before it dawned on him. "Sure, that's the hole where I stole Judy's supper."

"That's the place. Jude was one helluva soldier, wasn't he?"

"Yeah, he was that." Mac stood looking at the hole, his eyes misty.

"Remember how he and John Gallagher hung together?" He asked. "Judy such a wild sort, and John so quiet and straight."

Harris had his own opinion. "Well, I don't know. John was all you say, but there was more to Judy than any of us knew. His main trouble was, he was hard to deceive. His bullshit meter was always turned on. He could see straight and figure straight, and he wasn't fooled by sham or hypocrisy, no matter what it was wrapped in. He could spot a fake in an instant, and he laughed at all the rules the world uses to hide its insincerity and pretense."

"Yeah, that was Jude." Mac's eyes still looked a little misty. They left the shell hole and moved slowly across the field toward the village whose roofs showed above the fields.

"By the way," Harris asked. "What about John Gallagher's grave? Do we have it down?"

"Got it," Mac assured him. "We didn't need to see it. The burial detail located it. I have it in the book."

The sun hung low in the west as they passed through the village where such a short time before they'd had to put up a savage fight. The villagers had returned to their homes, rebuilding with a will. The pair was greeted cordially by the villagers as they passed. Harris suggested they make arrangements to spend the night there when they were done searching the fields beyond the town. Mac agreed, and Harris set off looking for a place to stay. Mac continued the search for graves until Harris returned after having made a successful arrangement for a nights lodging.

They moved slowly lest the last resting place of one of their friends be overlooked.

"Boy, we sure caught hell here."

"I'll tell a man we did." Mac shook his head as though to dispel some dark memory. "Whose grave is that, Harris?"

"MacGregor's." Mac got out his book.

"Here's Judy's." Harris called from a little distance ahead.

Mac walked slowly over to join him and two old soldiers stood staring at the bare patch of earth. There was no cross. Someone, probably the burial detail, had driven his bayonet deep into the ground and hung his helmet on it.

"A very appropriate cross." Harris stood at the foot of the grave, hands behind his back.

Mac reached out to touch the helmet. "That's his helmet, all right. See where the piece of shell hit it up in the Aracourt sector. Look. There are both his dog tags. I'm gonna take one of them and send it to that girl in Paris if you can give me her address, Harris."

He stooped and detached one of the metal disks from where it was fastened to the bayonet hilt, then took a paper from his pocket and looked at it silently. "You know," he said, "I wish Judy could have lasted long enough to see this. It would have pleased him. He put a high value on citations and decorations and such. Seeing that this is the only one of its kind put out in the entire war, he certainly would have been pleased."

Harris reached for the paper, unfolded it and read silently. Then in a clear, distinct voice, he read:

GHQ, AMERICAN EXPEDITIONARY FORCES
General Orders, France. Nov. 19, 1918
No. 201

1. The Commander in Chief desires to make record in the General Orders of the American Expeditionary Forces his extreme satisfaction with the conduct of the officers and men of the First Division in its advance west of the Meuse between October 4th and 11th 1918 During this period the Division gained a distance of 7 kilometers over a country which presented not only remarkable facilities for enemy defense but also great difficulties of terrain for the operations of our troops.

2. The Division met with resistance from elements of either hostile divisions most of which were first class troops and some of which were completely rested The enemy chose to defend his position to death and the fighting was always of the most desperate kind Throughout the operations the officers and men of the Division displayed the highest type of courage fortitude and self sacrificing devotion to duty In addition to many enemy killed the Division captured 1407 of the enemy thirteen 77 mm field guns 10 trench mortars and numerous machine guns and stores.

3. The success of the Division in driving a deep advance into the enemy's territory enabled an assault to be made on the left by the neighboring division against the northeastern portion of the Forest of Argonne and enabled the First Division to advance to the right and outflank the enemy's position in front of the division on that flank

4. The Commander in Chief has noted in this Division a special pride of service and a high state of morale never broken by hardship nor battle.

5. This order will be read to all organizations at the first assembly formation after its receipt.

By command of General Pershing:

Official: James W. Mc Andrew,
                              Chief of Staff

Robert C. Davis,
Adjutant General

As he finished, Sgt. Harris stooped and placed the folded copy of the citation in the ring of the bayonet hilt and whispered softly, "There, Judy, old boy, maybe you can see it. Who knows?"

Mac sniffed, then spoke. "I like that part where it says the Commander in Chief has noticed in this division a special pride of service and a high state of morale, never broken by hardship nor battle."

"Never broken by hardship nor battle," Harris nodded. "You bet, Mister President."

The sun had sunk and dusk had turned into darkness as they turned away and started for the village, their figures merging with the shadows until they lost the solidity of being and became one with the approaching darkness. Their footsteps died away, the low sound of their voices stilled.

* * *

BERLIN
JANUARY, 1919

Jeanne

The Hotel zur Post in Berlin was one of the truly fine hostelries of Europe, composed of many luxuriant suites of rooms, none more comfortable or more lavishly furnished than the one then occupied by Mlle. Jeanne Trevost. Peace had come to the nation, but in its coming it seemed to have passed her by. For eight weeks she'd been staying here among glittering surroundings. Each day Ludwig Von Boehm called to take her on a shopping tour or for a drive. At night they attended the theaters and the cafés, but no amount of pleasure could alleviate the sorrow that lived in her heart.

She'd received two letters from her brother René. In both, he approved of her course and assured her that her American lover would understand and not censure her. Ever since the Armistice, she'd looked for word from him, but in vain. At times, she'd been on the point of backing out of her bargain with Ludwig, but still she hesitated. Even though the war was over and she was no longer in mortal danger, Ludwig still seemed determined to hold her to the bargain.

Her telephone rang, jarring her out of thoughts of Sgt Redding. She lifted the receiver. A guttural voice stated that there was mail for her. "Shall I send it to your suite, Fräulein?"

"Yes, please." She hung up and smiled. "Ah, joy of joys! This may be it."

Maybe now the uncertainty would end. Oh, hurry. Hurry. She went to the door, opened it and stared down the hall with impatience. Why didn't the man hurry? At last, she heard the elevator stop at her floor. The gates clanged and she heard footsteps in the hall. The messenger turned a corner and came into view, carrying a small thin packet on a silver tray. She ran to him and grabbed the packet, tearing it open without so much as a 'thank you'.

"Your mail, Fräulein."

The man lingered. Oh, why didn't he go? What did he want? Then she realized and ran for her handbag, tucking the packet under her arm. A small coin changed hands, the man bowed and turned away. She slammed the door and tore at the string with fumbling fingers.

The handwriting was strange. It was postmarked Montabau which she knew was headquarters for the American First Division. Ah, this must be it. She had it open now, and a small metal disk dropped to the floor. News at last! She bent to pick it up. Inscribed on the face of the disk was: Redding, Emmet Co C, 1st Engineers Serial Number xxxxxxx. She stared at it for a moment, perplexed. What was this? She turned it over, still unsure what it meant. There, rudely carved into the reverse side was the inscription: *Killed in action, Oct 7, 1918, near Gesnes, France.*

She sank down upon her sofa, the packet in her hand, staring into space. There was nothing left. She looked down at the little box that had housed the disk and found a folded paper which had escaped her notice. She unfolded it and read:

Dear Mlle, Trevost:

We are sorry to have to inform you that Sgt Emmet (Judy) Redding was killed in action on Oct 7, 1918, just south of Gesnes, France. His body is buried where he fell. The grave is about three hundred yards from the village, and any of the villagers can direct you to it. He was killed by machine gun fire, and we think he died instantly and without pain.

Again, we express our sorrow at having to report this news.

 We are Yours Sincerely,
 Sergeants MacCarthy and Harris

She read the note several times, then rose with a purpose. She would break her bargain with Ludwig, locate Judy's grave, and have his body raised and reburied in the family plot in Paris. She sat back, grief stricken. She didn't even hear the knock on her door until the third time. She rose and opened the door. Herr Von Boehm stood there in civilian clothes, radiant with smiles. Since the revolution, his type of office was not popular in the Army, so he had resigned. He noticed Jeanne's sorrowful manner but attributed it to general conditions.

"Come, my dear." He kissed her on the cheek. "We must go to the railroad station."

"Why, what for?" She looked bewildered.

"There is a trainload of American wounded from the First Division going through. Perhaps your friend will be among them, and matters can be discussed among the three of us."

She gave a little moan and dropped down on the couch. "No. No, it's too late." She held the crumpled packet out to him.

He took the disk and read both sides, then the note. "Ah," he whispered. "So." He sat silent for a long time. "So they missed us." He was talking to himself. "Missed us by almost a day. Well, I almost wish we'd have stayed. You would be happy now, and I would have been spared seeing many things I hoped would never happen to my country."

He rose and crossed the room. After a few moments he leaned over and took Jeanne's chin between his thumb and forefinger. Raising her tear stained face, he looked long and deep into her eyes. "Our bargain is ended, dear Jeanne," he whispered. "It is over."

She rose, struggling to control her grief. "Dear friend, I can't express my gratitude. Your action proves that kindness and generosity are not limited to any one people."

"True, Jeanne." He smiled sadly. "Neither are courage and self sacrifice. Don't grieve for your fiancé. Comfort yourself with the fact that he died gallantly, moving forward with his face to the enemy. Be proud that he was faithful to his nation, asking no one to relieve him of his responsibilities. He was loyal when loyalty meant hardship and suffering and, above all, facing death. You are free. Go and mourn your dead."